INNOCENTS ABOARD

✦

INNOCENTS
ABOARD

NEW FANTASY STORIES

✦

GENE WOLFE

A Tom Doherty Associates Book
New York

INNOCENTS ABOARD: NEW FANTASY STORIES

Edited by David G. Hartwell

Book design by Kathryn Parise

A Tor Book
Published by Tom Doherty Associates, LLC
175 Fifth Avenue
New York, NY 10010

www.tor.com

Tor® is a registered trademark of Tom Doherty Associates, LLC.

LIBRARY OF CONGRESS CATALOGING-IN-PUBLICATION DATA
Wolfe, Gene.
    Innocents aboard : new fantasy stories / Gene Wolfe.—1st ed.
      p. cm.
    "A Tom Doherty Associates book."
    ISBN 0-765-30790-1 (alk. paper)
    EAN 978-0765-30790-3
    1. Fantasy fiction, American. I. Title.

PS3573.O52I56 2004
813'.54—dc22

                            2003071143

First Edition: June 2004

Printed in the United States of America

0 9 8 7 6 5 4 3 2 1

Copyright Acknowledgments

✦

For John Cramer, Ph.D., Captain Wesley Besse,
and everyone else who attended
—or is attending—
Edgar Allan Poe Elementary School

✦

Contents

✦

Introduction

✦

Yºou will find fantasy and horror stories in the book that follows, and nothing else. Okay, magic realism, maybe, depending on how you define it. But no science fiction and no mainstream literary stories. Not that I have anything against stories of those kinds, though you may.

Oh, ghost stories. If you want to count those as a separate category, well, "The Walking Sticks" is certainly a ghost story, and ghosts make cameo appearances in some of the others. To tell you the truth, I believe in ghosts (having had Certain Experiences). And as a result often find them creeping into stories.

Let's see . . . Perhaps I should tell you that "The Tree Is My Hat" was done as a radio play at the World Horror Convention; Neil Gaiman played Reverend Robbins, and I'm proud of that.

"The Old Woman Whose Rolling Pin Is the Sun" is a bedtime story for my granddaughter Becca; perhaps she'll read it here for the first time ever.

Well, I could comment in one way or another on all of them; but I don't want to, and you wouldn't read it if I did. So just a few . . .

"The Friendship Light" is one of those stories the author likes better than anyone else. Like "The Friendship Light," "Slow Children at Play" was based in part on an actual light—a mysterious light, in this case—which I saw once and have never seen again. It's also based on a traffic sign about half a block north of this house.

"Under Hill" was very pleasant to write because I fell for Princess Apple Blossom. What a great little person! Perhaps you'll like her, too.

"The Monday Man" refers, of course, to those sad and frightening men who steal women's underwear. When I was growing up no one had clothes dryers, and Monday men were a perennial problem for my poor mother.

"The Waif" has been praised by Gordon Van Gelder. That should be enough for you.

"The Legend of Xi Cygnus" is a dream story. Once or twice I have had a dream that sparks a story; it reveals itself as a story-dream by demanding to be written down.

"The Sailor Who Sailed After the Sun" is a favorite story of Joan Gordon's. Joan is an academic who knows a lot about this kind of story and was disappointed that it wasn't in my previous collection *Strange Travelers*. So here it is.

There really are islands like the one in "How the Bishop Sailed to Inniskeen" off the coast of Ireland, islands with ruined monasteries on them. It's hard for us to understand how happy monks are, for the most part. Yet they are, and pity us, and pray for us.

"Houston, 1943" is sort of autobiographical. I grew up in Houston, with a very nice mama and a very nice daddy and a fat spaniel named Boots. In 1943, I was twelve; and that's my family, my bedroom, and so forth. There were bugs and tarantulas, alligators, poisonous snakes, Nazi submarines, and housemaids who practiced voodoo. All that is real.

So are various other things in the rest of the stories. I sincerely hope you'll read and enjoy them all, especially the made-up parts.

—Gene Wolfe

INNOCENTS
ABOARD

✦

The Tree Is My Hat

✦

3 0 Jan. I saw a strange stranger on the beach this morning. I had been swimming in the little bay between here and the village; that may have had something to do with it, although I did not feel tired. Dived down and thought I saw a shark coming around the big staghorn coral. Got out fast. The whole swim cannot have been more than ten minutes. Ran out of the water and started walking.

There it is. I have begun this journal at last. (Thought I never would.) So let us return to all the things I ought to have put in and did not. I bought this the day after I came back from Africa.

No, the day I got out of the hospital—I remember now. I was wandering around, wondering when I would have another attack, and went into a little shop on Forty-second Street. There was a nice-looking woman in there, one of those good-looking black women, and I thought it might be nice to talk to her, so I had to buy something. I said, "I just got back from Africa."

She: "Really. How was it?" Me: "Hot."

Anyway, I came out with this notebook and told myself I had not wasted my money because I would keep a journal, writing down my attacks, what I had been doing and eating, as instructed; but all I could think of was how she looked when she turned to go to the back of the shop. Her legs and how she held her head. Her hips.

After that I planned to write down everything I remember from Africa, and what we said if Mary returned my calls. Then it was going to be about this assignment.

———

31 Jan. Setting up my new Mac. Who would think this place would have phones? But there are wires to Kololahi, and a dish. I can chat with people all over the world, for which the agency pays. (Talk about soft!) Nothing like this in Africa. Just the radio, and good luck with that.

I was full of enthusiasm. "A remote Pacific island chain." Wait . . .

P.D.: "Baden, we're going to send you to the Takanga Group."

No doubt I looked blank.

"It's a remote Pacific island chain." She cleared her throat and seemed to have swallowed a bone. "It's not going to be like Africa, Bad. You'll be on your own out there."

Me: "I thought you were going to fire me."

P.D.: "No, no! We wouldn't do that."

"Permanent sick leave."

"No, no, no! But, Bad." She leaned across her desk and for a minute I was afraid she was going to squeeze my hand. "This will be rough. I'm not going to try to fool you."

Hah!

Cut to the chase. This is nothing. This is a bungalow with rotten boards in the floors that has been here since before the British pulled out, a mile from the village and less than half that from the beach, close enough that the Pacific-smell is in all the rooms. The people are fat and happy, and my guess is not more than half are dumb. (Try and match that around Chicago.) Once or twice a year one gets yaws or some such, and Rev. Robbins gives him arsenic. *Which cures it.* Pooey!

There are fish in the ocean, plenty of them. Wild fruit in the jungle, and they know which you can eat. They plant yams and breadfruit, and if they need money or just want something, they dive for pearls and trade them when Jack's boat comes. Or do a big holiday boat trip to Kololahi.

There are coconuts, too, which I forgot. They know how to open them. Or perhaps I am just not strong enough yet. (I look in the mirror, and ugh.) I used to weigh two hundred pounds.

"You skinny," the king says. "Ha, ha, ha!" He is really a good guy, I think. He has a primitive sense of humor, but there are worse things. He can take a jungle chopper (we said upanga but they say heletay) and open a coconut like a pack of gum. I have coconuts and a heletay but I might as well try to open them with a spoon.

1 Feb. Nothing to report except a couple of wonderful swims. I did not swim at all for the first couple of weeks. There are sharks. I know they are really out there because I have seen them once or twice. According to what I was told, there are saltwater crocs, too, up to fourteen feet long. I have never seen any of those and am skeptical, although I know they have them in Queensland. Every so often you hear about somebody who was killed by a shark, but that does not stop the people from swimming all the time, and I do not see why it should stop me. Good luck so far.

2 Feb. Saturday. I was supposed to write about the dwarf I saw on the beach that time, but I never got the nerve. Sometimes I used to see things in the hospital. Afraid it may be coming back. I decided to take a walk on the beach. All right, did I get sunstroke?

Pooey.

He was just a little man, shorter even than Mary's father. He was too small for any adult in the village. He was certainly not a child, and was too pale to have been one of the islanders at all.

He cannot have been here long; he was whiter than I am.

Rev. Robbins will know—ask tomorrow.

3 Feb. Hot and getting hotter. Jan. is the hottest month here, according to Rob Robbins. Well, I got here the first week in Jan. and it has never been this hot.

Got up early while it was still cool. Went down the beach to the village. (Stopped to have a look at the rocks where the dwarf disappeared.) Waited around for the service to begin but could not talk to Rob, he was rehearsing the choir—"Nearer My God to Thee."

Half the village came, and the service went on for almost two hours.

When it was over I was able to get Rob alone. I said if he would drive us into Kololahi I would buy our Sunday dinner. (He has a jeep.) He was nice, but no—too far and the bad roads. I told him I had personal troubles I wanted his advice on, and he said, "Why don't we go to your place, Baden, and have a talk? I'd invite you for lemonade, but they'd be after me every minute."

So we walked back. It was hotter than hell, and this time I tried not to look. I got cold Cokes out of my rusty little fridge, and we sat on the porch (Rob calls it the veranda) and fanned ourselves. He knew I felt bad about not being able to do anything for these people, and urged patience. My chance would come.

I said, "I've given up on that, Reverend."

(That was when he told me to call him Rob. His first name is Mervyn.) "Never give up, Baden. Never." He looked so serious I almost laughed.

"All right, I'll keep my eyes open, and maybe someday the Agency will send me someplace where I'm needed."

"Back to Uganda?"

I explained that the A.O.A.A. almost never sends anyone to the same area twice. "That wasn't really what I wanted to talk to you about. It's my personal life. Well, really two things, but that's one of them. I'd like to get back together with my ex-wife. You're going to advise me to forget it, because I'm here and she's in Chicago; but I can send e-mail, and I'd like to put the bitterness behind us."

"Were there children? Sorry, Baden. I didn't intend it to hurt."

I explained how Mary had wanted them and I had not, and he gave me some advice. I have not e-mailed yet, but I will tonight after I write it out here.

"You're afraid that you were hallucinating. Did you feel feverish?" He got out his thermometer and took my temperature, which was nearly normal. "Let's look at it logically, Baden. This island is a hundred miles long and about thirty miles at the widest point. There are eight villages I know of. The population of Kololahi is over twelve hundred."

I said I understood all that.

"Twice a week, the plane from Cairns brings new tourists."

"Who almost never go five miles from Kololahi."

"Almost never, Baden. Not never. You say it wasn't one of the villagers. All right, I accept that. Was it me?"

"Of course not."

"Then it was someone from outside the village, someone from another village, from Kololahi, or a tourist. Why shake your head?"

I told him.

"I doubt there's a leprosarium nearer than the Marshalls. Anyway, I don't know of one closer. Unless you saw something else, some other sign of the disease, I doubt that this little man you saw had leprosy. It's a lot more likely that you saw a tourist with pasty white skin greased with sun blocker. As for his disappearing, the explanation seems pretty obvious. He dived off the rocks into the bay."

"There wasn't anybody there. I looked."

"There wasn't anybody there you saw, you mean. He would have been up to his neck in water, and the sun was glaring on the water, wasn't it?"

"I suppose so."

"It must have been. The weather's been clear." Rob drained his Coke and pushed it away. "As for his not leaving footprints, stop playing Sherlock Holmes. That's harsh, I realize, but I say it for your own good. Footprints in soft sand are shapeless indentations at best."

"I could see mine."

"You knew where to look. Did you try to backtrack yourself? I thought not. May I ask a few questions? When you saw him, did you think he was real?"

"Yes, absolutely. Would you like another one? Or something to eat?"

"No, thanks. When was the last time you had an attack?"

"A bad one? About six weeks."

"How about a not-bad one?"

"Last night, but it didn't amount to much. Two hours of chills, and it went away."

"That must have been a relief. No, I see it wasn't. Baden, the next time you have an attack, severe or not, I want you to come and see me. Understand?"

I promised.

———

This is Bad. I still love you. That's all I have to say, but I want to say it. I was wrong, and I know it. I hope you've forgiven me. And sign off.

4 Feb. Saw him again last night, and he has pointed teeth. I was shaking under the netting, and he looked through the window and smiled. Told Rob, and said I read somewhere that cannibals used to file their teeth. I know these people were cannibals three or four generations back, and I asked if they had done it. He thinks not but will ask the king.

I have been very ill, Mary, but I feel better now. It is evening here, and I am going to bed. I love you. Good night. I love you. Sign off.

5 Feb. Two men with spears came to take me to the king. I asked if I was under arrest, and they laughed. No ha, ha, ha from His Majesty this time, though. He was in the big house, but he came out and we went some distance among hardwoods the size of office buildings smothered in flowering vines, stopping in a circle of stones: the king, the men with spears, and an old man with a drum. The men with spears built a fire, and the drum made soft sounds like waves while the king made a speech or recited a poem, mocked all the while by invisible birds with eerie voices.

When the king was finished, he hung this piece of carved bone around my neck. While we were walking back to the village, he put his arm around me, which surprised me more than anything. He is bigger than a tackle in the NFL, and must weigh four hundred pounds. It felt like I was carrying a calf.

Horrible, *horrible* dreams! Swimming in boiling blood. Too scared to sleep anymore. Logged on and tried to find something on dreams and what they mean. Stumbled onto a witch in L.A.—her home page, then the lady herself. (I'll get you and your little dog, too!) Actually, she seemed nice.

Got out the carved bone thing the king gave me. Old, and probably ought to be in a museum, but I suppose I had better wear it as long as I stay here, at least when I go out. Suppose I were to offend him? He might sit on me! Seems to be a fish with pictures scratched into both sides. More fish, man in a hat, etc. Cord through the eye. Wish I had a magnifying glass.

6 Feb. Still haven't gone back to bed, but my watch says Wednesday. Wrote a long e-mail, typing it in as it came to me. Told her where I am and what I'm doing, and begged her to respond. After that I went outside and swam naked in the moonlit sea. Tomorrow I want to look for the place where the king hung this fish charm on me. Back to bed.

Morning, and beautiful. Why has it taken me so long to see what a beautiful place this is? (Maybe my heart just got back from Africa.) Palms swaying forever in the trade winds, and people like heroic bronze statues. How small, how stunted and pale we have to look to them!

Took a real swim to get the screaming out of my ears. Will I laugh in a year when I see that I said my midnight swim made me understand these people better? Maybe I will. But it did. They have been swimming in the moon like that for hundreds of years.

E-mail! God bless e-mail and whoever invented it! Just checked mine and found I had a message. Tried to guess who it might be. I wanted Mary, and was about certain it would be from the witch, from Annys. Read the name and it was *Julius R. Christmas.* Pops! Mary's Pops! Got up and ran around the room, so excited I could not read it. Now I have printed it out, and I am going to copy it here.

———

She went to Uganda looking for you, Bad. Coming back tomorrow, Kennedy, AA 47 from Heathrow. I'll tell her where you are. Watch out for those hula-hula girls.

SHE WENT TO UGANDA LOOKING FOR ME

7 Feb. More dreams—little man with pointed teeth smiling through the window. I doubt that I should write it all down, but I knew (in the dream) that he hurt people, and he kept telling me he would not hurt me. Maybe the first time was a dream, too. More screams.

Anyway, I talked to Rob again yesterday afternoon, although I had not planned on it. By the time I got back here I was too sick to do anything except lie on the bed. The worst since I left the hospital, I think.

Went looking for the place the king took me to. Did not want to start from the village, kids might have followed me, so I tried to circle and come at it from the other side. Found two old buildings, small and no roofs, and a bone that looked human. More about that later. Did not see any marks, but did not look for them either. It was black on one end like it had been in a fire, though.

Kept going about three hours and wore myself out. Tripped on a chunk of stone and stopped to wipe off the sweat, and Blam! I was there! Found the ashes and where the king and I stood. Looked around wishing I had my camera, and there was Rob, sitting up on four stones that were still together and looking down at me. I said, "Hey, why didn't you say something?"

And he said, "I wanted to see what you would do." So he had been spying on me; I did not say it, but that was what it was.

I told him about going there with the king, and how he gave me a charm. I said I was sorry I had not worn it, but anytime he wanted a Coke I would show it to him.

"It doesn't matter. He knows you're sick, and I imagine he gave you something to heal you. It might even work, because God hears all sorts of prayers. That's not what they teach in the seminary, or even what it says in the Bible. But I've been out in the missions long enough to know. When somebody with good intentions talks to the God who created him, he's heard. Pretty often the answer is yes. Why did you come back here?"

"I wanted to see it again, that's all. At first I thought it was just a circle of rocks, then when I thought about it, it seemed like it must have been more."

Rob kept quiet; so I explained that I had been thinking of Stonehenge. Stonehenge was a circle of big rocks, but the idea had been to look at the positions of certain stars and where the sun rose. But this could not be the same kind of thing, because of the trees. Stonehenge is out in the open on Salisbury Plain. I asked if it was some kind of a temple.

"It was a palace once, Baden." Rob cleared his throat. "If I tell you something about it in confidence, can you keep it to yourself?"

I promised.

"These are good people now. I want to make that clear. They seem a little childlike to us, as all primitives do. If we were primitives ourselves—and we were, Bad, not so long ago—they wouldn't. Can you imagine how they'd seem to us if they didn't seem a little childlike?"

I said, "I was thinking about that this morning before I left the bungalow."

Rob nodded. "Now I understand why you wanted to come back here. The Polynesians are scattered all over the South Pacific. Did you know that? Captain Cook, a British naval officer, was the first to explore the Pacific with any thoroughness, and he was absolutely astounded to find that after he'd sailed for weeks his interpreter could still talk to the natives. We know, for example, that Polynesians came down from Hawaii in sufficient numbers to conquer New Zealand. The historians hadn't admitted it the last time I looked, but it's a fact, recorded by the Maori themselves in their own history. The distance is about four thousand miles."

"Impressive."

"But you wonder what I'm getting at. I don't blame you. They're supposed to have come from Malaya originally. I won't go into all the reasons for thinking that they didn't, beyond saying that if it were the case they should be in New Guinea and Australia, and they're not."

I asked where they had come from, and for a minute or two he just rubbed his chin; then he said, "I'm not going to tell you that either. You wouldn't believe me, so why waste breath on it? Think of a distant land, a mountainous country with buildings and monuments to rival Ancient Egypt's, and gods worse than any demon Cotton Mather could have imagined. The time . . ." He shrugged. "After Moses but before Christ."

"Babylon?"

He shook his head. "They developed a ruling class, and in time those rulers, their priests and warriors, became something like another race, bigger and stronger than the peasants they treated like slaves. They drenched the altars of their gods with blood, the blood of enemies when they could capture enough, and the blood of peasants when they couldn't. Their peasants rebelled and drove them from the mountains to the sea, and into the sea."

I think he was waiting for me to say something; but I kept quiet, thinking over what he had said and wondering if it were true.

"They sailed away in terror of the thing they had awakened in the hearts of the nation that had been their own. I doubt very much if there were more than a few thousand, and there may well have been fewer than a thousand. They learned seamanship, and learned it well. They had to. In the Ancient World they were the only people to rival the Phoenicians, and they surpassed even the Phoenicians."

I asked whether he believed all that, and he said, "It doesn't matter whether I believe it, because it's true."

He pointed to one of the stones. "I called them primitives, and they are. But they weren't always as primitive as they are now. This was a palace, and there are ruins like this all over Polynesia, great buildings of coral rock falling to pieces. A palace and thus a sacred place, because the king was holy, the gods' representative. That was why he brought you here."

Rob was going to leave, but I told him about the buildings I found earlier and he wanted to see them. "There is a temple, too, Baden, although I've never been able to find it. When it was built, it must have been evil beyond our imagining. . . ." He grinned then, surprising the hell out of me. "You must get teased about your name."

"Ever since elementary school. It doesn't bother me." But the truth is it does, sometimes.

More later.

———————

Well, I have met the little man I saw on the beach, and to tell the truth (what's the sense of one of these if you are not going to tell the truth?) I like him. I am going to write about all that in a minute.

Rob and I looked for the buildings I had seen when I was looking for the palace but could not find them. Described them, but Rob did not think they were the temple he has been looking for since he came. "They know where it is. Certainly the older people do. Once in a while I catch little oblique references to it. Not jokes. They joke about the place you found, but not about that."

I asked what the place I had found had been.

"A Japanese camp. The Japanese were here during World War Two."

I had not known that.

"There were no battles. They built those buildings you found, pre-sumably, and they dug caves in the hills from which to fight. I've found some of those myself. But the Americans and Australians simply bypassed this island, as they did many other islands. The Japanese soldiers re-mained here, stranded. There must have been about a company, origi-nally."

"What happened to them?"

"Some surrendered. Some came out of the jungle to surrender and were killed. A few held out, twenty or twenty-five from what I've heard. They left their caves and went back to the camp they had built when they thought Japan would win and control the entire Pacific. That was what you found, I believe, and that's why I'd like to see it."

I said I could not understand how we could have missed it, and he said, "Look at this jungle, Baden. One of those buildings could be within ten feet of us."

After that we went on for another mile or two and came out on the beach. I did not know where we were, but Rob did. "This is where we sep-arate. The village is that way, and your bungalow the other way, beyond the bay."

I had been thinking about the Japs, and asked if they were all dead, and he said they were. "They were older every year and fewer every year, and a time came when the rifles and machine guns that had kept the villages in terror no longer worked. And after that, a time when the people realized they didn't. They went to the Japanese camp one night with their spears and war clubs. They killed the remaining Japanese and ate them, and sometimes they make sly little jokes about it when they want to get my goat."

I was feeling rocky and knew I was in for a bad time, so I came back here. I was sick the rest of the afternoon and all night, chills, fever, headache, the works. I remember watching the little vase on the bureau get up and walk to the other side, and sit back down, and seeing an American in a baseball cap float in. He took off his cap and combed his hair in front of the mirror, and floated back out. It was a Cardinals cap.

Now about Hanga, the little man I see on the beach.

After I wrote all that about the palace, I wanted to ask Rob a couple of questions, and tell him Mary was coming. All right, no one has actually said she was, and so far I have heard nothing from her directly, only the one e-mail from Pops. But she went to Africa, so why not here? I thanked Pops and told him where I am again. He knows how much I want to see her. If she comes, I am going to ask Rob to re-marry us, if she will.

Started down the beach, and I saw him; but after half a minute or so he seemed to melt into the haze. I told myself I was still seeing things, and I was still sick; and I reminded myself that I promised to go by Rob's mission next time I felt bad. But when I got to the end of the bay, there he was, perfectly real, sitting in the shade of one of the young palms. I wanted to talk to him, so I said, "Okay if I sit down, too? This sun's frying my brains."

He smiled (the pointed teeth are real) and said, "The tree is my hat."

I thought he just meant the shade, but after I sat he showed me, biting off a palm frond and peeling a strip from it, then showing me how to peel them and weave them into a rough sort of straw hat, with a high crown and a wide brim.

We talked a little, although he does not speak English as well as some of the others. He does not live in the village, and the people who do, do not like him although he likes them. They are afraid of him, he says, and give him things because they are. They prefer he stay away. "No village, no boat."

I said it must be lonely, but he only stared out to sea. I doubt that he knows the word.

He wanted to know about the charm the king gave me. I described it and asked if it brings good luck. He shook his head. "No malhoi." Picking up a single palm fiber, "This malhoi." Not knowing what "malhoi" meant, I was in no position to argue.

That is pretty much all, except that I told him to visit when he wants company; and he told me I must eat fish to restore my health. (I have no idea who told him I am ill sometimes, but I never tried to keep it a secret.) Also that I would never have to fear an attack (I think that must have been what he meant) while he was with me.

His skin is rough and hard, much lighter in color than the skin of my forearm, but I have no idea whether that is a symptom or a birth defect. When I got up to leave, he stood, too, and came no higher than my chest. Poor little man.

One more thing. I had not intended to put it down, but after what Rob said maybe I should. When I had walked some distance toward the village, I turned back to wave to Hanga, and he was gone. I walked back, thinking that the shade of the palm had fooled me; he was not there. I went to the bay thinking he was in the water as Rob suggested. It is a beautiful little cove, but Hanga was not there, either. I am beginning to feel sympathy for the old mariners. These islands vanished when they approached.

At any rate, Rob says that "malhoi" means *strong*. Since a palm fiber is not as strong as a cotton thread, there must be something wrong somewhere. (More likely, something I do not understand.) Maybe the word has more than one meaning.

"Hanga" means *shark*, Rob says, but he does not know my friend Hanga. Nearly all the men are named for fish.

More e-mail, this time the witch. "There is danger hanging over you. I feel it and know some higher power guided you to me. Be careful. Stay away from places of worship, my tarot shows trouble for you there. Tell me about the fetish you mentioned."

I doubt that I should, and that I will e-mail her again.

9 Feb. I guess I wore myself out on writing Thursday. I see I wrote nothing yesterday. To tell the truth, there was nothing to write about except my swim in Hanga's bay. And I cannot write about that in a way that makes sense. Beautiful beyond description. That is all I can say. To tell the truth, I am afraid to go back. Afraid I will be disappointed. No spot on earth, even under the sea, can be as lovely as I remember it. Colored coral, and the little sea-animals that look like flowers, and schools of blue and red and orange fish like live jewels.

Today when I went to see Rob (all right, Annys warned me; but I think she is full of it) I said he probably likes to think God made this beautiful world so we could admire it; but if He had, He would have given us gills.

"Do I also think that He made the stars for us, Baden? All those flaming suns hundreds and thousands of light-years away? Did God create whole galaxies so that once or twice in our lives we might chance to look up and glimpse them?"

When he said that I had to wonder about people like me, who work for the Federal Government. Would we be driven out someday, like the people Rob talked about? A lot of us do not care any more about ordinary people than they did. I know P.D. does not.

A woman who had cut her hand came in about then. Rob talked to her in her own language while he treated her, and she talked a good deal more, chattering away. When she left I asked whether he had really understood everything she said. He said, "I did and I didn't. I knew all the words she used, if that's what you mean. How long have you been here now, Baden?"

I told him and he said, "About five weeks? That's perfect. I've been here about five years. I don't speak as well as they do. Sometimes I have to stop to think of the right word, and sometimes I can't think of it at all.

But I understand when I hear them. It's not an elaborate language. Are you troubled by ghosts?"

I suppose I gawked.

"That was one of the things she said. The king has sent for a woman from another village to rid you of them, a sort of witch-doctress, I imagine. Her name is Langitokoua."

I said the only ghost bothering me was my dead marriage's, and I hoped to resuscitate it with his help.

He tried to look through me and may have succeeded; he has that kind of eyes. "You still don't know when Mary's coming?"

I shook my head.

"She'll want to rest a few days after her trip to Africa. I hope you're allowing for that."

"And she'll have to fly from Chicago to Los Angeles, from Los Angeles to Melbourne, and from there to Cairns, after which she'll have to wait for the next plane to Kololahi. Believe me, Rob, I've taken all that into consideration."

"Good. Has it occurred to you that your little friend Hanga might be a ghost? I mean, has it occurred to you since you spoke to him?"

Right then, I had that "what am I doing here" feeling I used to get in the bush. There I sat in that bright, flimsy little room with the medicine smell, and a jar of cotton balls at my elbow, and the noise of the surf coming in the window, about a thousand miles from anyplace that matters; and I could not remember the decisions I had made and the plans that had worked or not worked to get me there.

"Let me tell you a story, Baden. You don't have to believe it. The first year I was here, I had to go to town to see about some building supplies we were buying. As things fell out, there was a day there when I had nothing to do, and I decided to drive up to North Point. People had told me it was the most scenic part of the island, and I convinced myself I ought to see it. Have you ever been there?"

I had not even heard of it.

"The road only goes as far as the closest village. After that there's a footpath that takes two hours or so. It really is beautiful, rocks standing above the waves, and dramatic cliffs overlooking the ocean. I stayed there long enough to get the lovely, lonely feel of the place and make some sketches. Then I hiked back to the village where I'd left the jeep and started to drive back to Kololahi. It was almost dark.

"I hadn't gone far when I saw a man from our village walking along the road. Back then I didn't know everybody, but I knew him. I stopped, and we chatted for a minute. He said he was on his way to see his parents, and I thought they must live in the place I had just left. I told him to get into the jeep, and drove back, and let him out. He thanked me over and over, and when I got out to look at one of the tires I was worried about, he hugged me and kissed my eyes. I've never forgotten that."

I said something stupid about how warmhearted the people here are.

"You're right, of course. But, Baden, when I got back, I learned that North Point is a haunted place. It's where the souls of the dead go to make their farewell to the land of the living. The man I'd picked up had been killed by a shark the day I left, four days before I gave him a ride."

I did not know what to say, and at last I blurted out, "They lied to you. They had to be lying."

"No doubt—or I'm lying to you. At any rate, I'd like you to bring your friend Hanga here to see me if you can."

I promised I would try to bring Rob to see Hanga, since Hanga will not go into the village.

Swimming in the little bay again. I never thought of myself as a strong swimmer, never even had much chance to swim, but have been swimming like a dolphin, diving underwater and swimming with my eyes open for what has got to be two or two and a half minutes if not longer. Incredible! My God, wait till I show Mary!

You can buy scuba gear in Kololahi. I'll rent Rob's jeep or pay one of the men to take me in his canoe.

11 Feb. I let this slide again, and need to catch up. Yesterday was very odd. So was Saturday.

After I went to bed (still full of Rob's ghost story and the new world underwater) and *crash!* Jumped up scared as hell, and my bureau had fallen on its face. Dry rot in the legs, apparently. A couple of drawers broke, and stuff scattered all over.

I propped it back up and started cleaning up the mess, and found a book I never saw before, *The Light Garden of the Angel King,* about traveling through Afghanistan. In front is somebody's name and a date, and "American Overseas Assistance Agency." None of it registered right then.

But there it was, spelled out for me. And here is where he was, Larry Scribble. He was an Agency man, had bought the book three years ago (when he was posted to Afghanistan, most likely) and brought it with him when he was sent here. I only use the top three drawers, and it had been in one of the others and got overlooked when somebody (who?) cleared out his things.

Why was he gone when I got here? He should have been here to brief me, and stayed for a week or so. No one has so much as mentioned his name, and there must be a reason for that.

Intended to go to services at the mission and bring the book, but was sick again. Hundred and nine. Took medicine and went to bed, too weak to move, and had this very strange dream. Somehow I knew somebody was in the house. (I suppose steps, although I cannot remember any.) Sat up, and there was Hanga smiling by my bed. "I knock. You not come."

I said, "I'm sorry. I've been sick." I felt fine. Got up and offered to get him a Coke or something to eat, but he wanted to see the charm. I said sure, and got it off the bureau.

He looked at it, grunting and tracing the little drawings on its sides with his forefinger. "No tie? You take loose?" He pointed to the knot.

I said there was no reason to, that it would go over my head without untying the cord.

"Want friend?" He pointed to himself, and it was pathetic. "Hanga friend? Bad friend?"

"Yes," I said. "Absolutely."

"Untie."

I said I would cut the cord if he wanted me to.

"Untie, please. Blood friend." (He took my arm then, repeating, "Blood friend!")

I said all right and began to pick at the knot, which was complex; and at that moment, I swear, I heard someone else in the bungalow, some third person who pounded on the walls. I believe I would have gone to see who it was then, but Hanga was still holding my arm. He has big hands on those short arms, with a lot of strength in them.

In a minute or two I got the cord loose and asked if he wanted it, and he said eagerly that he did. I gave it to him, and there was one of those changes you get in dreams. He straightened up, and was at least as tall as I am. Holding my arm, he cut it quickly and neatly with his teeth and licked the blood, and seemed to grow again. It was as if some sort of defilement had been wiped away. He looked intelligent and almost handsome.

Then he cut the skin of his own arm just like mine. He offered it to me, and I licked his blood like he had licked mine. For some reason I expected it to taste horrible, but it did not; it was as if I had gotten seawater in my mouth while I was swimming.

"We are Blood friends now, Bad," Hanga told me. "I shall not harm you, and you must not harm me."

That was the end of the dream. The next thing I remember is lying in bed and smelling something sweet, while something tickled my ear. I thought the mosquito netting had come loose, and looked to see, and there was a woman with a flower in her hair lying beside me. I rolled over; and she, seeing that I was awake, embraced and kissed me.

She is Langitokoua, the woman Rob told me the king had sent for, but I call her Langi. She says she does not know how old she is, and is fibbing. Her size (she is about six feet tall, and must weigh a good two-fifty) makes her look older than she is, I feel sure. Twenty-five, maybe. Or seventeen. I asked her about ghosts, and she said very matter-of-factly that there is one in the house but he means no harm.

Pooey.

After that, naturally I asked her why the king wanted her to stay with me; and she solemnly explained that it is not good for a man to live by himself, that a man should have someone to cook and sweep, and take care of him when he is ill. That was my chance, and I went for it. I explained that I am expecting a woman from American soon, that American women are jealous, and that I would have to tell the American woman Langi was there to nurse me. Langi agreed without any fuss.

What else?

Hanga's visit was a dream, and I know it; but it seems I was sleepwalking. (Perhaps I wandered around the bungalow delirious.) The charm was where I left it on the dresser, but the cord was gone. I found it under my bed and tried to put it back through the fish's eye, but it would not go.

E-mail from Annys: "The hounds of hell are loosed. For heaven's sake be careful. Benign influences rising, so have hope." Crazy if you ask me.

E-mail from Pops: "How are you? We haven't heard from you. Have you found a place for Mary and the kids? She is on her way."

What kids? Why the old puritan!

Sent a long e-mail back saying I had been very ill but was better, and there were several places where Mary could stay, including this bungalow, and I would leave the final choice to her. In fairness to Pops, he has no idea where or how I live, and may have imagined a rented room in Kololahi with a monkish cot. I should send another e-mail asking about her flight from Cairns; I doubt he knows, but it may be worth a try.

Almost midnight, and Langi is asleep. We sat on the beach to watch the sunset, drank rum-and-Coke and rum-and-coconut-milk when the Coke ran out, looked at the stars, talked, and made love. Talked some more, drank some more, and made love again.

There. I had to put that down. Now I have to figure out where I can hide this so Mary never sees it. I will not destroy it and I will not lie. (Nothing is worse than lying to yourself. *Nothing.* I ought to know.)

Something else in the was-it-a-dream category, but I do not think it was. I was lying on my back on the sand, looking up at the stars with Langi beside me asleep; and I saw a UFO. It was somewhere between me and the stars, sleek, dark, and torpedo-shaped, but with a big fin on the back, like a rocket ship in an old comic. Circled over us two or three times, and was gone. Haunting, though.

It made me think. Those stars are like the islands here, only a million billion times bigger. Nobody really knows how many islands there are, and there are probably a few to this day that nobody has ever been on. At night they look up at the stars and the stars look down on them, and they tell each other, "They're coming!"

Langi's name means *sky sister* so I am not the only one who ever thought like that.

Found the temple!!! Even now I cannot believe it. Rob has been looking for it for five years, and I found it in six weeks. God, but I would love to tell him!

Which I cannot do. I gave Langi my word, so it is out of the question.

We went swimming in the little bay. I dove down, showing her corals and things that she has probably been seeing since she was old enough to walk, and she showed the temple to me. The roof is gone if it ever had one, and the walls are covered with coral and the sea-creatures that look like flowers; you can hardly see it unless somebody shows you. But once you do it is all there, the long straight walls, the main entrance, the little rooms at the sides, everything. It is as if you were looking at the ruins of a cathedral, but they were decked in flowers and bunting for a fiesta. (I know that is not clear, but it is what it was like, the nearest I can come.) They built it on land, and the water rose; but it is still there. It looks hidden, not abandoned. Too old to see, and too big.

I will never forget this: How one minute it was just rocks and coral, and the next it was walls and altar, with a fifty-foot branched coral like a big tree growing right out of it. Then an enormous gray-white shark with eyes like a man's came out of the shadow of the coral tree to look at us, worse than a lion or a leopard. My God, was I ever scared!

When we were both back up on the rocks, Langi explained that the shark had not meant to harm us, that we would both be dead if it had. (I cannot argue with that.) Then we picked flowers, and she made wreaths out of them and threw them in the water and sang a song. Afterward she said it was all right for me to know, because we are us; but I must never tell other *mulis*. I promised faithfully that I would not.

She has gone to the village to buy groceries. I asked her whether they worshipped Rob's God in the temple underwater. (I had to say it like that for her to understand.) She laughed and said no, they worshipped the shark god so the sharks would not eat them. I have been thinking about that.

It seems to me that they must have brought other gods from the mountains where they lived, a couple of thousand years ago, and they settled here and built that temple to their old gods. Later, probably hundreds of years later, the sea came up and swallowed it. Those old gods went away, but they left the sharks to guard their house. Someday the water will go down again. The ice will grow thick and strong on Antarctica once more, the Pacific will recede, and those murderous old mountain gods will return. That is how it seems to me, and if it is true I am glad I will not be around to see it.

I do not believe in Rob's God, so logically I should not believe in them either. But I do. It is a new millennium, but we are still playing by the old rules. They are going to come to teach us the new ones, or that is what I am afraid of.

Valentine's Day. Mary passed away. That is how Mom would have said it, and I have to say it like that, too. Print it. I cannot make these fingers print the other yet.

Can anybody read this?

Langi and I had presented her with a wreath of orchids, and she was wearing them. It was so fast, so crazy.

So much blood, and Mary and the kids screaming.

I had better backtrack or give this up altogether.

There was a boar hunt. I did not go, remembering how sick I had been after tramping through the jungle with Rob, but Langi and I went to the pig roast afterward. Boar-hunting is the men's favorite pastime; she says it is the only thing that the men like better than dancing. They do not have dogs and do not use bows and arrows. It is all a matter of tracking, and the boars are killed with spears when they find them, which must be really dangerous. I got to talk to the king about this hunt, and he told me how they get the boar they want to a place where it cannot run away anymore. It turns then and defies them, and may charge; but if it does not, four or five men all throw their spears at once. It was the king's spear, he said, that pierced the heart of this boar.

Anyway it was a grand feast with pineapples and native beer, and my rum, and lots of pork. It was nearly morning by the time we got back here, where Mary was asleep with Mark and Adam.

Which was a very good thing, since it gave us a chance to swim and otherwise freshen up. By the time they woke up, Langi had prepared a fruit tray for breakfast and woven the orchids, and I had picked them for her and made coffee. Little boys, in my experience, are generally cranky in the morning (could it be because we do not allow them coffee?) but Adam and Mark were sufficiently overwhelmed by the presence of a brown lady giant and a live skeleton that conversation was possible. They are fraternal twins, and I think they really are mine; certainly they look very much like I did at their age. The wind had begun to rise, but we thought nothing of it.

"Were you surprised to see me?" Mary was older than I remembered, and had the beginnings of a double chin.

"Delighted. But Pops told me you'd gone to Uganda, and you were on your way here."

"To the end of the earth." (She smiled, and my heart leaped.) "I never realized the end would be as pretty as this."

I told her that in another generation the beach would be lined with condos.

"Then let's be glad that we're in this one." She turned to the boys. "You have to take in everything as long as we're here. You'll never get another chance like this."

I said, "Which will be a long time, I hope."

"You mean that you and . . . ?"

"Langitokoua." I shook my head. (Here it was, and all my lies had melted away.) "Was I ever honest with you, Mary?"

"Certainly. Often."

"I wasn't, and you know it. So do I. I've got no right to expect you to believe me now. But I'm going to tell you, and myself, God's own truth. It's in remission now. Langi and I were able to go to a banquet last night, and eat, and talk to people, and enjoy ourselves. But when it's bad, it's horrible. I'm too sick to do anything but shake and sweat and moan, and I see things that aren't there. I—"

Mary interrupted me, trying to be kind. "You don't look as sick as I expected."

"I know how I look. My mirror tells me every morning while I shave. I look like death in a microwave oven, and that's not very far from the truth. It's liable to kill me this year. If it doesn't, I'll probably get attacks on and off for the rest of my life, which is apt to be short."

There was a silence that Langi filled by asking whether the boys wanted some coconut milk. They said they did, and she got my heletay and showed them how to open a green coconut with one chop. Mary and I stopped talking to watch her, and that's when I heard the surf. It was the first time that the sound of waves hitting the beach had ever reached as far inland as my bungalow.

Mary said, "I rented a Range Rover at the airport." It was the tone she used when she had to bring up something she really did not want to bring up.

"I know. I saw it."

"It's fifty dollars a day, Bad, plus mileage. I won't be able to keep it long."

I said, "I understand."

"We tried to phone. I had hoped you would be well enough to come for us, or send someone."

I said I would have had to borrow Rob's jeep if I had gotten her call.

"I wouldn't have known where you were, but we met a native, a very handsome man who says he knows you. He came along to show us the way." (At that point, the boys' expressions told me something was seriously wrong.) "He wouldn't take any money for it. Was I wrong to offer to pay him? He didn't seem angry."

"No," I said, and would have given anything to get the boys alone. But would it have been different if I had? When I read this, when I really get to where I can face it, the thing I will miss on was how fast it was—how fast the whole thing went. It cannot have been a hour between the time Mary woke up and the time Langi ran to the village to get Rob.

Mark lying there whiter than the sand. So thin and white, and looking just like me.

"He thought you were down on the beach, and wanted us to look for you there, but we were too tired," Mary said.

That is all for now, and in fact it is too much. I can barely read this left-handed printing, and my stump aches from holding down the book. I am going to go to bed, where I will cry, I know, and Langi will cuddle me like a kid.

Again tomorrow.

17 Feb. Hospital sent its plane for Mark, but no room for us. Doctor a lot more interested in my disease than my stump. "Dr. Robbins" did a fine job there, he said. We will catch the Cairns plane Monday.

I should catch up. But first: I am going to steal Rob's jeep tomorrow. He will not lend it, does not think I can drive. It will be slow, but I know I can.

19 Feb. Parked on the tarmac, something wrong with one engine. Have I got up nerve enough to write about it now? We will see.

Mary was telling us about her guide, how good-looking, and all he told her about the islands, lots I had not known myself. As if she were surprised she had not seen him sooner, she pointed and said, "Here he is now."

There was nobody there. Or rather, there was nobody Langi and I or the boys could see. I talked to Adam (to my son Adam, I have to get used to that) when it was over, while Rob was working on Mark and Mary. I had a bunch of surgical gauze and had to hold it as tight as I could. There was no strength left in my hand.

Adam said Mary had stopped and the door opened, and she made him get in back with Mark. *The door opened by itself.* That is the part he remembers most clearly, and the part of his story I will always remember, too. After that Mary seemed to be talking all the time to somebody he and his brother could not see or hear.

She screamed, and there, for just an instant, was the shark. He was as big as a boat, and the wind was like a current in the ocean, blowing us down to the water. I really do not see how I can ever explain this.

No takeoff yet, so I have to try. It is easy to say what was not happening. What is hard is saying what was, because there are no words. The shark was not swimming in air. I know that is what it will sound like, but it (he) was not. We were not under the water, either. We could breathe and walk and run just as he could swim, although not nearly so fast, and even fight the current a little.

The worst thing of all was he came and went and came and went, so that it seemed almost that we were running or fighting him by flashes of lightning, and sometimes he was Hanga, taller than the king and smiling at me while he herded us.

No. The most worst thing was really that he was herding everybody but me. He drove them toward the beach the way a dog drives sheep, Mary, Langi, Adam, and Mark, and he would have let me escape. (I wonder sometimes why I did not. This was a new me, a me I doubt I will ever see again.)

His jaws were real, and sometimes I could hear them snap when I could not see him. I shouted, calling him by name, and I believe I shouted that he was breaking our agreement, that to hurt my wives and my sons was to hurt me. To give the devil his due, I do not think he understood. The old gods are very wise, as the king told me today; still, there are limits to their understanding.

I ran for the knife, the heletay Langi opened coconuts with. I thought of the boar, and by God I charged them. I must have been terrified. I do not remember, only slashing at something and someone huge that was and was not there, and in an instant was back again. The sting of the windblown sand, and then up to my arms in foaming water, and cutting and stabbing, and the hammerhead with my knife and my hand in its mouth.

We got them all out, Langi and I did. But Mark has lost his leg, and jaws three feet across had closed on Mary. That was Hanga himself, I feel sure.

Here is what I think. I think he could only make one of us see him at a time, and that was why he flashed in and out. He is real. (God knows he is real!) Not really physical the way a stone is, but physical in other ways that I do not understand. Physical like and unlike light and radiation. He showed himself to each of us, each time for less than a second.

Mary wanted children, so she stopped the pill and did not tell me. That was what she told me when I drove Rob's jeep out to North Point. I was afraid. Not so much afraid of Hanga (though there was that, too) but afraid she would not be there. Then somebody said, "Banzai!" It was exactly as if he were sitting next to me in the jeep, except that there was nobody there. I said, "Banzai," back, and I never heard him again; but after that I knew I would find her, and I waited for her at the edge of the cliff.

She came back to me when the sun touched the Pacific, and the darker the night and the brighter the stars, the more real she was. Most of the time it was as if she were really in my arms. When the stars got dim and the first light showed in the east, she whispered, "I have to go," and walked over the edge, walking north with the sun to her right and getting dimmer and dimmer.

I got dressed again and drove back and it was finished. That was the last thing Mary ever said to me, spoken a couple of days after she died.

She was not going to get back together with me at all; then she heard how sick I was in Uganda, and she thought the disease might have changed me. (It has. What does it matter about people at the "end of the earth" if you cannot be good to your own people, most of all to your own family?)

Taking off.

We are airborne at last. Oh, Mary! Mary starlight!

Langi and I will take Adam to his grandfather's, then come back and stay with Mark (Brisbane or Melbourne) until he is well enough to come home.

The stewardess is serving lunch, and for the first time since it happened, I think I may be able to eat more than a mouthful. One stewardess, twenty or thirty people, which is all this plane will hold. News of the shark attack is driving tourists off the island.

As you see, I can print better with my left hand. I should be able to write eventually. The back of my right hand itches, even though it is gone. I wish I could scratch it.

Here comes the food.

An engine has quit. Pilot says no danger.

He is out there, swimming beside the plane. I watched him for a minute or more until he disappeared into a thunderhead. "The tree is my hat." Oh, God.

Oh my God!

My blood brother.

What can I do?

The Old Woman Whose Rolling Pin Is the Sun

✦

In the years before the river changed its course, both men and women understood all the things that are above the air, though they did not teach these things, as they themselves understood them, to their grandchildren. This is what they said:

This sky that bows over your head is a field, O most cherished Becca, and is of the best black land. So you may see it even now. Look up, until your eyes have forgotten the fire. Look between the stars.

This greatest of all fields belongs to an old man and his wife—I know their names, though I may not reveal to you such sacred things until you are tall and wise. When the weather is fair, and the night wind makes it pleasant to walk about, the old man seeds his whole field. Before you ate, wrapping your meat in the good bread your mother baked for us today on her flat stone, you watched the seeds fall. Remember? Each seed that the old man sows is a shining star. Because it is from his hand that those seeds fall, they shape themselves into men and beasts and many other things, the Little Bear and the Great Bear, the Hunter and his Hounds, and all the rest that you see now. And until their seeds have sprouted, all of these things are free to dash across the sky.

Then comes the rain. Its clouds cover them, and they grow, and we never see those beasts and men again until, on the next fine night, the old man sows the sky-field with new stars. If you were to walk among them, O cherished Becca, as our own longfather did, who himself ran and played in the old man's field, you would be dazzled by their beauty, just as our longfather was, for they grow higher and ever higher, and brighter and ever brighter. No flowers in our fields are ever so beautiful or so many-colored as they are. And even as a single grain of corn grows to a fine, tall plant bearing a hundred grains such as once it was, so with all of these stars.

Then the old woman, who is the old man's wife, picks them, every one except those that have grown from the Tree of the South. Them she leaves to the old man as seed for the morrow, but the rest she heaps on her bakestone. From the birch she cuts a new, white pestle and pounds it across the sky until she has ground all of the stars to powder. At dawn she moistens her flour with water dipped from the lake, and more drops are scattered from her fingers than you and I together could ever count. You will see these drops when you wake, on grass and bush and stone, and even on the new elk hide that I pegged to dry.

Then out comes the old woman's rolling pin, the finest that has ever been, a rolling pin of the strong and magical gold of the old time. Here, we see only one round end of it, which we call the sun. With it she rolls out the world upon her blue baking stone.

This she has been doing for many, many years. Indeed, before our longfather was born, she was doing her work in this same way, day after day, because the old man who sows the stars is always hungry and eats all that she bakes, so that after every day there is hardly a scrap of world left for tomorrow. Can you wonder then, O cherished Becca, that when she has done a whole year of such hard work the old woman wearies? Less and less she toils, so that our days wane, shorter and shorter. And the dry white flour that she has pounded from the stars sifts down upon us, out of the sky. Catch one single speck of it on a fleck of walnut bark and look at it very closely, and you may see that her flour is of stars still. Or find a golden leaf that has fled the maple, piece it with a locust thorn, and place a single drop of clear water on the hole that the thorn has made. Look through that drop at your snowflake upon the bark, and you will see that it is a star truly.

But she tires, as I told you, of so much grinding and rolling and baking. She grows careless even of treasures. Then come the Hounds, leaving the side of the Hunter, their master, and the pursuit of the Great Bear, which is their proper business. And together the Hounds make off with the old woman's rolling pin. With her golden rolling pin in their jaws, each striving to snatch it from the other, those bad Hounds run away, far, far to the south.

Do not laugh, O cherished Becca! For this is a serious matter for you and me. So far to the south, the golden sun seems small and cold. The deer are lean then, there are no berries, apples freeze and rot no matter how many leaves we heap upon their pit, and wolves, made bold by the Hounds' absence, sniff 'round the camp at night, caring nothing for our fire. At that time, children who venture out into the freezing dark without their fathers are torn to pieces. Do not forget!

See where I point, just above the blasted spruce? There course the Hounds, so far in the south that before we sleep they will be running through the trees. Asterion and Chara are their names, dog and bitch. Do you see them bounding between the racing clouds, O cherished Becca? Cor Caroli, La Supera, the Spiral Nebula, and all the rest. All these names I shall teach you when summer comes again, and you are taller.

It would go ill with us, O cherished Becca, if those bad Hounds were allowed to play with the golden sun until they tired of it. We should have nights without days, and see fair Skuld, winter's Morning Star, rise and set, with never a glimpse of morning.

But away to the south, the child rides his goat. We cannot see them now from our camp, though soon we will. The child loves us, perhaps. So at least we hope. Certainly his goat hates Hounds, as goats always do. Thus, as the Hounds approach him, he lowers his head to butt and drives them north again, their game ended for another year.

Or their task done. Perhaps that is how we should say it. Having so nearly lost her golden rolling pin, the old woman understands once more how dear a thing it is that she treated so carelessly, and returns to her task. Can you guess, O cherished Becca, what shapes she has cut from her dough? Yes, I am one, but not the only one by any means. Tree and rock and stream are her work as much as I—or you. The rabbit that you chased today is hers. So are the feet upon which you ran after it.

No, one does not see her in the sky, though there are other women there. One sees—

You did? And taller than the trees? Bent and stern?

No, those were not bulls you heard, but the roaring of her lions. I did not know. Yes, this is the time at which one sees her. Her rolling pin is gone, as I told you, and she herself left free to stroll about the world as she desires. I do not wonder that she smiled at you. Who would not? But, oh, cherished Becca, you must be careful, very careful, all your life. Those who see such things, even in the sky, must always have a care. I am glad she did not speak to you.

I see.

That is an old name of hers—a name I would have said that all but I had forgotten.

Fauna.

It was Fauna, the Bona Dea, some say, who sent the she-wolf that . . . Well, never mind. Nature, we call her now. But you must call her Fauna, O cherished Becca, because she has told you to. She is lonely, perhaps, for her old name; nor is the sun the only thing that leaves us and returns. Yes, I know that I said I could not tell you yet. It was because I did not think you old enough, O cherished Becca. But I was wrong. When Nature says that a child is grown, the child is grown. Even I know that, though I have never counted myself among the wise.

The names of the Hounds I have taught you already. The goat has many, of which the best and safest is Capricorn. Him, too, you may meet in wood or field, most often at noon, they say. Possibly that is because he must be back at his place in the sky by nightfall. Capricorn or Stonebuck, both are safe. But flee him, O cherished Becca. Fly from him, or he will butt you or do worse. Flee any goat, or any man with a goat's feet and horns. If you see the print of his cloven hoof beside water, turn away. And whether you see him on earth or in the sky, know that he brings heat and storm.

Now lay you down, O cherished Becca. You will see the stars better so. Count them, if you would see their true shapes.

That is well, and here is your blanket snug about you. There is the Swan, and there the Harp. See how beautiful they are! Cygnus and Lyra, we call them.

The old man? No, I will not tell you his name. Not I! Neither now nor ever. You will learn it soon enough. Close your eyes.

That is well. Sleep for a moment, and the stars will wait for you.

Sleep.

Forget the old man and his name while still you may. I am glad, very glad, O small and much-cherished Becca, that I shall not be present when you find it out at last.

The Friendship Light

✦

For my own part I have my journal; for my late brother-in-law's, his tape. I will refer to myself as "Ty" and to him as "Jack." That, I think, with careful concealment of our location, should prove sufficient. Ours is a mountainous—or at least, a hilly—area, more rural than Jack can have liked. My sister's house (I insist upon calling it that, as does the law) is set back two hundred yards from the county road. My own is yet more obscure, being precisely three miles down the gravel road that leaves the county road to the north, three-quarters of a mile west of poor Tessie's drive. I hope that these distances will be of help to you.

It began three months ago, and it was over—properly over, that is to say—in less than a week.

Though I have a telephone, I seldom answer it. Jack knew this; thus I had received a note from him in the mail asking me to come to him on the very day on which his note was delivered. Typically, he failed to so much as mention the matter he wished to discuss with me, but wrote that he would be gone for several days. He was to leave that night.

He was a heavy-limbed blond man, large and strong. Tessie says he played football in college, which I can well believe. I know he played baseball professionally for several seasons after graduation, because he never tired of talking about it. For me to specify his team would be counterproductive.

I found him at the end of the drive, eyeing the hole that the men from the gas company had dug; he smiled when he saw me. "I was afraid you weren't coming," he said.

I told him I had received his note only that day.

"I have to go away," he said. "The judge wants to see me." He named the city.

I offered to accompany him.

"No, no. I need you here. To look after the place, and—You see this hole?"

I was very tempted to leave him then and there. To spit, perhaps, and stroll back to my car. Even though he was so much stronger, he would have done nothing. I contented myself with pointing out that it was nearly a yard across, and that we were standing before it. As I ought to have anticipated, it had no effect upon him.

"It's for a friendship light. One of those gas things, you know? Tess ordered it last fall. . . ."

"Before you had her committed," I added helpfully.

"Before she got so sick. Only they wouldn't put it in then because they were busy tuning up furnaces." He paused to wipe the sweat from his forehead with his index finger, flinging the moisture into the hole. I could see he did not like talking to me, and I resolved to stay for as long as I could tolerate him.

"And they don't like doing it in the winter because of the ground's being frozen and hard to dig. Then in the spring it's all mushy."

I said, "But here we are at last. I suppose it will be made to look like a carriage lamp? With a little arm for your name? They're so nice."

He would not look at me. "I would have canceled the order if I'd remembered it, but some damned woman phoned me about it a couple days ago, and I don't know—Because Tess ordered it—See that trench there?"

Again, I could hardly have failed to notice it.

"It's for the pipe that'll tap into the gas line. They'll be back tomorrow to run the pipe and put up the lamp and so on. Somebody's got to be here to sign for it. And somebody ought to see to Tess's cats and everything. I've still got them. You're the only one I could think of."

I said that I was flattered that he had so much confidence in me.

"Besides, I want to visit her while I'm away. It's been a couple of months. I'll let her know that you're looking after things. Maybe that will make her happy."

How little he knew of her!

"And I've got some business of my own to take care of."

It would have given me enormous pleasure to have refused, making some excuse. But to see my old home again—the room in which Tessie and I slept as children—I would have done a great deal more. "I'll need a key," I told him. "Do you know when the workmen will come?"

"About nine-thirty or ten, they said." Jack hesitated. "The cats are outside. I don't let them in the house anymore."

"I am certainly not going to take any responsibility for a property I am not allowed to enter," I told him. "What if there were some emergency? I would have to drive back to my own house to use the telephone. Do you keep your cat food outside, too? What about the can-opener? The milk?"

"All right—all right." Reluctantly, he fished his keys from his pocket. I smiled when I saw that there was a rabbit's foot on the ring. I had nearly forgotten how superstitious he was.

I arrived at the house, which for so many years had been my home, before nine. Tessie's cats seemed as happy to see me as I was to see them— Marmaduke and Millicent "talked" and rubbed my legs, and Princess actually sprang into my arms. Jack has had them neutered, I believed. It struck me that it would be fairly easy to take one of the females— Princess, let us say—home with me, substituting an unaltered female of similar appearance who would doubtless soon present Jack with an unexpected litter of alley kittens. One seal-point Siamese, I reflected, looks very like another; and most of the kittens—very possibly all of them— would be black, blacks being exceedingly common when Siamese are outcrossed.

I would have had to pay for the new female, however—fifty dollars at least. I dropped the idea as a practical possibility as I opened a can of cat food and extended it with one of tuna. But it had set my mental wheels in motion, so to speak.

It was after eleven when the men from the gas company came, and after two before their supervisor rang the bell. He asked if I was Jack, and to save trouble I told him I was and prepared to sign whatever paper he might thrust under my nose.

"Come out here for a minute, will you?" he said. "I want to show you how it works."

Docilely, I followed him down the long drive.

"This is the control valve." He tapped it with his pencil. "You turn this knob to raise and lower the flame."

I nodded to show I understood.

"Now when you light it, you've got to hold this button in until it gets hot—otherwise, it'll go out, see? That's so if it goes out somehow, it'll turn off."

He applied his cigarette lighter, and the flame came on with a *whoosh*.

"Don't try to turn it off in the daytime. You'll ruin the mantle if you light it a lot. Just let it burn, and it'll last you maybe ten years. Should be hot enough now."

He removed his hand. The blue and yellow flame seemed to die, blazed up, then appeared almost to die once more.

"Flickering a little."

He paused and glanced at his watch. I could see that he did not want to take the time to change the valve. Thinking of Jack's irritation, I said, "It will probably be all right when it gets a bit hotter." It flared again as I spoke.

"Yeah. I better turn it down a little. I got it set kind of high." The sullen flickering persisted, though in somewhat muted fashion.

The supervisor pointed. "Right over here's your cutoff. You see how long that valve-stem is? When the boys get through filling in the trench, it'll be just about level with the ground so you don't hit it with the mower. But if you've got to put in a new light—like, if somebody wracks up this one with his car—that's where you can turn off the gas."

I lingered in the house. If you knew how spartanly I live, in a house that my grandfather had thought scarcely fit for his tenant farmers, you would understand why. Jack had liquor, and plenty of good food. (Trust him for that.) My sister's books still lined her shelves, and there was an excellent stereo. It was with something of a shock that I glanced up from *A Rebours* and realized that night had fallen. Far away, at the very end of the long, winding driveway, the new friendship light glared fitfully. It was then that I conceived my little plan.

In the morning I found the handle of the cutoff valve the supervisor had shown me and took it off, employing one of Jack's screwdrivers. Though I am not really mechanically inclined, I had observed that the screws holding the plate over the control valve had shallow heads and poorly formed slots; they had given the supervisor some difficulty when he replaced them. I told a clerk at our hardware store in the village that I frequently had to retighten a screw in my stove, which (although there was never any need to take it out) repeatedly worked loose. The product he recommended is called an anaerobic adhesive, I believe. It was available in four grades: Wicking, Medium (General Purpose), High Strength, and Permanent Installation. I selected the last, though the clerk warned me that I would have to heat the screw thoroughly with a propane torch if I ever wished to remove it.

Back at my sister's, I turned the flame higher, treated the screws with the adhesive, and tightened them as much as I could. At that time, I did not know that Jack kept a journal of his own on cassette tapes. He had locked them away from my prying ears before he left, you may be sure; but I found the current number when the end-of-tape alarm sounded following his demise, and it may be time now to give old Jack the floor—time for a bit of fun.

"Well, here we are. Nicolette's in the bedroom switching into something a lot more comfortable as they always say, so I'm going to take a minute here to wrap things up.

"The judge said okay to selling the beach property, but all the money's got to go into the fund. I'll knock down the price a little and take a finder's fee. Nicolette and I had a couple of good days, and I thought—"

"Jack! Jack!"

"Okay, here's what happened. Nicolette says she was trying out some of Tess's lipsticks, and looking in the mirror she saw somebody down at the end of the driveway watching her. I told her she ought to have shut the drapes, but she said she thought way out in the country like this she wouldn't have to. Anyway, she saw this guy, standing there and not moving. Then the gas died down, and when it came back up he was still there, only a little nearer the house. Then it died down again, and when it came back up he was gone. She was looking out of the window by that time, she says in her slip. I went down to the end of the drive with a flashlight and looked around, but there's so many footprints from the guys that put up the friendship light you can't tell anything. If you ask me it was Ty. He stopped to look when he saw lights in the windows. It would be just like that sneaky son of a bitch not to come by or say anything, but I've got to admit I'm glad he didn't.

"Well, when I got back to the house, Nicolette told me she heard the back door open and close again while I was gone. I went back there, and it was shut and locked. I remembered how it was while Tess was here, and I thought, that bastard has let those cats in, so I went, 'Kitty-kitty-kitty,' and sure as hell the big tom came out of the pantry to see if there was anything to eat. I got him by the neck and chucked him out."

"Got some good pix of Nicolette and me by using the bulb with the motor drive. What I did was put the bulb under the mattress. Every once in a while it would get shoved down hard enough to trip the shutter, then the motor would advance the film. Shot up a whole roll of twenty-four that way last night. She laughed and said, 'Put in a big roll tomorrow,' but I don't think so. I'm going to try to get her to go back Thursday—got to think about that. Can't take *this* roll to Berry's in town, that's for sure. I'll wait till I go to sign the transfer of title, then turn it in to one of the big camera stores. Maybe they'll mail the prints to me, too.

"She wanted me to call Ty and ask if anything funny went on while we were away. I said okay, thinking he wouldn't answer, but he did. He said there was nothing funny while I was gone, but last night he was driving past, and he saw what looked like lightning at an upstairs window. I said I'd been fooling around with my camera equipment and set off the flash a couple of times to test it out. I said I was calling to thank him and see when I could drop by and get my key back. He said he'd already put it in the mail.

"If you ask me he knows Nicolette's here. That was him out there last night as sure as hell. He's been watching the house, and a few minutes ago on the phone he was playing a little game. Okay by me. I've loaded the Savage and stuck it under the bed. Next time he comes snooping around, he's going to have bullets buzzing around his ears. If he gets hit—Hell, no jury around here's going to blame a man for shooting at trespassers on his property at night.

"Either there's more cats now, or the coons are eating the cat food again."

"Nicolette got real scared tonight as soon as it got dark. I kept saying what's the matter? And she kept saying she didn't know, but there was something out there, moving around. I got the Savage, thinking that would make her feel better. Every so often the phone would ring and keep on ringing, but there'd be nobody on the line when I picked it up. I mixed us a couple of stiff drinks, but it was like she'd never touched hers—when she finished, she was just as scared as ever.

"Finally I got smart and told her, 'Listen, honey, if this old place bothers you so much, why don't I just drive you to the airport tonight and put you on a plane home?' She jumped on it. 'Would you? Oh, Lord, Jack, I love you! Just a minute and I'll run up and get packed.'

"Until then there hadn't really been anything to be scared of that I could see, but then something really spooky happened. The phone rang again. I picked it up out of habit, and instead of nobody being there like before, I heard a car start up—over the God-damned phone! I was mad as hell and banged it down, and right then Nicolette screamed.

"I grabbed the rifle and ran upstairs, only she was crying too much to say what it was. The damn drapes were still open, and I figured she'd seen Ty out by the friendship light again, so I closed them. Later she said it wasn't the guy she'd seen before, but something big with wings. It could have been a big owl, or maybe just her imagination and too much liquor. Anyway we wasted a lot of time before she got straightened out enough to pack.

"Then I heard something moving around downstairs. While I was going down the stairs, I heard it run—I guess to hide, and the sack of garbage falling over. After I saw the mess in the kitchen, I thought sure it was one of those damned cats, and I still do, but it seemed like it made too much noise running to be a cat—more like a dog, maybe.

"Nicolette didn't want to go out to the garage with me, so I said I'd bring the car around and pick her up out front. The car and jeep looked okay when I raised the door and switched on the light, but as soon as I opened the car door I knew something was wrong, because the dome light didn't come on. I tossed the rifle in back, meaning to take a look under the hood, and there was the God-damnedest noise you ever heard in your life. It's a hell of a good thing I wasn't still holding the gun.

"It was a cat, and not one of ours. I guess he was asleep on the back seat and I hit him with the Savage when I tossed it inside.

"He came out of there like a buzz saw and it feels like he peeled off half my face. I yelled—that scared the shit out of Nicolette in the house—and grabbed the hammer off my bench. I was going to kill that son of a bitch if I could find him. The moon was up, and I saw him scooting past the pond. I chucked the hammer at him but missed him by a mile. He'd been yowling like crazy, but all of a sudden he shut up, and I went back into the house to get a bandage for my face.

"I was a mess, too. That bastard took a lot of skin off my cheek, and a lot of blood had run onto my shirt and jacket.

"Nicolette was helping me when we heard something fall on the roof. She yelled, 'Where's your gun?' and I told her it was still out in the God-damned car, which it was. She wanted me to go out and get it, and I wanted to find out what had hit on the roof, but I went out first and got the Savage. Everything was okay, too—the garage light was still on, and the gun was lying on the seat of the car. But when I tried to start the car, it wouldn't turn over. Finally I checked the headlights, and sure enough the switch was pulled out. I must have left the lights on last night. The battery's as dead as a doornail.

"I was pulling out the folding steps to the attic when the phone rang. Nicolette got it, and she said all she could hear was a car starting up, the same as I'd heard.

"I went up into the attic with a flashlight, and opened the window and went out onto the roof. It took a lot of looking to find what had hit. I should have just chucked it out into the yard, but like a jerk I picked it up by the ear and carried it downstairs and scared Nicolette half to death. It's the head of a big tomcat, if you ask me, or maybe a wildcat. Not one of ours, a black one.

"Okay, when I was outside and that cat got quiet all of a sudden, I felt a breeze—only cold like somebody had opened the door of a big freezer. There wasn't a noise, but then owls can fly without making a sound. So it's pretty clear what happened.

"We've got a big owl around here. That was probably what Nicolette saw out the window, and it was sure as hell what got the cat. The cat must have come around to eat our cat food, and got into the garage sometime when I opened the door. None of this has got anything to do with the phone. That's just kids.

"Nicolette wanted me to take her to the airport in the jeep right away, but after all that had happened I didn't feel like doing it, so I told her it would be too late to catch a flight and the jeep wasn't running anyhow. I told her tomorrow we'll call the garage and get somebody to come out and give us a jump.

"We yelled about that for a while until I gave her some of Tess's sleeping pills. She took two or three. Now she's out like a light. I've pulled the jack on every God-damned phone in the house. I took a couple aspirins, but my cheek still hurt so bad I couldn't sleep, so I got up and fixed a drink and tried to talk all this out. Now I'm going back to bed."

"This is bad—I've called the sheriff, and the ambulance is supposed to come out. It will be all over the damned paper, and the judge will see it as sure as hell, but what else could I do? Just now I mopped up the blood with a couple of dirty shirts. I threw them out back, and as soon as I shut the door I could hear them out there. I should've opened the door and shot. I don't know why I didn't, except Nicolette was making that noise that drives me crazy. I damn near hit her with the rifle. I've done everything I can. She needs an ambulance—a hospital."

—————

"Now, honey, I want you to say—right into here—that it wasn't me, understand?"

"Water . . ."

"I'll get you plenty of water. You say it, and I'll get it right away. Tell them what happened."

"The tape ran out. Had to turn it over.

"Okay, then I'll say it. It wasn't me—wasn't Jack. Maybe I ought to start right at the beginning.

"Nicolette shot at a coon. I was sound asleep, but I must have jumped damned near through the ceiling. I came up yelling and fighting, and it was dark as hell. I hit the light switch, but the lights wouldn't come on. The only light in the whole place was the little crack between the drapes. I pulled them open. It was just the damned friendship light way down at the end of the drive, but that was better than nothing.

"I saw she had the gun, so I grabbed it. She'd been trying to work it, but she hadn't pulled the lever down far enough to chamber a fresh round. If she had, she'd probably have killed us both.

"I said, 'Listen, the power's just gone off—that happens a lot out here.' She said she got up to go to the bathroom, and she saw eyes, green eyes shining. She turned on the hall light, but it was gone. She tried to wake me up but I just grabbed for her, so she got the gun. Pretty soon all the lights went out. She thought she heard it coming and fired.

"I got my flashlight and looked around. The bullet went right through the wall of Tess's room and hit the bed—I think it stopped in the mattress somewhere.

"Nicolette kept saying, 'Give me the keys—I'll go to the airport by myself.' I smacked her good and hard a few times to make her shut up, once with the flashlight.

"Then I saw the green eyes, too, but as soon as I got the light on it, I knew what it was—just a coon, not even a real big one.

"I didn't want to shoot again, because even if I'd hit, it would have made a hell of a mess, so I told Nicolette to open the door. She did, and that's when I saw them, two or three of them, flying around down by the friendship light. Jesus!"

"They're outside now. I know they are. I took a shot at one through the big window, but I don't think I hit it.

"Where the hell's the sheriff's guy? He should've been here an hour ago—the ambulance, too. It's starting to get light outside."

"The coon got in through the God-damned cat door. I ought to have guessed. When Ty was here he had the cats in the house with him, so he unbolted it—that was how Marmaduke got in last night.

"I tried to switch this thing off, but I'm shaking too bad. I damn near dropped it. I might as well get on with it anyway. This isn't getting us any-where. I gave her the keys and I told her, 'Okay, you want to go to the God-damn airport so bad, here. Leave the keys and the ticket in the dash compartment and I'll go out and pick it up when I can.'

"I didn't think she'd do it, but she took the keys and ran outside. I went to the window. I heard the jeep start up, and it sounded like she was tearing out the whole damn transmission. Pretty soon she came roaring down the driveway. I guess she had it in second and the pedal all the way to the floor. I didn't think any were close to her, and all of a sudden there was one right above her, dropping down. The wings made it look like the jeep was blinking on and off, too.

"The jeep went across the road and into the ditch. I never thought I'd see her again, but it dropped her on the front lawn. I shouldn't have gone out to get her. I could've been killed.

"It was looking for something in her, that's what I think. I didn't know there was so much blood when you cut a person open like that. What the hell do the doctors do?

"I think she's dead now."

———

"The sheriff's men just left. They say the power's off all over. It looks like a plane hit the wires, they said, without crashing. Jesus.

"Here's what I told them. Nicolette and I had a fight. I keep the gun loaded in case of prowlers, and she took a couple of shots at me. They said, 'How do we know you didn't shoot at her?' I said, 'You think I'd miss a woman twice, with my deer rifle, inside the house?' I could see they bought it.

"I said I gave her the keys to the jeep and said to leave it at the airport—the truth in other words. They said, 'Didn't you give her any money?' I told them, 'Not then, but I'd given her some before, back when we were still in the hotel.' I told them that she floorboarded it down the drive and couldn't make the turn. I saw her hit and went out and got her, and brought her back into the house.

"They said, 'You ripped her up the belly with a knife.' I said, 'No way. Sure, I slapped her a couple times for shooting at me, but I never knifed her.' I showed them my hunting knife, and they checked out all the kitchen knives. They said, 'How'd she get ripped up the middle like that?' and I said, 'How the hell should I know? She got thrown out of the jeep.'

"I'm not supposed to leave the county, not supposed to stay anyplace but here. They took the Savage, but I've still got my shotgun and the twenty-two."

"Power's back on. The tow truck came out for the jeep and gave me a jump for the Cadillac.

"The way I see it, they've never even tried to get into the house, so if I stay in here I ought to be all right. I'm going to wait until after dark, then see if I can get Ty to come over. If he gets in okay, fine—I'll string him along for a while. If he doesn't, I'll leave tomorrow and the sheriff can go to hell. I'll let his office know where I am, and tell them I'll come in for questioning any time they want to see me."

———

"I just phoned Ty. I said I'd like to give him something for looking after the place while I was gone. And that I was going away again, this time for quite a while, and I wanted him to take care of things like he did before. I told him I've been using the spare key, but the one he mailed was probably in the box, down by the friendship light, because I haven't picked up my mail yet. I said for him to check the box before he came to the house. He said okay, he'd be right over. It seems to be taking him . . ."

Ty again. At this point in the tape, my knock can be heard quite distinctly, followed by Jack's footfalls as he went to the door; it would seem that he was too rattled to turn off his tape recorder. (Liquor, as I have observed several times, does not in fact prevent nervousness, merely allowing it to accumulate.) I would be very happy to transcribe his scream here, if only I knew how to express it by means of the twenty-six letters of the Roman alphabet.

You took him, as you promised, whole and entire. I have no grounds for complaint upon that score, or indeed upon any. And I feel certain he met his well-deserved death firmly convinced that he was in the grip of demons, or some such thing, which I find enormously satisfying.

Why, then, do I write? Permit me to be frank now: I am in need of your assistance. I will not pretend that I deserve it (you would quite correctly care nothing for that), or that it is owed me; I carried out my part of the agreement we made at the friendship light, and you carried out yours. But I find myself in difficulties.

Poor Tessie will probably never be discharged. Even the most progressive of our hospitals are now loath to grant release in cases of her type—there were so many unfortunate incidents earlier, and although society really has very little invested in children aged two to four, it overvalues them absurdly.

As her husband, Jack was charged with administration of the estate in which (though it was by right mine) I shared only to a minuscule degree through the perversity of my mother. Were Jack legally dead, I, as Tessie's brother, would almost certainly be appointed administrator—so my attorney assures me. But as long as Jack is considered by the law a mere fugitive, a suspect in the suspicious death of Nicolette Corso, the entire matter is in abeyance.

True, I have access to the house; but I have been unable to persuade the conservator that I am the obvious person to look after the property. Nor can I vote the stock, complete the sale of the beach acreage, or do any other of many such useful and possibly remunerative things.

Thus I appeal to you. (And to any privileged human being who may read this. Please forward my message to the appropriate recipients.) I urgently require proof of Jack's demise. The nature of that proof I shall leave entirely at your discretion. I venture to point out, however, that identifications based on dental records are in most cases accepted by our courts without question. If Jack's skull, for example, were discovered some fifty or more miles from here, there should be little difficulty.

In return, I stand ready to do whatever may be of value to you. Let us discuss this matter, openly and in good faith. I will arrange for this account to be reproduced in a variety of media.

It was I, of course, as even old Jack surmised, whom Jack's whore saw the first time near the friendship light. To a human being its morose dance appeared quite threatening, a point I had grasped from the beginning.

It was I also who pulled out Jack's headlight switch and put the black tom—I obtained it from the Humane Society—in his car. And it was I who telephoned; at first I did it merely to annoy him—a symbolic revenge on all those (himself included) who have employed that means to render my existence miserable. Later I permitted him to hear my vehicle start, knowing as I did that his would not. Childish, all of them, to be sure; and yet I dare hope they were of some service to you.

Before I replaced the handle of the valve and extinguished Tessie's friendship light, I contrived that my Coleman lantern should be made to flicker at the signal frequency. Each evening I hoist it high into the branches of the large maple in front of my home. Consider it, please, a beacon of welcome. I am most anxious to speak with you again.

Slow Children at Play

✦

Possibly I am the only one who understands how they have come to live in our building, Doctor, and it is possible that I am the only one who has ever wondered; certainly they themselves neither wonder nor understand. They are Mark and Joe, and although Mark can be quick at times, both in movement and in apprehension, the two in combination have not infrequently recalled to my mind the admonitory sign outside our building.

For there is always something childlike about them both, something childlike about their fear as the days (I had nearly said the years) dwindle, while the simplest tasks (their none-too-frequent baths, for example, or warming a can of soup) may require whole mornings, whole afternoons. They live by begging.

Ours is a red brick building, in which I live on the seventh floor. They are on the eighth, where the elevator does not run. There are three small apartments on that floor, but they occupy only one; the rest are vacant, I believe. Theirs is kept cleaner than one would expect, though it is not clean. To the west (one of my windows looks west) flows the river, moving as slowly as Joe and almost as placidly. Its silent gray ships have come to it from far away, from Yokohama and Christchurch and Guayaquil, and now that they have reached port at last they are in no hurry to set forth again. Mark and Joe are like them in that.

To the east stand a few more buildings like our own, then silent streets traversed solely by trucks; to the north are many old homes, divided and subdivided; but to the south, ruin. Mark and Joe lived among those ruins (such, at least, is my theory) as many do, perhaps for several years. Slowly—for they do all things very slowly—they must have drifted north-ward in search of better lodgings, or perhaps only safer ones. Accus-tomed as they must surely have been to derelict buildings, ours must have appeared derelict, for more than half its apartments are empty, and the rest rented, for the most part, to unproductive scholars like myself, per-sons cognizant of the latest gossip concerning Pericles or Paracelsus, who neither know nor care which politico may be president or to what Gen-eral Foods or General Motors will lay siege next.

They would have used the stairs, I think, as they do now; and only on the uppermost floor, their eighth, would they have found a door un-bolted. The old man who cared for this building then never bothered much about the eighth floor, seldom showing the apartments there, for he did not like the steps. When they had lived there for a month or more, he encountered them in the lobby and asked them what they wanted. Joe told him, "Nothing," which made him suspicious, of course. I said, "Don't be afraid. Tell him about your sink." After that he left them alone. He died in March.

Since then we have had a whole chain of people, white and black, both men and women, who were supposed to take care of the building. None have remained more than a few weeks, for the pay is only the ground-floor back. I offered to check his book for one, a sallow man who could scarcely read, and told him it was wrong, that the eighth floor west was occupied, and taking his pencil marked it so. While I had his pencil, I indicated that rent had been paid in advance as well. Since then Mark and Joe have not been troubled, or at least have not been troubled much.

Joe is retarded, I feel sure. It would be conventional to say that he has the mind of a child of ten or some such age; but although I said they were childlike, there is little about him suggestive of a boy of ten, at least to me. He is not inclined to run or shout, and lacks that curiosity which is so marked a trait in most boys. He is silent as a rule, and when he speaks, un-willing to meet any eyes but Mark's. He considers long before he acts, and then acts slowly; and he has a remarkably retentive memory. All this seems the very opposite of a boy to me, or at least of such boys as I knew long ago.

Mark I am much less sure about. I will hazard a guess—I am no psychologist—and say that he is somewhat insane. As you will see, it may be that I am mistaken or worse.

He is as thin as Joe is thick, and at first glance as swift as Joe is deliberate. Yet it is not really so, for Mark begins everything a score of times before finishing, twists and turns, jerks forward and back like a shuttle, rolls his eyes and wags his head to no purpose, wiggles one foot then the other, then both. His hair, which is long, falls into his eyes fifty times an hour, and must be pushed away.

Some celestial power meditates his death; so Mark believes. I learned this because I was curious about his past, and Joe's. Had they, I wanted to know, really lived in ruined buildings for a while? And would they go on living in this building of ours, when it, too, was given over to decay? When old Hearn and I, and all the rest, were gone or dead? Had he and Joe no parents, no sisters or brothers? Where had they come from originally?

"I c-came from the sky," Mark told me. "J-Joe out of the ground, G-Gene. Yes! F-from the sky! I f-fell, oh, f-fell so many, many. I h-had wings."

Seated upon my piano bench, he extended not only his arms, but his legs. The effect was shocking, for it made me think not of a bird but of an insect, so many of which have four wings.

This Mark himself reinforced, saying, "He t-tore them off. Ne-ne-ne-never! Nevermore. Never more fly! Die, not fly, die now, fly! For bad."

Joe said, "We have to die, too, Mark," looking to me for confirmation.

"That's right," I told him. "Dust to dust."

Mark crossed to the window and pointed. "S-see that s-sun? He'll k-kill you, too, G-Gene?" The sun had set an hour before, behind clouds the color of butchers' meat; now a crimson beacon, bright but remote, gleamed like a lonely star on the other side of the river. "Today's *his* day. He takes your sun away."

I glanced at the calendar on my desk. "You're right, Mark. This's the solstice, the twenty-second of December, the shortest day of all."

I should not have said that, as I knew the moment the words left my lips. Sheer terror invaded Joe's normally placid face, and he pointed, trembling, as Mark had a moment before. "It's going. Flying away."

To tell the truth I do not like to look out of that window, or even to think about it, because it was from that window that David Arimaspian stepped to his death. And so I remained where I was, studying, or rather, pretending to study, G. T. Griffith's *Mercenaries of the Hellenistic World;* though when I thought of David, the nominal "best friend" of my childhood, the author's name became anathema to me and I covered it (for it appeared at the top of the page) with one hand. I said, "That's not really the sun, Joe."

Mark said, "He'll b-be b-bad tonight." It was one of those moments in which Mark seems quite sane.

"The sun's yellow," I reminded Joe, "or at least it usually is." I had remembered as I spoke that it would be red-shifted if it were in fact leaving us, but it seemed best to say nothing of that. "Mark, would you shut that window for me and draw the drapes?" It was cold in the apartment, as it had been for some time, and growing ever colder; but as I said, I do not care to approach that window too near.

"C-closed already, G-Gene." He drew the drapes, as I had asked.

Neither of us, I think, were in the least prepared for what happened next, which was that Joe tried to throw himself through the window. It was Mark who saved him, wrapping his arms around Joe's waist and heaving him backward with such force that they fell to the carpet.

"N-not the sun, Joe," Mark said when I had hold of Joe as well. "Really. Really. A light, a red light for st-stop."

Even if I could, I would not reconstruct that whole session with Joe. Calming him enough for even the simplest arguments to be of service required half an hour at least; but at last he was ready to listen to reason, insofar as he could comprehend it, and Mark promised that they would go across the river and find "the sun." If it was truly the sun, they would bring it back if they could, and they would at least be warm themselves. If it was not, Joe would know that there was nothing to worry about. Joe agreed that in that case he would return here and go to bed, and never try to jump after the sun again.

I should have said nothing, of course, but the thought of someone else going to his death through that window had shaken me to my core. Ever since David's death two years ago, I have felt that it was tugging at me; and I knew that if Joe had died as well, its pull would have been doubled. "I'll drive you," I told them. "If you have to walk, it'll take you all night." To test myself, I went to the window and parted the drapes. "Look carefully, Joe, and you'll see it's just above that second oil-storage tank. We'll go there and take another sighting."

And so we did, in my rusty station wagon, crossing the toll bridge and halting on the far side of the refinery. The crimson beacon shone high upon a hill, or so it seemed; and it was still some considerable distance away.

Slowly the industrial district through which I drove faded to shabby stores. In time—I am not sure how much time—these grew sleeker, and gave way to houses, and they to larger houses, ever more widely separated, until we sped along a straight road that climbed and climbed through mere darkness, with the beacon to our right at times and to our left at others. I thought then (for I could not resist the association) of the Magi, wise men who were in fact members of a certain Median tribe, who followed a star to Bethlehem. We three comprised a half-wit, a madman, and a fool. But perhaps those "three kings" had thought hardly better of themselves.

It was about then, I think, that I first saw the man in the fire—for a fire it was, and not an electric light of some sort, as I had been assuming. When I write "the man in the fire," I mean it only as one speaks of the Man in the Moon; for surely he was not actually standing among the flames, although he appeared to be. When I stopped the car and we got out, he was (this I am certain of) standing before it with his back toward it, as a man will, and his arms extended behind him as though his fingers were cold.

"It's not the sun!" Joe exclaimed happily.

"It is the sun," the man before the fire said.

He was much taller than I, though I am taller than Joe and much taller than Mark. Although his face was in shadow, framed as it was by leaping flames, it appeared noble and impressive; and so I said, "You don't understand—Joe takes people seriously when they say things like that."

As if to confirm it, Joe pleaded, "Don't take it away now! Bring it back."

"It has never gone," the man said, "but I will bring all of you again to it. Not for your sake." (His eyes had never left mine.) "And certainly not for yours," he looked disdainfully at Mark, "and not even for yours," he told Joe more kindly, "but because the time is not yet."

"It doesn't have to be for me," Joe said humbly, "if you'll just do it."

"I will. Now, for this is the hour." And with that he spun about.

It was here that my psychotic episode (if that was what it was) began. For in turning thus it seemed that he revealed, not his back, but an entire new being: a live griffin, eagle-clawed and many-winged. Its eagle's head screamed at me, a shriek that seemed to fill that whole chill night, and its golden eyes shone brighter than its fire.

I staggered backward. I do not remember how I reached the car; but I was driving again, backing it and twisting the wheel. Once I glanced behind us, because I had already begun to doubt what I had seen. The lofty figure we had first glimpsed still stood like a sentry before its fire, which appeared to revolve majestically now, grown even larger and more brilliant.

And that figure was horned like a Viking or a devil; and as I looked, it roared like a lion.

Joe came to see me this morning, which is why I am writing this for you, Doctor. Because of what he said, I am no longer certain I lost my reason for a time. I tried to explain to him that I had been ill last night. "We're all sick at one time or another, Joe," I tried to explain. "I'm sorry, really sorry, if I acted, well, oddly. But I couldn't help it."

Joe nodded, not meeting my eyes.

"You've been ill yourself a time or two, I imagine."

He nodded again, slowly. "From eating out of the Dumpster. Because they spray for flies."

I did not remember then that the devil was called the Baal of Flies by someone in a position to know. I have thought of it only now, but it may be significant.

"I'm going to see a doctor, a specialist." I felt sure Joe would not know what a clinical psychologist is. "He's a friend of a friend, and so he agreed to work me in this afternoon." My agony cried out: "I never thought this would happen to me."

"We were just playing," Joe told me very seriously. "You played, too."

"No! I really thought I saw it, Joe. I believed that it was real."

Joe shook his head stubbornly. "Mark plays, Gene. Shows me, and I play, too, because I'm there. Last night you played with us."

I could only gape at him.

"We were just playing." Joe nodded a solemn confirmation. "We don't get hurt, because we take care of each other." He went to the window and stood looking out, smiling his shy smile at the sunlit river.

They, all together, singing
in harmony and moving round
the heaven in their measured dance,
unite in one harmony whose cause is one,
and whose end is one.
It is this harmony which entitles the All
to be called Order, and not disorder.
—DE MUNDO

Under Hill

✦

Sir Bradwen, that famous paladin, had heard stories of the Hill of Glass in far-off Camelot. With Arthur's leave, he had ridden far and sailed perilous seas. For seventy days thereafter it seemed the tale fled even as he approached it, for at every village men pointed to the place where rose the sun, and swore it was but two days' journey more—or three. Or a fortnight.

And yet . . .

The tale gained substance at each new place. The size of the hill diminished. Likewise the difficulty of the lower slopes. It was not merely of glass, but of green glass of about the color of this leaf, sir. The princess, once only a beautiful lady from a remote country, gained a name: Apple Blossom. And when Sir Bradwen protested that neither he nor any other man in Christendom had heard of a lady so named, his informants merely shrugged, and declared that she ought to know—an argument he found difficult to refute.

At length he encountered a merchant, a solid no-nonsense trader in wool and fleeces, who declared that he had seen the glass hill himself, and even conversed with the princess. "A smallish woman," he continued, "with long black hair and big eyes. I prefer my women larger, and I like a bit more meat on them. But she's very pretty if you care for the type. Delicate, you know. One of those oval faces. Young, I would say. Very young, and stolen from far Cathay. Daughter of their king and all the rest. Think you can climb a hill of glass, Sir Bradwen?"

"By Saint Joseph!" Bradwen exclaimed, and raised his sword hand to attest the oath. "I have not come this far to fail."

"Well said." The merchant smiled as the point of his dagger carried half his chop to his mouth. "I like a young man of spirit."

"And he likes you," Bradwen declared. And then, seeing that the merchant expected to be asked for a loan, "I have gold sufficient for my modest needs, you understand. I've lands, and a castle that we wrenched from the Heathen Saxon. But in the matter of tidings I am poorer than any churl. May I ask how you came to speak with the princess?"

"With little difficulty," the merchant replied, clearly relieved, "for I have been blessed with good ears and a good, loud voice. She was on the battlements, where she appears to spend a good deal of her time. The slope of the lower levels is easy, and there are crevices in the glass with bushes sprouting out of them. It becomes steeper higher up, then levels off at the top." The merchant traced the outline of a bell with his hands.

"So I was able to get pretty close," he continued. "It's not a large castle, and the walls aren't terribly high. I asked her name and so forth. She's been enchanted, she says—a spell to replace her own tongue with ours. But anyone who rescues her can have her. The enchanter has promised her that.

"Let's see . . . What else? Well, the gates are open. I saw they were. She has food in there, she says, and springs of water and wine. Princess Apple Blossom's her name, her father's King of Cathay—"

Sir Bradwen, who had heard these things before, nodded somewhat curtly.

"And she wants to be rescued," the merchant finished, not the least discomfited. "I told her I wasn't a rescuer, that I was a married man and would leave rescuing to the younger fellows, but that I would try to find a rescuer and send him to her."

"You have succeeded," Sir Bradwen declared.

"I thought so." A draught of ale washed down the rest of the chop. "Is there anything else I can tell you?"

"Yes, indeed. I assumed she was locked in her castle. You say the gates are open. Why does she not walk through them?"

The merchant shrugged. "I can but speculate, though speculation feeds me well enough. It may be that she hopes for rescue, and prefers that to death. You see, my bold and knightly friend, with each step beyond the gate the slope grows steeper. Perhaps she might take ten steps, perhaps two. I don't know. But soon she would surely lose her footing, slip, and slide. The farther she slid the faster she would go. When she struck the stones and trees at the foot . . ." He shrugged again. "Suppose a kestrel, bold and young, were to fly full tilt into a wall of stone. For that matter, suppose that you were to ride at such a wall as you would a foe in the lists."

Sir Bradwen nodded thoughtfully. "Then one has only to reach the summit of the hill to enter the castle."

"So it appeared to me," the merchant declared, "though I did not try it—or see anybody else try it either. Have you more questions?"

"One, certainly. How can I reach the hill?"

"Oh, there's no difficulty about that. It's but a day's ride. Go down the road tomorrow until you reach the ford of the Sart. Turn left. There's a path along the river."

Sir Bradwen nodded.

"Follow it. Keep your eyes to your left, away from the river. If the weather's fair, you'll have no difficulty at all. The glass flashes in the sunshine. If the day is dark, you're looking for a smooth, grass-green hill with a small castle of gray stone at its top."

The merchant paused to clear his throat. "Tell Her Highness I sent you, will you? I swore I'd send somebody, and I'd like her to know I kept my promise."

"I will," quoth Sir Bradwen, "and I will rise next morning before the sky grows gray."

Which he did, waking both the sleepy grooms and his charger, saddling the latter, and rising forth while the morning star still gleamed above the eastern horizon, his good sword at his side, his lance in his hand, and another morning star (a weighty mace with a head of steel spikes) dangling from his saddlebow.

"For if I find Princess Apple Blossom half so easily as that merchant said I might," he murmured to Saint Joseph, "I may climb her slippery hill and claim her by sunset. Assist me, and Joseph shall be our firstborn son."

The sun was scarcely higher than the treetops when his road reached the ford of the Sart. To his left, narrow indeed but quite visible, stretched the path of which the merchant had spoken. Up it rode Sir Bradwen with a merry heart, and before tierce beheld a distant hill flashing in the sunshine. A little nearer, and he saw plainly that this dazzling hill was crowned with a small castle—scarcely more than a diminutive keep—of gray stone. Nearer still, and his keen eyes made out a figure on the battlements, a maiden, he felt sure, with long dark hair.

A maiden who tottered forward and back, wringing her hands at every step.

Dismounting and dropping his reins on the ground, he took a certain wallet he had secured before leaving Albion from a saddlebag and applied the fine powder it contained to the soles of his boots.

For a time it sufficed. He negotiated the lower slopes with little difficulty and was quickly seen by the maiden on the battlement, who waved a many-colored scarf so fine that sunlight freely penetrated it, and called, "Hail, illustrious stranger! Greeting and welcome! Should you be desirous of cushioned rest, delectable refreshment, cooling airs, and the attentions a humble maid overjoyed by the lightest smile from her courageous and ever-compassionate lord, be aware that all are to be found in this lowly dwelling which, should you wish it, will at once become your own."

He waved in return. "I am Sir Bradwen of the Forest Tower, Your Highness. Your friend the merchant sent me as your rescuer, as I had been seeking you earlier. I have ridden hard all the way from Camelot. I am a knight of Arthur's table. Have you heard of us?"

He essayed another step, and finding it difficult indeed powdered his boot soles again.

"Your glory, most goodly, most generous lord, reaches to the stars," replied the maiden on the battlement, "and now has attained even to my decayed dwelling, for I have seen you, radiant as the sun and of clean and glorious visage."

At which point the knight came near to falling. "Your Highness," he called, "I can climb no nearer. This slope is too steep, and grows even steeper farther up. Do not lose hope. I will return with some better means of ascent."

Although the face of the princess was still distant, he saw her joy fade. "This inconsiderable person sympathizes most deeply with your plight," she called. "This bewildered and imprisoned maid had dared think it possible that her lord—that her l-lord . . ."

"I will!" he shouted, under his breath adding, "Just not today."

There was a long silence between them, bridged only by desire. At last the princess called, "My lord, the wisest and most ingenious of men, has doubtless hit upon some slight of noble simplicity by whose means this unexceptional person might regain her liberty?"

He shook his head.

"As, for example, harnessing a hundred wild geese to a sedan chair? This slight was employed by the profound Lo Hi to pass over bandit-infested mountains."

"Unfortunately," called Sir Bradwen, "I have no sedan chair, Your Highness."

"Conceivably one might befriend the Storm Dragon, who would in magnanimity lift one up, even as the daring Sho Mee was borne among clouds to behold the earth?"

"Should I meet the Storm Dragon," declared Sir Bradwen, "I will surely oblige him so long as the matter involves no virgins. I have never made his acquaintance, however. Nor have I the smallest notion where he might be found."

Silence reigned once again, until the princess ventured, "This least of all persons has the honor to claim membership in a family highly favored by the August Personage of Jade. She herself, a poor weak woman, has often laid her wretched petitions at the feet of the Queen of Heaven. Perhaps if you were to petition her exalted husband . . . ?"

"Of course!" Sir Bradwen snapped his fingers. "I'll ask Saint Joseph. I should have thought of that at once."

With that brisk speed which optimism engenders, Sir Bradwen left the glass hill and returned to the village in which he had lodged the night before. There was no church there, but the villagers directed him to a chapel in the wood, not very distant. There he spent the afternoon and evening in prayer and retired, fasting, to the dubious shelter of a nearby bush.

Of horse and sword, mail and helm, no trace remained. Clad in the single simple garment of the poor, he stood at the entrance to the workshop. Inside that shop a patient craftsman labored, drilling holes and pounding pegs into them at measured intervals. Leaving off his work, he straightened up. And their eyes met.

In the village next day, he explained the contrivance he had been shown to an old peasant who knew some carpentry; the old peasant made a model of it: a peeled sapling, with twigs pushed into little holes along both its sides.

Later that same day, he and the old peasant showed the model to two young men he had selected. "Fell a tree," Sir Bradwen explained, "a straight, slender one with a lot of boughs. Cut off most of those completely, but leave the stubs of a few. You would have something like this."

They scratched, and nodded slowly.

"There can't be many trees with boughs all the way to the ground. I looked for some and couldn't find any. But we can drill holes and pound cut-off branches into them where we need them."

There was a lengthy silence, after which one muttered, "Ya."

"Old Lenz here will take care of the drilling and pounding. Your tasks will be choosing the trees, felling them, and getting them into place."

One ventured, "Oxen we will need? It could be."

Sir Bradwen shook his head. "If you need an ox to move it, the tree's too big. Cut slender trees."

The old peasant added, "The top you cut where it lies. The branches you trim. Then it you move."

Both muttered, "Ya . . ."

"Work hard," Sir Bradwen said, "and I will pay you one lushberg *per day,* paid at the end of each day."

As he spoke he held up two lushbergen, and both young men exclaimed, "Ya!" To which the one with the cast in his eye added, "We work hard!"

———

Days passed. The first pole had brought him nearer the princess indeed, but carried him only to a point at which the glass hill rose steeper still. A second pole, lashed to the first at the top, provided a base from which they raised a third. That third brought him so near that for the first time he was able to appreciate the beauty and the marvelous delicacy of her countenance. His whole being throbbed with longing for her—even as the longing in her own eyes, and the tears, broke his heart.

"We must build a second triangle like to the first," he told the old peasant. "We can mount another ladder-stick on that, tie it to the one we've got up there already, and put a seventh on top of them. That should do it."

The old peasant nodded, his assistants mumbled, "Ya . . ." in unison, and the great new work was begun.

At two per night to the old peasant, and one each to his assistants, Sir Bradwen's store of lushbergen had begun to run short. He took to the highroad to refresh it, and had the good fortune to encounter a merchant the very first day. "What ho, my bold knightly friend," quoth the merchant. "Have you rescued the princess?"

"My campaign is well begun," Sir Bradwen replied, "my troops advance even as we speak. We require, however, some small support from those well able to give it. May I count upon you for some trifling contribution?"

"Alas!" The merchant pulled a long face, an expression he had practiced and perfected. "My affairs go very ill. You spoke of a castle and lands when last we met. How I envied you, my bold knightly friend! For I have neither."

"Your contribution need not be large," Sir Bradwen explained. "A mere token of your support. What say you?"

The merchant sighed. "I cannot. I must buy wool with the few pence I yet retain, and if I cannot sell it at a profit I must starve."

"You appear remarkably well nourished at present," Sir Bradwen remarked.

"My difficulties, though very recent, are severe," the merchant declared. "Will you let me pass?"

"Alas!" Knowing that his own long face was wont to be interrupted by spasms of merriment, Sir Bradwen pulled down his visor instead. "Without a contribution, you may not pass this way. Doubtless there are other roads. There always are."

The merchant nodded. "There is one other. It is not as advantageous however. It is longer, for one thing. For another, it has the ill luck to pass the castle of Gifflet le Fils de Do, lord of these lands. As a loyal freeman thereof, I should think myself obliged to report your obstruction of the more convenient route."

"I would enjoy the contest," Sir Bradwen replied with perfect sincerity, "but before we engaged, honesty would oblige me to mention that I do not obstruct it, only seek to collect a trifling toll. Also that I am authorized to do so by a visiting princess, the daughter of the King of Cathay. Perhaps honesty would also oblige me to report that you were well apprised of these matters, and to ask whether you had communicated them in making your complaint."

"O my bold and knightly friend!" the merchant replied. "We were truly friends only a fortnight ago. Is it not a shame that two Christians should thus be at daggers drawn?"

"It is," Sir Bradwen replied, taking his morning star from his saddlebow and testing one of its points against his fingertip. "I rarely employ my dagger while on horseback, however, and I reserve my sword—a noble weapon with an attested relic of Saint Joseph in the pommel—for those well born. For the rest I employ this."

So saying, he rode hard at the merchant; and when the latter raised his arm to block the expected blow, struck him with the lower edge of his shield, knocking him from his saddle. In a trice Sir Bradwen had dismounted as well and seated himself upon the merchant's belly.

The merchant's dagger he swiftly snatched from the merchant's belt and flung into the bushes. The merchant's large and weighty purse he then decanted onto the ground before him, an act accompanied by much chinking and chiming.

When he had selected those coins he favored, he returned the remainder to the merchant's purse; and the merchant, when he had recovered from being sat upon by a powerful man in chain mail, and had ridden a safe distance along the road, was surprised to find that his gold was intact—only his brass lushbergen had been taken, with two Roman aeris, one denarius, and some other silver.

The great day came at last. Four overlapping triangles supported similar poles forming two triangles of their own. These (high up the glassy slope) supported another two, which with the addition of a bottom pole to brace them formed the final triangle that raised high the final pole— the one triumphantly climbed by Sir Bradwen, the one he stepped from where the slope was gentle enough.

The one at the top of which Princess Apple Blossom met him, a perfect, dainty maiden a head and a half shorter than he, perfumed and robed in magnificent brocade. The one at whose top they embraced and kissed, and kissed again and again. And yet again, until at last Sir Bradwen, fearing that he might be overwhelmed by his passion, suggested they go, saying, "If you cannot climb down, or hesitate to climb down for sweet modesty's sake, I will carry you down. I can hold you with one arm, and we will stand upon honest clay in a trice."

At this the princess smiled. "If my exalted lord will consent, this beggarly person retains a few poor possessions, and my all-wise lord must surely know that we miserable ones who have nothing greatly value what little we have. There is my inconsiderable jade figure of the Queen of Heaven, to whom I have no joss to burn though she is dear to me. There is my second-best gown, a contemptible thing in the eyes of every beholder, yet precious to me."

"I understand, Your Highness," quoth Sir Bradwen, "and I shall have one of the men in my employ climb here and carry down these things."

The princess lowered her eyes in shame. "There is also my chop—my seal, perhaps? Has this humble one committed some risible error, my lord?"

"No, indeed."

"And the ivory sticks with which I feed myself, the gift of my gently nurturing mother. Would my lord consent to view the debased quarters to which this wretched prisoner has been for three long years confined?"

"Eagerly," Sir Bradwen replied, "if Your Highness will consent to show them to me."

"There is a magic box—"

She smiled again, and he felt his love deepen.

"Which may be opened only at certain times, and behold! it is filled with rice and fruits. If it can be opened now, is it possible that the most gracious lordly rescuer would consent to sample its poor contents?"

"I would, Your Highness." Sir Bradwen bowed, for though he was eager to be gone he was far to well-bred to refuse the invitation of a princess.

Together they went into the castle, she tottering and half supported by his hand and arm; and if their words were the stately ones of their time and their disparate homelands, their hands spoke a language much older: *I am a woman and you—you are a man!* whispered the tiny hand; and *I am a man and you are a woman indeed!* replied the great one.

Soon they stood before the box of which the princess had spoken, which was in fact a cabinet or locker set into one of the interior walls of her castle. She explained that the sun was now high—one of the times at which the box might be opened. She further described the food they might expect to find within it, and having received Sir Bradwen's courteous consent, she touched the latch.

At which the floor gave way beneath them, dropping nearly as fast as a falling stone. Together, she clutching him in terror, they descended into the hill of green glass.

Their fall slowed, and at length it halted altogether. Soft green light bathed them; unguessable shapes surrounded them. "Welcome!" a small voice cried; and again, "Welcome!"

A very small man with a very small face in a very large head approached them riding in a silent and ugly little cart with invisible wheels.

"The unconscionable and tricksy person you see before you," whispered the princess, "is that very wicked magician who snatched me from the City of Peace."

Sir Bradwen bowed as he would have at Arthur's court. "Perhaps we meet as antagonists," he said politely, "yet I would much prefer to count among my friends a man so learned in all the ways of the Unseen World. You placed the lovely and royal lady at my side atop this mountain—"

"To find us a man of the Dark Ages who showed a glimmer of intelligence," the very small man in the cart replied. "She's done it, too, as I knew she would." He simpered, and seemed to be on the verge of laughter. "My name's 12BFW-CY-, by the way, and I come from the remote future."

The knight bowed deeper still. "Sir Bradwen of the Forest Tower am I, and in a larger sense of glorious Camelot. In a sense larger still, of Albion, the White Isle."

"This inconsiderable person," the princess said, "is called by the unattractive name of Apple Blossom. She has been torn, as may be known, from the Land of the Black-haired People, Kingdom of Ch'in, a country well governed by the most illustrious person whose light dazzles these inferior eyes, her father, here styled King of Far-Off Cathay."

12BFW-CY-'s smile broadened, becoming almost as wide as both the princess's thumbs. "You wish to return home, I'm sure. This knight has won you, though. He probably won't agree to it."

"On the contrary," Sir Bradwen declared, "if this lovely lady can be returned to her parents in safety, I could wish for no happier outcome. I declare her—" His voice wavered, and he paused to clear his throat. "I declare her free to go at once, and may God speed her on her way."

At this, the princess clung more tightly than ever. "This wr-wretched person, the m-m-most m-miserable of w-women, w-would—w-w-would . . ." She burst into tears.

With his free hand, Sir Bradwen patted her shoulder. "There, there. Do not weep, Your Highness. You will be in the arms of your royal mother almost before you know it. Do you have sisters?"

"She has five hundred and twenty-six," 12BFW-CY- put in somewhat dryly. "And six hundred and ten brothers. It was because she came from such an extensive family that we selected her—the removal of one very minor princess from so large a group is unlikely to result in historical—"

"I w-want to st-st-stay here!" wailed the unfortunate princess. "I w-w-want to be in *your* arms!"

Sir Bradwen's heart bounded like a stag. "Then you shall! As long as my hand can grasp a sword, no one shall take you from me. By good Saint Joseph I swear it! By the Holy Family! By my honor and my mother's grave!"

"Certainly not me," 12BFW-CY- remarked dryly. "*I* don't want her. As for your sword—" He tittered. "I am about to give you a more effectual weapon."

Sir Bradwen's eyebrows went up. "Do you mean a magic bow? An enchanted lance? Something of that kind?"

12BFW-CY- tittered again. "Precisely. It will enable you to overcome the most powerful opponent without fighting him at all. A little background must be filled in first, I think. If you'll indulge me.

"Hem, hem! My companions—vile and selfish creatures with whom you would not wish to speak—and I represent a sizable fraction of humanity in the year thirty-two thousand three hundred and eleven. In another generation or two the human gene pool will be too small to support a viable race, even with all that genetic engineering can do for us, and humanity will be irrevocably doomed. Finished. Ended. Headed to be shredded, eh?"

"This fribbling person weeps," declared the princess with feeling.

To which Sir Bradwen added, "I'm not sure I understood everything you said, the bit about the magic pool especially, but it sounded very bad. If my sword can be of service to you, you need but ask."

"Oh, we don't mind." 12BFW-CY- waved an airy hand. "We don't mind at all. In a way we rather enjoy it. Our race has always been a filthy mess, you know, and we feel it's high time we gave the daisies a turn at the hup-controller. Now I'll show you. Don't be afraid."

Sir Bradwen was sorely tempted, but said nothing.

"Here's what we've come up with, and very clever of us, too, if I may say it. Of me, especially, which is why I get to talk to you two."

It was a short staff with a bulging, lusterless crystal at one end.

"I won't point it at you," 12BFW-CY- continued, "and if I did, I wouldn't turn it on. That would be too dangerous for *you*. But you may point it at other people, you see. It's thought-controlled, of course, just like my car. Point it, think of it working, and you'll see a crimson flash, very short."

Sir Bradwen nodded slowly.

"Suppose an enemy knight comes into view. He doesn't have to attack you. If you can see him, that's plenty. You merely have to point my paciforcer at him, and think of him being paciforced. He will be incapable of any violence whatsoever, from that moment on."

Softly and involuntarily, the princess moaned.

"Yes! Yes, yes!" 12BFW-CY- paused to clear his throat. "But there's— hem, hem!—more. The same holds true for his descendants. Or at least for any conceived after ten days or so. No violence. None! Can't kill a chicken or bait a hook. And their own children will inherit the, er, tendency. If they have any. You appear troubled."

"I am," Sir Bradwen conceded. "You see, Sir Magician, many of my foes are Arthur's rebellious subjects. It is my task to return them to their loyalty, whether by killing them or by other means. With this . . . ?"

"Paciforcer."

"With this paciforcer they will be of no use to Arthur even if they renounce their rebellion. Knights and nobles who will not smite the heathen have no value."

"Why worry?" 12BFW-CY- smiled. "In such cases you need not use it. But against the—ah?"

"Heathen."

"Heathen themselves . . . Eh? Eh?"

"I hesitate—" Sir Bradwen began.

"Do not." 12BFW-CY- held out the paciforcer, and edging his cart nearer actually forced it into Sir Bradwen's hand. "I must warn you that should you decline, this toothsome lady will be restored to her family. I shall be compelled to use the paciforcer myself. On both of you."

Sir Bradwen bowed. "In that case I accept. No price is too great."

"Good. Good!"

Sir Bradwen's hand closed about the paciforcer.

And 12BFW-CY- released it with a sigh. "An infinity of pain and suffering is thus wiped away. Human history will be infinitely more peaceful. Shorter, of course. Much shorter. But delightfully peaceful. My own generation will never have been." For a moment he appeared radiantly happy. "We will have the oblivion we crave. Guard my paciforcer well. If it is not subjected to abuse, it will endure and continue to function for a thousand years."

"You may trust me," Sir Bradwen declared, "to do the right thing."

"Then go."

12BFW-CY- pointed down a long aisle between towering devices of sorcery, and suddenly Sir Bradwen beheld an opening at its termination, and sunlight beyond the opening.

"Blessings are without meaning," 12BFW-CY- murmured, "and yet, and yet . . ."

"Farewell!" Sir Bradwen told him, and flourished the paciforcer.

The princess bowed until her hair swept the floor. "This submissive person makes haste to remove her loathsome self from your august presence. Ten thousand blessings!"

No sooner had she and Sir Bradwen left the glass hill than its opening shut behind them. A pleasant walk of a quarter mile (over much of which he carried her) brought them to the old peasant and his helpers. Sir Bradwen gave each of them a full day's pay, though they had labored for less than half that.

That done, he lifted the princess into his great war saddle and mounted behind her; and together they rode away until they reached the path beside the River Sart. There he took the paciforcer from his belt and flung it into the water.

And the two of them rode on, upon a great white charger who felt and shared their joy, the princess singing and Sir Bradwen whistling.

The Monday Man

✦

I knew John Genaro more than forty years, I suppose, if you want to go all the way back to the beginning. When we were kids and the old Harry S Truman School split the tracks (as the saying was), we made up the finest softball battery in the eighth grade. I forgot John when I went off to college, but ran into him again when I came home to hang up my shingle in the window of what we used to call the world's smallest law office. By that time my dad had lost what little money he'd had. It killed him, and that killed Mom; but nothing had killed me yet, and I rented a walk-up in John's old neighborhood, writing wills for scrubwomen who'd saved five bucks a week and Korean families who wanted to split a little grocery among five sons.

I took all the criminal cases I could get in those days, so it wasn't very long before I found out that John was walking a beat a couple of blocks from my office: he'd collared a lot of the muggers and shoplifters I was defending. I tried to shake him the first few times he appeared as arresting officer, and found out I couldn't; I recall thinking it might be because he wasn't married.

Anyhow, we became friends again, between fights over those pitiful little cases; and we stayed friends. Every season we'd hunt together (it's mostly rabbits and pheasants in this part of the state), and we'd meet for lunch once or twice a month when there wasn't anything to hunt. On and off I tried to interest John in fishing, which has always outrated hunting with me, but I never even got him to get a line wet; before he died he told me why. Now that I'm close to going myself, I think I ought to pass his story along. You won't believe it, but perhaps you'll remember it just the same.

If only when it's too late.

My wife had gone to bed, and he and I were drinking in the kitchen. Perhaps he had a little too much that night; he rarely risked being disbelieved, but I think he'd kept it to himself so long it had started to fester, and the whiskey brought it out.

It happened while I was still in law school, according to John, and I'll let him take it from there.

"I was still a rookie," he said, "and it hit me harder than anything has since, though I've had a partner shot down beside me, and I was the one that opened the box they'd put the Rothman girl in. Know what a Monday man is, Gene?"

I said I didn't, and John kept talking.

"This was back before they had these laundromats and driers all over, or anyway before the people on my old beat had 'em. A Monday man was a guy who stole washing off clotheslines. Monday was when most washing got hung out, so that's when I'd have the most trouble with 'em. Sometimes they were the kind that steals women's underwear to keep—there's something wrong with those—but mostly they'd take anything that wasn't too worn, and wear it themselves or sell it. Very petty, petty larceny.

"I was strolling along one afternoon, enjoying the weather and feeling proud of my nice new blue uniform—which I was still new and green enough myself to do—when a woman ran out of one of the buildings yelling that somebody'd just taken her husband's overalls off the line. She'd seen him out the back window.

"I got around to the end of the block just in time to spot a little guy with overalls in his hand come out of the alley. I chased him, but I lost him before long; that's never been a good neighborhood for a cop to chase somebody in. It made me sore to lose him, because it was going to be my first pinch and I knew I'd get chewed out by my sergeant. They put guys in cars right away now and everybody's a stranger; but in those days a good cop was supposed to know everyone on his beat, and I hadn't recognized this Monday man.

"Like I said, I felt lousy about the whole thing. So when I saw a kid I knew sitting on a stoop, I went over and asked if he'd seen the guy I'd been chasing, and did he know him. This kid had been in trouble before—mostly vandalism—so I suppose he wanted to get on the good side of the law. Anyway he told me he didn't know the guy, but he'd seen where he'd gone."

I poured John another one. "Ah, the police informer."

"Yeah. Today that kid's in the Assembly, but he still calls me Johnny, as democratic as you please.

"Anyway the kid pointed out the place. These days it'd be full of addicts, but back then you didn't see so much of that. I went through it, floor by floor, and when I got to the fourth I could hear somebody moving around up on the fifth—that was the top floor. I figured I had him if it was him, because there wasn't but the one stairway and no fire escape.

"By the time I got up there, he'd locked himself in one of the apartments. I rapped on the door with my billy and yelled, 'Police!' All by the book and just like he really lived there. But when he didn't open up, I kicked down the door.

"He was just standing in the middle of the room, with the overalls still in his hand. I figured he'd been looking for a place to hide 'em and couldn't find one, because that was about as bare a room as you could find. There was an empty bottle on the floor and a closet, and that was all there was except for the guy himself. He was pretty ordinary-looking, or at least I thought so then. Had on an old sportcoat a little too big for him."

I asked whether the Monday man had been living there, and if so, where he had slept.

John shook his head. "I doubt that he did," he said.

"I yelled that he was under arrest and grabbed his arm with my left hand, just above the cuff of that old plaid sportcoat. Like this, see?" John grasped my forearm. "That was what saved me, even though I didn't know it then. Every once in a while I still dream about it.

"With my right I snapped my handcuffs over both our wrists, and I told him to come along. We were about halfway down the first flight when he started to pull back. I gave a hard jerk on the cuffs and went down two or three more steps. Then he pulled me right off my feet."

I said, "It sounds as though your Monday man was stronger than he looked."

"He dragged me clear back to the landing before I could get my legs under me again. I got pretty mad about that; I rapped him alongside the head and told him to cut it out. His knees gave a little and he stopped pulling, but he never said a word.

"I started back down and got a little farther before the same thing happened. "I'd have sworn there wasn't a man alive that could drag me up a flight of stairs if I didn't want to go, but here was this little guy who didn't look like he weighed a hundred and forty doing it. I dropped my billy and the overalls when that pull came, and he got me back almost to the door of the apartment. Well, that was more than enough for me—I pasted him one on the jaw that ought to have broken it."

I asked, "But it didn't?"

John rubbed the white scars on his knuckles reflectively. "No. But he stopped pulling. You want to shove that bottle over a little?

"The funny thing was that my fist stayed right on his chin. You ever touch a piece of bare metal that's been in a freezer? It was just like that, except he didn't feel cold. It was like when you get Krazy Glue on your fingers, except we didn't have Krazy Glue then. I tried to shake my hand loose and couldn't—all it did was hurt.

"Naturally I looked at my hand and his jaw, trying to see what was wrong, and I think that was the first time I'd really looked at this Monday man. He was such an ordinary little bum that I hadn't paid any more attention to him than I would to one particular match in a folder. I had his face turned up so I could see my knuckles, and I noticed his nostrils."

"What was the matter?" I asked. "Were they square?"

"No, that wouldn't have been so bad. He didn't have any, not real ones. Where they should've been there were two little black depressions. His eyes were the same way—they didn't have any depth. Oh, the look was there all right, just like a good photo has it, when you can scrape it with a fingernail and hit paper just below the surface."

I said, "In other words, your Monday man had on a mask."

John shook his head. "A mask ends someplace. It was more like he was a dummy, like they have in department stores. Only I've never seen one half as good as he was.

"While I was getting used to what I had hanging off the end of my hand, he began pulling hard again, trying to drag me back into that apartment. I pulled the other way, doing most of it with the cuffs. It hurt like hell when I tried to pull with the stuck hand. With the cuffs on my left and my right stuck like that, I didn't have a free hand, which scared the hell out of me. Being scared can make you strong sometimes, and I was able to drag him clear down to the first floor, although I lost ground once or twice.

"When I'd got him out the front door I'd gone as far as I could go, and I knew it. He'd stopped pulling steady and was making sudden jerks whenever he could catch me off balance. I'd wrenched a knee going down the last flight and between that and my hand and my left wrist the pain was awful. I yelled—screamed is a lot more like it—but you know how much chance a cop has of getting help in that neighborhood. I could hear windows banging shut and people hustling to get off the street. Then he dragged me back inside the building.

"I kicked at his feet as we went upstairs, but it didn't do any good and after I'd kicked him half a dozen times I finally got wise. His legs weren't really what was holding him up. He was like one of those bass lures you're always bragging about—they wiggle a lot when they go through the water, but it isn't the wiggle that makes 'em go.

"Then I got the idea that if I could get my hand out of the cuffs I could get to my gun. I still thought it was the little guy himself I was fighting, see? The key was in my watch pocket, and by rushing him as we got to the top of the stairs I was able to get my fingers in there. I couldn't use my right, naturally, but I got the key between my teeth and managed to stick it into the lock just as we stumbled through the door of that apartment. The feeling I got when those cuffs dropped off was the greatest damned feeling I've ever had in my whole life.

"This time the door that I'd thought probably belonged to a closet was standing wide open, but there wasn't a closet in back of it—it was as black as an alderman's heart. I can see you're not buying a God-damned word of this. Well, I was about through drinking anyway."

I told John that I was willing to believe it if he said it was true, but that it was a story that took some thinking about.

"It does. But I've been thinking about it for twenty-eight years, and I've never come up with a better answer than the one that hit me as soon as I saw that open door. There was somebody inside there, on the other side of the dark, get me? I couldn't make him out, but I could feel him just like you can feel death at the scene of a murder. I call him the Fisherman."

I told John I wasn't sure I understood him.

"Well, what do you guys do when you want to catch something? You buy yourself a little hunk of wood painted up to look like a bug, or maybe a frog or a little fish that a big one might like to eat, and it's got a hook hidden in it someplace so the poor fish can't let it go once he's grabbed it. And you try to make your Colorado wobbler or whatever you call it act just as much like a real fish as you can.

"That's what the Fisherman had done, and now he was reeling me in, probably getting a hell of a charge out of it every time I pulled back. I wore a crossdraw then—which regulations won't allow anymore—and I was able to make what you call a cavalry draw with my left hand. I let the Monday man have three, and then I fired more into that closet. Neither one did any good, and the Monday man was dragging me closer and closer to it. I heaved with everything I had, then, and got my right hand free. Tore off a bunch of skin.

"You see, my cuffs had fooled the Fisherman into thinking he had his hook set good, when I was only caught by the knuckles, where I'd hit his lure on the chin.

"I've been thinking about that Fisherman, on and off, ever since it happened. That's why I won't fish, and why I always look real carefully at everybody I run into, which is what got me my captain's bars. I'm not too worried about meeting another lure like the Monday man—I'd know one of those the minute I laid eyes on it.

"But I keep wondering whether the Fisherman ever uses live bait."

The Waif

✦

The soft sigh of breath might have come from a puppy, and Bin hoped
it did. Quietly, hoping that it was a sleeping puppy and not a piglet
(though he would very willingly have petted a piglet), he went to see, the
heavy stick forgotten in his hands.

It was a boy, sound asleep on straw, and covered with more straw and
feed sacks. The boy's face was white, and so delicate it might almost have
been a girl's; his hair was as black as a crow's wing. Bin stood watching
him for a long time, feeling something he could put no name to. He had
never had a friend. Fil and Gid were not really his friends, but he had not
known that.

At length he turned over a bucket and sat on it. That was the way you
got the rats to come out, you just waited, real still, not hardly breathing,
till they thought you had gone; but the other boy's breath made faint
plumes of steam, and Bin's big, greasy coat with the wool on the inside
did not keep him warm enough. He found an old shingle and a bent nail,
and printed: IF YOU HUNGRY COME MY HOUSE LATE WHISTLE BY WINDOW.
On the other side: LITTLE ONE WEST NO ROAD.

Propping up the shingle near the sleeping boy, where he would be
sure to see it, Bin tiptoed to the door. Niman Corin was nowhere in sight,
and that was good. Niman Joel's punishments for trespassing had been
light; but they had burned Niman Joel, and who could say what Niman
Corin might do? It was better not to be whacked at all.

Supper had been bread and soup, as it nearly always was. Bin lay in bed listening to Gam's wheezing inhalations and speculating on the difficulties of giving the other boy soup. The bowl and spoon would have to be returned. There could be no getting around that. Could he trust the other boy to do it?

Everyone had trusted Niman Joel, even the grown-ups.

He should have gone to see the reverend, after, like Gam said. He had not, had lied about it. Gam had put his finger on the stove, not for lying but just so he would know how burning felt. He had been punished for the lie, even if Gam had believed him. That was something to remember.

To remember always.

Outside a saw-whet called, probably from the big pine at the edge of the woods.

It would have been better to have gone to the reverend. The reverend would have said what Fil had said, that Niman Joel had been punished on Earth and was in heaven now and all that. But it would have been better to have gone. One lie, and you have to watch everything you say forever.

But Gid had not been lying when he said he had killed that rat. He had showed it, almost as big as a cat. Or he had been, because somebody else had killed it, maybe. It had been poisoned or something.

The saw-whet cried again, a little nearer this time, like on a fence post. The mice would not come out in this cold, they had already come into Gam's house to keep warm. As he had.

Gam had caught two in her trap, and one had drowned trying to drink out of the scrub bucket. Cats were no good, Gam said. When a old lady like her had a cat, folks said she talked to the Flying People. Maybe helped them like Niman Joel.

The saw-whet was perched on the chimney, probably. Its shrill whistle came again, and Bin sat up, threw off quilt and blanket, and sprang from his bed.

A shadowy figure was waiting outside in the snow beyond the window.

Bin pushed his feet into his boots, snatched up his coat and what remained of the bread, and hurried outside.

"Aren't you cold?" he asked the boy waiting in the snow. The moon was bright, and it seemed to him that the other boy was dressed in rags, and thin rags at that.

"Very cold." When the other boy took the bread his hand shook. "Can't I come inside? Please?"

Bin shook his head.

"I could eat this in front of the fire, and warm myself. Just for a moment."

"You'd wake Gam. She'd be mad."

The other boy chewed and swallowed. "I wouldn't, but suppose I did. Hasn't she ever been angry before?"

"Sure. Lots."

"Was it worse than my freezing to death?"

In the cabin, the other boy crouched in the ashes and ate the bread while Bin brought him a bowl of soup. There was still a little fire in the stove, banked for breakfast, so the soup was warm. "There isn't any meat," Bin explained, " 'cause we don't have any. It's just carrots and potatoes, mostly."

"It smells wonderful."

While the other boy was eating his soup, Bin said, "You'll have to go out when that's finished."

The other boy looked up, smiling. "Then I won't eat so fast. It's wonderful to be warm."

"You could build a fire in the woods."

The other boy said nothing, eating soup.

"Does Niman Corin know you sleep in his new barn?"

The other boy's shoulders rose and fell. "I suppose. Some of them do."

"They let you?"

The other boy dipped what was left of his bread into his soup and ate it. "Not exactly, but they know I'm there sometimes."

"What's your name?"

"They call me the Cold Lad." The other boy smiled. "But that's not really my name. My name is Ariael."

"Mine's Bin."

Bin had smiled, too, when he spoke, but the other boy's smile faded. "What are you going to do when I leave, Bin?"

"I guess go back to bed."

"I'm tired, too. Probably more tired than you are." The other boy spooned up the last of his soup and drank it. "I want you to let me hide in here, where it's warm. Gam won't find me. Will you do that?"

"You don't have no boots?" Bin was looking at the other boy's bare feet; one had been bleeding, and the blood was caked with ashes now.

"No. None."

"Gam bought me these." Bin indicated his own boots, sheepskin boots with thick wooden soles. "They're big so I can wear 'em next year, too."

The other boy said nothing.

"I guess I could give you one."

The other boy grinned and hugged him, which surprised him very much indeed. "I won't take it," he whispered.

He let Bin go.

"But, Bin, think how Gam would feel if you gave me a boot. You'd have to say you lost it, and she'd be terribly hurt."

"I guess."

"So instead of giving me one of your boots, I want you to do something much easier. I want you to let me hide in bed with you. I won't take up much room, and I'll get down under the covers so Gam won't see me. Watch."

Handing Bin his bowl and spoon, the other boy ran soundlessly to Bin's bed and slipped beneath the old quilt. The quilt rose—or so it seemed to Bin, watching it by firelight. For a moment or two it twitched and settled itself.

After that it seemed clear that the other boy had gone. Thinking about it, Bin decided that the other boy had slipped over to the side of the bed and slid over the edge, and was hiding under it. He took off his coat and hung it on the peg, pulled off his boots, stood them at the foot of his bed the way Gam liked, and got under the covers. The other boy was in there, too, small and thin and very cold. He huddled against Bin for warmth, and Bin found that he was no longer little, as he had been all his life. He was someone large and warm, someone strong, generous, and protecting. It felt good, but it felt serious, too.

The other boy was still there when he got out of bed in the morning. He washed the way he always did, trying not to look, got dressed, and went outside to cut a twig to clean his teeth the way you were supposed to.

When he came back in, Gam said, "Cold out?"

"Pretty cold."

"There was bread left last night. It was going to be our breakfast."

"I'll be late for school," Bin told her.

"You ate it, didn't you, Bin? You got up in the night and ate it."

"Yes'm."

"Don't cry. It wasn't no sin."

Gam held him for a minute. She was warm and smelled bad and he loved her.

"There's soup left for me, and I'll bake more bread, if I can get salt. It'll be spring real soon now, Bin, and things will be easier."

Gam had been right, Bin decided as he walked to school. Yes, it was still cold. Yes, there was still snow on the ground, a lot of it. But there was something new in the air, something that made him think of the other boy, a promise not in words. He had straightened up his bed because Gam had made him, and it had seemed like there was nothing in that bed, nothing at all. Or only the promise.

The other boy could whistle like a saw-whet. He himself could whistle like a wren, and he did as he walked to school, then fell silent as he clattered up the rickety wooden steps and shuffled into the long gloomy room with sheets of scarred wood for walls.

When the schoolmaster arrived, Bin rose with the others to greet him. *"Good morning, Niman Pryderi!"*

"Good morning, class. I trust you had a good holiday?"

Several nodded.

"You did not go to see Niman Joel burned?"

Bin, who had, said nothing.

"What about you, Shula?"

Shula had been toying nervously with one of her skinny braids; she let it fall as she spoke. "I didn't go, Niman Pryderi. I didn't want to."

"That is well. Fil?"

Fil sat up straight. "Yes, sir. I went. I felt like I ought to see it."

"That is well, too." The schoolmaster rose, selected a stick from the woodbox, opened the door of the stove, poked the fire with it, and tossed it in to burn. The sky around the hole in the weathered aluminum roof was bright blue. As he had often before, Bin stared at it, sick for the freedom temporarily denied him.

"Do you understand why I said that, class? I said it was good that Shula didn't want to watch Niman Joel burned, and good that Fil felt he should. Who will explain that? Bin?"

He rose as slowly as he could, his mind racing. "'Cause boys 'n girls are different?"

"They are, of course, but that's not the reason." Hands were up. The schoolmaster said, "Dionne?"

She stood, taller and wider than anyone else in the class, and ever defiant. "You said it was good that Fil watched, because we ought to know about it—about what happens to people that get mixed up with the Flying People. But we shouldn't *want* to watch it, because it was horrible. Nobody ought to want to see somebody else burned to death. That's sick."

"Excellent, Dionne."

Bin, who never raised his hand, had raised it now. For a moment the schoolmaster looked at it in surprise. Then he said, "Yes, Bin. What is it?"

He rose again, as slowly as ever. "I—I . . ."

The schoolmaster thought he understood, and said, "You were there, too. With Fil, I imagine."

"Yes, sir. Yes, sir, I was. I seen it. Only—only if we don't want to see it, we could just not do it. Folks do it, Niman Pryderi. It don't just happen."

There was laughter. Some light object struck the back of his head, and he sat down.

"We have lost a world," the schoolmaster explained almost gently, "and it was the only world we had. All our nations collapsed as our raw materials were exhausted, Bin, and no sooner had we begun to rebuild than the Flying People arrived."

The class was satisfied and seemed ready to move on, but the schoolmaster was not. He went to his desk, sat down, and regarded them, his soft, dark eyes traveling from face to face. "Their presence prevents us from rebuilding it. How can we bring back the science we lost, when we know that human beings not much different from ourselves are watching all we do, and our lost science is child's play to them?"

He paused. "That was a rhetorical question. Do you know what a rhetorical question is?"

About half the class nodded.

"It's a question we ask because it cannot be answered, or because the answer is so obvious that no one needs to say it. In this case, the answer is that we can't. You may say that our shame, embarrassment, and humiliation ought not to prevent us from doing what we should. If you won't say it, I will. I do. But the fact is that we are so prevented. It's why so many of you have only one pair of shoes, and less than enough to eat. That's why you have to go to school in an old truck. Burning our neighbors is horrible, very horrible indeed. But having neighbors who would side with the Flying People is intolerable—which means that we do not tolerate it."

Dionne approached Bin at recess; and Bin, who was terrified of her, tried to back away.

She smiled. "I just wanted to say I never knew what a good little kid you are. They pick on you sometimes, don't they?"

He shrugged. "They make fun. Gam 'n me's poor."

"Yeah. Let me tell you a secret." She bent, her mouth at his ear. "We all are."

Bin had not yet recovered his emotional balance when Fil took him aside. "Look, Bin, somebody's gotta tell you this, so I guess it's me. What you said in class? You know what I mean?"

He nodded.

"There's a dozen kids that will tell their folks, all right? What happened to Niman Joel could happen to you. It don't take much. You keep your mouth shut from now on. Or you say he got what he had comin'. You say, show me another one and I'll bring the wood. Understand?"

"It was dumb," Bin said. "I know that."

"It was dumb, and if you keep on like that I won't know you anymore, understand? You're going to be too risky to know, so you shut up."

Bin joined the kickball game, and scored. Fil slapped his back, but none of the others said anything. As soon as the game had resumed, a big hand grasped his shoulder. "Come in," the schoolmaster said. "I must speak with you."

Docilely, Bin followed him back into the school.

"Sit down. You can pull up that stool. We're not going to stand on formality until your classmates return." The schoolmaster's smile was touched with bitterness.

Bin did as he was told. "I guess I know what this is about, Niman Pryderi. I'm sorry."

"I doubt that you do, Bin—though I've no doubt that you're sorry. Do you know why I'm called Niman, Bin? Or why Niman Joel was, or any other man?"

Bin shook his head.

"When the Flying People came, we started calling each other Neighbor. Neighbor meant that a man was one of us, and not one of them. Then we wanted to burn our neighbors." The bitter smile returned. "Which our religion—some people's religion, at least—teaches us we should not do. So we changed it to Near-man, then to Niman. It wasn't all that long ago. About the time I was born."

Bin nodded again.

"Have I ever used my switch on you, Bin?"

"Last year." Bin gulped. "For talkin' in class."

"I'm going to do it again, when class resumes. I am going to make the dust fly. Did you cry, last year?"

"A little, Niman Pryderi."

"Are you going to cry this time?"

Bin shook his head. "I'm bigger."

"You will cry, this time," the schoolmaster told him. "You'll scream. When class resumes, I'm going to ask you questions, and they will be questions you can't answer. I'll see to that. Then I'll bend you over my desk and whale away. It will hurt and you'll cry, but the boys who are ready to league against you will like you after that. And the girls will talk about how you were beaten when they go home this afternoon, not about what you said. Do you understand?"

"I think so, Niman Pryderi."

The schoolmaster's voice softened. "Guilt is the worst part, Bin. Knowing that we were on the devil's side, and that what we got was less than we deserved. I want to spare you that. You've done nothing wrong. Have you ever raked something out of the fire with a stick?"

Bin nodded.

"That's what I'll be doing, with my switch. Remember that."

Gam saw the tracks the tears had left down a face not particularly clean and said, "What happened?" and hugged him, and he ate his supper standing up. There was fresh bread for supper, and to divert him from his sufferings she told him about the salt some kind neighbor had surely left for them, a nice big sack of clean white salt just sitting there on the doorstep when she had gone to the well. "Spring was in the air, Bin. I guess you noticed, too, when you children went outside to play? I was thinking about it, it felt so nice, and I turned around and carried my bucket back in, and there it was, sitting on the step."

By a great effort of will, Bin succeeded in not looking at his bed; it seemed likely the other boy would not have gone to bed so early anyway. He would want some of the new bread after Gam had gone to sleep, Bin decided, and he had earned it, too.

"You want to study your book now?"

He shook his head. "I'm goin' out to play. It'll be dark soon. I'll study then."

"You got switched for not knowing the answers, Bin. You know them now?"

"That's why I'd like you to help me study when I come back."

Once outside, he found his stick and made straight for the barn that had been Niman Joel's. There was still snow on the ground here and there, and ice that cracked beneath the hard wooden soles of his boots; but there was water, as well, puddles to splash in, and cold drippings that fell from the eaves of the barn onto his head and down the

back of his neck, finding their way inside the greasy wool and the old
gray shirt.

Most of all, there was the new-year feeling in the air, as Gam had said.
It would be kite-flying time before long, and the first kite-flying time in
which he was not youngest flier. Emlyn and Cu and Sid would look to him
for help with their kites, just as—

Footsteps. He froze.

It was Gid; Bin relaxed a little.

Gid looked around. "Bin? Bin, I know you're in here. Where are you?"

Bin stepped forward. "Here I am. I thought maybe I could kill a big
rat, Gid, like you did. So I stayed real quiet."

"This's our barn now."

Bin nodded.

"We don't want nobody thinkin' it don't belong to nobody. It's ours."

Bin nodded again.

"Niman Joel's dead, and his wife's run out. So we took his place for
what he owed. Who you got with you?"

"Nobody." The question had taken Bin by surprise.

"Yes, you do. I seen you comin' across our new field."

"I did," Bin admitted, "only there wasn't nobody with me."

"I seen him." Gid stepped nearer—larger, older, and stronger. "You
better tell me, an' I mean now."

Bin resorted to logic. "If there was anybody, he'd be in here."

Gid's fist struck him under the left eye, and he yelped with pain, backing away.

"Don't you yell when I hit you!" Gid waded in, fists flying, and Bin fell.
The kicks were worse—much worse—than the blows of Gid's fists.

And then the heavy stick Bin had brought to kill rats was above Gid's
head. It came down hard with a noise like a sack of feed dropped from
high up, catching Gid where his neck joined his shoulder. Gid swung
around, and it hit his forehead with the sound of a hammer pounding a
board, and he fell.

The stick fell, too; for an instant, Bin caught sight of the other boy in
the dimness of the barn. Then he was gone.

So was Bin, taking his stick with him, as soon as he could get to his feet. The wood was not a comfortable place in weather like this, full of ice and water, with snow-water dripping from every tree; but it was a familiar place, and he remembered the saw-whet. If the other boy had come here one time, he might come here again.

"Hello, Bin."

Bin whirled, and found the other boy behind him. "That was good," Bin said with solemn sincerity, "what you done for me. I owe you."

The other boy smiled. "Owe me what? A pair of boots like yours?"

"Sure! Lemme find a place to set, 'n I'll take 'em off."

The other boy shook his head. "I don't want them, Bin. They're too heavy for me. I was testing you, and I shouldn't do that. I won't, ever again."

"Then I won't test you, neither."

"Good. Why did you go into that barn? Were you looking for me?"

Bin nodded. "About school. The salt, too. It was right of you, 'n I wanted to say I'd give some a' the bread tonight. You goin' to be in my bed again?"

"If you don't object."

"Then I could a' said there, only I didn't know."

"You wanted to tell me something about your school, too."

"Yeah." Bin ran his fingers through his unruly hair, spat, and ran his fingers through his hair again. "'Bout school 'n Niman Joel. All that. They said how bad it was to burn him. It didn't seem so bad to me when they was doin' it. Everybody was yellin' 'n carryin' on. I was, too."

"I understand, Bin, and I don't blame you."

"Course I couldn't see much. I said I did, after, only it was a lie. I seen a little, but they was crowdin' around the fire too close."

He waited for some comment from the other boy, but none came.

"So then today in school they said how bad it was, burnin' a neighbor like that, 'n I said why do it if you don't like to? 'N I got warmed for it pretty good. Just for sayin' that. He said it wasn't for that, only it was. So I got to wonderin' what Niman Joel done, you know? The Flyin' People's rich, they say, 'n whatever they say, why that's got to go. Fil said he most likely told on them that talked against 'em, only everybody does, 'n they got to know that. So what'd he do? 'N I remembered you used to sleep in his barn, sometimes anyhow, so maybe you'd know."

"He was very poor," the other boy said.

Bin nodded. "He didn't have but the one mule. I know that."

"Hatred is a luxury, Bin. Like whiskey. Do you know about whiskey?"

"Sure."

"People who have good farms make it and drink it, and for the most part it does them little harm. But those who are truly poor must choose between whiskey and food, and if they choose whiskey they die. Hatred is like that. Niman Joel had to devote all his energy to feeding himself and his family. He carved spoons and bowls and pannikins in winter, and sold them, though he got very little for them. From spring until fall he worked from sunrise to sunset, trying to grow enough food, and hay enough to carry his mule through the winter. I tried to help him now and then, and sometimes I succeeded."

"That's good."

"I think myself very rich, Bin. You may not believe me, but I do. This whole, beautiful world of yours lies open before me. I can go wherever I want to, and do whatever I want to. I watch the sun go down, and I watch the moon come up. Its mountains and its seas are all mine. I can see them and play on them anytime I want, and I wish that I could show them to you as well."

"Did you show him?"

Sadly, the other boy shook his head. "I couldn't. But I helped him sometimes, as I said, and as I said, he was too poor to hate. He didn't hate—he couldn't afford to, and I think that the others must have seen that. I tried—"

"Wait up!" Bin made an urgent gesture. "You're one?"

"Would you hate me, Bin? If you thought I was?"

"Sure!"

"Then I am not, because I know you can't afford it. I'm cold, and you're cold, too. I can see you are. I think we both ought to go inside and warm ourselves before Gam's fire. You promised her you'd study tonight, and she was going to help you. Remember?"

"You better not let her see you," Bin said as he turned away. "She'll have a fit."

Behind him, the other boy said, *"She won't see me, Bin. I promise you."* Bin had the feeling that if he turned around he would not see the other boy either.

Gam had finished washing up and was waiting for him inside, with Bin's tattered little arithmetic book on her lap. They had finished with IF JON HAS FIVE APPLES, JORJ HAS FOUR APPLES, AND JAK HAS THREE APPLES, HOW MANY APPLES DO THE BOYS HAVE? And were starting on IT IS FOUR O'CLOCK AND OTO WANTS TO SLED when someone knocked. Bin opened the door and Niman Corin came in without asking, with Gid behind him. "Another boy hit my son with a stick," Niman Corin told Gam. "He was playing with your grandson, and this other boy came up behind him and hit him." He looked around at Gid, who nodded.

"I'm sorry to hear," Gam said politely. "I hope he's not hurt bad."

"He saw that boy go in here with your grandson." Niman Corin did not bother looking around this time. "Didn't you, Gid?"

"Yes, sir," Gid said.

Gam shook her head. "Bin came in to study a bit ago, but there wasn't anybody with him. Were you playing with somebody outside, Bin?"

Bin said, "Yes'm."

"Who with?"

"Him. Gid."

Gam looked severe. "You didn't hit him with any stick, I hope, Bin."

"No, ma'am. I never." Privately Bin considered that it might be nice to hit Gid with a stick in the future.

"Did anybody?"

"Yes, ma'am. This one boy did."

Niman Corin aimed a thick forefinger at Bin. "A boy that was playing with you and Gid?"

"No, sir, Niman Corin. He just come up behind Gid 'n whapped him. I never seen he's there till he done it."

Niman Corin looked angrier than ever. "What's his name?"

Bin strove to remember, hoping he could not. "I don't know. He told me once, only I forget."

"Does he live around here?"

"I don't know, Niman Corin. I don't think so."

Gam cleared her throat, the sound of a woman with much of import to say. "'It's four o'clock and Oto wants to sled. If it takes half an hour to walk to the hill, and Oto must be home for supper by six, how long will he have to sled?'"

"Why you old bitch!" Niman Corin glared at her.

She looked up from Bin's arithmetic. "You take that back."

Niman Corin's face, red already, grew redder still. "You look at my son's head."

"I've seen it," Gam declared. "Now I want you to look at Bin's bottom. Take off your trousers, Bin."

Bin did not.

"He was switched for not getting his lessons," Gam explained, "beat harder than a lot would beat a mule. I'm sure Niman Pryderi had reason, but I don't like it. I'm going to see to it he's never switched so bad again. Now you take back what you said or you clear out of my house."

Gid said, "He's hidin' in here, Pa. I seen him come in." He lay down to look under Gam's bed.

Bin had been thinking about the other boy, and not about Oto. He said, "Two hours?"

Gam stood up and closed the arithmetic. "You listen here," she told Niman Corin. "I don't give a rap for what your Gid thinks he seen. I was sitting right there when Bin came in, and there wasn't nobody with him. You've came in my house and called me a name that will stand between us when these boys are grown men. You get out."

"I've been a friend to you," Niman Corin told her.

"Not so I've noticed. Get out!"

He left, and Gid left with him after looking under Bin's bed, and after that Gam began to cry.

———

Shula's mother stopped Bin on the way to school. "I see you've got a new boy living in your house, Bin. What's his name?"

"There isn't none," Bin told her, and knew he lied.

"I saw your grandma going to market yesterday," Shula's mother insisted, "and there was a little boy with her. It wasn't you."

Bin shrugged.

"I come up to talk, and he wasn't there anymore. It was like he'd just flown away."

After recess, Shula herself told the schoolmaster, "Bin was talkin' to some boy that don't go to our school. I seen them way over by the trees." Nor was that the only such report.

They found Bin in the woods one day when the first bold trees had donned their spring green. Niman Adken caught him by one arm and, when he tried to pull away, Niman Corin by the other; and they walked him back to town, saying hardly a word between them. The stake was being driven in as they got there, Niman Torn with a sledge and Niman Rasmos with a maul, so the sounds of the blows they struck (standing in a wagon and pounding down the stake until it stood no taller than a man) differed: *Bang! Bam! Bang! Bam! Bang! Bam!* On and on.

They kept Bin there while the wood was unloaded from another wagon, and when Niman Smit and Niman Kruk brought a bottle of kero. There were other boys watching by then, shouting to each other just as he had shouted when Niman Joel had burned, and helping unload wood. But Bin did not shout, and could not have helped unload, because Niman Adken had his left arm, and Niman Corin his right. And when the grownups chased the boys and crowded them out so they themselves could see better, Bin was not chased and not crowded at all. He stood way up front instead, where he could see everything that was being done, and they would not let him go.

He thought then of the game in the wood, and how he would hide in the hollow log next time where the other boy would never be able to find him; but he knew that there would never be a next time, not really, and the other boy had flown into the leaves up above, and through the leaves, and up into the sky when Niman Adken and Niman Corin had come, working hard to do it even if he had no wings that you could see. They would never play together in the woods anymore, or sit in front of the fire hearing stories, or huddle together under the old quilt and the blanket on cold nights. No, never.

Then Niman Adken bent down and sort of whispered, "Maybe it'd be better if you shut your eyes," and some men brought Gam with her hands tied and a rope around her neck like a dog would have; and they took it off and tied her to the stake with it, and everybody threw wood and some of it hit her, and Niman Smit and Niman Kruk poured their kero on it.

Niman Lipa puffed his cigar hard after that, and when it was going good he lit a rag tied on a stick from it; and the reverend came and went right up to Gam like he was going to cut her loose and talked to her, and she talked back, and he nodded a lot and gave her a tract to hold. But he never cut her loose, and when he went away he walked like he was never coming back, right through everybody that was watching, and on out. Niman Lipa puffed again and lit another rag on another stick (or maybe the same one, if he had put the first one out) and threw it. And the kero caught pretty slow, but it caught, the fire jumping up and dying down, and fire got into the wood, too, just little flames here and there, only it was wood burning and you could smell it through the smell of kero, bright little tongues of yellow flame climbing up the pile closer to Gam all the time.

Bin yelled for somebody to help her, and Niman Adken and Niman Corin held him tighter, and he saw Fil between a couple grown-ups, and Fil was not yelling and did not look happy or sad or anything, just watching. He wiggled out of his coat then and ran up onto the wood and stamped the little flames. And it was funny, but nobody came to catch him. Nobody.

The fire got bigger anyway, and Bin stamped as fast as he could and yelled, "They're nicer 'n we are! They really are nicer! *You don't know!*"

Slowly at first—a few big drops—then harder and harder, it began to rain.

The Legend of Xi Cygnus

✦

In the fall sky, not long after sundown, you may see Cygnus the Swan, which the Greeks called Ornis. In its right wing is the small yellow star that the Arabs (the only people to have named it as far as I know) call Gienah. Its legend is ancient, having reached us at the speed of light.

A small world circling that star was ruled by a giant. To be sure, he was not such a giant as we have here, a giant with eyes and arms and legs all like a man's, only larger. But he was a giant indeed among his own kind, both huge and strong, and so we will call him that. Like most giants, he was inclined to be tolerant and rather lazy; but like other giants, he could be roused to anger, and his size and strength were so great that when thus roused he was terrible indeed. The legend concerns him, his life, and his death.

There was, upon the world ruled by this giant, a race of Dwarves, numerous, malevolent, and proud, much given to cruel jests and small thefts, the bane of the Centaurs, the Sylphs, the Demons, and all the other peoples of that world, detested and feared. And so it was that when the giant had at last unified it under his rule, he punished these Dwarves severely, to the applause of all those whom they had so long vexed and despoiled. Their fortresses, castles, citadels, and other strong places he pulled down, so that they might no longer mock their neighbors from their ramparts. Into the many mouths of their mines (which were rich and extensive, and very deep) he directed the waters of a hundred rivers and streams.

Nor was that all. He burned their towns and villages, gave over their flocks and their herds to the bears and the wolves, returned their fields to the herbs and the thronging wildflowers from which they had been taken, and set free the bondsmen who had worked them. Lastly, he caused all of the Dwarves to be counted; and finding them too many, with his own hand he slew every tenth.

This done, he declared their chastisement at an end; but in order that they might never return to their evil ways, he made them his slaves, to sweep and scrub his palace, hoe and manure his flower beds, catch, cook, and serve his food, and answer his door; and very busy he kept them, that they might have no time for evildoing.

That they hated him goes without saying. Whispering one to another while they labored, by nod and wink and gesture and secret word, they brewed the First Plot. Thus it was that one cold winter night, while the giant slept, a hundred of their largest, strongest, and most courageous entered his bedchamber with scythes, cleavers, pruning hooks, pickaxes, and such-like implements. Five stood at each foot to cut the tendon there, and five more at each hand. Forty took their places upon his belly, ready at the signal agreed-upon to plunge their weapons into his vitals. On either side of his neck there waited twenty more, the chiefs and bullies of the whole hundred, to cut the giant's throat. On them was the greatest reliance placed.

When each was well positioned, the strongest and slyest of them all gave the signal. His trumpeter put lip to horn and blew a mighty blast; and at the sound, all hundred struck as one. Then were broadaxe and hatchet laid to tendon, and sickle, shears, and saw to artery! Scarlet blood spurted to the ceiling of that high chamber, till every Dwarf was dyed with it, and the sheet, and coverlet, and pillow, too, until the tallest stood knee-deep in the hot reeking rush of it, and those small creatures that dwell in the blood of those who live upon that world of the star called by Arabs Gienah clambered out of it, rosy or pale, and clung to the skirts, and beards, and faces of the Dwarves, murmuring and muttering with soft tongues in an unknown speech, and in that fashion saying many things that no one could know.

Then the giant waked, and rose roaring. Those Dwarves who were yet in his bedchamber when he slammed shut its great door, he slew. And when day came, he most carefully examined all the rest, blinding any upon whom he discovered the least trace of his blood. And lastly, he declared an end to the stipend he had previously granted to each Dwarf for bread and meat. Thenceforward they were made to beg those who had been their victims in times past for peelings and stale crusts, and were made to work harder than ever, toiling for the giant from the first light of the star that the Arabs call Gienah until the last stall in the market closed.

That they hated him goes without saying. Year followed year, and in all those years there came not a night in which they did not dream of murder. To their children and their grandchildren they whispered of revenge about the fire, and they painted their doorposts and lintels with certain uncouth signs, red or black, whose signification they themselves well understood.

At last the giant grew old. His step was no longer so quick as it had been, nor his voice so loud, nor his eyes so keen. He fell ill, and when word of it went abroad, Shee and Sidhe, Fairy and Sprite, Kobold, Nisse, and Centaur, Goblin and Demon trooped to his palace, bringing with them gifts they hoped might bring him pleasure: hams smoked with rare woods, so great in size that no champion of the Trolls could lift one to his shoulder; tuns brimming with wine, ale, and strong beer; salt whales, their tails in their mouths, with pickled melons for eyes; perfumes in crystal and incense in thuribles hollowed from diamonds, and with these many meadows of blossoms: yellow, red, incarnadine, mauve, and celestine. And weapons of hammered steel, chased with gold. The old giant received them in the Great Court and blessed them, smiled upon them, spoke with them for a time, and sent them away. Sadly they returned to their own homes and countries, there to pray for him, and sacrifice, and sing.

But the Dwarves, seeing how many, and how vast and rich, were the gifts that had been brought him, and seeing, too, that he himself was no longer the great and terrible foe of whom their fathers had spoken, then contrived the Second Plot.

And when the last Nixie had departed, leaving behind her gift of silver foam, and the giant dozed in his chair, they heaped about it all the wood that they could gather—that which had been meant to feed the palace fires, and furniture, and precious painted carvings, too, the work of the great xyloglyphists of old, whereby might be seen many a figure quaint yet imbued with a curious grace, and even the sticks and stumps of their own huts, with all their thatching and daubed doorposts. And to all this mass, which at last rose higher than the giant's waist, they put fire in a score of places.

So terrified were they of the giant, that the first had fled before the last torch was applied. Yet some few stayed behind to watch—a dozen (or so the legend reports) through the crevice of a certain door, half a hundred peering between the petals and leaves of the hills of blossoms, each thinking himself or herself alone.

Up climbed the smoke, and the flames after it. Burned through, some accidental prop in the mountainous pile of heaped wood broke, and half the whole shifted with a grinding roar, so that a column of sparks vied for a time with all the watching stars.

At last the giant stirred, and blinked, and closed his great, slow eyes again. Perhaps he heard the twittering of the Dwarves' distress through the crackling of the flames. Perhaps not. However that may have been, it is certain that he shouted so loudly that the very walls of his palace shook, rose and kicked the fire apart, and with a half-burned brand for a club hunted and slew all he found that night, battering the trees till showers of Dwarves dropped like ripe fruit, and stamping, stamping, stamping, until scarcely one of the fallen Dwarves still drew breath.

When the kindly light of that star which the Arabs call Gienah returned, however, he took to his bed, and summoned physicians from among the Centaurs, who are famous healers. These buttered his many burns with ointments, peered into his eyes, examined his great tongue as so many merchants might a carpet, and stamped upon his chest in order that each might know for himself, through all his feet, the beating of that mighty heart.

And when all that had been done, they shook their heads, and spoke brave words of comfort and encouragement, and went away.

For eight days and eight nights, those Dwarves who yet lived waited outside the giant's bedchamber door with food and drink, and spoke among themselves of poisons (though none dared to fetch them), and turned back such Peris, Ouphes, and Titans as would have brought the giant comfort if they could. On the ninth day, however, a great Worm, white and blind and thicker through the body than any Dwarf, wriggled from beneath the door of the giant's bedchamber.

They entered, first a few pushed forward by the rest, and afterward the whole of them, or rather all that remained alive. This they called the Third Plot. They climbed his sheets, explored the great foul cavern of his open mouth, danced clogs and reels where the Centaurs had stamped, and pierced and slashed his blind eyes again and again with hedge bills and pokers. Then they carved those rude signs that they had aforetime scrawled upon their own doorposts and lintels into the dead giant's forehead, and nose, and cheeks, slicing away the putrescent flesh with their knives until each sign stood out boldly in sullen, weeping crimson. And when the last had been cut deep, they emptied their bowels and bladders wherever they stood, each boasting of what he had done, and where he had done it, and telling the rest how in years to come Dwarf children yet unborn would learn, when they were come to the age of understanding, what he, their ancestor had once done, and glory in it.

Thus they were speaking when the thunderous voice came. So mighty it was that it filled every hall and chamber of the palace; and its first word dashed the pictures from the walls so that their crash and smash added to the roar, though they were lost in it.

Its second word broke all the crockery in the palace and set the shards to sliding like screes of stones, so that they burst open cabinets and cupboards and descended to the floors in avalanches.

Its third word toppled all the statues along the broad avenue that led up to the Great Gate; its fourth stopped the fountain and snapped off both arms of the marble nymph who blessed the waters; and its fifth cracked the basin itself.

Its sixth, seventh, and eighth words maddened every cat in the place, struck dead seventeen bat-winged black rooks of the flock that swept the sky about the Grand Campanile, and set all the bells to ringing.

Its ninth soured every cask in the cellars, while its tenth word stove them in. Its eleventh stopped the clocks and started the hounds to howling.

Its twelfth and last (which was an especially big word) knocked the

Dwarves off their feet and sent every one of them rolling and somer-saulting amongst all their foulnesses while they held their ears and screeched.

And what that voice said was, *"What vermin are these who dare defile the body of a **Giant**?"*

Oh, my friends! Let us of this star, who are ourselves but Dwarves, heed well the warning.

> *But if the great sun move not of himself;*
> *but is an errand boy in heaven . . .*
> —*MELVILLE*

The Sailor Who Sailed
After the Sun

✦

In the good days now lost, when cranky, old-fashioned people still wore three-cornered hats and knee breeches, a lanky farm boy with hair like tow walked to New Bedford with all his possessions tied up in a red-and-white kerchief. Reuben was his name. He gawked at the high wooden houses so close together (for he had never seen the like), at the horses and the wagons, and at all the people—hundreds of men and dozens of women all shoulder-to-shoulder and pushing one another up and down the streets. Most of all, he gawked at the towering ships in the harbor; and when, after an hour or so, a big man with a bushy black beard asked whether he was looking for work, he nodded readily, and followed the big man (who was the chief mate) aboard, and signed a paper.

Next morning the third mate, a man no older than Reuben himself, escorted Reuben to a chandler's, where he bought two pairs of white duck trousers, three striped shirts, a hammock, a pea-jacket, a seabag, and some other things, the cost of everything to be deducted from his pay. And on the day after that, the ship set sail.

Of its passage 'round the Horn to the great whaling grounds of the Southeast Pacific, I shall say little, save that it was very hard indeed. There were storms and more storms; nor were they the right sort of storms, which blow one in the direction in which one wishes to go. These were emphatically storms of the wrong sort. They blew the ship back into the Atlantic time after time; and Reuben believed that was what made them storms of the wrong sort until one blew the man who slung his hammock aft of Reuben's own from the mizzen yard and into the churning waters of the West Scotia Basin. The man who had slung his hammock aft of Reuben's had been the only man aboard with whom Reuben had forged the beginnings of a friendship, and the emptiness of that hammock, as it swung back and forth with the labored pitching of the ship, weighed heavily against him until it was taken down.

At last the storms relented. From open boats tossed and rolled in frigid seas, they took two right whales (which are whales of the right sort) and one sperm whale (which is not). There is no more onerous work done at sea than the butchering and rendering of whales. It is without danger and thus without excitement; nor does it involve monotony of the sort that frees the sailor's mind to go elsewhere. It means working twelve hours a day in a cold, cramped, and reeking factory in which one also lives, and everything—men, clothes, hammocks, blankets, decks, bulkheads, masts, spars, rigging, and sails—gets intolerably greasy.

One dark day when the ice wind from the south punished the ship worse even than usual, and patches of freezing fog raced like great cold ghosts across the black swell, and the old, gray-bearded captain rubbed his greasy eyeglasses upon the sleeve of his greasy blue greatcoat and cursed, and five minutes afterward rubbed them there again, and cursed again, they were stove by a great sperm whale the color of coffee rich with cream. For a moment only they saw him, his great head dashing aside the waves, and the wrecks of two harpoons behind his eye, and the round, pale scars (like so many bubbles in the coffee) two feet across left by the suckers of giant squid.

He vanished and struck. The whole ship shivered and rolled.

In an instant everything seemed to have gone wrong.

In the next it appeared that everything was as right as it had ever been, foursquare and shipshape, after all; and that the crash and shock and splintered planks had been an evil dream.

Yet they were stove, nevertheless. The ship was taking green water forward, and all the pumps together could not keep pace with it. They plugged the hole as well as they could with caps and coats and an old foresail, and when, after three days that even the big, black-bearded mate called hellish, they reached calmer waters, they passed lines under the bow, and hauled into place (there in the darkness below the waterline) a great square of doubled sailcloth like a bandage.

After that they sailed for nearly a month with the pumps going night and day, through waters ever bluer and warmer, until they reached a green island with a white, sloping beach. Whether it lay among those lands first explored by Captain Cook, or on the edge of the Indies, or somewhere east of Africa, Reuben did not know and could not discover. Some mentioned the Friendly Islands; some spoke of the Cocos, some of the Maldives, and still others of Île-de-France or Madagascar. It is probable, indeed, that no one knew except the captain, and perhaps even he did not know.

Wherever it was, it seemed a kindly sort of place to poor Reuben. There, through long, sunny days and moonlit nights, they lightened the ship as much as possible, until it rode as high in the water as a puffin, and at high tide warped it as near the beach as they could get it, and at low tide rolled it on its side to get at the stove-in planking.

One day, when the work was nearly done and his watch dismissed, Reuben wandered farther inland than he usually ventured. There was a spring there, he knew, for he had fetched water from it; he thought that he recalled the way, and he longed for a drink from its cool, clear, up-welling pool. But most of all (if the truth be told) he wished to become lost—to be lost and left behind on that island, which was the finest place that he had ever known save his mother's lap.

And so of course he *was* lost, for people who wish to be lost always get their way. He found a spring that might (or might not) have been the one he recalled. He drank from it, and lay down beside it and slept; and when he woke, a large gray monkey had climbed down out of a banyan tree and thrust a long, careful gray hand into his pocket, and was looking at his clasp knife.

"That's mine," Reuben said, sitting up.

The monkey nodded solemnly, and as much as said, "I know."

But here I have to explain all the ways in which this monkey talked, because you think that monkeys do not often do it. Mostly, at first, he talked with his face and eyes and head, looking away or looking up, grinning or pulling down the corners of his mouth. Later he talked with his hands as well, just as I do. And subsequently he came to make actual sounds, grunting like the mate or sighing like the captain, and pushing his lips in or out. All this until eventually—and long before he had finished talking with Reuben—he spoke at least as well as most of the crew and better than some of them.

"Give it back," Reuben said.

"Wait a bit," replied the monkey, opening and closing the marlinspike, and testing the point with his finger. "That may not be necessary. How much will you take for it? I offer fifteen round, ripe coconuts, delivered here to you immediately upon your agreement."

"Don't want coconuts." Reuben held out his hand.

The monkey raised his shoulders and let them fall. "I don't blame you. Neither do I." Regretfully, he returned the knife to Reuben. "You're from that big ship in the lagoon, aren't you? And you'll be going away in a day or two."

"I wish," Reuben told the monkey, "that I didn't have to go away."

The monkey scratched his head with his left hand, then with his right. His gray arms were long and thin, but very muscular. "Your mother would miss you."

"My mother's dead," Reuben confessed sadly. "My father, too."

"Your sisters and brothers, then."

"I have only one brother," Reuben explained. "While my father was alive, my brother and I helped on the farm. But when my father died, my brother got it and I had to leave."

"Your troop, on the ship. Unless you had someone to take your place."

"No one would do that," Reuben said.

"Don't be too sure," the monkey told him. "I would trade this island for your clasp knife, those trousers, your striped shirt, your cap, and your place on the ship."

Reuben shook his head in wonder. "This beautiful island is worth a great deal more than our whole ship."

"Not to me," said the monkey. "You see, I have owned this island ever since I was born, and have never seen any other place."

Reuben nodded. "That was the way our farm was. When I could live there I didn't really care about it, so that when my brother told me I had to go, I felt that I'd just as soon do it, because I didn't want to work for him. But now it seems the dearest spot in all the world, next to this one."

Thus it was arranged. The monkey dressed himself in Reuben's clothes, putting his beautiful, curled tail down the left leg of Reuben's white duck trousers and the clasp knife into the pocket. And Reuben dressed himself in the monkey's (who had none). And when they heard some of the crew coming, he hid behind the banyan tree.

It was a watering party with buckets, for the ship had been mended, and refloated again, and they had come to refill its barrels and butts. Each sailor had two buckets, and when one set a full bucket down to fill another, the monkey picked it up and waited for him to object. He did not, and the monkey became quite friendly with him by the time that they had carried their buckets back to the ship.

The mates were not fooled. Let me say that at the outset, neither the bushy-black-bearded chief mate, nor the youthful third mate, nor the sleepy-eyed second mate, who never even appears in this story. All three knew perfectly well that the monkey was not Reuben; and if they did not imagine that he was a monkey, they must nonetheless have suspected that he was something not quite human and perhaps of the ape kind. This is shown clearly by the name they gave him, which was Jacko. But since Jacko was a better sailor than Reuben had ever been, and a prankish, lively fellow as well, they did not say a great deal about it.

As for the captain, his eyeglasses were so greasy that Jacko in Reuben's shirt looked the very image of Reuben to him. Once, it is true, the chief mate mentioned the matter to him, saying, "There's somethin' perqu'ler about one of our topmen, Capt'n."

"And what is that, Mr. Blackmire?" the captain had replied, looking at the chief mate over his eyeglasses in order to see him.

"Well, Capt'n, he's shorter than all the rest. And he's hairy, sir. Terribly hairy. Gray hair."

Scratching his own greasy gray beard with the point of his pen, the captain had inquired, "A disciplinary problem, Mr. Blackmire?"

"No, sir."

"Does his work?"

"Yes, sir." The chief mate had taken a step backward as he spoke, having divined whither their talk was bound.

"Keep an eye on him, Mr. Blackmire. Just keep an eye on him."

That was the end of it; and indeed, Jacko soon became such a valuable member of the crew that the chief mate was sorry he had brought the matter up.

But to explain to you how that was, I am going to have to explain first how whaling was carried on in those days, before the invention of the modern harpoon gun, and the equally modern explosive harpoon, and all the rest of the improvements and astonishing devices that have made whaling so easy and pleasant for everyone except the whales.

Those old harpoons, you see, hardly ever killed the whale—they did not penetrate deeply enough for that. The old harpoons were, in fact, really no more than big spears with barbed heads to which a long rope was attached as a sort of fishing line.

When the harpooner, standing in bow of his whaleboat (you have seen pictures of Washington crossing the Delaware doing this) had thrown his harpoon, and it had gone a foot or two into the hump, as it usually was, of the poor whale, the whalers had only hooked their catch, not landed it. They had to play it, and when it was so tired that it could hardly swim and could not dive, though its life depended on it, they had to pull their boat alongside it and kill it with their whale lances, either by stabbing it from the boat, or actually springing out of the boat and onto the whale. And to say that all this was a difficult and a very dangerous business is like saying that learning to ride a tiger requires tenacity and a scratch-proof surface far above the common.

For a whale is as much bigger than the biggest tiger as the planet Jupiter is bigger than the big globe in a country school, and it is as much stronger than the strongest tiger as a full, round bumper of nitroglycerin is stronger than a cup of tea. And though it is not as savage as a tiger, the whale is fighting for its life.

Which Jacko, as I have implied, became very skilled in taking. No sailor on the ship was bolder than he with the whaling lance, none more ready to spring from the whaleboat onto the great, dark, slippery back, or to plunge the razor-sharp steel lancehead between his own feet, and raise the lance, and plunge it again and again till the whale's bright blood gushed forth not like a spring but like a full-grown river, and the whole of the sea for a mile around was dyed scarlet by it—just as certain rivers we have, that are bleeding their continents to death, dye the very oceans themselves for whole leagues beyond land with red or yellow mud that they have stolen away.

A day arrived (and in part it came as quickly as it did as a result of Jacko's efforts, let there be no doubt of that) when the great tuns in the ship's hold were nearly full. Then the captain, and the crew as well, calculated that one more whale would fill them to the brim. It was a pleasant prospect. Already the captain was thinking of his high white house in New Bedford and his grandchildren; and the sailors of weeks and even months ashore, of living well in an inn, and eating and drinking whenever they wished and never working, of farms and cottages and village girls, and stories around the fire.

Jacko was in the fo'c'sle that day, enlightening a few select friends as to the way the chief mate walked, and the way the captain lit his pipe, and the way in which a clever fellow may look between his own legs and see the world new, and other such things, when they heard the thrilling cry of "There . . . there . . . *thar* she blows!" from the maintop.

Three whales!

Jacko was the first on deck, the first at the davits, and the first into the first of the half-dozen whaleboats they launched. No oarsman pulled harder than he, his thin, gray back straining against Reuben's second-best striped shirt; and not a man on board cheered more heartily than he when Savannah Jefferson, the big brown harpooner with arms thicker than most men's thighs and a child's soft, sweet voice, cast his harpoon up and out, rising, bending, and falling like lightning to strike deep into the whale's back a boat's length behind the tail.

What a ride that whale gave them! There is nothing like it now, nothing at all. Mile after mile, as fast as the fastest speedboat, through mist and fog and floating ice. They could not slow or steer, and they would not cut free. At one moment they were sitting in water and bailing like so many madmen, nine-tenths swamped. At the next the whale was sounding, and like to pull them down with it. Long, long before it stopped and they were able to draw their boat up to it, they had lost sight of their ship.

But stop it did, eventually, and lie on the rough and heaving swell like the black keel of a capsized hulk, with its breath smoking in the air, and the long summer day (it was the twenty-first of December), like the whale, nearly spent.

"Lances!" bellowed the chief mate from his place in the stern.

Jacko was the first with his lance; nor did he content himself, as many another would have, with a mere jab at the whale from the boat. No, not he! As in times past he had leaped from the top of one tall palm to another, now he sprang from the gunnel of the whaleboat onto the whale's board back.

And as he did, the whale, with one powerful blow of its tail, upset the whaleboat and tossed crew, oars, lances, and spare harpoons into the freezing water.

A hand reached up—one lone hand, and that only for a moment—as though to grasp the top of a small wave. Jacko extended the shaft of his lance toward it, but the shaft was not long enough, nor Jacko quick enough, quick though he was. The hand vanished below the wave it had tried to grasp and never reappeared.

Then Jacko looked at the whale, or rather, as I should say, at the little round eye of it; and the whale at Jacko; and Jacko saw the whale for what it was, and himself for what *he* was, too. He took off Reuben's cap then and threw it into the sea, where it floated. Ruben's second-best shirt followed it, and floated, too. Reuben's white duck trousers followed them both; but those trousers did not float like a duck or like anything else, for the weight of Reuben's clasp knife in the pocket sunk them.

"I am an animal like you," Jacko told the whale. "Not really like you, because you're very big, while I'm very small. And you're where you belong, while I'm thousands and thousands of miles from where I belong.

But we're both animals—that's all I meant to say. If I don't molest you anymore, ever again, will you let me right the boat, and bail it, and live on this terrible sea if I can?"

To which the whale said, "I will."

Then Jacko cut the harpoon line with the head of his lance, and let it slide into the sea. It is hard, very hard, to pull out a harpoon, because of the big, swiveling barbs on the head that open out and resist the pull. But Jacko worked the head back and forth with his long, gray, clever fingers, and cut when he had to with the head of the lance (those lanceheads look very much like the blades of daggers), and eventually he got it out, and threw it into the sea, and the lance after it.

By that time it was nearly dark—so dark that he could hardly make out the upturned bottom of the whaleboat; but the whale knew where it was, and swam over to it until it bumped against its side. Jacko braced his long monkey-feet against the whale, grasped the gunnel through the freezing waves, and by heaving till it seemed his arms must break righted the whaleboat again, although it was still half full of seawater.

He leaped in with a loud splash, and the whale slid, silently and with hardly a ripple, beneath the dark sea.

Jacko bailed with his hands all that night, scooping out the cold seawater and throwing it over the side; and it is a good thing he did, for he would certainly have frozen to death otherwise. His thoughts were freed, as I have explained, and he thought about a great many things—about the beautiful island he had left behind, and how the sun had joined him there every morning in the top of his tall banyan tree; about finding bright shells and things to eat on the beach, and how he had scolded, sometimes, certain friendly little waves that came up to play with his toes.

All of which was pleasant enough. But again and again he thought of the ship, and wondered whether he would see it in the morning. He did not want to go back to it. In fact, he discovered that he hated the very thought of it, and its greasy smoke, and its cold, and the brutal treatment that he and others had received there, and the more brutal hunting of the peaceable whales. Yet he felt that if he did not see the ship in the morning he would certainly die.

Nor was that the worst of that terrible night, for he found himself haunted by the men who had been his companions in the whaleboat. When he went to the bow, it seemed to him that he could make out the shadowy form of Mr. Blackmire, the chief mate, seated in the stern with his hand upon the tiller. When he went to the stern, there was no one there; yet it seemed to him that he could make out the dark, dim shape of Savannah Jefferson in the bow, crouched and ready, grasping a harpoon.

Worst of all, he sometimes glimpsed the faces of the drowned sailors floating just beneath the waves, and he could not be certain that they were mere shenanigans of his imagination; their still lips seemed to ask him, silently and patiently, how it was that he deserved to live and they to die. At times he talked to them as he had when they were alive, and he found he had no answer to give them, save that it might be that he was only destined to die more slowly and more miserably. When he spoke to them in this way, he felt sure that the night would never end.

But that night, which seemed so very long to him, was actually quite short as measured by your clock. Our winter, in this northern hemisphere, is summer in the southern, so that at the same time that we have our longest winter night they have their shortest summer one. Morning came, and the water in the bottom of the whaleboat was no deeper than his ankles, but the ship was nowhere in sight.

Morning came, I said. But there was more to it than that, and it was far more beautiful than those plain words imply. Night faded—that was how it began. The stars winked out, one by one at first, and then by whole dozens and scores. A beautiful rosy flush touched the horizon, deepened, strengthened, and drove the night away before it as ten thousand angels with swords and bows and rods of power fanned out across the sky, more beautiful than birds and more terrible than the wildest storm. Jacko waved and called out to them, but if they heard him or saw him they gave no sign of it.

Soon the sun revealed its face, in the beginning no more than a sliver of golden light but rounded and lovely just the same, peeping above clouds in the northeast. Then the whole sun itself, warm and dazzling, and its friendly beams showed Jacko a little pole mast and a toy-like boom, wrapped in a sail and lashed beneath the seats.

He set up the mast and climbed to the top (at which the whaleboat rolled alarmingly), but no ship could he see.

When he had climbed down again, he gave his head a good scratching, something that always seemed to help his thought processes. Since the ship was not here, it was clear to him that it was very likely somewhere else. And if that was the case, there seemed no point at all in his remaining where he was.

So he fitted the boom, which was not much thicker than a broomstick, to his little mast, and bent the small, three-cornered sail, and steered for the sun.

That was a very foolish thing to do, to be sure. The sun was in the northeast when it rose, but in the north at noon, and in the northwest as the long afternoon wore on, so that if you were to plot Jacko's course you would find that it looked rather like a banana, generally northward, but inclined to the east in the morning and rather favoring the west toward afternoon. But Jacko did not know much about navigation (which he had always left to the captain), it was comforting to feel himself drawing ever nearer to the sun, and if the truth be told it was probably as good a course for looking for the ship as any of the other incorrect ones.

That day, which was in fact long, as I have tried to explain, seemed terribly short to poor Jacko. Soon evening came, the angels streamed back to the sun, night rose from the sea and spread her black wings, and Jacko was left alone, cold, hungry, and thirsty. He climbed his mast again so that he could keep the vanishing sun in sight as long as possible; and when it was gone, he dropped down into the bilges of the whaleboat and wept. In those days there were no laboratories, and so we may be fairly sure that he was the most miserable monkey in the world.

Still, it was not until the tenth hour of the night, when the new dawn was almost upon him, that his heart broke. When that happened, something that had always lived there, something that was very like Jacko himself, yet not at all like a monkey, went out from him. It left his broken heart, and left his skin as well, and left the whaleboat, and shot like an arrow over the dark sea, northeast after the sun. Jacko could not see it, but he knew that it was gone and that he was more alone now than he had ever been.

At which point a very strange thing happened. Among the many, many stars that had kindled in the northeast when the last light of the sun had gone, a new star rose (or so it seemed) and flew toward him—a star no different from countless others, but different indeed because it left its place in the heavens and approached him, nearer and nearer, until it hung just above his head.

"You mistake me," said the star.

"I don't even know you," replied Jacko, "but can you help me? Oh, please, help me if you can."

"You have seen me every day, throughout your entire life," replied the star. "I have always helped all of you, and I will help you again. But first you must tell me your story, so that I will know how to proceed."

And so Jacko told, more or less as you have heard it here, but in many more words, and with a wealth of gesture and expression, which I should strive in vain to reproduce. It took quite a long time, as you have already seen. And during that long time the star said nothing, but floated above his head, a minute pinpoint of light; so that when he had finished at last Jacko said, "Are you really a star, and not a firefly?"

"I am a star," the star answered. If a small silver bell could form words when it spoke, it would no doubt sound very much like that star. "And this is my true appearance—or at least, it is as near my true appearance as you are able to comprehend. I am the star you call the sun, the star you pursued all day."

Jacko's mouth opened and shut. Then it opened and shut again—all this without saying one word.

"You think me large and very strong," the star said, "but there are many stars that are far larger and stronger than I. It is only because you stand so close to me that you think me a giant. Thus I show myself to you now as I really am, among my peers: a smallish, quite common and ordinary-looking star."

Jacko, who did not understand in the least, but who had been taught manners by the chief mate, said, "It's very kind of you to show yourself to me at all, sir."

"I do it every day," the star reminded him.

Jacko nodded humbly.

"Here is how I judge your case," the star continued. "Please interrupt if you feel that I am mistaken in anything that I say."

Jacko nodded, resolving not to object (as he too often had in the fo'c'sle) about trifles.

"You do not desire to be where you are."

Jacko nodded again, emphatically, both his hands across his mouth.

"You would prefer some me-warmed place, where fruiting trees were plentiful and men treated monkeys with great kindness. A place where there are wonderful things to see and climb on, of the sort you imagined when you left your island—monuments, and the like."

Jacko nodded a third time, more enthusiastically than ever, his hands still tight across his mouth.

"And yet you believe that you could be happy now, if only you might return to the island that was yours." The star sighed. "In that you are mistaken. Your island—it is no longer yours in any event—is visited from time to time by the ships of men. The first man, as you know, has already made his home there, and more will be moving in soon. This age is not a good one for monkeys, and the age to come will be far worse."

At these words, Jacko felt his heart sink within him; it was only then that he realized it was whole once more—that the part of himself which had run away from him when his heart had broken had returned to him.

"Steer as I tell you," said the star, "and do not be afraid."

So poor Jacko took the tiller again, and trimmed their little sail; and it was a good thing he did, for the wind was rising and seemed almost to blow the star as though it were a firefly after all. For a few minutes he could still see it bright against the sail. By degrees it appeared to climb the mast, and for a long while it remained there, as if the whaleboat had hoisted a lantern with a little candle in it. But at last it blew forward and dropped lower, until it was hidden by the sail.

"Are you still there?" Jacko called.

"I am sitting in the bow," the star replied.

But while that was happening, far stranger things were taking place outside the boat. Night had backed away, and twilight had come again. A fiery arch, like a burning rainbow, stretched clear across the sky. Ships came into view, only to vanish before Jacko could hail them; and very strange ships they were—a towering junk, like a pagoda afloat; a stately galleon with a big cross upon its crimson foresail; and at last an odd, beaked craft, so long and narrow that it seemed almost a lance put to sea, that flew over the water on three pairs of wings.

"A point to starboard, helmsman," called the star. As it spoke, the twilight vanished. The shadow of their sail fell upon the water as sharp and black as that of the gnomen of a sundial, and around it every little wave sparkled and danced in the sunlight. Jacko steered a point to starboard, as he had been told, then turned his face toward the sun, grinned with happiness, and shut his eyes for a moment.

The sound of many voices made him open them again. A river's mouth was swallowing their whaleboat between sandy lips, and both those lips were black with people, thousands upon thousands of them, chanting and shouting.

"Where are we?" Jacko asked.

"This is Now." The star's clear voice came from the other side of the sail. "It is always Now, wherever I am." Beneath the lower edge of the sail, Jacko could see a man's bare, brown feet.

"Here and Now is your new home," the star continued. "They will treat you well—better than you deserve—because you have come with me. But you must watch out for crocodiles."

"I will," Jacko promised.

"Then let down the sail so that they can see you. Our way will carry us as near the shore as we wish to go."

So Jacko freed the halyard, letting the little sail slip down the mast, and bounced up onto the tiller.

"Come here," said the star, "and sit upon my shoulder." Which now made perfect sense, because the star had become a tall, slender, brown man. Jacko leaped from the tiller to the mast, and from the mast onto the star's shoulder just as he had been told, though the great gold disc of the star's headdress was so bright it nearly blinded him. And at that a great cheer went up from all those thousands of people.

"Ra!" they shouted. "Ra, Ra, *Ra!*," so that Jacko might have thought that they were watching a game, if he had known more about games. But some shouted "Thoth!" as well.

"Ra is the name by which I am known Now," explained the star. "Do you see that old man with the necklace? He is my chief mistaker in this place. When I give the word, you must jump to him and take his hand. It will seem very far, but you must jump anyway. Do you understand?"

Jacko nodded. "I hope I don't fall in the water."

"You have my promise," the star said. "You will not fall in the water."

As he spoke, the whaleboat soared upward. It seemed to Jacko that some new kind of water, water so clear it could not be seen, must have been raining down on them, creating a new sea above the sea and leaving the river's mouth and all of its thousands of bowing people on the bottom.

Then the star said, "Go!" and he leaped over the side and seemed almost to fly.

If you that love books should ever come across *The Book of That Which Is in Tuat,* which is one of the very oldest books we have, I hope that you will look carefully at the picture called "The Tenth Hour of the Night." There you will see, marching to the right of Ra's glorious sunboat, twelve men holding paddles. These are the twelve hours of the day. Beyond them march twelve women, all holding one long cord; these twelve women are the twelve hours of the night. Beyond even them—and thus almost at the head of this lengthy procession—are four gods, two with the heads of men and two with the heads of animals. Their names are Bant, Seshsha, Ka-Ament, and Renen-sebu.

And in front of *them,* standing upon the tiller of a boat, is one monkey.

It seems strange, to be sure, to find a monkey in such a procession as Ra's, but there is something about this particular monkey that is stranger still. Unlike the four gods, and the twelve women with the cord, and the twelve men with paddles, this monkey is actually looking back at Ra in his glorious sunboat. And waving. Above this monkey's head, I should add, floats something that you will not find anywhere else in the whole of *The Book of That Which Is in Tuat.* It is a smallish, quite common and ordinary-looking, five-pointed star.

How the Bishop Sailed
to Inniskeen

✦

There was a King to rule the islands then,
Chosen for might, who had his Admiral
Of all the Inniskeas. The Priest's sick call
Was this cold pasture's only festival.

—T. H. WHITE

This is the story Hogan told as we sat before our fire in the unroofed
chapel, looking up at the niche above the door—the niche that had
held the holy stone.

" 'Twas Saint Cian's pillow," said Hogan, "an' rough when he got it—
rough as a pike's kiss. Smooth it was when he died, for his head had
smoothed it sixty years. Couldn't a maid have done it nicer, an' where the
stone had worn away was the Virgin. Her picture, belike, sir, in the
markin's that'd been in the stone."

It sounded as if he meant to talk no more, so I said, "What would he
want with a stone pillow, Pat?" This though I knew the answer, simply because the night and the lonesome wind sweeping in off the Atlantic had
made me hungry for a human voice.

"Not for his own sins, sure, for he'd none. But for yours, sir, an' mine.
There was others, too, that come to live on this island."

"Other hermits, you mean?"

Hogan nodded. "An' when they was gone the fisherfolk come, me own folk with them. 'Twas they that built this chapel here, an' they set the holy stone above the door, for he was dead an' didn't want it. When it was stormin' they'd make a broom, an' dip it in the water, an' sprinkle the holy stone, an' the storm would pass. But if it was stormin' bad, they'd carry the stone to the water an' dip it in."

I nodded, thinking how hard and how lonely life must have been for them on the Inniskeas, and of fishermen drowned. "What happened to it, Pat?"

" 'Twas sunk in the bay in me grandfather's time." Hogan paused, but I could see that he was thinking—still talking in himself, as he himself would have said. "Some says it was the pirates an' some the Protestants. They told that to the woman that come from Dublin, an' she believed them."

I had been in Hogan's company for three days, and was too sage a hound to go haring off after the woman from Dublin; in any event, I knew already that she was the one who had fenced the cromlech at the summit of the island. So I said, "But what do you think, Pat? What really happened to it?"

"The bishop took it. Me own grandfather saw him, him that was dead when I was born. Or me great-grandfather it might be, one or the other don't matter. But me father told me, an' the bishop took it Christmas Eve."

The wind was rising. Hogan's boat was snug enough down in the little harbor, but I could hear the breakers crash not two hundred yards from where we sat.

"There was never a priest here, only this an' a man to take care of it. O'Dea his name was."

Because I was already thinking of writing about some of the things he told me (though in the event I have waited so long) I said, "That was your grandfather, Pat, I feel certain."

"A relative, no doubt, sir," Hogan conceded, "for they were all relations on this island, more or less. But me grandfather was only a lad. O'Dea cared for the place when he wasn't out in his boat. 'Twas the women, you see, that wetted the holy stone, when the men were away."

I said, "It's a pity we haven't got it now, but if it's in the bay it ought to be wet enough."

" 'Tis not, sir. 'Tis in Dublin, in their big museum there, an' dry as a bone. The woman from there fetched it this summer."

"I thought you said the bishop threw it into the bay."

"She had a mask for her face," Hogan continued, as though he had not heard me, "an' a rubber bathin' costume for the rest of her, an' air in a tin tied to her back, just like you see." (He meant, "as I have seen it on television.") "Three days she dove from Kilkelly's boat. Friday it was she brought it up in two pieces. Some say she broke it under the water to make the bringing up easier." Hogan paused to light his pipe.

I asked, "Did the bishop throw it into the bay?"

"In a manner of speakin', sir. It all began when he was just a young priest, do you see? The bishop that was before him had stuck close to the cathedral, as sometimes they will. In the old days it was not easy, journeyin'. Very bad, it was, in winter. 'If you'd seen the roads before they were made, you'd thank the Lord for General Wade.' "

Having had difficulties of my own in traveling around the west of Ireland in a newish Ford Fiesta, I nodded sympathetically.

"So this one, when he got the job, he made a speech. 'The devil take me,' he says, 'if ever I say mass Christmas Eve twice in the same church.' "

"And the devil took him," I suggested.

"That he did not, sir, for the bishop was as good as his word. As the times wore on, there was many a one that begged him to stop, but there was no holdin' him. Come the tag end of Advent, off he'd go. An' if he heard that there was one place worse than another, it's where he went. One year a priest from Ballycroy went on the pilgrimage, an' he told the bishop a bit about Inniskeen, havin' been once or twice. 'Send word,' says the bishop, 'to this good man O'Dea. Tell him to have a boat waitin' for me at Erris.'

"They settled it by a fight, an' it was me grandfather's own father that was to bring him."

"Ah," I said.

"Me grandfather wanted to come along to help with the boat, sure, but his father wouldn't allow it, it was that rough, an' he had to wait in the chapel—right here, sir—with his mother. They was all here a long time before midnight, sure, talkin' the one to the other an' waitin' on the bishop, an' me grandfather—recollect he was but a little lad, sir—he fell asleep.

"Next thing he knew, his mother was shakin' him. 'Wake up, Sean, for he's come!' He wakes an' sits up, rubbin' his eyes, an' there's the bishop. But Lord, sir, there wasn't half there that should've been! Late as the sun rises at Christmas, it was near the time.

"It didn't matter a hair to His Excellency. He shook all the men by the hand, an' smiled at all the women, an' patted me grandfather's head, an' blessed everybody. Then he begun the mass. You never heard the like, sir. When they sang, there was angels singin' with them. Sure they couldn't see them, but they knew that they was there an' they could hear them. An' when the bishop preached, they saw the Gates an' got the smell of Heaven. It was like cryin' for happiness, an' it was forever. Me father said the good man used to cry a bit himself when he talked of it—which he did, sir, every year about this time, until he left this world.

"When the mass was over the bishop blessed them all again, an' he give O'Dea a letter, an' O'Dea kissed his ring, which was an honor to him after. Me grandfather saw his father waiting to take the bishop back to Erris, an' knew he'd been in the back of them. Right back there, sir."

We were burning wreckage we had picked up on the beach earlier. Hogan paused to throw a broken timber on the fire.

"The stone, Pat," I said.

"The bishop took it, sir, sure. After he give the letter, he points at it, do you see," Hogan pointed to the empty niche, "an' he says, 'Sorry I am, O'Dea, but I must have that.' Then O'Dea gets up on a stool—'twas what they sat on here—an' gives it to him, an' off he goes with me grandfather's father.

"All natural, sir. But me grandfather lagged behind when the women went home, an' as soon as there wasn't one lookin', off he runs after the bishop, for he'd hopes his father'd allow him this time, it bein' not so rough as the night before. You know where the rock juts, sir? You took a picture from there."

"Of course," I said.

"Me grandfather run out onto that rock, sir, for there's a bit of a moon by then an' he's wantin' to see if they'd put out. They hadn't, sir. He sees his father there in the boat, holdin' it close in for the bishop. An' he sees the bishop, holdin' the holy stone an' steppin' into it. Up comes the sun, an' devil a boat, or bishop, or father, or holy stone there is.

"Me grandfather's father's body washed up on Duvillaun, but never the bishop's. He'd wanted the holy stone, do you see, to weight him. Or some say to sleep on, there on the bottom. 'Tis the same thing, maybe."

I nodded. In that place, with the wind moaning around the ruined stone chapel, it did not seem impossible or even strange.

"They're all dead now, sir. There's not a man alive that was born on these islands, or a woman, either. But they do say the ghosts of them that missed midnight mass can be seen comin' over the bay Christmas Eve, for they was buried on the mainland, sir, most of 'em, or died at sea like the bishop. I never seen 'em, mind, an' don't want to."

Hogan was silent for a long time after that, and so was I.

At last I said, "You're suggesting that I come back here and have a look."

Hogan knocked out his pipe. "You've an interest in such things, sir, an' so I thought I ought to mention it. I could take you out by daylight an' leave you here with your food an' sleepin' bag, an' your camera. Christmas Day, I'd come by for you again."

"I have to go to Bangor, Pat."

"I know you do, sir."

"Let me think about it. What was in the letter?"

" 'Twas after New Year's when they read it, sir, for O'Dea wouldn't let it out of his hands. Sure there wasn't a soul on the island that could read, an' no school. It says the bishop had drowned on his way to Inniskeen to say the midnight mass, an' asked the good people to make a novena for his soul. The priest at Erris wrote it, two days after Christmas."

Hogan lay down after that, but I could not. I went outside with a flashlight and roamed over the island for an hour or more, cold though it was.

I had come to Inniskeen, to the westernmost of Ireland's westernmost island group, in search of the remote past. For I am, among various other things, a writer of novels about that past, a chronicler of Xerxes and

"King" Pausanias. And indeed the past was here in plenty. Sinking vessels from the Spanish Armada had been run aground here. Vikings had strode the very beaches I paced, and earlier still, neolithic people had lived here largely upon shellfish, or so their middens suggested.

And yet it seemed to me that night that I had not found the past, but the future; for they were all gone, as Hogan had said. The neolithic people had fallen, presumably, before the modern, Celtic Irish, becoming one of the chief strands of Irish fairy lore. The last of Saint Cian's hermits had died in grace, leaving no disciple. The fishermen had lived here for two hundred years or more, generation after generation, harvesting the treacherous sea and tiny gardens of potatoes; and for a few years there had actually been a whaling station on North Island.

No more.

The Norwegians sailed from their whaling station for the last time long ago. Long ago the Irish Land Commission removed the fisherfolk and resettled them; their thatched stone cottages are tumbling down, as the hermits' huts did earlier. Gray sea-geese nest upon Inniskeen again, and otters whistle above the whistling wind. A few shaggy black cattle are humanity's sole contribution; I cannot call them wild, because they do not know human beings well enough for fear. In the Inniskeas our race is already extinct. We stayed a hundred centuries, and are gone.

I drove to Bangor the following day, December twenty-second. There I sent two cables and made transatlantic calls, learning only that my literary agent, who might perhaps have acted, had not the slightest intention of doing so before the holidays, and that my publishers, who might certainly have acted if they chose, would not.

Already all of Ireland, which delights in closing at every opportunity, was gleefully locking its doors. I would have to stay in Bangor over Christmas, or drive on to Dublin (praying the while for an open petrol station), or go back to Erris. I filled my rented Ford's tank until I could literally dabble my forefinger in gasoline and returned to Erris.

I will not regale you here with everything that went wrong on the twenty-fourth. Hogan had an errand that could neither be neglected nor postponed. His usually dependable motor would not start, so that eventually we were forced to beg the proprietor of the only store that carried such things to leave his dinner to sell us a spark plug. It was nearly dark before we pushed off, and the storm that had been brewing all day was ready to burst upon us.

"We're mad, you know," Hogan told me. "Me as much as you." He was at the tiller, his pipe clenched between his teeth; I was huddled in the bow in a life jacket, my hat pulled over my ears. "How'll you make a fire, sir? Tell me that."

Through chattering teeth, I said that I would manage somehow.

"No you won't, sir, for we'll never get there."

I said that if he was waiting for me to tell him to turn back, he would have to wait until we reached Inniskeen; and I added—bitterly—that if Hogan wanted to turn back I could not prevent him.

"I've taken your money an' given me word."

"We'll make it, Pat."

As though to give me the lie, lightning lit the bay.

"Did you see the island, then?"

"No," I said, and added that we were surely miles from it still.

"I must know if I'm steerin' right," Hogan said.

"Don't you have a compass?"

"It's no good for this, sir. We're shakin' too much." It was an ordinary pocket compass, as I should have remembered, and not a regular boat's compass in a binnacle.

After that I kept a sharp lookout forward. Low-lying North Island was invisible to my right, but from time to time I caught sight of higher, closer, South Island. The land I glimpsed at times to our left might have been Duvillaun or Innisglora, or even Achill, or all three. Black Rock Light was visible only occasionally, which was somewhat reassuring. At last, when the final, sullen twilight had vanished, I caught sight of Inniskeen only slightly to our left. Pointing, I half rose in the bow as Hogan swung it around to meet a particularly dangerous comber. It lifted us so high that it seemed certain we were being flipped end-for-end; we raced down its back and plunged into the trough, only to be lifted again at once.

"Hang on!" Hogan shouted. At that moment lightning cut the dark bowl of the sky from one horizon to the other.

I pointed indeed, but I pointed back toward Erris. I would have spoken if I could, but I did not need to. In two hours or less we were sitting comfortably in Hogan's parlor, over whiskey toddies. The German tradition of the Christmas tree, which we Americans now count among American customs, has not taken much root in Ireland. But there was an Advent Calendar with all its postage-stamp-sized windows wide, and gifts done up in brightly colored papers. And the little crèche (we would call it a crib set) with its as-yet empty manger, cracked, ethereal Mary, and devoted Joseph, had more to say about Christmas than any tree I have ever seen.

"Perhaps you'll come back next year," Hogan suggested after we had related our adventures, "an' then we'll have another go."

I shook my head.

His wife looked up from her knitting, and with that single glance understood everything I had been at pains to hide. "What was it you saw?" she asked.

I did not tell her, then or later. Nor am I certain that I can tell you. It was no ghost, or at least there was nothing of sheet or skull or ectoplasm, none of the conventional claptrap of movies and Halloween. In appearance, it was no more than the floating corpse of a rather small man with longish white hair. He was dressed in dark clothes, and his eyes—I saw them plainly as he rolled in the wave—were open. No doubt it was the motion of the water; but as I stared at him for half a second or so in the lightning's glare, it appeared to me that he raised his arm and gestured, invitingly and with the utmost good will, in the direction of Inniskeen.

I have never returned to Ireland, and never will. And yet I have no doubt at all that the time will soon come when I, too, shall attend his midnight mass in the ruined chapel. What will follow that service, I cannot guess.

In Christ's name, I implore mercy for my soul.

Houston, 1943

✦

The voice woke Roddie in the middle of the night. Or rather, it did not wake him at first. It seeped into his sleep, so that he dreamed he was at his desk in Poe School reading "The Murders in the Rue Morgue"; and through the open windows with smeared gray panes (the smear was to keep their shattered glass from cutting Mrs. Butcher and her class when the first Nazi bombs fell on the playground outside), and above the rising, fading hum of the big electric fan that shook its head forever *no, no, no* (because the room was so hot, boiling with the merciless Gulf heat that would endure not for days or weeks but for almost a year, a heat that soaked everything and that no fan could blow away), he heard his father's voice calling him.

His father was gone, as always except on Friday nights, on Saturdays, and on Sundays until evening, gone selling "systems" to defense plants. Roddie sat up in bed.

"Come."

He went to the window. His was a large bedroom in a small house that had only four rooms and a tiny bathroom; there were four windows at the side (facing Mrs. Smith's) and three at the rear. It was to one of the rear windows that he went.

A boy stood in the middle of the back yard, distinct in the moonlight. The boy was small and thin, almost frail; but his eyes caught the moonlight like a cat's eyes, and the moon filled them with a colorless glow. He waved, gesturing for Roddie to join him, silently saying that they must go somewhere together. The window was already thrown wide; Roddie un-hooked the screen and climbed out, dropping four feet into his mother's fragrant bed of mint.

"Who are you?" he asked.

"Jim." The strange boy's voice was high and reedy, laced with an ac-cent Roddie had never heard before. He had expected some neighbor-hood friend; this was a boy he did not know at all. The strange boy gripped him by the arm and pointed toward the crawlspace beneath the house. His grasp was cold and damp, as if he had been groping after something lost in water.

"We'll get dirty."

The boy pointed again. At the edge of the shadow of the fig tree there was something Roddie took for a tarantula. He had seen many tarantu-las, big, hairy spiders found lurking under old boards or in firewood; this was the biggest ever, big enough to kill birds, something that only the largest did. It rose on five legs, ran swiftly to him, and climbed his pajama bottoms.

He slapped at it just as it reached his waist. Although it was as hard as his cast-iron clown bank, it seemed to slip for a moment, to lose its hold.

A moment more and it was climbing again, pinching the soft skin of his bare chest between sharp legs. He grasped it, felt its stiff hair and gouging nails, and knew he held a human hand. With all his strength, he flung it from him and heard it thump against the wall of the Jacobsons' garage. In the shadow of the eaves, it fell softly to earth.

"Foul weather," Jim whispered. " 'E don't like 'avin' 'is 'awser crossed. Better cut it."

Roddie said, "I'm going back inside."

He returned to the window, and the thin boy, Jim, followed him, not trying to stop him. "Better cut," Jim repeated.

Roddie raised the screen and pushed his head under it, put a bare foot on the narrow white-painted finale that was the last board down the wall of the house.

There was a boy, another boy, sleeping in his bed. Roddie scrambled through the window, ran to the switch, and turned on the light.

The other boy did not wake up or even stir. Roddie thought vaguely of offering to share the bed if the other boy—like Jim, perhaps—needed a place to sleep. He shook the other boy by the shoulder; his eyes opened at once, and he screamed.

Roddie heard his mother in the front bedroom, the click of the switch on her reading light, the patter of bare feet.

The boy in the bed screamed again, his eyes huge, his face empty of everything save fear. A thin line of spit ran from one corner of his mouth and wet his chin.

The door banged open. Roddie's mother flew in, her hair in curl papers, her pale face a study in terror and anger. "It's a dream, Roddie! Only a bad dream, see? Oh, that awful school! I'm right here. It's all right, Roddie—everything's all right." She hugged the blank-faced boy, crushing him against her breasts, rocking back and forth as she held him.

Icy fingers touched Roddie's shoulder. "Best cut, we 'ad. 'E'll be in main soon, if we don't. 'E'll be after 'e, but 'e might get 'er."

Baffled, Roddie backed away, out of the bedroom and into the little hallway. The phone rang as they passed; he jerked with fear, and at the sound of his mother's steps he followed Jim into the twilight of the big room that was living room and dining room together.

The phone rang again before his mother picked it up.

"Hello?"

"Oh, good evening, Mrs. Smith. No, we're fine. Roddie had a nightmare.

"Really? In our yard?

"What did he look like? Do you think I should call the police?"

There were already past the hulking Crosley radio. " 'E'll be waitin' at the back."

"*I'm* Roddie," Roddie said. It sounded false even to him as he said it, as false as the lies he told at times to get out of trouble. "Where we going?"

"Old man's."

The streets were hot, dark, and silent. They saw a single car on Old Spanish Trail, a black de Soto that hummed past them meditating upon secrets.

———

The old man's house looked like dozens Roddie passed every time he rode his bike to the Y, a tiny clapboard cottage with a sagging roof.

" 'E's 'ome," Jim said. "Open the door."

Roddie asked, "Shouldn't we knock?"

Jim made no reply; when Roddie looked around for him he was gone, and Roddy stood alone on the crooked little porch beside a rickety rocking chair. Tentatively, mostly because it seemed so silly to come way out here without doing anything, he knocked at the peeling door.

Someone inside laughed, a high, cracked cackling. "They hear. They hear. Sister, hear them!"

Somebody else moaned softly.

Roddie waited. And at last, when no one opened the door, he knocked again. This time a bell jangled inside the cottage, giving him the crazy feeling that he had pushed a button somehow instead of knocking, though he knew that he had knocked. He tried the knob, and it turned in his hand. There was a rattle and squeak as the latch crept back. The door seemed strangely heavy but swung ponderously away from him.

The interior of the cottage was a single room; even so it was smaller than his bedroom at home. A narrow cot stood in one corner, a commode with a broken seat in another.

In the center of the room, in place of a carpet or a rug, was a spreading pool of blood. It came from a black chicken hanging by its feet from the light fixture. The chicken's neck had been cut though its head was still attached. Its wings hung down as though to sweep up its own blood from the cracked boards of the floor.

Because both were so still, a second or more passed before Roddie saw the people. There were two, a shriveled old man with a beard as white as cotton, and a slender girl who to Roddie's unpracticed eyes appeared to be about nineteen. The old man was naked except for a long necklace of broken bones, the girl naked entirely. Designs had been traced upon their bodies in red and white—in places their sweat had made the designs run. The old man held a cracked leather strap with three brass bells sewn on it, and that and his beard made Roddie think of Santa Claus.

Roddie stepped into the room. "I'm really sorry. I didn't mean—"

The thing that had climbed his pajama bottoms in the back yard dropped onto his shoulder. As he grabbed for it, he felt it turn around like a dog lying down; its fingers closed on his neck.

He yelled; but the yell did not leave his lips as noise but as something else, a strong wild thing that he had never known he could make, as if the fingers around his throat had reshaped it, just as those of Miss Smith (who lived next door with her widowed mother and taught art) could reshape the witless wax of his broken Crayolas into rearing horses and roaring flames. The wild thing smashed the light bulb, casting tinkling shards all over the room, which at the same instant became pitch-dark. The strong wild thing vanished then, and something else dropped to the floor with a thud.

"Now 'ear me," rasped a voice at Roddie's ear. "Put down them 'ands, for they don't answer. 'E stand to."

It was no longer merely a hand, Roddie felt certain. Now there was an arm behind the hand, and a big man at the other end of the arm. He could sense the man's big body behind him and smell the big man's foul breath.

"Ask him, Doc!" It had to be the naked girl's voice. It was answered by a terrified mumble: "Jes', Mar', Jos'f . . ." The girl's voice again, clear and sweet: "Glory hand, you lead us! Petro man, you know the places, don' do you no good. Show us, and whatever you want, that you shall receive. Anythin'. Doc an' me swear to it."

The hand was gone, and the man with it. Roddie would have bolted like a jackrabbit, but he misjudged the position of the door and ran full tilt into the wall instead—the crash of his body a whisper like a weary sigh. Aerial salutes burst orange and blue somewhere behind his eyes; he fell half-stunned.

"On thy feet! Stand to!"

He tried, but somehow, fell again.

"Take 'im, Jim lad. Make 'im look."

There was a flare of light and the smell of sulfur—a match framed by the girl's disheveled hair. She held the match to the wick of a mishappen little candle, and it blazed and sputtered.

"Go on with you," Jim whispered. "You 'eard 'im."

"Okay," he said, floundering forward toward the girl and the light.

The hand lay on its back before her, darkly spattered with the chicken's blood. She placed the candle on its forefinger, shaping the greasy tallow to hold it there, and lit another from it. The dead chicken sprawled in its own gore now, a black isle rising from a crimson sea. Roddie could smell the dust in its feathers over the sweet-salt tang of its blood.

Though the hand was gone, the big man's hand was on him, forcing him forward, forcing his head down.

Weakly, Doc said, "You take care, Sheba. Don' know what you got."

The fifth candle was burning. Sheba positioned it on the smallest finger and lifted the hand by the wrist. A new voice—the big man's voice—boomed from the old man's mouth. "Look, 'e slut! In the bloodpool. Mine! *MINE!*"

Sheba peered down into the thicking blood. Roddie looked, too, and saw Sheba's face reflected there, startled and eager beside his own.

The cottage seemed to spin, though Roddie knew that it did not. He felt that a long time had passed—not minutes or hours, but months and years and something larger. Jim and the big man were gone. He was alone except for Sheba and Doc, and happy to be thus alone. Still holding the hand, Sheba was snuffing out its candles, one by one.

"What you see, Sheba?"

"Li'l boy's face. White boy."

"That what he want, then. That one—got to be that special one."

As Roddie went through the doorway, he heard Sheba mutter, "He gone get him."

It was black night still, but not quite night long before he reached South Boulevard where he went to school. Doug, an older boy, was riding no-hands down the street, folding papers and throwing them as he went. Roddie waved to Doug, but Doug paid no attention to him. Doug seldom did.

There were lights in the kitchen window already. The front door stood open, and the living-room-dining-room was full of the morning smells of coffee and bacon. The green enameled door to the kitchen swung both ways—but not for Roddie, not today. He shoved against it hard with his shoulder, but could move it barely an inch; the springs in its double hinges seemed to have stiffened like cast iron.

"Mom!"

She had the radio on in the kitchen, as she always did. It was "The Wide-Awake Hour" this early, drums and big brass horns that blew *ta-dah, ta-dah!* Roddie usually liked "The Wide-Awake Hour."

"Momma!"

He could hear her moving around in the kitchen, the scrape of her spatula on the bottom of the frying pan. But there was no reply.

Mysteriously, he felt that he was somehow in bed, bound in bed, only dreaming that he stood helpless at the kitchen door; and after a moment or two he went into his bedroom to see if he could find himself.

And did. He lay on his back in the bed, covered with a sheet, eyes closed, forehead beaded with sweat, even his arms beneath the sheet.

"Wake up," he said. "Hey, wake up."

The sleeping self did not stir.

Roddie knelt on the mattress beside it. He had never liked his face, with its chubby cheeks and insignificant mouth; but he had to admit that it was his face. He might have been looking into a mirror, except that his own mouth was closed, that of the sleeper slightly open. "Wake up!" he said again, and it seemed to him that the sleeper stirred.

He grabbed the sleeper's shoulders then and shook him. For an instant it seemed to him that his fingertips penetrated those shoulders ever so slightly. The sleeper opened his eyes and sat up, bumping him hard.

The sleeper could see him. He knew it because the sleeper recoiled just as he himself would have if he had bumped someone, and when he slid off the bed, the sleeper followed him with his eyes.

"Hello," Roddie said. "I'm you."

The sleeper did not answer, or even seem to understand.

"You're—"

His mother's voice interrupted him. "Get out of bed now, Roddie. You'll be late for school."

The sleeper only stared at her, and Roddie saw her face fall. "You're really sick, aren't you? Ever since last night."

Slowly, the sleeper nodded, his mouth still gaping.

"That does it. No school today—you're going to see Dr. Johnson. But first I'm going to take your temperature. Are you hungry?"

There was no reply. Roddie tugged at his mother's apron; but she only smoothed it absently as if it had been twitched by a breeze. Her eyes had filled with tears, and he was glad when she went back to the kitchen.

It was a long time before she returned with bacon, toast, and two fried eggs, all of them cold. Roddie took a strip of bacon while his mother fed the sleeper like an infant, but he found he could not chew it, and it made him gag. He did not have the heart to follow them when his mother led the sleeper to the bus stop.

By then Boots had returned from her morning patrol of the neighborhood and lay, beautifully black-and-white, on the front porch, ever alert for strangers and food. In theory, Boots was Roddie's dog; in actuality she was his father's, and both he and Boots knew it. But Boots was generally tolerant and even protective of him, and when it was not too hot she sometimes consented to chase the sticks and balls he threw for her. She only rolled her soulful brown eyes now when Roddie spoke to her. When he patted her head, she snarled.

There were plenty of books in his room, but he discovered that it required all of his strength just to pull one from the shelf, and he let it fall to the floor. It was *Peter Pan* with wonderful colored illustrations; but he had read it before and the story seemed dull and stupid now, so that even turning the page took effort; it was as if the pages had become sheets of lead, heavier than the foil that he was supposed to save from his parents' cigarettes. After a time he realized that he was not thinking of the story at all, but only of himself lying on the rug and turning the pages, invisible to everyone but Boots and the sleeper. He recalled seeing pages turn themselves when he and the sleeper had been one boy. He wondered who had been reading them, or at least looking at the pictures. Possibly it had been Jim, reading his books.

That's all right, Roddie thought. I don't care if you read them, just as long as you don't tear them up.

Jim had been able to see him, but where was Jim? He was not even sure he wanted to find Jim.

But Jim had not been the only one. The naked girl, Sheba, had seen his reflection. Then Sheba and Doc had said they were going to get him for the big man; but that was wrong, because the big man had been right there and could have taken him for himself if he had wanted to. Roddie poked among his toys, then lay down on his bed, feeling very tired.

The front door opened and closed, and Roddie went out to look. It was his father, carrying his suitcase as he always did, sweating as he always did in his navy-blue business suit. Boots frisked around on the living room carpet, her stump of a tail wagging frantically. His father tossed his hat onto the floor lamp and did not see Roddie either.

It was boiling outside. It had seemed hot already in the house, but outside the sun struck like a blow, a heavy, burning weight that had to be carried like a sack of meal. Squinting up at the sun, Roddie decided it was already afternoon. Today was Friday, because that was the day his father came home. But his father never came home before noon—even on Friday—and anyway the sun was over the house at the end of the block. Or at least it looked that way.

A stinking orange diesel bus roared by on Mandell. There was a squeal of air brakes as it halted at the stop on the next corner. Roddie waited, then watched his mother and the sleeper walk slowly along Vassar and go up on the porch. His mother was wearing her best gray dress, the sleeper Roddie's own jeans and red-and-white striped pullover. Roddie was glad to see that his mother was no longer crying, although her face was grim as she went into the house, towing the sleeper behind her. Through the screen door, he heard his father say, "Oh. There you are."

Roddie went back onto the porch to listen. His mother was telling about taking the sleeper (whom to his disgust she called *Roddie*) to the doctor. The doctor had made an appointment for Roddie to see a specialist.

"I'll call him up," Roddie's father said. "I want to hear what he has to say about this." Like just about everybody, the doctor was a friend of his.

"Do you think we could go to the beach tonight?" his mother asked. "Do you have enough gas? I think the cool air might do Roddie good."

"Sure," his father answered. "Why not?" Because he was a salesman, his father had a "C" card.

Roddie left the porch, and in leaving it discovered that he could not hear his own footsteps. He stopped, stamped hard, and shuffled his feet; but there was no sound. He could make noise, though, he remembered—he had knocked on the peeling white door. He knocked on a fender of his father's black Plymouth and heard his knock crisp and clear.

That encouraged him so much that he skipped awhile despite the heat, though he knew that he would be tired and hot before he reached Old Spanish Trail. Whenever he could, he stopped in air-conditioned stores; the clerks could not see him either, or at least did not chase him out. That was good, he told himself; yet he would have given everything he owned to be chased out, to be seen and yelled at again.

The sun was under the phone wires when he found the cottage, so that he was afraid he would have to look for it in the dark. Yet instinct led him to it, and he knew at once that it was the only place he wanted to be. Sheba would look into a mirror, he thought. Girls were always looking at the mirror, always fixing their hair, as if anybody cared. Sheba would look, he would put his face close by hers, and then she would see him. That would be sufficient, he felt. If Sheba saw him, he knew that he would feel better; then he would think of some way she could help him, and some way in which he could tell her to.

"Ah," Jim's voice said. " 'Ere 'e are."

Jim was at his elbow, seeming to have come from no place, a thin, ragged boy with hair the color of sawdust and a bruise on one cheek.

"I have to go in there," Roddie told him. "I have to see Sheba." It was not until he had said it that he realized it was really the other way around.

"Course 'e do." Jim grinned and nodded.

"Are you coming, too?"

"Course I am."

Roddie pushed the door. It swung back even more slowly, even more heavily, than before; but it swung, and he and Jim slipped inside.

The small room was crowded. Besides Doc and Sheba (Roddie had been afraid she would not be there, and sighed with relief to see that she was), there was a stiff old man with tobacco-stained whiskers, a thin woman who seemed almost like a shadow, another boy, and Captain

Hook. Roddie recognized Captain Hook from his picture in *Peter Pan*, even though he was handsome there and had nicer clothes. They do that for the pictures they put in books, Roddie thought. They make everybody look nicer. The shadowy woman stroked him. "Aren't you *pretty*."

Roddie shook his head violently. "No, I'm not!"

She laughed, a faint, thin sound Roddie remembered having heard at night. "Well, *I* think so. Do you know what they're going to do here to-night? Do you go to church?"

Roddie shook his head again.

"That's a pity—it's so *useful*. Anyway, they are honoring us. It's a religious ceremony. 'Where two are gathered in my name—' "

The old man spat tobacco juice toward the toilet with the broken seat. Jim said, "You was drawn, same as us, same as 'er and 'im. They got the wrong 'un, but we was drawn all the same, and we'll 'ave slum out o' it."

The other boy had been lying naked on the narrow cot. Doc lifted him and laid him on the little red-covered table that now stood in the center of the crowded room. Slowly, muttering as if to himself, Doc placed various objects around him. They were mostly pieces of dead people and animals, Roddie decided. From time to time Sheba spoke in response to Doc's muttered prayers: "Oh, yes. Yes, yes. You know. *Arrivez!*"

The boy's feet were not tied, and Roddie wondered why he did not get up off the table when he saw the old butcher knife in Doc's hand, and the bright, new edge on its big blade. He tried to help the boy, but Captain Hook elbowed him out of the way.

Sheba had lit the candles of the hand again. She spread the boy's legs and placed it between them, then switched off the light. Other candles burned with blue flames near the walls of the room, though Roddie had not seen them until the light went out, big homemade candles with curling wicks.

"We'll get to 'e," Captain Hook growled. "Stand to."

Doc whispered a name Roddie did not know and raised the old knife above his head. It trembled with the thin hands that held it, so that blue candlelight danced along its edge; Roddie heard the faint rattle of Doc's necklace of bones.

"No!" Roddie shouted. The shadowy woman smoothed his hair as his mother sometimes did, and laughed at him.

Doc did not even hear them; Captain Hook's hand held his, and the old man's hands closed upon all three; the knife came down, splitting the boy's unprotected chest like a watermelon. Roddie turned away, retching, but Jim held him by the collar. " 'Ere. 'E'll want it, if there's somat left for us."

And he did.

He knew it instantly, and had known it even before Jim told him. So it had been when his father had killed his pet duck—it had been awful to watch Donald die, his wings flapping uselessly and his white feathers dyed with his own blood. But once Donald was truly dead it had seemed to Roddie that there was no harm in eating him, though Roddie's parents could hardly touch a bite.

The shadowy woman whispered, "He was drugged, my darling. Believe me, he didn't feel a thing."

Roddie nodded absently. He was watching Captain Hook and the old man. For an instant the two big men stood eye to eye. When Captain Hook turned away, his face was twisted with rage. But turn away he did, and the old man smiled and bent over the dying boy.

"Pig," the shadowy woman whispered.

For half a minute, the cottage was silent. Roddie could hear the hum of a mosquito roused by Doc from its post on the pull-string of the light. The candles filled the room with a smell like burning garbage.

Inch by inch, the scarlet hue of life vanished from the dying boy's clotting blood as the old man drank, leaving it a rusty brown; as more blood welled forth, he drank more. The shadowy woman made a tiny gesture of impatience, and there was black death in Captain Hook's eyes.

At last the old man straightened up, wiped his discolored beard on his sleeve and sauntered out of the cottage. At once Captain Hook took his place, drinking, it seemed to Roddie, even more greedily.

Sheba asked Doc, "Is he comin'?"

Doc shook his head and shrugged. Roddie whispered, *"Look at a mirror!"* but Sheba did not hear him.

"This a murder," Sheba murmured, "do they find out. You go to Huntsville, won't never see the outside again. You know?"

Captain Hook rose.

Instantly, Jim sprang toward the dying boy, but the shadowy woman tripped him expertly. He fell with a slight creak of the floorboards, and she bent over the blood as Captain Hook had.

All this Roddie saw only from a corner of his eye. He was watching Doc, suddenly metamorphosed, his back straight and his shoulders squared, his face somehow longer. With one hand he seized Sheba's throat and slammed her to the wall with a crash that threatened to bring it down. "'E slut! 'E stupid *slut!*" Sheba's mouth gaped wide. Her tongue protruded farther than Roddie would have believed possible, and her eyes seemed about to leap from their sockets. Doc shook her and dropped her to the floor.

"That was very *nice.*" The shadowy woman—no longer quite so shadowy as she had been—patted her lips. "I haven't had such a nice drink in a long time."

Jim was drinking eagerly now, though the new, bright blood had nearly ceased to flow.

"Stand to," Doc told Sheba, "I'll show 'e the lad we wants. On with thy slops." He had snatched a pair of old trousers from the foot of the cot and was thrusting his legs into them as he spoke.

Roddie put his mouth to Jim's ear. "That's the captain, isn't it? That's him. How did he do that?" Jim only pushed him away.

Sheba staggered to her feet, staring at Doc with fear-crazed eyes.

"There's a wench. I never minded drinkin' from the tar bucket." Doc tossed her a purple dress spotted with yellow flowers.

Jim wiped his lips on his forearm. "Course that's 'im. The blood let 'im, woter 'e thinks?"

"Would it let me . . . ?" Roddie could not find words for the thing he wanted to say.

"Jury-rig 'im 'e left behind 'e? Might, and there's any left."

Doc glanced toward Roddie. "Do it, lad. 'Andsomely, now."

"You can see me!" Roddie exclaimed.

Sheba was backing away, holding her purple dress in front of her. Her cheeks were streaked with tears, and Roddie felt sorry for her.

Jim said, "We 'ave to cut. Drink up."

Roddie still hesitated. "Where are we going?"

"Takin' 'e 'ome. We've need o' a lad, 'im and me do. But we 'ave to 'ave the other 'alf, twig?"

Doc took off his necklace of bones and held it out. "See 'em, lad?"

Roddie nodded.

"Know 'ose they be?"

"No, sir." Roddie shook his head.

"Mine, lad. Jim's and mine. 'E seen the 'and." Doc bent over Roddie exactly as if Roddie were a real person, and that made Roddie feel wonderful. " 'Ose 'and do it be, do 'e think?"

"Yours, sir."

"A likely lad! Oh, Jim, 'e's a promising 'un!"

Jim nodded. " 'E's that."

Doc crouched until his eyes were at Roddie's level. "They 'anged me in chains, lad. Now do 'e know what 'tis to 'ang in chains?"

"No, sir," Roddie admitted.

"After 'e've 'anged, they tars thy remains, same as to tar the bottom of a boat."

Roddie nodded to show that he understood.

"And they wraps the 'ole in chains for to keep it together. They hangs the 'ole wear it may do the most good. So I 'ung—and a long time it seemed to me. Me 'and was taken then, and various."

Roddie asked, "Did they hang Jim, too?"

"Oh, aye."

Jim said, "We want a Christian grave, we do, and 'e must give it to us. One for both."

"I will, honest," Roddie promised. "If you'll put me back together."

"Me own thought, lad." Doc smiled with satisfaction, then whirled to face Sheba. "And 'e, 'e wants treasure, wench, don't 'e?"

Sheba shook her head.

"Wot!" Doc laughed; it sounded almost as though two voices were laughing together, one shrill, one roaring.

"You let me go—" Sheba swallowed, edging toward the back door.

"Ah there, lass." Doc tossed the string of bones rattling onto the cot; with one swift stride he was before her, a hand against the door. "No rubies, lass, great as pigeon eggs? No gold? No em'ralds cut square, full o' green fire?"

Sheba shook her head. "I don't want them."

Doc laughed again. (Roddie wondered what the people next door thought, hearing that laugh.) "But we want 'e, lass. We must 'ave the lad, and 'e to 'elp us get 'im. Now drink, lad. No more nonsense, 'ear? Drink up!"

Roddie bent over the dying boy. For the first time, he truly noticed the boy's face; it was a little like his own, he decided, but not very much.

"Drink!"

Roddie discovered that he wanted to, that he was hungry and thirsty. Very thirsty. He tried to remember the last time that he had eaten, the last time he had drunk.

Jim said, " 'E don't like 'avin' 'is 'awser crossed. Best be at it."

Roddie nodded, studying the blood. For a moment it seemed that all life had already been drawn from it, leaving it as dry and unappealing as so much dust. No: one single, shining drop remained, far down in the deep wound. He would have to put his lips against the edges of that wound, as if he were kissing it.

The dying boy's eyes opened, wandered vaguely, fastened on his. For a moment Roddie saw the dying boy and the boy saw him.

"DRINK!"

Roddie lowered his head until he felt his lips smeared with the dead blood, extended his tongue; the dying boy's eyes rolled upward, no longer together, one drifting aside. Roddie shut his own, sought with his tongue for the drop and found it.

His father had given him a scrap of raw steak once. Though he had been so strongly attracted to the blood, he had supposed it would be like that—cold, wet, and nearly flavorless. It was hot instead; not hot like the sun, or his room by night, but hot like music sometimes, or like nothing else that he could think of, energizing and delightful.

"Main good, 'tis." Doc's hand dropped heavily on Roddie's shoulder, bigger and stronger than he would have imagined Doc's hand could be. "Now I wants 'e to do somat for me, 'ear? See 'em bones on the bunk? 'E're not asceered o' 'em?"

Roddie shook his head.

"There's a lad! Go lift 'em up."

Roddie did as he had been told, and Doc filled the little room with his strange laughter.

"Which way?" Sheba looked at Doc, and Doc at Roddie.

Roddie shrugged helplessly. "Just the beach, that's all. I can't drive."

"Wears the beach, lass?"

"They got two." Sheba was resentful, now that she was no longer terrified. "East Beach and West Beach." After a moment she added, "An' Stewart Beach."

"The closest 'un."

Another driver blew his horn behind them. Sheba punched down the long clutch pedal and shoved the old Ford into gear.

West Beach was practically deserted at this time of night, though a few diehard fishermen still cast into the surf. The wind was rising, shaving grains of sand from the crests of dark dunes to carry across the road. To feel it, Roddie thrust his head from the rear window, just as Boots did whenever she rode on his mother's lap. Almost at once, he saw his father's black Plymouth coupe. *"There they are!"*

"Stop 'ere," Doc told Sheba. "Now, lad, 'ear me wile I gives 'e thy orders, and say 'em back after."

When he was finished, Roddie asked, "But will they see me?"

"Oh, aye. 'Tis 'ard, but 'e can do it, 'avin' drunk. By night, mind. By day, 'e'd be sailin' into the wind, do 'e twig? Up anchor now."

Though Roddie tugged at the handle of the Ford's rear door, he could not move it; and at last, at Jim's urging, he slipped out through the window. They separated as soon as they had left the car, he going to his father's, Jim into the waves. As he had been directed, he climbed into the rumble seat.

He did not think that his parents would have seen him even if they could see him; they were staring at the horizon, at the faint orange glow there that was—as his father had told him on a previous occasion—a burning tanker. But the sleeper had seen him; the sleeper cared less for torpedoed ships even than Roddie himself. The sleeper stared vacantly at this and that, and now and then at Roddie. It seemed a long time before Jim called.

Or perhaps neither Roddie nor the sleeper had heard Jim at first. Jim's call was so faint, so much a part (it seemed) of the sighing of the night wind and the sobbing of the waves that it hardly seemed a voice at all.

Yet the sleeper heard it. He rose from his place between Roddie's mother and his father and walked down the sloping sand toward Jim. Roddie's mother stood, too, but his father said, "He just wants to splash around a little. Let him alone." After a moment's hesitation, she sat down again.

Boots ran after the sleeper, then back to Roddie's father, a study in canine concern. "Keep an eye on him," his father said, and patted her head.

The sleeper hesitated at the edge of the water. Jim called to him; for a moment, as he listened to Jim's call, it seemed to Roddie that he saw a second vessel in the night, nearer than the burning tanker: a dark ship with raked masts and ragged sails.

Sheba had pulled the Ford off the road and onto the beach some distance away. She and Doc were sitting side by side on the sand in front of its bumper. Roddie remembered that people like them were not supposed to use the beach and wondered what would happen if the police came; perhaps the police did not care when the beach was so nearly empty.

Already, the gentle little inshore waves were washing the sleeper's thighs. Roddie's father called, "Roddie! Come back here!" But the sleeper did not even look around.

Boots dashed out to him. Roddie noted the moment at which she could no longer wade and had to swim. She paddled in front of the sleeper, barking, lifted by the surf like a small, noisy boat.

Roddie's mother was on her feet. "I'll get him, Ray."

Boots had run back to his father, appealing far from mutely to that highest of all courts. "I'll do it," he said. He was pulling off his shoes and socks, rolling up his trouser legs.

Roddie looked for the sleeper again. He was hard to see, so far from the shore lights; but it seemed to Roddie that the waves had reached his neck. If Jim were still calling, Roddie could not hear him.

Roddie hunkered down in the rumble seat, thinking about the moment when he would have to make himself visible to his parents. It would come very soon now, and he was not sure he could do it. How did you make yourself visible? The only way he could think of was by jumping out of the bushes, but that was for when they were playing cowboys, he and Wes and John.

"Roddie! Roddie! Roddie!" His parents' voices sounded far away.

Raising his head, he saw them waist-high in surging waves. Boots was with them, or perhaps even farther out—her barking could hardly be heard above the pounding of the surf. He stood up, pretending he was pushing the bushes aside, cupped his hands around his mouth. *"Here I am, Mom!"*

They did not hear him, but perhaps that was only because it was so far. He tried to inflate his body, to render it real and substantial. *"HERE! Over here!"*

He could not quite hear what his mother said; but he saw her touch his father's arm and point, and his heart seemed to swell. He jumped up and down in the seat, shouting and waving. *"Here! Here! Here! IT'S ME!"*

His father had seen him and was splashing toward shore. His mother was ordering Boots to abandon the search, her faint "Here, Bootsie!" and the clap of her hands borne on the salt sea-breeze. His father would be angry for a while; but when he was angry with Roddie, he would not speak to him, or even look at him. So that part would be all right.

His father shouted, "Roddie, are you still in the car?" and he strained to make himself visible again.

"Roddie, stand up!"

His mother was just coming out of the water. "Is he gone again, Ray?"

"No, he's hiding back there. He thinks that's very funny."

"Ray—"

"Let him alone. He and I are going to have a talk about this when we get home. Get the dog in the car. Make her stay on the floor." Soaked to the shirt pocket, angry and dripping, his father got behind the wheel.

Softly his mother asked, "Roddie, are you well now?"

Again that swelling in his chest. He answered, "Yes," and although she did not appear to see him, she smiled and took her place beside her husband. Boots came up panting and climbed in next to her feet.

Roddie slipped out of the rumble seat as the car began to move.

The road had shrunk until it was no more than a single lane surfaced with oyster shells. Roddie hated oyster shells, which snapped under the wheels of cars and trucks to release a choking white dust. He had rolled up his window, and he wished that Doc and Sheba would close theirs, too. But the car was much too hot for that; the sleeper's face was beaded with sweat. So was his; he had taken off his shirt, and he used it now to wipe his face. He thought of wiping the sleeper's as well but decided it would do no good. "Why can't I go back in?" he asked Jim.

"Couldn't nobody here," Jim said.

"Because of the car, you mean?"

Jim did not reply. He seemed to be studying the sleeper.

Doc had not spoken for a long while, making Roddie wonder if he was really Doc again. Now Sheba said, "We got to get some gas. You got any money?"

Doc only stared at her.

"Ain' got none—don' look at me like that." After a moment she added, "Probably not no stations 'long this ol' road anyhow."

" 'E's been here. 'E told me."

"Only that one time, an' that 'bout a year ago."

" 'E said they wouldn't know."

"Those police was back at the house? Don' think so. They Houston police anyway, ain' come out here. This here out in the county. They has to call the sheriff, get the sheriff to send them out a deputy."

The narrow road bent about a clump of moss-hung live oak to reveal a one-pump gas station. An elderly black man came out as Sheba pulled the old Ford up to the pump. "Evenin', folks. How many tonight?"

Sheba looked at Doc, but Doc said nothing. She said, "Fill it up."

Doc got out and walked into the station, a shack smaller even than the cottage. Roddie could not imagine what he was doing in there, and whatever it was made no noise. There was only the gurgle of gasoline from the hose and the singing of millions of frogs.

"That boy sick?"

Sheba nodded.

"You tell his mama, take him to the doctor."

"His mama gone," Sheba said. "I takin' care of him. We gone take him tomorrow, that why we need so much gas."

"That old man goin' to pay?"

Sheba nodded again. "He probably lookin' to buy some cut plug, too. I tol' him you might have some."

The man hung up the hose and went into the station. Roddie heard a dull tap, as if someone had thumped a melon; then he saw a foot through the doorway, its toe pointed downward as though the man had lain down inside. After a minute or two, Doc came out and got back into the car. Sheba drove on.

They crossed a creek on a rattling wooden bridge, turned, and turned again. The road lost its coat of oyster shells and became no more than a jolting track of red dirt. Roddie rolled his window down, but the car was moving so slowly now that the air coming through the window seemed only to add to the heat. Mosquitoes clustered on the sleeper's cheeks and neck, darkened his forehead until his hairline appeared to reach his eyebrows; from time to time he tried languidly to brush them away. Sheba waved a hand before her face as she drove.

A gator bellowed not far off, a noise not very different from the bellowing of a bull. "That's an alligator," Roddie said. "A real big one, too."

Jim said nothing.

Trees, bearded but dead, gave way to clearings that looked like meadows. Sheba stopped the car, pulled up the long handle of the emergency brake, and switched off the lights. "Road don' go no farther. They a boat over there, but it look like we got to pour the water out."

She and Doc left the car, and Roddie climbed over the front seat to follow them.

"Sheba, honey," Doc said, "what we doin' way out here?"

"This where he want to come," Sheba told him. She had hold of the half-sunken skiff's painter. "He'p me." Together they turned the skiff on its side, flooding the already-soft soil at their feet and revealing two oars and a rusty bailing can. "We should of bring a flashlight."

Doc said, "He want go to the cabin?"

Though a thin crescent moon had risen, Sheba's nod was next to invisible.

Roddie had been looking around for Captain Hook, but could not find him. While Doc and Sheba were putting the skiff back into the water, he went to the window of the car. "Is he still in there?"

Jim nodded.

Doc climbed onto the board seat in the middle of the skiff and took the oars. Sheba said, "Wait a minute, I got get the boy."

"We got a boy?"

"In the back, ain' you see? When the last you remember?"

"Back my house, offerin' up that white boy," Doc said. "We gone to throw him in?"

"This 'nother 'un," Sheba told him. She opened the car's rear door and took the sleeper by the hand; when he came out, Jim followed. All of them crowded into the skiff, Roddie and Jim slipping past Doc to the bow, the sleeper sitting in the stern beside Sheba.

"They hear with us," Doc muttered. "I ain' move an' you ain' move, but this hear boat move. You feel it?"

Sheba shook her head. "You don' remember 'bout that old man back at the gas station?"

"Isrul Caruthers? What 'bout him?"

Sheba cast off the painter. "Nothin'. Jus' I think maybe you kill him."

Doc shook his head, pulling at the oars. "I hope not. I know him ever since twenty-six."

Sheba said, "Then how come he don' know you?"

"He don'?"

"No, sir. He say, 'That ol' man goin' pay?' "

"He ain' Isrul then," Doc said. "Isrul know me any time, day or night."

"That good. How far now?"

"Jes' a bit. Mr. J.J. Randall, he build this place only it be drier then. It flood hear sometime, though, so he put it up on the big pilin's. I done the roof—that back when I work for him. Then the big storm come, and it be wet an' Mr. J.J. don' come no more. I use it ever since. Mr. J.J., he gone now."

Uninterested, Sheba said, "Uh huh."

"You think I really kill him?" Doc asked.

"That man at the gas station? I don' know."

Something large slithered into the water at their approach.

"That li'l boy."

"Course you did."

Doc did not speak again. Their voices and the plash of his oars had quieted the frogs, so that it seemed to Roddie that he could hear the most minute noises, the most faraway sounds—cars and trucks and buses back in town, his mother calling him. He felt, too, that if he spoke, Doc and Sheba would hear him; but he did not want to speak to them and did not know what to say. He no longer believed that Captain Hook was somehow in Doc, and he wondered whether Jim still believed it.

Sheba said, "You want me row awhile? You mus' be gettin' tired."

Doc shook his head and continued to row. After a moment he chuckled, the stridulous merriment of an old man.

"What you laughin' at?" Sheba asked him.

"That Isrul Caruthers. He think I come way out here with a young gal, maybe I don' want nobody know. So he ask you if the old man pay." Doc chuckled again.

"Uh huh. You goin' go to his funeral?"

"I s'pose," Doc said. "I know Isrul since twenty-six."

"You bes' not. The police gone be after you for killin' that boy back in Houston. You don' remember, but the police be all over your place when we get back. That why we come out here." Sheba was silent for a moment. "Maybe we could tell them we be out here together, somebody else use your house."

"Maybe. You know I never didn't mean for all this. Not killin' no li'l boy."

Sheba did not reply. In the silence, Roddie heard a faint, slow ticking, as though a grandfather clock stood somewhere in the darkness beneath the trees, its hands raised in horror, its pendulum telling the hours of the salt marsh through which they rowed with more precision than the beating of Doc's oars.

"Used, I think they's way away," Doc said softly. "I try to make them hear me. I ever tell you 'bout Big Mike?"

"Huh uh," Sheba said.

"That Big Mike, he be a panther, used to kill all the deers 'round hear, cows, too. Mr. J.J., he hunt Big Mike many a time. One time he out hear huntin' quail, it gettin' dark, so Mr. J.J. and Jess start for home. Jess his bird dog."

Sheba said, "Uh huh."

"Mr. J.J., he hear Big Mike holler, you know how they do? Like a woman that's scared, almos'. It sound like he way off, so Mr. J.J. don't pay it no mind. Jus' 'bout then Jess give a holler, and Big Mike rear up in front of her. Mr. J.J. say he mus' of shot twice with that li'l bitty bird gun, 'cause there was empties in it after an' he been goin' loaded case Jess put up some birds comin' back. He don' remember a-tall. I ask do he hit Big Mike, and he say he don' know, he jus' glad he ain' hit Jess."

Sheba laughed softly. "Better be glad he don' shoot off his own foot."

"So then I say, Mr. J.J., how come Big Mike right there when you jus' hear him way off? An' he say, I think that big ol' panther put his head right down at the dirt when he holler so I think he way off. He wait for me to come by, and if Jess ain' see him first, he kill me sure. Sheba, these what we been messin' with, I think they jus' the same. They be not no long ways away. They jus' be waitin' till we get a li'l closer."

"You think they still goin' give us that treasure?"

Softly, Jim said, "Aye," and Doc dropped one oar. Roddie had to cover his mouth to keep from laughing.

Sheba asked, "What the matter with you, old man?"

"Didn't you hear somethin'?"

Sheba shook her head. "I didn't hear nothin'."

"It behind me, closer to me than you," Doc muttered. He bent over the gunnel of the skiff, feeling with one hand in the dark water for the oar.

It was then that Roddie saw where the ticking came from. Something that seemed almost a sunken log was drifting slowly toward the skiff—toward Doc's groping hand—when nothing else in the water moved. The ticking came from that, the slow, slow beating of its heart.

Doc said, "Pull it out, Sheba. It back by you." He took his hand from the water.

Sheba thrust hers in, grasped the oar near the blade, and swung the loom to him. "You keep on droppin' these, we never gone get there."

Doc glanced behind him. "We there now, don' you see?"

"I ain'—"

There was a scream from the darkness before them, a paean to hate and agony worthy of a damned soul charring in the flames of Hell. Sheba froze, her mouth wide open, a hand upraised; the sleeper's eyes went wide, so that it appeared for a moment that he was about to wake. Doc continued to row, the slow beating of his oars unaltered.

Sheba gasped, "What the matter with you?"

"Nothin' the matter with me," Doc replied placidly.

"You hear some itty-bitty noise and drop the oar. You hear *that* and don' even look 'round again."

" 'Cause I know what holler," Doc told her. "That be a li'l ol' bobcat. What you think, gal? It be Big Mike? Big Mike, he gone 'fore Mr. J.J."

Roddie had spotted the cabin, a black bulk against the less solid blackness of mere night; he pointed it out to Jim a minute or two before the side of the skiff scraped the little landing stage moored at the foot of its steps. The screamer yowled, a softer sound this time, and Roddie thought he caught a flash of green.

Doc shipped oars and pulled a kitchen match from his shirt pocket. Striking it on his thumbnail, he held it up so that its flare of blue and yellow drove the night into sudden retreat. A large black cat arched its back at the top of the cabin steps, glaring at them through a single green eye.

"Not even no bobcat." Doc chuckled. "Jus' a li'l pussycat got lost out hear, maybe throwed out somebody's car." Tossing the match into the water, he rose and stepped onto the stage. "Now pass me that rope, gal, so I can tie the boat up, and don' talk no more 'bout who scared and who ain'."

As though in a dream, the sleeper followed Sheba out of the skiff. Roddie saw the hungry way in which Jim eyed him.

Sheba was looking at him, too. "We gon' do it tonight?"

Doc jerked his half hitches tight and grasped the sleeper's arm without replying, leading him up the rotting steps. The cat spat at them, then moved aside.

Jim said, "This won't be like town. 'Im an' me, an' 'e. That's all there be."

"You said you wanted both parts of me," Roddie protested.

"Said we needed both." Jim grinned as he followed Sheba up the steps, slipping through the doorway just as she closed the door.

Roddie heard it shut, and the rattle of its old-fashioned latch. For half a minute or more he stood on the little landing stage, wondering whether Doc and Sheba would open for him if he knocked, as they had back at the cottage. Light poured from the wide windows of the cabin; Doc had struck another match and lit a candle, or perhaps a lantern of some kind.

Something moved uneasily in the water. Roddie watched it for a moment, then went up the steps and caught the cat by the loose skin at the back of its neck. It yowled and clawed, but its claws seemed no more than feathers stroking Roddie's arms. He tried to quiet it, then decided that its cries and frantic movements might actually be helpful.

It liked the water even less than it liked Roddie, wailing and splashing as he pushed it under.

The cabin door flew open. Looking up, Roddie saw Doc with a rifle in his hands. Captain Hook stood behind him, his hand upon Doc's shoulder. Roddie let go of the cat, which scrambled back onto the stage. Fire flashed from the muzzle of the rifle—the report struck Roddie's ears like a blow. The cat shrieked with pain, and with a backhanded swipe Roddie knocked it into the water again.

Apparently satisfied, Doc shut the door.

The big gator was coming, swimming with astonishing speed: even the slow tick of its heart sounded faster. Roddie helped the wounded cat onto the stage and urged it up the steps. He had wondered vaguely whether the gator would have difficulty in getting up onto the floating stage; it took it with a rush, its body propelled by a powerful stroke of its tail. It was larger than Roddie would have guessed, eight feet long at least and as thick through as one of the empty drums buoying the stage.

Bleeding and frantic, the cat scrambled up the cabin door. Roddie pounded on the rough planks with his fists. Inside, he heard Sheba say, "They here." The door swung open again.

The gator's charge knocked her down like a tenpin. With a sinuosity that seemed almost that of a python, it turned. Sheba screamed as its jaws closed on her body.

The rifle was leaning in a corner, and both Doc and Roddie scrambled for it. Roddie had fired a twenty-two in a shooting gallery once; he knew that rifles had safeties, buttons to keep them from working. Captain Hook's curved iron hand pierced his cheek, knocking out a milk tooth— he was jerked backward like a hooked fish. The sleeper yelled, hands grabbing his empty face.

It seemed to Roddie that Sheba should be dead, and yet she screamed and struggled, clutching the edge of the doorway. Doc had the rifle at his shoulder. With two fast motions, he pulled its lever down and shoved it up again; *klu-klux-klan,* whispered the mechanism. He fired, the noise of the shot deafening in the little cabin.

"'E bleedin' bugger!" Something slammed against Roddie's temple. The cabin seemed to spin around him, tossed upon wild seas as though it were really the cabin of a ship; he saw Doc's necklace of bones and the mummified hand beside a kerosene lamp on a greasy table before Doc fired again and a sweep of the gator's tail knocked the table to kindling. The lamp's glass chimney shattered. Kerosene splashed the floor. For an instant it was only a spilled liquid, darkening the boards like so much water; but flames raced after it.

"'Ere," Jim shouted. "Take 'em quick." He thrust the hand and the necklace at Roddie. An empty cartridge case flew before his face. At point-blank range, Doc fired at the gator's head. Sheba still screamed, her long black hair blazing.

The hand wriggled dryly in Roddie's grasp like a spider; instinctively, he flung it and the bones out of the closest window.

At once the hook vanished from his cheek. Faintly, as if an unseen artist had traced their pictures in the smoke, he saw Captain Hook and Jim back toward the flames. The captain's hard face and Jim's haunted eyes seemed far away—old, half-forgotten things lost in the reality of the present.

"Rest in peace," Roddie told them. He had remembered that it was the thing you were supposed to say over dead people. He swallowed. "You're sailors, and this's the way they bury them, in the water." He could see them still, see the fire licking at their legs. "In peace in the name of God and Jesus and the Holy Ghost and—and Mary [Mary was his mother's name] and everybody."

They were gone. Roddie put his hand to his cheek; it hurt, but he could feel no blood.

The sleeper was standing up, his blank eyes wild. Roddie ran at him, trying to drive himself back into the sleeper's body by main force. The sleeper's face changed, briefly, as though from a shadow cast by the flames. Roddie grabbed him, shouting and coughing, and pushed him toward the doorway, past Doc, over Sheba and the still-living gator, the sleeper stumbling on the gator's moving, armored back, tumbling head-long down the steps and hitting the landing stage with a bang.

Roddie leaped after him, landed lightly and picked himself up, and turned to look back at the cabin. Doc had the barrel of his rifle between the gator's jaws, prying, and Roddie thought that was the bravest thing he had even seen.

The whole cabin crackled a thousand times louder than wood in a bar-becue; a moment afterward, its roof fell. There was a ball of flame and a great *whoosh!* followed by a cloud of sparks. Roddie pulled the sleeper away from the heat and forced him into the skiff. The black cat was crouched in the prow. It licked its side and stared at Roddie as he made the sleeper sit down and take the oars. "I understand all this now," Roddie said as he cast off. "Row, won't you?"

He was forced to guide the sleeper's arms through the first three strokes; after that the sleeper rowed on without coaching, though even more slowly than Doc, and much more clumsily.

"It's a bad dream I'm having," Roddie told him as the skiff moved sluggishly away from the firelight and reentered the realm of night.

The sleeper did not speak.

"You know the cat in back of you? It's in a story by Edgar Allan Poe. Jim was from one called *Treasure Island*, and Captain Hook and the alligator are from *Peter Pan*. This is a nightmare, that's all."

It seemed to Roddie that the sleeper shook his head, though in the flickering light it was hard to be sure. Roddie said, "I think that when we come back together, we'll wake up."

He waited for some reaction, but the sleeper rowed on; and whenever Roddie tried to return to him, his face became that of the dead boy whose blood Roddie had drunk.

This through an endless dark to which there came no day.

A Fish Story

◆

I am always embarrassed by the truth. For one thing, I am a writer of fiction, and know that coming from me it will not be believed; nor does it lend itself to neat conclusions in which the hero and heroine discover the lost silver mine. So bear with me, or read something else. This is true—and because it is, not quite satisfactory.

We three were on a fishing trip along a certain river in Minnesota. We had put Bruce's boat in the water that morning and made our way in a most dilatory fashion downstream, stopping for an hour or two at any spot we thought might have a muskie in it. That night we camped on shore. The next day we would make our way to the lake, where Bruce's wife and mine would meet us about six. Rab, who had never married, would ride as far as Madison with my wife and me. We had not caught much, as I remember; but we had enough to make a decent meal, and were eating it when we saw the UFO.

I do not mean that we saw a saucer-shaped mother ship from a far-off galaxy full of cute green people with feelers. When I say it was a UFO, I mean merely what those three letters indicate—something in the air (lights, in our case) we could not identify. They hovered over us for a half minute, drifted off to the northeast, then receded very fast and vanished. That was all there was to it; in my opinion, we had witnessed a natural phenomenon of some sort, or seen some type of aircraft.

But of course we started talking about them, and Roswell, and all that;

and after a while Bruce suggested we tell ghost stories. "We've all had some supernatural experience," Bruce said.

And Rab said, "No."

"Oh, of course you have." Bruce winked at me.

"I didn't mean that nothing like this has ever happened to me," Rab said, "just that I don't want to talk about it."

I looked at him then. It was not easy to read his face in the firelight, but I thought he seemed frightened.

It took about half an hour to get the story out of him. Here it is. I make no comment because I have none to make; I do not know what it means, if it means anything.

"I've always hated ghosts and all that sort of thing," Rab began, "because I had an aunt who was a spiritualist. She used to read tea leaves, and bring her Ouija board when she came to dinner, and hold séances, and so on and so forth. When I was a little boy it scared me silly. I had nightmares, really terrible nightmares, and used to wake up screaming. All that ended when I was thirteen or fourteen, and since then I've despised the whole stupid business. Pretty soon one of you is going to ask if I've ever seen a ghost, so I'll answer that right now. No. Never.

"Well, you don't want my life history. Let's just say that I grew up, and after a while my mother and father weren't around anymore, or married to each other either. My sister was living in England. She's moved to Greece, but I still hear from her at Christmas.

"One day I got home from work, and there was a message from Dane County Hospital on my machine. Aunt Elspeth was dying, and if I wanted to see her one last time, I had better get over there. I didn't want to. I had disliked her all my life, and I was pretty sure the feeling was mutual. But I thought of her alone in one of those high, narrow beds, dying and knowing that nobody cared that she was dying. So I went.

"It was the most miserable four or five hours I've ever spent. She looked like hell, and even though they had her in an oxygen tent, she couldn't breathe. She kept taking these great gasping breaths. . . ."

Rab demonstrated.

"And in between breaths she talked. She talked about my grandparents' house, which I've never seen, and how it had been there when she and Mom were kids. Not just about them and my grandparents, but the neighbors, the dogs and cats they'd owned, and everything. The furniture. The linoleum on the kitchen floor. Everything. After a while I realized that she was still talking even when she wasn't talking. Do you know what I mean? She would be taking one of those horrible breaths, and I'd still hear her voice inside my head.

"It was getting pretty late, and I thought I'd better go. But there was something I wanted to say to her first—I told you how much I hate ghosts and all that kind of crazy talk. Anyway, I cut her off while she was telling about how she and my mother used to help my grandmother can tomatoes, and I said, 'Aunt Elspeth, I'd like you to promise me something. I want your word of honor on it. Will you do that? Will you give it to me?'

"She didn't say anything, but she nodded.

" 'I want you to promise me that when you're gone, if there's any possible way for you to speak to me, or send me a message—make any kind of signal of any sort—to say that there's another life after the life we know here, another existence on the other side of the grave, you won't do it. Will you give me your solemn promise about that, Aunt Elspeth? Please? And mean it?'

"She didn't say anything more after that, just lay there and glared at me. I wanted to go, and I tried to a couple of times, but I couldn't make myself do it. There she was, about the only person still left from my childhood, and she was dying—would probably die that night, they had said. So I sat there instead, and I wanted to take her hand but I couldn't because of the oxygen tent, and she kept on glaring at me and making those horrible sounds trying to breathe, and neither of us said anything. It must have been for about an hour.

"I guess I shut my eyes—I know I didn't want to look at her—and leaned back in the chair. And then, all of a sudden, the noises stopped. I leaned forward and turned on the little light at the head of her bed, and she wasn't trying to breathe anymore. She was still glaring as if she wanted to run me through a grinder, but when I got up and took a step toward the door, her eyes didn't move. So I knew she was dead, and I ought to call the nurse or something, but I didn't."

Rab fell silent at that point, and Bruce said, "What did you do?"

"I just went out. Out of the room, and out of the Intensive Care Wing, and out into the corridor. It was a pretty long corridor, and I had to walk, oh, maybe a hundred steps before I came to the waiting room. It was late by then, and there was only one person in it, and that one person was me."

Rab gave us a chance to say something, but neither of us did.

"I don't mean I went in. I didn't. I just stood out in the corridor and looked inside. And there I was, sitting in there. I had on a black turtleneck and a whiskey-colored suede sports jacket. I remember that, because I've never owned those clothes. It was my face behind my glasses, though. It was even my haircut. He—I—was reading *Reader's Digest* and didn't see me. But I saw myself, and I must have stood there for five minutes just staring at him.

"Then a nurse pushed past me and said, 'You can go in and see your aunt now, Mister Sammon.' He put down his magazine and stood up and said, 'Call me Rab.' And she smiled and said, 'You can see your Aunt Elspeth now, Rab.'

"I stepped out of the way and the nurse and I went past me and down the corridor toward the Intensive Care Wing. I watched till they had gone through the big double doors and I couldn't see them anymore. Then I went into the waiting room and picked up that copy of the *Reader's Digest* that I had laid down and slipped it into my pocket, and went home and went to bed. I still have it, but I've never gotten up the nerve to read it."

Rab sighed. "That's my story. I don't imagine that yours will be true—I know both of you too well for that. But mine is."

"When you woke up in the morning, was your aunt still dead?" Bruce wanted to know.

Rab said, "Yes, of course. The hospital called me at work."

That bothered me, and I said, "When you started telling us about this, you said that there was a message from the hospital on your answering machine when you got home from the office. So the hospital didn't have your number there, presumably at least."

Rab nodded. "I suppose he gave it to them."

Nobody said much after that, and pretty soon we undressed and got into our sleeping bags. When we had been asleep for two or three hours, Rab screamed.

It brought me bolt upright, and Bruce, too. I sat up just in time to see Rab scream again. Then he blinked and looked around and said, "Somebody yelled. Did you hear it?"

Bruce was a great deal wiser than I. He said, "It was an animal, Rab. Maybe an owl. Go back to sleep."

Rab lay back down, and so did I; but I did not go back to sleep. I lay awake looking at the clouds, the moon, and the stars, and thinking about that midnight hospital waiting room in which the man who stood outside sat reading a magazine, and wondering just how much power the recently dead may have to twist our reality, and their own.

There actually was something shrieking up on the bluff, but I cannot say with any confidence what it was. A wildcat, perhaps, or a cougar.

Wolfer

♦

She dropped the bar, she shot the bolt, she fed the fire anew,
For she heard a whimper under the sill and a great grey paw
came through.

Janet listened with attention and an eerie foreboding while the lecturer spoke forcefully and knowledgeably, talking about things he clearly knew well and had known for a long time.

"With only trifling exceptions, our surnames originated as notations on tax rolls. There were a great many Johns and Williams and so on, just as there are now. Some means had to be found to distinguish between them. Let us suppose that a certain man named John, living in England, had been born in Ireland. The tax collector would record his name, John . . ."

A haunting wail overpowered the calm and reasonable words—a sound no one but she could hear. Later, when she was walking through the snow to the bus stop, the howl would be louder and more insistent; but it was frightening even now.

"And so a notation appeared after John's name, Ireland or perhaps Irish. Check the telephone directory in any big city and you will find those names, borne by John's descendants to this day. Franz and Francis are familiar names of this type, both indicating that the bearer was originally French. Not long ago I read, with a certain amusement, about historians searching the archives of Liège, a city in Belgium, for mention of

Jacques de Liège, the inventor of the jackknife. Anyone who knew any-thing about the history of surnames could have told them that the very last place to look for Monsieur de Liège was in Liège itself." The lecturer paused, smiling as he glanced from face to face.

Kyoto howls like that sometimes, Janet thought. Kyoto was one of the Scotties she was caring for while Rachael and Andy were in Europe; but she knew Kyoto did not really sound like that, and that the howl was in her mind, not in the freezing February night outside the lecture hall. What would the dogs say when she told them about it?

"Physical peculiarities presented another fertile source of surnames. Thus we have John Short, John Stout, John Small, and even John Talman. John White had white or at least light-colored hair. John Black had a dark complexion in an area in which fair complexions were the rule.

"Trades were the exception at a time when most people farmed the land. John Hooper made barrels, while John Fletcher made arrows. I need not explain names like Smith and Taylor, I hope. Thus we know that Oliver Goldsmith's ancestor made jewelry, and that Geoffrey Chaucer's made shoes."

Janet fidgeted, and tried to still the wild wailing in her mind. What a fool she had been to come!

"And now I'd like to learn your own surnames, each of which I will endeavor to explain as well as I can. I must warn you that those drawn from Slavic languages—Polish and Russian, for example—are liable to stump me."

He studied the audience, and pointed. "How about you, sir? Are you willing to stand and tell us your name?"

A middle-aged man rose, straightening his heavy overcoat. "I don't mind, but you will. I'm George Dembinski."

The lecturer smiled again. "I said that some Slavic names might stump me, not that all of them would. Your ancestor lived in an oak wood, sir. If he had lived in England instead of Poland, your name would be Oakely, or something of the sort.

"Which brings us back to place names. In addition to such names as French and England, derived from nations, we find many names like Mis-ter Dembinski's. John Ford's house was near the point at which you could wade the river, for example. Somewhat less obviously, John Clough lived in a clearing in the forest."

He scanned his audience again. "Are you willing to stand up so I can explain your surname, madam?"

The gray-haired woman he had indicated stood, proving to be taller than Janet expected. "You'll be talking about Bishop John," she told him. "My name is Margaret Bishop."

"Ah. That's an interesting class, names taken from an employer's position. Your ancestor—or your husband's—was not the bishop but the bishop's servant, probably an upper servant. The author Stephen King furnishes a good example of this type of name. His ancestor was John Who-serves-the-king."

Another search. "What about you, sir?"

A man younger than Janet, in jeans and a leather jacket. "Bill Noble."

"Another name of the same type. I came across a very clear example recently. The gentleman's name was James M'Lady. Your ancestor, sir, was John Who-serves-the-noble-family, just as his was John Who-serves-my-lady. Most of you are probably familiar with the very interesting name of a chain of bookstores—Barnes and Noble. John Barnes may have been John Who-cares-for-barns or John Who-lives-near-barns. But the name Barnes is most often derived from the old Scottish word *bairn*, meaning a child and especially a younger son in a noble Scottish family. Mr. Barnes and his junior partner Mr. Noble, show how frequently these old relationships are continued or resumed when their thousand-year-old origins are utterly forgotten. Forgotten, I should say, except by me.

"What about you, madam?"

Here it was.

"Will you give us your name?"

Janet stood, conscious that her knees were trembling and perfectly certain that the lecturer knew it. "Of course I will. That was why I came. I'm . . . You said that—that Ms. Bishop's ancestor . . . Or her husband's. So I ought to tell you I'm not married anymore, and it's my maiden name. I'm Janet Woolf." She paused, floundering mentally. "You know. Like Virginia Woolf? With two *o*'s. Does that matter?"

The lecturer shook his head. "All such names are merely variants of *Wolf*. I take it you're not Jewish?"

"No, I'm a—no."

"If you were, your name would indicate membership in the tribe of Benjamin. Since you're not, you're presumably descended from someone called Wolf or Vulf—"

Janet wanted to protest, but did not.

"Someone who exhibited the courage and ferocity thought characteristic of wolves."

Too softly she murmured, "I don't think so."

"I might note that though the various forms of *wolf* are unusual as first names, they remain in use. The Irish patriot Wolfe Tone is an example, as is Jack London's fictional captain, Wolf Larson. You're shaking your head."

"I don't believe any of that." Janet took a deep breath. "I think my name—" Louder! "Belongs to the same group as that other woman's. That it's really a servant name and maybe even a friend name, because back then a servant wasn't just somebody who cooked and cleaned, he was somebody who went out and fought for you when that was what you needed. I think that we were John and Joan and Jane Who-serve-the-wolves, once."

The lecturer started to say something, but she raised her voice again, overriding him shrilly. "I can't prove it, but I feel it. You'll make fun of me, I know, but half the time I was listening I was laughing at you. You're so sure you know everything that went on back when people like us were savages with bows and spears. Where everybody lived. What everybody did."

The audience was buzzing; she had to shout to make herself heard. "But I know what I feel in my heart! And I don't believe you know nearly as much as you think you do!"

She dropped back into her seat, her face burning. Somewhere high overhead, the lecturer was saying something—something presumably crushing. She did not hear it.

————

As she left the lecture hall, a tall, gaunt, gray-haired woman edged closer to her. Mentally Janet snapped her fingers. Margaret Bishop.

"Wolves! Take the crosstown bus."

Abruptly, Margaret Bishop strode ahead and vanished into the crowd.

She's crazy, Janet thought; but there had been something so urgent and compelling in that whisper that she went to the bus stop, all the while worrying frantically about her little Geo in the parking lot. There were two men at the bus stop; both looked tired, and neither so much as glanced at her. No, she thought, Margaret Bishop's perfectly sane—I'm the one who's crazy.

When the almost-empty bus arrived, Margaret Bishop was sitting by herself in the last seat. A slight motion of her head and something welcoming in her eyes indicated that Janet was to sit beside her.

Janet did. "I guess I went to the wrong stop. I thought that was the closest."

"It is." Margaret Bishop spoke under her breath. "You're a godsend, Janet. Is it all right if I call you Janet? You're gold and diamonds and rubies to me. Do you have some kind of big car, a van, or a minivan? Anything at all like that? Don't look at me when you answer."

Responding to the last, Janet said, "Yes. All right."

"I knew you would!" There was heady exultation in Margaret Bishop's whisper. "You listen, you follow instructions, and you don't ask questions. You're perfectly wonderful!"

I've often tried to be, Janet thought. Maybe this time I'm succeeding.

"We need somebody to transport three young wolves. You'll do it. I know you will."

"Wolves?" She nodded. "I'll certainly try."

"We're trying to re-establish wolves throughout the United States. Maybe you've heard about us?"

"I've read something, I think."

"They call us wolfers, and there are a lot more of us than they think. Ranchers who doom thousands of cattle every year," the whisper grew bitter, "and rent thousands of acres of public land for pennies, are afraid that somewhere, sometime, a wolf may kill a calf. But wolves are a vital part of this country's ecology."

"I know," Janet whispered back. "I've read a great deal about them."

The bus lurched to a stop; a tired-looking man got off and an even tireder-looking one got on, stamping snow from his overshoes. "That's not one of them," Margaret Bishop whispered, "or I don't think so. They're behind us in a car."

Janet forgot about not asking questions. "Who are they?"

"Feds. Probably Fish and Game, but it might be the FBI or even the ATF."

"That's scary."

"Of course it is, and there are dozens of those secret police agencies, though nobody's got the guts to call them the Secret Police. Are you particularly frightened of the ATF? You shouldn't be, because they're really all the same. Someone who shows you a United States Marshal's badge today may show somebody else credentials from the CIA tomorrow." A slight smile tugged at Margaret Bishop's thin lips. "Their names aren't like Woolf and Bishop, you see, Janet. Theirs mean nothing."

"Young wolves, you said. You want me to take them somewhere."

"Yes, three. Two females and a male." Margaret Bishop opened her purse and rummaged through it. "To a certain park in Michigan. There's a new place in Texas, too, but I'm going to send you to Michigan. I assume you work."

Janet nodded—almost imperceptibly, she hoped.

"Can you take a few days off work?"

"I already am. I won't have to go back until a week from Monday. I— do you mind if I tell you something personal? I don't want to burden you with my problems. I really don't."

"I'd *love* for you to tell me something personal, Janet. I'm eager to get to know you."

"It was because I was getting so depressed, because of the divorce. I divorced Steve, you see. He didn't want it, but . . ."

"You just didn't get along." Margaret Bishop sounded sympathetic.

"He was always bossing me, always crowding me. I'd say stop, stop. You're killing me and you're killing the last bit of the love we used to have."

"Yes."

"And he'd say, why can't you be sensible, Janet? And then when I filed, it was all my fault and he started talking about the good times we'd had. That was what he said, the good times. Only they hadn't been good times for me, and I could never make Steve understand that."

Margaret Bishop's hand found hers.

"The day he moved out, I threw a frying pan at Wasabe—at dear little Wasabe! She's the best little dog anybody ever saw, but I threw a great big cast-iron skillet at her. I could've killed her."

"You had been hurt, and wanted to hurt someone else."

"Yes, exactly. So I explained to my boss and he let me take my two weeks of vacation. I'd been planning to fly to Florida, but I couldn't because of the dogs, so I thought I'd just stay here at home and go to museums and, you know, cultural things, and get some extra sleep and snap out of it. Only I didn't. And because of taking my old name back I kept thinking about wolves, real wolves and werewolves and all the rest of it, and getting bluer and bluer, until you came along. But now I'm not depressed at all. When you get off this bus I'll get off, too—"

"No you won't," Margaret Bishop told her. "We can't let them see us together. Stay on for another two stops."

"All right, I'll stay on for another two stops, and then I'll get off and take another bus back to the campus and get my Geo. That's not the big car I told you about. It's just little. The big one's a Ford Expedition."

"Perfect!"

"And I can start tomorrow. I will, if that's all right."

For the first time, Margaret Bishop turned and looked at her. "If you're caught, caught with the wolves, you'll be fined. You could even be sent to prison. I doubt that it will happen, but it could. Do you understand?"

"Yes. I'll try very hard not to be caught. Kyoto and Wasabe and I will, because I'll have to take them with me. And we won't be."

"Let us pray," Margaret Bishop had said, and had handed her this piece of paper. At the top was the name and address of the man in Minnesota who had the wolves—and, supposedly at least, cages for them. At the bottom was the name and address of the Michigan man who knew all the back roads around the new park and would sneak the wolves in, one at a time and at night.

Home at last, Janet was showing the paper to Kyoto, the wheaten Scottie, who sniffed and inspected it, and cocked her head wisely. "This is very important information," Janet told Kyoto. "You're not to tear it up! Not under any circumstances. Understand?"

I don't do that, Kyoto said quite plainly. It's Wasabe who tears things up, and she mostly tears up house plants burying her toy.

"Let me rephrase that. You are not to tear this up unless we're raided by the Feds. That's what Margaret Bishop calls them, Feds. If we're raided by Feds, I want you to bark as loud as you can, and eat it."

Eat what? Wasabe inquired, interested. (Wasabe was the black Scottie.)

"This is a very valuable paper." Janet showed it to Wasabe, who sniffed it even more thoroughly than Kyoto had.

"It doesn't have phone numbers because their phones might be tapped. The Feds might even be putting a tap on *our* phone right now, so if either of you make a call, don't speak English. Speak Dog."

We will, Kyoto and Wasabe declared in unison.

"Tomorrow I'm going to have to see Steve. It will be ugly, I know it will, but I've got to do it. After that, we'll go to Minnesota and get three wolves, fierce big animals that eat little puppy dogs for lunch. Understand? You two have Japanese names so you ought to be polite, but I can't really say I've noticed it so far. You'd darned well better be polite to the wolves though, and keep your distance, too. And so had I."

Don't worry, Janet, Kyoto said. I'll protect you.

They had said hi, how are you, and not listened to the answers, and Steve had invited Janet in. Now she sat on the edge of a chair big enough to hold a man bigger even than Steve, and clutched her purse in both hands. "When we separated I swore I would never ask you for help."

Steve nodded, his hard, handsome face guarded.

"Now I am. I have to borrow your truck. It shouldn't be for more than two days, and you'll have my Geo to drive to work." She hesitated. "It could be three, I hope not, but it could be. Not any longer than that."

"It's not a truck. It's a sport utility vehicle."

This was encouraging—he had not said no. "I'm sorry. I really am. Your sport utility vehicle. I simply have to have it. I'll take good care of it, and I'll owe you a big, big favor if you let me borrow it. I know that. Will you, Steve? Please?"

A guarded nod. "What do you want it for?"

"Thank you! Oh, Steve, thank you very, very much." It would be too dangerous to kiss him, she decided, although she wanted to. "Do you remember Rachael's dogs?"

"With the funny names? Sure."

"Well I stuck my neck out. I shouldn't have, but I did. I promised to take some other dogs for another woman, a new friend. And they're big, really big dogs—"

He chuckled.

"I said I'd take them to Michigan for her." Janet's voice fell. "Three of them."

"If they piss on my upholstery, Janet . . ."

"They won't! They'll be in a cage in back. You've seen big dog cages like that. Everybody has. They'll never get near your upholstery, I promise, and if they—you know—relieve themselves, I'll clean it up."

"You'd better."

"I will Steve. Really, I will." She paused to swallow; there was the money for Florida, money that she would never use now. "In fact, before I bring it back to you I'll take it to that detailing place. They charge a lot, I know—"

"It'll be two hundred if it's a dime," Steve declared.

"But I will. It'll be just like a new car—I mean sport utility vehicle— when you see it again."

She gave him the keys to her Geo, and he gave her his, which she put in her purse.

"Steve . . . ?"

He cocked an eyebrow. "You need another favor?"

"No. But—but I'd like one. I said I'd be careful with your car? I'll be twice as careful with this. I want you to lend me a gun."

"What?"

"I know I never liked them. I know I always complained about your having them. But these are really big dogs, and they're not nice dogs like Kyoto and Wasabe. Do you know what I mean? And there are three of them, and I'll have to—to let them out to exercise them, I guess. So will you? Not one of your hunting rifles, the little one, the pistol."

"The Smith & Wesson?"

She swallowed again. "I guess so. I don't think I'll need it. I certainly hope I don't. . . ."

To her surprise he nodded sympathetically.

The Smith & Wesson was in the pocket of Janet's parka as she drove up to the Minnesota farmhouse. The house was dark, the barnyard brilliantly illuminated by a light on a high pole. She switched off her headlights before the Expedition rolled to a stop, jumped out, and ran up the steps onto the dark front porch, joyfully accompanied by Wasabe and Kyoto.

There was no response to her knock. She listened for a time, found the bell and rang it, looked back at the dark front yard and the darker road, watched the silent ghost that was her breath floating in the frigid air, and knocked a second time. Nothing.

Wasabe was sticking close, an almost invisible furry presence around her feet; Kyoto had decided the wolves were probably in the rusty hulk of an old truck on the other side of the driveway, and was investigating. A third knock, as loud as she could make it.

Nothing.

Janet whistled Kyoto to her and went back to the Expedition, sat in it for ten minutes or so watching the front door, and restarted the engine. "Nobody." She scratched Kyoto's ears and switched the headlights back on.

"A farm's not like a house," she told Kyoto. "You can't just go off and leave it. Who's going to feed the chickens?"

It seemed a compelling argument, but as is the case with most compelling arguments, nobody listened. Slowly she backed up and out onto the road again. "Well, I'm not going back to Margaret Bishop and say I tried once but there was nobody home. No way!"

Not us! Kyoto declared. As usual, Wasabe seconded her: Not us, right, Janet?

"No indeed. I'm going back to—what was the name of that little town?"

Thief River Falls, Kyoto declared. Wasabe laid a paw on Janet's arm. Viking.

"Whatever." She put the Expedition in drive and glanced at the instruments. "There's bound to be someplace to stay there. A motel or a bed-and-breakfast or something. Tomorrow we'll come back—"

She hit the brakes as a big man in a red cap and a big red checkered coat appeared in her headlights. The Expedition skidded a little on the icy asphalt and came to a stop.

The man in the checkered coat came to her window and the Smith & Wesson into her hand without her consciously wanting either one of them. There seemed to be little to do with the latter except point it at the face of the former, so she did and said, "I darned near killed you. What do you want?"

"A ride." He held up one big hand as though its leathery palm would stop a bullet. "You are looking for me? Granstrom is my name."

"You weren't at your house." Janet hesitated. "Are you afraid they're watching it?"

"Put that away." Granstrom took a deep breath. "I get in the car, all right?"

"This?" She glanced at the Smith & Wesson and put it back into the pocket of her parka. "Yes. Get in. You'll have to chase the dogs into the back."

He did, settling himself into the deep bucket seat. "Nice car. You come to get my wolfs, ya?"

"Wolves. Yes, I did."

"All right."

She waited for him to say more; when he did not, she asked, "Should we go back to your house?"

He shook his head and pointed. "Go slow."

"Right." She let the big Expedition drift ahead.

"There." He pointed again.

"You want to go through all that snow?"

"Ya."

Her headlights showed an opening in a sagging fence of rusty wire. Cautiously the Expedition edged forward, crossing what might or might not have been cattle bars.

"I say turn off those light, you do that?"

"Ya," Janet said, and did. Dark pines and white snow, lost in inky darkness when the moon vanished behind snow-laden clouds.

"Go slow."

It was impossible to go much slower, but she tried. No doubt there was a dirt road under the snow; presumably the Expedition was on it, more or less. "Are the Feds watching your house?" she asked him.

He scratched his head without removing his cap, knocking it to one side. "I don't think so."

"But you went outside in this cold to wait for me half a mile down the road."

"Ya. A certain fellow, he said you would be coming."

"A friend of yours."

"Oh, ya."

"And of Margaret Bishop's."

He turned to look at her. "Ya, her, too."

"You let me go past you so you could look me over, and maybe so you could see if anybody came out of the bushes to grab me when I stopped at your place."

This time he did not speak.

"But you don't think your place is watched?"

"Here stop."

He got out, walked away at an angle until he was only just visible in the moonlight, then motioned for her to follow. She did, and in a minute and a half was enveloped in the deeper night of pines. A faint light motioned her forward. From outside the Expedition there came a throaty yelping cry that was not in her mind. The faint light shone down upon crisp, undisturbed snow: she was to stop. She put the transmission in park and got out, followed by the Scotties.

"They are here," Granstrom said. "My wolfs." He did not shine his flashlight on them, but their eyes glowed. Shadows in the shadows, they passed back and forth, moaning and whining, clinking faintly like icicles rattling down from the highest branches of a big tree. She felt Wasabe tremble as she pressed against her calf. Kyoto was broadside to the wolves, tail erect as an obelisk, fur on end making her look larger than Janet had ever seen her.

"That is a brave little dog you got." Granstrom had followed the direction of her eyes.

"Yes. She's not really mine, but she is."

"Don't let her get too close to my wolfs."

"I don't think we have to worry about that." Janet paused, looking around. "Don't you have cages for them?"

"A big pile of brush." Granstrom's light shot over the wolves' heads to illuminate it. "They go in there, ya? Get out of the wind, sleep all together. I got them on chains."

"You have to have a cage for them!"

He indicated the Expedition with a nod. "I chain them for you in back so they don't get at you."

For a moment they stared at each other. "Open the back," he said.

She did and he did. One wolf snapped at him, and he slapped its muzzle. When all three were inside the Expedition and the rear hatch was shut again, he motioned for her to get in.

"Aren't you coming? I could give you a ride back to where you live."

"No." When he saw that she expected some further answer he added, "I stay to clean up."

"In the dark?"

He did not reply.

She got back into the Expedition, followed reluctantly by Kyoto. Granstrom picked up Wasabe and handed her to Janet. "Thank you," she said. "Sure you don't want a ride home?"

He shook his head. "You go slow, ya? Till you get to the county road, you go slow."

"I will," she promised.

She had covered perhaps one-tenth of a mile when she saw him running behind her and stopped, and rolled down her window as she had before.

"My—wolfs." He was out of breath and panting. "Where do—you bring them?"

"I don't know if . . ."

"Where!"

Margaret Bishop had said nothing to indicate she should not tell him. "To a Larry Ventris in Michigan. There's a big park close to where he lives. He'll smuggle them into it and let them go."

"Good—good." Granstrom's hands, clutching the top of the Expedition's door, relaxed a trifle. "That is good. A good man." She had assumed unconsciously that Granstrom never smiled, but he smiled now. "Up Suicide Road he will take them. This he tells once. Suicide Road or else Harrison Road."

"You know him."

"Ya."

She waited for him to release the door so that she could roll up her window again, but he did not. At last she said, "If you don't want a lift . . . ?"

"The mother wolf, she is dead." He spoke slowly. "A trap or a hunter. Someone shoots, or else poisons. I don't know. Three days I watch their den, and the little wolfs, they are weaker each day."

Janet found herself nodding. "I understand."

"Littler than your dogs they are. I keep them in the house till they get big. Larry Ventris, he is a good man."

She nodded. "I feel sure he is."

"You." He did not point to her, but made a small gesture to indicate her; in the back of the Expedition one of the wolves whimpered. "You are a good woman. Such a good woman most men don't ever see."

She thanked him, sounding—to herself—exceedingly inadequate.

"I was going to tell you their names," Granstrom said, "but they are wild wolfs again now. Wild wolfs in the woods, they got no names."

———

Once they stopped beside the road, and she slept for two hours before the cold and Kyoto woke her. Once, too, she stopped for gasoline (careful to pay cash), bought five hamburgers and coffee at the gas station, and a mile down the road stopped again to eat a hamburger herself, share another between the Scotties, and feed the remaining three to the wolves, throwing the pieces at first, then letting them eat—each growling to keep the others away—from her fingers as Granstrom must have.

No one answered her repeated knocks at the Ventrises', and at last a neighbor came to tell her that neither Ventris nor his wife were at home. Her voice dropped. "I think he was arrested. He always seemed like such a nice, nice man, but I think that they've arrested him."

Janet said, "That was why they arrested him, I suppose." But she did not say it loudly, and said it only to Wasabe and Kyoto after she was back in the Expedition with the doors closed and locked.

She looked into the rearview mirror, and one of the wolves, meeting her eyes there, spoke in Wolf: Aren't we ever going to be free?

"You will," Janet told it. "I swear you will. You'll be free today. Kyoto, do you remember where in that park—Suicide Road. That was one. Who could forget Suicide Road?"

Nobody, Kyoto declared; to which Wasabe added, We only need one.

In another gas station, this one quite near the park, a mechanic who looked as weary as she felt gave her directions to Suicide Road. "It's a pretty place, ma'am. Lot of people go snowmobiling there." He himself looked out at the snow with longing. "This's probably the last big fall this winter. Should be real pretty out there."

"It sounds awful, but it's where my boyfriend said he was going to go, so I've got to find it." She had forgotten already who was dying—the father or the mother; it probably did not matter, she decided.

"Well, you just take Ninety-four and stay with it, then turn off where you see the red barns, like I said. I don't believe there's a sign though."

"Will I be in much danger of going off the edge? Suicide Road sounds so scary." One of the wolves was starting to howl. Janet wondered whether the mechanic heard it.

He grinned, weary still. "Not 'less you jump. It goes up to Suicide Cliff. That's why they call it that."

"How far?" she asked Kyoto. "That's the question. We're about a mile into this park already."

A little farther, Kyoto advised. So they won't run out right away and get shot.

She nodded, too tired to be sleepy. Kyoto was right as always. Go in deep, let out the wolves . . .

For the first time it occurred to her that she, unaided by Larry Ventris, Granstrom, Margaret Bishop, or anyone else, was going to have to unchain the wolves and release them. "You wolves," she spoke to them over her shoulder, "had darned well better remember that I'm your friend and I've got a gun."

One howled, then another; Wasabe began to yip in sympathy.

"Shut up!" She tapped the horn, and they did. "What I'm going to do is drive way deep in this park. Have you noticed that we haven't seen any other cars?"

Kyoto had, and said so.

"I'm going to enjoy this winter scenery, which really is spectacular. Then I'm going to stop and let you wolves out. Let me do it, and you're free. Bite me while I'm trying to unchain you, and you're going to have a fight on your hands. Understand?"

A wolf met her eyes in the mirror but said nothing.

"You think you're big, tough wolves, but you're not even half grown up yet. It'll be three against three if we fight. Speaking for myself and the dogs, we don't want to. It's entirely up to you."

A second wolf appeared in the mirror, saying in Wolf, Let us out here.

"Okay," Janet told it. "That sign said there was a scenic overlook up ahead. We can pull off right up there."

She did and got out, followed by both Scotties. "We'll go on through the park," she told them. "Did I say that?"

Wasabe nodded. I think so, Janet.

"Then we'll find someplace that will take dogs and I'll have a bath and sleep till next Wednesday." She unlocked the hatch of Steve's Expedition and held out her hand to the most docile-looking wolf. "That is the hand of friendship. Remember the hamburgers?"

The wolf said nothing, but allowed her to unsnap the chain around its neck. She took three quick steps backward as Kyoto barked a warning.

Almost fearfully the wolf stood for a moment on the rear of the Expedition, looking at her and the dogs, the rocks, the snow, and the trees. It lifted its head, sniffed the wind, and jumped down, loped across the little snow-covered parking lot and across Suicide Road to what appeared to be a sheer cliff so steep that the snow had found only scattered points in which to lodge. Passing behind a roadside bush, it never reappeared.

Janet discovered that she had been holding her breath and let it out with a whoosh. "That was the greatest moment of my life," she told the emptiness beyond the railing.

Wasabe, sniffing at the wolf's trail, looked up with snow on her nose. Mine, too, Janet.

She had almost gotten up the courage to release the second wolf when the park ranger's car pulled in. He marched grimly toward her, a good foot taller than she in his Smoky Bear hat. "Miss—" he began. His eyes opened very wide when he saw the Smith & Wesson.

"Were you about to say that I'm under arrest?"

He shook his head, the motion almost imperceptible.

"That's good," Janet told him. "Because if you do I'm going to shoot you and roll your body over that drop." For a moment it seemed to her that she might actually do it.

"You're bringing in wolves." There was an odd, undecided quality to his voice.

She pointed to the back of the Expedition. "There they are."

"Letting them go in the park."

"I *was*. But that was before you came." Something in her voice made Wasabe bark at him and Kyoto growl. "Now you are. If you want to keep breathing, you get over there and unchain them."

He looked at the two remaining wolves, and back at her. "You don't need that gun, Miss."

"I'm glad to hear it. Get busy."

"In a minute."

She raised the gun. "The trigger was pretty stiff when I got it, but I had a gunsmith smooth it out." It was something Steve had said. On her own she added, "I don't have strong hands, but I can pull this trigger now, and it's a lot easier to pull after the first time. It's called double action."

"I know what it's called," the park ranger said.

"Sure you do. And you know that if you can keep me talking somebody will come by. Get over there and unchain them."

He took a hesitant step toward the wolves.

"I'm going to count to ten." She tried to make her voice hard, and at least succeeded in frightening herself. "Is that understood? I don't want to, but on the count of ten I shoot. One. Two. Three . . ."

Like playing hide-and-seek, she thought.

"Four. Five. Six. I am not joking. Do it!"

He edged nearer the wolves, but one lunged at him snarling.

"Never mind, I'll do it."

She was no longer tired. It's getting out of the truck and into the fresh air, she thought, or it's getting to stretch my legs, and whatever it is, it's wonderful.

She gestured with the Smith & Wesson. "Get over closer to your car, but don't get in."

"I am not going to rush you," he said. He sounded sincere.

"That's good. If you're not going to rush me I'm not going to shoot you, and that's the way we both like it."

"I was going to warn you, that's all. Tell you to come in at night, because if somebody else saw you I'd have to—"

She made an angry gesture, and he backed away. She said, "I'm going to put this in my pocket. See?"

He nodded.

"If you can get to me before I can get it out again, you win. But you'd better be careful not to slip in the snow." The wolf that had snarled at him snapped at her; she cuffed its muzzle and unhooked its chain. "Now get out of here," she told it. "We're tired of feeding you. Go kill a gopher or something."

When she looked around at the ranger, his hands were no longer raised. "There," she told him, "that's another one. You arrested a friend of mine yesterday, but you still haven't stopped us." *Us* was Margaret Bishop, Granstrom, Larry Ventris, and how many others? It really wasn't a question of how many others, she decided; it was a question of how many wolves.

The ranger had spoken, but she had been too occupied with her thoughts to hear him. As she unchained the third wolf she said, "Come again?"

"I said I was sorry about your friend. It wasn't me."

The third wolf jumped from the back of the Expedition and for perhaps fifteen seconds stood nose-to-nose with Kyoto and Wasabe. I'm going to live in these woods and have cubs, the third wolf said in Wolf, because that's what I want to do.

It's up to you, Kyoto declared in Dog. We want to stay with Janet.

Wasabe added, Until Rachael and Andy get back.

Kyoto glanced up at Janet, saying, How long? And the third wolf trotted away as if she meant to trot straight down Suicide Road, but went someplace else before she reached it.

Good-bye, Kyoto called; and Wasabe, Janet, and the ranger joined her. Good-bye! "Good-bye!" "Good-bye!"

"Do you know what I worry about?" Janet asked him.

"Sure. You're afraid one might bite a kid."

She nodded. "I'm afraid one may kill a child. How did you know?"

"Because I worry, too. I worry about every kid that comes into this park, but we have bears and wildcats. Do you know how many kids have been bitten by bears and wildcats put together since I've been here? I've been here six years."

She shook her head.

"Not a one. They've got wolves in Canada, just about everywhere except in the cities, and they've got wolves in Minnesota that came down from Canada. Do you think the TV news in Minneapolis and Toronto is yelling every day about kids torn to pieces by wolves?"

When she did not reply, his voice softened. "Can I tell you something? Wolves aren't half as dangerous as deer. Deer aren't nearly as smart, and the males get very aggressive in the fall. We've got more than a thousand deer in this park."

She pointed toward his car. "You've got a radio in there?"

He nodded. "I'm not going to use it, though."

"But if I put a bullet in it, you'll have to explain what happened."

He nodded again.

"All right." With her hand on the gun in her pocket, she shut the Expedition's hatch. "I'll take my chances."

"Thanks . . ." he said.

"What is it?"

He pointed to her left hand. "You're not married."

"No."

He tried to smile. It was not something he did well. "My name's Jerry, Miss. Jerry Baumgarten."

She got back into the Expedition and whistled for the dogs. "This is the wild, wild woods," she told him. A glance took in rocks and pines and snow that she knew she would never forget. "In the wild woods, we Woolfs have no names."

As the Expedition pulled away, she watched its side mirror to see whether he ran for his car and its radio. He did not.

Suicide Road struck another road, a Michigan state highway, and she turned onto it singing under her breath, a happy little song about a winter wonderland. There were curves and more curves, hills and valleys, pines, white birch, and snow-covered bushes.

Then suddenly and incredibly an impossibly tall man in snowy white, with outstretched arms and the finest smile she had ever seen. She slammed on the brakes so hard that the Expedition nearly skidded off into the ditch.

In the blinking of an eye, the man in white was gone. Where he had stood, three snowmobiles flashed across the road.

Janet turned off the ignition, told the dogs to stay inside, and got out. There were no footprints where the man in white had stood, only the tracks of the racing snowmobiles that, if she had not seen him and braked . . .

It did not bear thinking about. She looked up and down the empty road, and listened to the sound of their racing engines until they faded to bright winter sunshine and clear blue sky. Slowly and stiffly she knelt in the snow, clasped her hands, and closed her eyes. *Thank you. Thank you very, very much. It was a pleasure, Lord, a pleasure and an honor to look after your dogs, even if it was only for a day. I'll be happy to do it again anytime.*

Back in the Expedition, traveling the state highway at a cautious twenty-five miles an hour, she waited for some word of thanks and approval from Him. There was none; instead, a vast questioning, as though God (too big to be seen) were waiting expectantly for something more from her.

What was it Margaret Bishop had said? Michigan, and another park someplace? Janet cast her mind back to the dark, crawling, jolting bus. A certain park in Michigan, and a new place . . .

"Saddle up, you li'l Scottie gals." She risked a small nudge of the accelerator. "Round up them wolves 'n head 'em on out. We're a-goin' to Texas."

"Yip-yip-yippee!" the wheaten Scottie replied, speaking even more plainly than usual.

Ever loyal, Wasabe seconded her. "Yippee-ki-yi, Kyoto!"

> *She loosed the bar, she slid the bolt, she opened the door anon,*
> *And a grey bitch-wolf came out of the dark and fawned on the*
> *Only Son!*
>
> —KIPLING

The Eleventh City

✦

April 18, 2003
Franklin A. Abraham, Ph.D., Chair
Comparative Religion and Folklore
U. of Nebraska Lincoln
Lincoln NE 68501
Estados Unidos

Dear Frank,

I am in the little town of San Marcos del Lago, in the province of Córdoba. You can write me here poste restante. I have asked that my mail be forwarded from Buenos Aires, but you never can tell. E-mail should reach me if phone service is ever restored.

This is the happy hunting-ground of the folklorist, exactly as Adolfo promised—not only is there the rich folklore of the Native American tribes of the Chaco (who are actually inclined to be rather close-mouthed with a stranger) but Spanish folklore and Spanish-American folklore, which is often a strange mixture of the two. Every day I rove the town or range the countryside on horseback, a method of operation I find much more effectual than driving around in my rented jeep. At night I haunt the cantinas, nursing a cerveza or three and buying one for anybody with a good story. The plentiful fruits of my labors you shall read when my book appears. What will follow in this present letter is somewhat different. I give it to you now in the hope of obtaining your advice. To tell the truth, I do not know what to do with it. Is it American or Spanish-American? Is it folklore at all, properly considered? Advise me, Frank, if you have any counsel to give.

From time to time I have seen an elderly man, quite well dressed, drinking in the cantina closest to this house. Somebody or other told me that he was a gringo, too (he is from St. Louis originally, as it turns out) and so I made no effort to engage him in conversation. He is generally quiet, pays cash, and keeps to himself. His name is Wendell Zane, he asked me to call him Dell, and for the present that is all you need to know about him.

As I was riding past the old Catholic cemetery yesterday evening, I was accosted by a madwoman. The sun was low, the shadows were long, and the incident was unsettling to say the least. She shouted at me in a language that was neither Spanish nor English, shrieked like a banshee, and tried to pull me off my horse; and when my horse bolted, she threw stones at us in much the same way that a rifle throws bullets. If this were some tale of romance, no doubt she would be beautiful. Believe me, Frank, she is anything but.

In the cantina that evening I mentioned the incident to the barman, suggesting as diplomatically as I could that she be confined for her own protection. He shrugged and said that it had been tried many times and was perfectly useless. "Soon she gets away, señor, always." He glanced at the man I had been told was a fellow American as he spoke. "She is so strong! Nothing can hold her."

Later Dell introduced himself. My recorder was on by that time, so I can give you his story as he told it:

I'm a civil engineer, Doctor Cooper, and I came down here when they were running the new line to Tucuman. I was pretty close to retirement already, and I made friends here and got myself a young wife—that's why I'm in San Marcos—and what with one thing and another, I never went back. The trains here run over a couple of bridges I helped design and build, and I could say the same thing just about anywhere north of La Pampa.

Anyway, it happened the second year I was here. Or maybe it was the third, I'm not sure anymore. I was ready to pack it in after a long day on the job when I heard a funny noise way down the track, and all the men stopped work to cross themselves. I asked about it, and they said it was *el jabalí encadenados,* the pig-in-chains. They said it ran up and down the tracks all over the world and brought bad luck wherever it went. Well, I told them I'd done a lot of work around railroads in the States and I'd never heard of it. And they said maybe it hadn't gotten there yet, because it had been looking around their country for a long time.

Next day we lost Pepe Cardoza and two more. It was one of those damned stupid accidents where the plans say you've got to build A before you even start on B, but somebody decides he'll go ahead with B anyhow, because A is waiting for parts. The welds cracked and the beams fell, like any damned fool could have told you they would. And they fell right on three good men. That night I heard the noise again, and I— well, I got out of bed and got my clothes on and went out on the line to have a look.

After a while the girl I was shacking up with then caught up with me. This wasn't my wife, you understand. I hadn't met my wife yet when all this happened. This was just a girl, not bad-looking, who had slept around some. A friend had told me to buy her a couple of drinks and she might show me a good time that night. So I did, and I sort of hooked on to her, or she hooked on to me. Her name was Jacinta.

Anyway my shutting the door woke her up, and she thought I might be sneaking out to see another woman. So I told her about the pig, a sort of ghost pig according to the men I'd talked to, and she said she'd heard of it and she knew a woman that was real good with ghosts, she'd talk to her tomorrow but it would probably cost me money. I said all right, we'll try her if it's not too much.

So this old witch was there waiting for me when I got back the next day. I told her about the pig-in-chains, everything the men had said, and she said there were a lot of things like that and she'd have to find out. She threw her head back and sang to herself without much music in it, drumming on the table. That lasted a long time. I remember Jacinta and I about did for a pack of cigarettes waiting for her to stop it and tell us something.

Then she shut up. It was dark out by that time. This is going to be sort of hard to tell you about.

[Here I assured Dell at some length that I would give full credit to whatever he might tell me.]

It got to be too quiet. Usually you could hear somebody singing in the cantina down the street, and street vendors, and so forth and so on; but there wasn't any of that anymore. Just quiet little noises that told you there were other things in the room that you couldn't see. It was like rats in the walls, only you knew it wasn't rats. There was an electric light over the table, just the bare bulb, we used to have them all over, and it got dim. It didn't go out, but it didn't give near as much light as it should have either. It was like the voltage had dropped.

Then the witch got to talking to the things we couldn't see. Some of it was in Spanish, and I remember her saying, *"Qué busca él?"* over and over. A lot of it was names, or at any rate that was how it seemed to me. Funny names, and maybe they were Toba names. I don't know.

Finally she came out of it. You're not going to believe any of this, and I didn't either. But this is what she said. She said that back when Christ walked this earth he had put devils into a bunch of pigs, and the pigs had drowned themselves to get rid of them. The men who owned the pigs had tried to save them, and they had saved this one, pulling it out of the water before it died. After that it couldn't kill itself anymore, because the devil inside wouldn't let it. The whole story's in the Bible somewhere. I looked it up and read it once, but that was a long time ago.

[As did I, Frank, after Dell and I separated. Slightly condensed from the Fifth Chapter of the Gospel According to Mark:

[*Now a great herd of swine was there on the mountainside, feeding. And the devils kept entreating Him, saying, "Send us into the swine, that we may enter into them." And Jesus gave them leave. And the devils came out and entered into the swine; and the herd, in number about two thousand, rushed down with great violence into the sea, and were drowned.*

[*But the swineherds fled and reported it; and people came out to see what was happening. And they came to Jesus and saw the man who had been afflicted by the devil sitting clothed and in his right mind, and they were afraid. And they began to entreat him to depart from their midst. . . . And he departed and began to publish in the Ten Cities all that Jesus had done for him. And all marveled.*]

This pig, she said, was still alive. The devil inside wouldn't let it die, and because that devil was in it, it knew more than any man. People had tried to catch it and pen it up and they had even fastened big chains around its neck, but it had broken all those chains and run away, always looking for somebody that would free it from the devil Jesus had put into it. It brought bad luck, naturally, because it carried that devil with it wherever it want.

I asked her if she couldn't do something about it, and she said she'd try but she'd have to have a piece of the blessed sacrament to work with. She said the priest would never give her one because he didn't trust her. Jacinta said she'd get it, steal it some way.

To make a long story short, Jacinta did it the next Sunday, and the witch tacked it onto a long cross she'd made out of two sticks that she could use about like a leveling rod. After that we'd make a date, her and Jacinta and me, and wait along the tracks someplace at night, usually for three or four hours. It must have gone on like that for about a month before we finally got it.

It didn't look like a pig, not to me anyway. There was a green glow, with something dark behind it that I never could see right. But it stopped when the witch stepped out onto the tracks with her cross, and she talked to it a little and the dark thing said, "Cast me into the woman." I had never heard a voice like that before, and I've never heard another one like that since. I don't want to, either.

There was a lot of talk about that between Jacinta and the witch and me. But eventually the witch did it, putting it into Jacinta like it wanted. After that, we never heard the pig-in-chains again, and I don't think anybody else has heard it either.

And that's all there is to tell, Doctor Cooper. You saw Jacinta today, so you know the rest.

That was his story, Frank. I asked him whether she had consented, and he said she had, that the witch had promised her she would be wiser than anyone alive and would live forever, and she had believed her. I did not ask him how much he had paid the witch or what had become of her, but he volunteered the information that she had died not long after that. He did not say how, but there was a certain dark satisfaction in his voice when he talked about it.

As I said earlier, Frank, I would appreciate your advice. Is this folklore? The madwoman is real enough; I saw her and was stoned by her. I still have the bruises. If it is folklore, is it Spanish-American? I heard it from an American in this godforsaken little town in Argentina, and I suspect that I might have heard much the same tale from the barman if Dell himself had not been present.

Should I put it in my book or just try to forget about it?

I trust that everything is going well back in Lincoln. Give Joe and Rusty, and the whole department, my regards and tell them I will see them again in the fall and regale them with my adventures. Although I should not say it, I can hardly wait to get out of this place.

> Sincerely,
>
> Sam Cooper

P.S. I spent most of this morning wandering around the town, but this afternoon I rode out to the cemetery to look for the madwoman. I did not find her; but between the road and the closest grave markers someone had sculpted a surrealistic and truly horrible pig from mud and straw, with padlocks and broken chains lying at its feet. That was Jacinta's work, I believe; no sane person could have done it and remained sane. I have photographed it.

The Night Chough

✦

Silk was gone, the black bird reminded itself. There was no point in
thinking about him.

No, it itself had gone.

Which was the same.

A gleaming pool caught its eye, reminding it of its thirst. It looked at
the water and its margins, seeing no danger, dropped from the threatening sky to an overhanging branch and scanned its surroundings.

Croaked. Sometimes hungry things moved when you croaked.

Nothing moved here.

Water below. Cold and still and dark. Cool. Inviting.

It fluttered across to the highest point on a half-submerged log,
sharply recalling that it was hungry, too. Bent, stretching its neck, spreading dark wings to keep its balance. Its polished bill was the color of old
blood, not quite straight. That bill was beautiful in its cruel way, but the
bird was too accustomed to it to admire it anymore—so it told itself, and
turned its head to see it better, knowing (as most birds did not) that it was
the bird in the water as well as the bird on the log, just as the log itself was
partly in the water and partly above it.

"Good bird!" The bird pronounced judgment. "Pretty bird!" These
were its own words, not words that forced themselves past its throat at
times, the words it spoke that were not its own. "Good bird," it repeated. "Bird see." Speaking as humans did was an accomplishment
that had earned it both food and admiration in the recent past, and it

was proud of its ability. More loudly it said, "Talk good!" And stooped to drink.

There was someone else in the water, a blank and livid face that stared into its own with sightless blue eyes that looked good to eat. The bird pecked at them, but refraction disturbed its aim. Its bill stabbed soft flesh instead, flesh that at once sank deeper and vanished. The bird whistled with surprise, then drank as it had intended.

Already a third countenance was forming, a young woman's snarling face framed by floating tendrils of dark hair. This new young woman had a profusion of arms, some with two elbows and some with three—some, even, that required no elbows at all, arms without hands, as sinuous as serpents. She struggled to speak, mouthing angry phrases without sound.

"Bad bird!" It had not intended to say that, and was angry at itself for having done so. "Bad bad! No eat!" It had not intended to say those things either.

"Bad eat!"

It had been trying to drink again, tilting back its head at the moment that the words emerged; it nearly choked. "Bad talk!" it sputtered.

Then, "Bad god! No talk!"

"Is somebody here?" A slender young man was approaching the pool, threading his way dolefully among fragrant incense willows. "Anybody besides Lily?" He carried an instrument for landing large fish, a pole topped with a sharp iron hook.

Reminded of its owner, the bird inquired, "Fish heads?"

"Who is that?" The young man looked around. "Are you making fun of me?"

"Good bird!" It was still hoping to be fed.

"I see you." For a moment, the young man almost smiled. "What are you, a crow?"

The bird repeated, "Good bird!" and flew up from the log to light on a branch nearer the young man.

"I've never seen a crow with a red topknot like that," the young man told it, "or a crow that talked, either. I guess you must be some new kind of crow they've got here." He groped the dark water with his hook, heedless of the distant rumble of thunder.

"Fish heads?"

"Yes," the young man agreed. "I'm fishing for Lily's head. I suppose you could say that." An audible swallow. "And the rest of her. I'm hoping to hook her gown, actually. This hook is sharp, and I'm afraid it may tear her face, if that's what we find."

The black bird whistled softly.

"When I heard you, I was hoping there was somebody else here, somebody who would help me pull Lily out of the water. Water lily. That's funny isn't it?" Tears streamed down his cheeks.

"No cry," the bird urged, its usual stridency muted.

Still weeping, the young man plunged his pole into the dark water, groping its inky recesses with the hook, which he drew out from time to time bringing forth mud and tangled, rotting sticks. "She's here in this pond," he told the bird. "Serval said so."

The bird recalled its vision. "Girl here. In pond."

"She was walking into town," the young man spoke half to himself. "Walking to the fair. They stopped her. Serval did, and Bushdog and Marten. They made her go with them, and they took her here."

He paused, and there was that in his eyes that made the bird flutter nervously. At length he said, "They made her do everything they wanted. That was what he said, what Serval said, drinking last night at Kob's. He bragged about it. He boasted. I had it from Moonrat and Caracal, independently."

Suddenly, he laughed; and his merriment was more frightening than his anger. "Listen to me! Just listen! 'Independently.' I've been reading for the law you see, dear birdie. Going to be an advocate and buy Lily furs. And pearls. And a big house of her own. All—all . . ."

He had begun to weep again. "All so she'd love me. But she did already." His voice rose to a frenzied scream. *"She told me so!"* He dropped his pole and sat down, heedless of the muddy ground, his face in his hands; the bird, who had more than a little experience of emotional outbursts, edged cautiously nearer.

At length the weeping stopped. The young man pulled something wrapped in a clean rag from a side pocket of his jacket. Unwrapping the rag revealed a thick sandwich, which he opened to inspect the meat inside. "Mother made me take this," he told the bird. "I don't really want it. Would you like a piece?"

"Bird like!"

The young man removed a slice of meat and hooked it on a twig, then sat down to re-close and re-wrap his sandwich.

"Find girl?" Those words had not been the bird's own, and it shook its head angrily.

"Not yet." The young man shrugged. "Of course there's a lot of pool yet. I'll keep looking."

He returned the sandwich to his pocket. "This might not be the place. Moonrat may have gotten it wrong."

The meat was dangerously near him, in the bird's opinion; and it occurred to the bird that the situation would be much improved if the stirring of the pool with the hook and pole were resumed. "Girl here!" it declared. "Find girl." Again it recalled its vision. "Big wet. Have arms."

The young man stood up. "I don't have any," he told the bird quite calmly. "If I had arms, a slug gun or even a sword, I'd kill them for killing her, all three of them."

"Have arms!" the bird reiterated testily. "Girl wet."

"I don't," the young man protested, "and I haven't forgotten Lily. I will never forget her."

"Have arms!" Then something that it had no intention of saying: "Your hook."

"You mean this?" Wondering, the young man examined the cruel steel hook on the end of his pole; rendered bold by hunger, the bird took flight and snatched the red slice of beef he had hung on the twig.

"I wonder where he is now," the young man whispered to himself. "Several. Bushdog. Marten. I wonder where they all are right now."

He turned away from the pool; and the bird (mindful of the sandwich still in his pocket) followed him, carrying its slice of half-raw beef in its beak, and pausing from time to time to tear at it.

It had begun to rain. In the hitherto silent pool where Lily waited beneath the water with the exemplary patience of the dead, the first big drops tore the water like shot. Thunder rumbled in the distance. By the time the young man and the bird reached the raw, new streets and hastily erected houses, it was raining hard, solid sheets of pounding silver rain that turned the streets to oozing mire—sheets that were whisked away by the wind at the very moment they arrived, replaced within a second or so by new sheets from elsewhere, more beautiful and more violent than their predecessors.

They went from house to house, the bird seeking shelter under each low, overhanging roof only to fly frantically to the next as the young man moved on. When the young man himself stood beneath the eaves at a door or window, the bird perched upon his shoulder, bedraggled and dripping, nursing vague hopes of food and fire, and did its best to explain things: "Bad man. Go where? Bad man!"

"There's one," the young man whispered, pointing. Through the twenty-second window (or perhaps the forty-third) could be seen three men and a woman seated around a rough table on which stood three dark bottles and five cheap wineglasses among scattered playing cards.

"That's Marten. That's Locust and Lacewing with him. They're brothers. I think the woman's Gillyflower."

The bird only shook itself, spreading its sable wings and fluffing out its feathers in an effort to become, if not dry, at least some trifle less wet.

"Lacewing has a slug gun. See there in the corner? They'll all have knives, even Gillyflower. If I were to gaff Marten now, they'd come out and kill me, and—" A flash that might have revealed his tense features to those inside, if anyone had been looking toward the window, was followed by a peal of thunder that swept aside his final words.

"I was going to kill myself," the young man's tones were unnaturally flat, "once I'd found Lily's body and seen that it had a proper burial."

"Bad, bad."

"Yes, it is—was." A smile tugged on his lips, became a broad grin. "I'd be killing the wrong person, wouldn't I? But I'm going to kill both Marten and myself tonight. You'd better get out of the way before Lacewing starts shooting, birdie."

The steel hook crashed through the window. There was just time enough for Marten to jerk his head around, half turning in his chair, before the sharp point caught him in the back of the neck.

It did not sever his spine, or either jugular vein; there was no terrify-ing gush of blood as there is when those (they are in fact arteries) are cut; but it stabbed through the thick muscles there, his gullet, and his wind-pipe, and emerged from the front of his throat after having destroyed his larynx.

He was jerked from his seat and pulled irresistibly toward the window. For what seemed almost an eternity, and was perhaps a full half second in reality, he braced both his hands against the wall.

"Hook good!" the black bird exclaimed, its head bobbing.

Marten's own head and neck emerged, the latter bleeding copiously now. After them came his shoulders, softer and more pliable than would have seemed possible before the hook. His knife was in his right hand, making it appear that he had hoped—perhaps even intended—to stab the young man with it when he emerged.

Nothing of the kind remained within his power. The young man braced his feet as well as he could in the liquefying street, and stiffened his body against the lead slug that he expected from the window or the front door, and heaved with all his might, drawing the dying Marten out beyond the overhanging thatch into the pounding rain, until his body tumbled through the window to a deafening drumroll of thunder and sprawled twitching in the mud. Scarlet streams of blood trickled from its open mouth only to be washed away at once by a silver flood.

"And now," the young man told the black bird beneath the eaves, "now they will come out and kill me, and I will be with her."

No one came out of the front door, and the young man was unable to nerve himself sufficiently to look through the shattered window again.

At length he knelt in the mud and took the knife from Marten's flac-cid hand. "This killed her," he told the bird. "I'm going to throw it into that pond." He paused, gnawing at his lower lip while his imagination showed him the knife plunging through the water until chance drove its long, keen blade into Lily's throat.

"But not till I have her out of there."

"Knife good," announced the bird, who had not in the least intended to do so. On its own, it urged nonviolence: "No cut!"

The young man gave no attention to either remark, and perhaps did not hear them. With a small pocketknife, he cut the dead Marten's belt. He himself wore none; but he thrust the knife into the sheath he had taken from Marten's, and put knife and sheath into the waistband of his soaking trousers behind his right hip.

When he had freed his hook, he straightened up. For a second or two he stood waiting, staring at the shattered window, which had gone dark. "They're not coming," he told the bird, and laughed softly. "They're more afraid of me than I am of them, for the present anyway."

He set off up the rain-swept street, walking slowly with long strides, each of which ended ankle-deep in mud and water. "We're hunting Serval now," he muttered when he had left the house with the shattered window behind, thinking that the bird had accompanied him. "We were always hunting Serval, really."

Having gulped Marten's right eye, the bird was in the process of extracting the left, and paid scant attention.

It overtook the young man outside a tavern, plunging from chimney-height to thump down wetly on his shoulder. The three drunken men whose presence in the doorway had prevented him from entering gathered around to look at the bird, and he was able to step through them, entering an atmosphere of warmth and smoke, redolent of beer.

The bird, seeing the blaze at the farther end of the room and discovering with unfeigned delight that it was no longer rained upon, exclaimed, "Good place!" and flew straight to the hearth, landing there in a small cloud of ash and spreading its wings to dry with much satisfaction.

The man behind the bar laughed aloud (as did half his patrons) and poured the young man a small beer. "Just to get you started."

The young man ignored it. His eyes were on a burly man, younger even than he, at the table in the middle of the room. Softly he said, "Bad evening, Bushdog."

Noisy as the room was, it seemed that Bushdog had heard him; for a second or two he glared, while the young man looked back at him as a cat watches a mousehole.

The black bird's voice sounded from the chimneypiece, "Bad man! Cut girl!"; and Bushdog shouted, "Get that out of here," and threw his glass at the bird.

It smashed against the stones of the chimney, showering the bird with broken glass. For a heartbeat, the room was noisy no longer. Then the young man picked up the small beer he had been given a moment before and threw it at Bushdog.

"Get out!" It was Kob, and as he spoke he motioned to a pair of big men nursing beers at a table in the back. They rose as one.

Resting the hooked gaff against his shoulder, the young man raised both his hands. "You don't have to throw me out. I agree completely. I am leaving." As he went out the door, the bird flew to his shoulder.

Together, they waited in the rain, he leaning on the pole, the black bird perched dismally upon the hook that had killed Marten. "No fair," something in the bird that was not the bird muttered urgently to the young man, and the bird repeated it again and again: "No fair! *No fair!*"

From within the tavern came a snarl of angry voices, followed by the double smack of two blows struck so quickly they might almost have been one.

"Here. Take it. You'll need it." The object was a slug gun, thrust at the young man by somebody as damp as he who had stepped from a shadow.

"Moonrat? Is that you?"

The light spilling from the tavern's doorway was blocked by the bulky bodies of Bushdog and another man who shoved Bushdog out and slammed the door; holding a finger to his lips, Moonrat retreated down the street.

The young man thrust his pole into the mud and leveled the slug gun he had been given, and the bird flew to the shelter of the eaves, perching upon a windowsill from which it repeated, "Watch out! No fair!"

The young man's index finger had located the trigger. He had never fired a slug gun, and was not particularly eager to begin.

Slowly, Bushdog put up his hands. "You going to take me in, Starling?"

The young man shook his head. "You killed Lily yesterday, and I—"

"I didn't! It was Serval, Pas's my witness."

"Am going to kill you tonight." There was supposed to be a safety catch somewhere that had to be released with the thumb; he recalled that from a conversation years ago, and his thumb groped for the button, or lever, or whatever that catch was.

"Perhaps it was Serval. I don't know or care. If it was, you helped him, which is enough for me." He tried to tighten his finger on the trigger, and discovered that he could not.

"They'll get you." Bushdog's voice was thick with brandy. "They'll get you, and you'll get a slug in the belly, just like me."

The young man hesitated. Was there a cartridge ready to fire? Slug guns, he knew, were often carried without one—only the magazine was loaded. You were supposed to move the handle in front to make the gun ready. He tried, tugging it with his left hand; it would not budge.

"You can't just kill me in cold blood."

He swallowed. "All right, I won't. I won't, if you do as I tell you. You've got a knife. Get it out."

"No fair," the bird muttered from the eaves. And again, "No fair!"

"So you can shoot me soon as I've got it in my hand?"

"No," the young man said. "Get it out. I won't shoot you unless you attack me."

Rain heavier than any he had yet seen lashed the street, rain so hard that for an instant he lost sight of Bushdog altogether. Because of that, perhaps, he was suddenly aware that the window of the tavern was full of faces, as a bowl or a basket may be full of cherries.

"I got it." Bushdog displayed his knife.

"Throw it away."

Bushdog shook his head.

His thumb had found the safety. He pushed it, unable to hear the click in the pounding rain, and unsure of what he had done. "Throw it away." He struggled to keep his uncertainty out of his voice. "Or this will be over very, very soon. Now!" His finger tightened on the trigger, but there was no shot. He had applied the safety, in that case—assuming that there was a cartridge in line with the barrel.

As Bushdog's knife flew off into the blind night, the young man returned the safety to its original position. "I'm taking out mine," he said. "I've got to take my hand away from the trigger to do it, so if you think you can rush me, now's the time."

Bushdog shook his head again. "In this shaggy mud?" He spat in the young man's direction, but his spittle was drowned by the rain almost before it left his lips.

He was swaying a little, the young man noticed; probably swaying quite a lot, in fact, for it to be visible in such small light as spilled through the tavern's window. The young man wondered vaguely whether that would make it better or worse as he pulled Marten's knife from the sheath, displayed it, and flung it behind him.

"No fair!" the bird croaked urgently.

"He's right, it isn't—not as long as I've got this." The young man held up the slug gun. "So I'm going to lean it against the wall. I won't try to get it—or my gaff—if you don't. Do I have your word?"

For a moment Bushdog stared. He nodded.

"I've killed your friend Marten already tonight. Did you know that?"

Bushdog said nothing.

"I gave him no chance at all, which is to say I gave him the same chance that you and he and Serval gave Lily. I feel bad about that, so I'm giving you more chance than I should—"

"No fair! Shoot! Shoot!" the bird urged.

"To make up for that. I'm going to fight you on even terms, and I warn you that if I beat you I'm going to kill you. If you beat me, I expect you to kill me as well. But of course that's up to you."

"I got it."

Pointing his slug gun at the ground between them, the young man pulled the trigger. The booming report was louder than he had expected. The gun jumped in his grasp like a live thing, and a geyser of mud leaped into the air. Stepping to his left, he propped the gun next to the window.

Bushdog was on him in an instant, knocking him off his feet, big hands closing on his throat.

Something in him exploded, and he was on top of Bushdog, hammering Bushdog's face with his fists, driving it down into the water and the liquid mud. As if that moment had never been, Bushdog was astride him, biting at some dark thing that was abruptly a knife. It plunged toward him; with a convulsive effort, he wrenched away.

There was a wild cry as the black bird struck furiously at Bushdog's face, vanishing as quickly as it had come. At once the knife was gone, and both Bushdog's hands were at the socket of his right eye. He roared with pain and shouted for help before the muddy water filled his nose and mouth and his solid, muscular body ceased to struggle, stiffened. . . . And relaxed.

"Good," the bird croaked, and returned to the eaves. "Good, good!"

It is, the young man thought. (He would have wiped his mouth if he could, but both his hands were still locked around Bushdog's throat, although Bushdog was limp and unresisting.) It shouldn't be good to take the life of another human being, the young man told himself, yet it is. I'll never feel rain, or hear thunder, without thinking about this and being glad.

Moonrat caught up with the young man as he was scouring the town for Serval. *"Starling! Starling! Wait up!"* Moonrat was running, his feet splashing mud and water. "How's that gun I gave you, Starling? It work all right for you?"

"It was fine," the young man told him. "I haven't put a fresh cartridge into place—is that how you say it?"

"Into the chamber."

"Into the chamber, then. I haven't done that, because I thought it was safer this way. But I will."

"You're right. Wait till you're ready to shoot. Is Bushdog dead?"

From the young man's shoulder, the black bird muttered, "Bad man," and "Watch out."

"Yes," the young man said. His voice was flat.

"Good! That's wonderful, Starling."

"But Serval's really the one, isn't he? The one who put Marten and Bushdog up to it. I've seen him around town pretty often—more than I liked, in fact. But I have no idea where he lives."

"I thought you were going there." Moonrat glanced at the houses on the left side of the street.

"No. I was just hoping to find someone who would tell me where he might be."

"Well, you've found him." Moonrat edged closer. "Listen, Starling . . ."

"Yes?"

"I—I want to help you. I mean, I already did. I loaned you my slug gun."

The young man, who had it slung behind his right shoulder, unslung it and offered it to its owner. "Do you want it back? Here it is."

"No, you keep it." Moonrat backed away. "You may need it worse than I do. I've got my knife."

The bird muttered, "Watch out."

"Are you joining me?" The young man hesitated, torn between caution and hope. "In a way you already have. I realize that. You told me what Serval's been saying and gave me this. But are you willing to help me kill him?"

"That's it. That's it exactly." Moonrat moved to his left until he stood beneath the overhanging roof of a lightless house. "Won't you come over here, so we don't have to stand in the rain?"

"If you like." The young man joined him. "It doesn't bother me. Not tonight. It's as though I had a fire in me. The bird complains about it, though."

"Good bird." It shook itself, and aired out its feathers as all birds do when they wish to be warmer.

"Can I ask you something?" Hesitantly, Moonrat took the young man by the sleeve.

"If I may ask a question of my own in return."

"I—I've been following you. Not ever since I gave you my gun, I went away then. I didn't want him to see me. But I started back when I heard the shot."

"I understand."

"You were gone by then, and your bird was pecking at Bushdog's. . . . At his face. So I was sure you were going to Serval's, so I ran down the street to catch up to you. Maybe you didn't hear me, because of the storm."

"I didn't," the young man said.

"Then your bird flew past and lit on your shoulder, and a girl was with you, walking beside you. The—your bird had brought her. That was what it seemed like."

"Lily's ghost?" The young man was silent, pensive.

"I don't think so." Moonrat's voice quavered. "I've seen Lily, you know? Around town sometimes with you. It didn't look like her. Not—not at all like Lily."

"I wish I'd seen her." The young man might not have heard him.

"You had to. She was right beside you. In the, you know, the lightning flashes I could see her better than I can see you right now. I wanted to ask who she was."

"*Scylla.*" That was the bird. And not the bird.

"I didn't see her," the young man declared, "and in fact, I don't believe you. She was beside me, when the bird was on my shoulder, and you were running up behind us?"

He sensed rather than saw Moonrat's nod.

"Well, what happened to her?"

"I don't know. She wasn't with you when I got to you."

The young man shook himself, perhaps from cold, possibly in unconscious imitation of the bird. "We're wasting time. "Where does Serval live? I want to get this over."

"I'll show you." Moonrat stepped out into the rain once more. "I'm going to go with you, and—and help out, if that's all right."

They pounded on the door; and when Serval answered it, the young man put his hook around Serval's neck and jerked him out into the storm, then knocked him down with the steel back of it. A woman screamed inside. A moment after Moonrat had closed the door, they heard the clank of a heavy bar dropped into place.

"You killed Lily," the young man told Serval. "You raped her, and then you killed her." He had passed his gaff to Moonrat, and he held Moonrat's slug gun so that Serval could see the pit of oblivion that was its muzzle.

"Shoot," Moonrat whispered, and the bird took up the word, croaking, "Shoot! Shoot!"

Serval himself said nothing, wiping mud from his eyes and cheeks, then rising slowly and cautiously. He had been holding a poker when the young man's hook had caught him, but that had vanished into the mud.

"Since you killed her," the young man said, "I think it only fitting that you help me give her a proper burial. If you do it, I suppose it's conceivable that I may not be able to bring myself to kill you."

Serval cleared his throat and spat, taking a half step backward toward the door, as if he expected it to open behind him.

"Shoot!" the bird urged, and lightning lit the street. Serval looked at Moonrat, whose gray steel blade seemed almost to glow in the flash.

"Refuse," the young man urged him as the thunder died away. "Why don't you refuse and make it easy for me?"

"I got to go in and get my clothes." Save for mud that the rain was quickly washing from his body, Serval was naked.

"No." The young man shook his head. "Do you refuse?"

"I'll do it. What do I have to do?"

"How did you dispose of Lily's body? You seem to have told the rest of the town, so tell me."

"There's a pond in the woods." Serval's voice was husky, his eyes upon the muzzle of the slug gun, though it was almost invisible in the dark and the rain. "We threw it in, then we threw rocks and stuff at it till it sank."

"Take us there," the young man said.

"If I do—"

"Take us!"

When the town was behind them, and the roar of countless raindrops upon uncounted millions of leaves filled their ears, Serval said, "I didn't kill her. You know?"

The young man said nothing.

"You know?" Serval repeated. "I didn't have her neither."

"You said you did last night in the Keg and Barrel."

"In the cock and bull, you mean." Serval actually sounded chastened. "I couldn't say I didn't, you know?"

"Bad man!" the bird declared damply, and clacked its bill for emphasis.

The young man remained silent; so did Moonrat.

"Listen. If I'd had her, would I pay that little slut Foxglove tonight? That was who it was with me back there in my place. You must have heard her."

Moonrat urged Serval forward with the butt of the young man's gaff.

"I tried, all right? I tried, and I held one leg for the other culls. But she was about dead already, 'cause somebody'd put his knife in her, you know? So I couldn't. It wasn't, you know, fun no more."

"Had it ever been fun for Lily?" the young man asked him. "Say yes, and die."

Serval did not.

"Who were those others? You said you held one of her legs for them. Who were they?"

Moonrat said loudly, "You might as well tell him. They're already dead, both of them. He killed them."

Lightning showed the rain-whipped pool gleaming like a mirror through the trees.

"Why do I have to I tell him, then? He knows."

"Yes," the young man said. "I know." He fingered the cracked fore-end of the slug gun. "Give him my gaff, Moonrat."

Moonrat passed the pole and its cruel-looking hook to Serval, saying, "Here. This did for Marten."

The young man nodded. "Go to the water. You threw Lily into it. Now you can fish her out."

Serval went, and the bird flew after him, alighting upon the half-submerged log it remembered. The rain was no longer quite so violent, it decided; still it longed for the heat and cheer of the tavern fire, and the dry and smoky room with food on half a dozen tables. "Here girl," it told Serval loudly. "Girl wet."

Serval looked at it incredulously, then returned to groping with the hooked gaff in a part of the pool far from its perch.

"Girl here!" the bird insisted. "Wet girl!" Its bill snapped with impatience. "Here! Here! Bird say!"

Stepping into the shallows, the young man poked Serval's back with the muzzle of the slug gun. "Go over there and have a look."

Sullenly, Serval waded out to the bird's half-submerged log.

"Good! Good!" Excited, the bird flapped its wings, hopping up from the log itself to a stub that protruded from it. "Girl here!"

The steel hook splashed, and the pole stirred the black waters of the pool. For the young man waiting upon the bank, the seconds plodded past like so many dripping pack mules, laboring mules carrying the universe to eternity, bit by bit.

By a final effort of the dying storm, lightning struck a dead tree on the far side of the pool, exploding it like a bomb and setting its ruins ablaze; and Serval screamed, turned, and fled, splashing through the shallows and slipping in the mud, but virtually invisible to all but the bird, who squawked and whistled, and whooped, "Man run! Bad man! Shoot! Shoot!"

The young man jerked back the slide of the slug gun, pulling harder than necessary because of his inexperience, then ramming it forward again, hearing the bolt thud and snick into place as it pushed a fresh cartridge into the chamber and locked up.

As if by the gun's own volition, the butt was tight against the hollow of his shoulder. He fired at a shadow and a sound, the flash from the muzzle lighting up the rain-dotted pool as the lighting had, and vanishing as quickly.

Serval shrieked with pain, and the young man nodded to himself, cycling the slide once more while he wondered vaguely just how many cartridges a slug gun held, and how many had been in this one when Moonrat had given it to him.

"You got him!" Moonrat slapped him on the back.

"I doubt that he's dead," the young man said. "I couldn't see him that well. In fact, I couldn't see him very well at all."

"Bird see!"

The young man nodded to the bird as though it were a person. "No doubt you did. Your eyes are much better than my own, I'm sure."

"Eyes good!"

"He eats them," the young man told Moonrat conversationally. "He ate Marten's, I believe, and from what you said, I would imagine that he ate Bushdog's, too."

Moonrat said, "I wonder what got into him. Into Serval, I mean."

"See girl," the bird informed them. "Arm girl."

The young man nodded, mostly to himself. "Lily's body is there. It has to be. He must have brought it to the surface just as the lightning struck. It was too much for his nerves."

"I don't think you killed him either." Moonrat's knife was out. "If you didn't, I'll finish him for you."

"Wait just a moment." The young man caught him by the elbow.

"You better let me go, Starling." Moonrat tried to shake free of his grasp. "He may not be dead."

"I'm sure he's not." Smoky flames from the burning tree illuminated a smiling face in which nothing at all could be read. "If he were dead the bird would know, and it would have gone for his eyes."

"No dead," the bird confirmed.

"But he's unarmed and wounded, and he's seen her face, down there in the water. I'll get him tomorrow. Or the day after that, or perhaps the day after that. Possibly Lily's brothers may get him first. Her brothers or her father. He'll realize that, when he's had time to think. He'll run, or barricade himself in his house with a slug gun. But we'll get him."

"I'll get him *now*," Moonrat declared.

"No." The young man released Moonrat's arm and held out his hand. "Give me your knife."

Moonrat hesitated.

"Give it to me. I want to see it."

Reluctantly, Moonrat handed it over. A flip of the young man's hand sent it spinning away to raise a splash in the middle of the pool.

"Now I want you to find Lily and bring her out," the young man said. "I think he dropped my gaff. The weight of the hook will have sunk it, but the handle will be standing straight up in the water, or nearly. It shouldn't be hard to find."

"Wet girl," the bird explained.

Moonrat started to speak, bit it back, and substituted, "All right if I take off my boots?"

Leveling the slug gun, the young man shook his head.

"Have knife," the bird announced. It had not intended to announce that; but it was true, and the bird was glad afterward that it had said it.

"In his boot." The young man nodded and smiled, smelling the rain and the wood smoke from the burning tree, and still practically unaware of the scene this combination of odors would invariably summon from memory as the years passed.

"In boot!"

"It may remain there. Go get her, Moonrat." The young man's finger tightened on the trigger. "Go now."

Moonrat waded out, ankle deep, knee deep, and at last waist deep in the pool. After half a minute he found the gaff and held it up for the young man to see. By that time it had nearly stopped raining, although the sky was still dark.

"Moonrat."

"What is it?" Moonrat's voice was sullen, his face expressionless.

"The end of the hook is very sharp. Try not to stab her with it, please."

If Moonrat nodded, it was too small and slight a nod to be seen.

When Lily's body lay on the sodden leaves, the young man ordered Moonrat back into the pool, leaned his slug gun against a white willow, and covered Lily with his tunic. She had been small, and his tunic reached—mercifully—from the top of her forehead to a point just below her naked loins.

When the young man picked up his slug gun again, Moonrat asked, "Can I get out of here now?"

The young man said nothing, wondering again whether there was a cartridge in the chamber. He pressed the slide lock and opened the action a little, but the faint light from the east was not sufficient to let him see the cartridge, if there was one. His fingertips found it, and he closed the action again.

"I won't go after Serval if you don't want me to." Moonrat took a tentative step toward the still-smoldering tree.

"I thought you might want to tell me about it," the young man said. His tone was almost conversational.

"What?"

"About raping Lily, and about killing her."

Moonrat said nothing.

"Bad man!" the bird announced virtuously.

"You couldn't be convicted in court unless Serval talks, and that may be the chief reason I'm going to kill you here and now. It may be. I can't be sure."

"I didn't."

There had been a tremor in Moonrat's voice, and something in the young man sang at the sound of it. "There were four of you. There had to be, because neither Marten nor Bushdog had scratched faces. Shall I tell you about that?"

The bird urged, "Man talk!"

"All right, I will. Serval said that he held a leg while the others raped her. Someone else, clearly, held her other leg, and there must also have been a third man holding her hands. Otherwise there would have been scratches, as I said. I got a good look at Marten when he was sitting at a table with a candle on it, and an even better look at Bushdog in the tavern. And neither of them had scratches or bruises. So there were four of you. At least four. Now do you want to tell me about it?"

Moonrat said, "No."

"I'm not going to let you pray or plead, or anything of that foolish kind. But if you'll confess—if you'll tell me in detail, and truthfully, just what you and the rest did and why you did it—you'll have those added minutes of life."

"No," Moonrat repeated.

"Man talk!" This time the bird was addressing Moonrat.

"Someone might come by while you're talking. You might be saved. You should think about that."

Moonrat was silent, possibly thinking.

"You were very, very anxious to help me—"

"I'm your friend!"

The young man shrugged and raised his slug gun, squinting down the barrel at the front sight and a trifle surprised to discover that there was light enough for him to see it. "You're an acquaintance. You came to me—so did Caracal—to tell me that Serval had been boasting about . . . about what you did. But you knew a lot more than Caracal did, or at least a lot more than he told me." The young man lowered the slug gun. Not yet.

"I said what Serval'd said." Moonrat sounded less than confident.

"Bad man!" The bird was cocksure. "Shoot! Shoot!"

"Soon," the young man promised, and spoke to Moonrat again. "Caracal only said that he had boasted of doing it. You said he had named Marten and Bushdog, and you even knew where they had disposed of Lily's body, and were able to tell me accurately enough for me to find the place—this pond. Do you want to hear some more?"

Moonrat shook his head, and the young man noted with some slight surprise he stood shoulder deep in the water—if indeed he were standing.

"Well, I do. I'm marshaling all my arguments, you see, so I can pardon myself afterward for having killed you, even though I've killed Marten and Bushdog already. Or perhaps I'm merely looking for a reason to let you run like Serval. You're planning to duck under the water when I'm about to fire, aren't you?"

Moonrat shook his head.

"No. Of course not. Well, we'll soon find out. Whcrc was I?"

"Say name," the bird prompted him; and it seemed to Moonrat, although only very briefly, that the woman of many arms whom he had seen earlier was standing in the water beside the log upon which the bird perched.

"I had finished with that." The young man was silent for a moment, thinking. "When I looked through the window of the house where I found Marten, I saw Lacewing and his brother Locust, and Lacewing's girl Gillyflower. They were sitting around a table talking to Marten, or perhaps playing some gambling game. There was a slug gun with a cracked fore-end in a corner. I assumed that was Lacewing's, and even imagined him coming out and killing me with it. He didn't, but later you gave me that same gun, so that I would kill Bushdog."

"I was trying to help you," Moonrat muttered, "so that doesn't prove anything."

"I didn't say I could prove anything," the young man replied. His tones were reasonable, his eyes wholly insane. "But then I don't have to prove, do I? I know." He sighted along the barrel. The pool was awash in gray light now, and tendrils of mist snaked upward from its surface.

"I wanted to be friends," Moonrat repeated stubbornly.

"You wanted someone else to commit your murders," the young man told him, "and you found me. Serval was talking, and even if he hadn't named you—or Marten or Bushdog—you knew that Lily's brothers would beat your name out of him. Then you would die. So you gave me their names and told me where her body was, thus establishing what we pettifoggers call a presumption of innocence. Where were you when I hooked Marten? Relieving yourself?"

"Watch out," the bird muttered, and snapped its bill. More forcefully it repeated, *"Watch out!"* Moonrat was straightening up or standing up, his torso emerging from the water until the ripples were scarcely higher than his waist.

"Before I killed Bushdog he cried out for help," the young man said. "Kob's tavern was full because of the fair, and I thought he was calling on the drinkers in there. But you were watching, at least in the beginning, and he had seen you and was calling to you, pleading for you to help him before I took his life. You'd been his friend, and he thought you'd come to his rescue. On whom will you call, Moonrat?"

Moonrat's hand and Moonrat's knife leaped from the water like fish, and the slug gun boomed.

The knife flashed past the young man's ear to thud against a tree behind him.

Moonrat's throw continued, his arm preceding his face, until he lay, as it were, upon the dark, mist-shrouded water, his legs still sunk by the weight of his boots. The bird left its log to fly out to the corpse and perch upon the back of its head, claws gripping its hair.

"No eyes for you," the young man said. "Get off there."

"All right." The bird regarded him with an intelligence that seemed almost human and flew to the overhanging limb of a threadwood tree. "No eat."

Recalling his sandwich, the young man took it from his pocket and unwrapped it again. The bread was torn and crumbled, but the meat remained largely intact. "Here, you can have this. But no eyes, understand?"

"Good, good!"

The bird was eyeing the sandwich, and the young man stepped away from it. "Take it and go. Take whatever you want—but after that you have to go back to wherever it is you come from, or keep on going to wherever you were going when you saw me. Understand?"

"Like bird?"

"Yes, I do." The young man hesitated. "But I'm going to have to leave Lily here while I go to tell her father and her mother, and I won't leave her with you. Not as long as you're alive."

"Take meat?"

"Yes. You may take it and eat it, but then you must go. Don't come back, I warn you."

The bird dove toward the meat and snatched it up, rising in circles, higher and higher, with the meat still clamped in its bill. At length it found a favoring wind and flew northwest, apparently following the coast.

The young man watched it go, a winged dot of black against the morning sky, until wings and dot vanished. Then he propped Moonrat's slug gun against the bole of the tree Moonrat's knife had struck and began to walk, wondering as he walked just how much of the life he had known might be salvaged, and how much, in addition to Lily, was gone forever.

The Wrapper

✦

It was so nice to see it again, the little meadows fenced with the walls of dry-laid fieldstones, and the architectural woods—big gray trees like columns written over with hieroglyphics. And the huts and little church, all thatch and sticks plastered over with mud, like muddy little mushrooms the trees let live there.

Before I went to sleep last night, I tried to remember as much as I could, scared I might forget it all. *Knowing* I will forget it all in a year or so, pretty soon after I have talked myself into thinking it was just a dream. That is why I am writing this. I am going to keep this on my hard disk, print out a copy for my desk, and back everything up.

This was real.

It started on Saturday when I took Joan to dinner. Joan used to work at Botha, too. She works at another company now, but we still get together about twice a month. There was a time when I thought I might marry Joan, and I think there was one when Joan thought she might marry me. But it was not the same time, if you know what I mean.

Let me start over, because this is really going off in the wrong direction. It began when the Zuccharas moved in across the hall. Not that I noticed them particularly either way. Mister is short and wide, with a big black mustache. Mrs. Dent says he is a chef, but that may not be right. He does not get drunk or want to talk, so that was all right with me. It still is.

Mrs. Z. is short and wide, too. Her mustache is smaller and she has about ten black dresses all pretty much alike. She wants to talk, but only to other women in the building, which suits me. They go to church a lot, I suppose to mass. They are the sort of people you imagine bowing down to a crucifix, and I guess they do. Well, why not? Mister wears a fresh carnation in his lapel when they go to church, and I like that.

Angelo never goes with them, though. It was a while before I noticed that.

Angelo is their son, about six. You are not supposed to have kids in this building, but I guess the Zuccharas know somebody. Or they could be related to the owners or something like that. Anyway, they seem to have gotten a variance or whatever you call it. An exemption?

Whatever.

I remember the first time I saw Angelo. I thought oh my God don't buy him a drum. But Angelo is a quiet kid, really. He is even quiet when his folks are away at church. Or more likely he is not in there. She probably takes him to stay with somebody else before they go. Like maybe Mister is her second, and her first is Angelo's father, and he takes him when it is not convenient for her to. Anyway, Angelo does not look much like them. He has that dark skin or anyway a wonderful tan, but he is blond. If Mrs. Z. is really his mother, there is just no way Mister can be the father.

Maybe Angelo is adopted.

One day I saw him playing in the hallway, and I sort of grinned at him. He said, "Hi," and started to grin back, but then he stopped and stared at me. He has these beautiful blue eyes about as big as jawbreakers. When Angelo stares at you, you know you have been stared at.

I said something to show I was not somebody he had to be scared of, and after that I would talk to him a little every time I saw him, which was about once a week. That is how I found out his name, and I saw him going into the place across the hall two/three times so I know that is where he lives.

Then Saturday night after I took Joan back to her place I guess I did not push my door all the way closed or put on the night bolt either. I logged on and was checking out my e-mail, and here was Angelo, right at my elbow and sort of reading over my shoulder. I said hello and how are you doing, and all that, because what would be the use of me being mad? Angelo is just a little kid and did not mean any harm or he would not have let me see him like that. I was his friend, wasn't I? So I would not be mad if he came for a visit.

We talked a little bit and I showed him some of my e-mail and tried to explain the difference between a computer screen and a TV. Then I remembered that the waiter had left a piece of candy for Joan on top of our bill, only she had not wanted it. She never does eat anything like that, and I stuck it in my pocket.

So I got it out and gave it to Angelo. He said, "Thank you," very polite and unwrapped it and put it in his mouth, and said "Thank you" again. After that I went to one of the tech boards where I knew they would be talking about automated sailing ships, something that interests me quite a lot.

It went on like that for quite a while and pretty soon it hit home to me that it was getting really late and Angelo ought to be home in bed. I looked around for him and he was over at the window looking down at the parked cars, only he was looking at them through the candy wrapper. Then he turned around and looked at the table lamp through it like that was really, really interesting. And after that he sort of smiled and gave it to me.

I put it up to my eyes like he had and looked at the screen.

This is where I have a really hard time. Because I want to say what it was I saw through the wrapper, and I want to say it so you will know (you being me five or ten years from now) what it was I saw. Only I want to say it so you will know that I did and this is not just some bullshit. That is going to be hard.

Here goes. It was a book, the biggest book anybody ever saw, bigger than I am. Taller, I mean. And wide, those pages must have been four or five feet across. It was open on a sort of a stand, and there were pictures and that business where the first letter is sort of a picture, too, like an *M* was two naked men carrying a naked girl like she was dead or had passed out.

I started reading and looking at the pictures, and there was no way you could read it all, it just went on and on without me ever turning the page, and after a while it sort of came to me that whatever I wanted to read was written on there someplace, high-tech, low-tech, you name it. There were circuits there that did things I had never thought of or read about anywhere, with little people in the drawings to point out the best parts, the kind of thing nobody has done for about five hundred years, and there was a poem next to one that made me feel like I'd spent my whole life at sea the way I used to want to. Lots of sex, too, and hunting lions with a spear. All kinds of stuff.

Anything I wanted to read about.

Anything.

This is another hard part. I do not want to write it, and I know that's going to make it hard for me to write it the way it really happened. I set the wrapper down, eventually, and looked around for Angelo, but he was gone.

Without looking through the wrapper, my PC was just my PC again. I thought about that, but to tell you the truth I was too dumb to be scared. I should have been, but I just kept trying to figure it out. I got up for a while and walked around, but that did not help either. Angelo had gone out and closed the door quietly behind him like a nice kid.

I think he really is one, too, even if his eyes do make me nervous.

He was not out in the hall playing, either. I thought about calling over to his parents, but how would it have looked, a grown man calling up to ask about their little boy at that time of night?

Finally I sat down here again and smoothed out the candy wrapper (it was sort of light-red-colored, more of a rose red than a pink) and picked it up and looked through. And there was the big book again, with everything (really everything!) written on just those two pages. My right hand kept the wrapper up in front of my eyes, and with my left I reached out to feel the computer.

That is when I got the surprise of my life, because what I felt was the big book. The boards were covered with leather like the oiled leather of a baseball glove, soft but strong, and there seemed to be actual wood underneath that. The pages felt like the head of a drum, except not stretched tight. I picked up the corner of one.

Wow, I thought. *Wow!*

I still think wow.

I took the wrapper away and looked at my hand, and it was touching the screen. That's when I started to be really scared. I put the wrapper on top of a box I keep floppies in and tried to think, but I never found a lot to think about. Not right then, and not anytime that night. I guess I was in shock.

Here I would like to start, "Next day at work—" Only I know not, because that was Saturday night. So there is Sunday there, and I do not know anymore what I did. I know I never did look through the wrapper again though, or even touch it.

Monday at work I tried to remember one of those circuits and draw it out. There were parts of it I could get and parts I could not. That night you would think I would have looked again, but I was afraid to touch the wrapper. I remember sitting in my living room making sketches and deleting them, and staring at it. I never picked it up.

Wednesday I got the circuit right, I think. I took the printout in to Mr. Koch and told him what I think they will do, which is hunt for an idea instead of words. I remember exactly what I said, "Put together a couple hundred of these, and you could say get everything about going crazy and it would get you all that, *The Man Who Mistook His Wife for a Hat* and all the rest of that stuff."

Mr. Koch looked at my circuit for a long time, then he said, "I'm going to have to study this. I'll get back to you." Just before quitting time, he gave me back my printout and said, "Either you're the biggest screwball anybody ever saw or you're a frigging genius. We're going to have to build some." (He said "frigging" because Dot and Sally were both listening.)

So after work I was not afraid of the wrapper anymore, or anyway not as much. When I got home I went over to the window and looked out, and it was not quite dark yet.

The thing was that when I had looked at the book, not the first time but the other one, I tried to turn the page. And I lost my nerve and could not do it. I have never thought I was a hero or anything, but that made me feel really scuzzy. So this time I decided I would not even look at my computer like before, I would look outside at the lawn and the parking lot.

I picked the wrapper up and carried it over carefully and got it with both hands and held it up to my eyes. That is when I saw those fields and the woods I told you about. It was like I was up in a tower, or it could have been floating over them like in a balloon.

I do not know.

It was beautiful, so beautiful it sort of caught inside my chest and I thought for a minute I might die. I kept telling myself I had to put the wrapper down, and finally I did, and after that I just sort of sat down and thought.

Then I went out to the Greek place and ate dinner, and thought some more. I swear I do not even remember what I had. Probably the moussaka.

The thing was, it was real. I kept on coming back to that. When I had reached out and touched it, the book was what I had felt. That big book, not my screen. It had only felt like my screen when I took the wrapper away. So it was real, what I saw through the wrapper. And I kept on thinking about his eyes.

This is really crazy, as crazy as those books I got from the library. I should not put it in, but if you have read this far why not?

The whole universe is *around* that wrapper.

Suppose the universe is infinite, which is what somebody said in *Scientific American*. If it is, then "middle" is just a way of thinking about it, a reference point, and we can put the middle anyplace that is convenient. One might be handier than all the others, but it really does not matter except for simplifying your equations.

So that wrapper is the middle as much as anyplace else is. But if it is the middle, you can say it is wrapping the whole universe. You define "in" as away from the wrapper, if the wrapper is the middle.

So if you are inside, in the candy, and you look through the wrapper— well, you see what I mean? Angelo is the one who gets to draw the axes, the crossing lines to measure from. He is the one who gets to say what the middle is.

I do not know why.

I thought about a lot of other stuff in the Greek place, but every time I try to write it down, I end up writing about his eyes. I have deleted a lot of that.

Like when I was looking out at the forest again just like it used to be, and it was night and I could see the windows of a little house over here and another one over there, little round windows as yellow as butter, and the trees great big shadows. I kept thinking how his eyes looked like eggs, like the blue eggs of some bird that does not have a name but nests in those trees or even around those little houses in under the thatch.

The next day, I guess that was Thursday, I tried to tell Sally just a little bit, just a hint like, and pretty soon I could see she thought I was nuts and she was trying to get away from me. So I went to Buck. Buck's about as good a friend as I have at work or anyplace, but he laughed at me. It was not friendly laughter, if you know what I mean. It was like the people in the crowd laugh in that movie *Freak Show,* and after that I called Joan.

I went home feeling really, really down. For a long time I just sort of walked around—living room, bedroom, kitchen, and living room again. Every time I saw the wrapper I started wondering all over again if it was real. Finally I went to the window and held it up like before.

(I have got to write this, or none of it will make any sense.)

It was already pretty dark, but down below me there were people dancing. I think they were singing, too, and dancing to their own singing, but I could not see them very well and I could not hear anything at all through the wrapper. I never could.

One of them looked up and saw me.

I swear she did.

She saw me and stopped singing for a minute and smiled. After that she looked at me every time the dance came around. This was not Joan, naturally, but her face made me think of Joan the way she used to be about five years ago. She was a lot thinner than Joan and probably quite a bit younger. Her smile was sort of like Angelo's eyes.

And that was when I did it. I took down the wrapper and crumpled it up into a little tiny wad, and then I opened the window and threw it out.

I think the wind must have caught it and blown it a long way away.

The thing was I did not want to be crazy, and I knew Sally thought I was and she was going to tell everybody. And the more I looked, the more different from them I was going to get, even if I was not crazy. I would be a grown-up man carrying around a little square of red plastic wrapper and looking through it all the time. It would be the same as crazy, there would be no difference at all.

Sooner or later somebody would try to take it away from me. That is what I thought, and I would yell and fight until they locked me up.

Because it was something I saw when I was just a little kid, not any bigger than Angelo is. I do not know where, but I saw it a long time ago.

For about a week I tried to forget it, but after that I was down on my knees looking through the grass everywhere and in the gutter and the cracks in the sidewalk, anyplace I could think of. If anybody asked, I was going to say I lost a contact lens. But nobody did.

Yesterday I stopped Angelo's dad in the hall and tried to talk to him, but he said his wife was sick and he had to get her prescription filled. I do not think he would have told me anything anyway. I thought Mrs. Dent would know where Angelo is because she seems to know everything, but she just said there are no children in our building and he must have been a visitor.

So here is what I did.

I bought a lot of candy, all different kinds but all of them with different-colored wrappers about like that one. I carry some in my jacket pocket, and here in the apartment I have bowls of it all over. I used to lock my door as soon as I got home, but I do not anymore. I do not even close it all the way until I go to bed.

Because you don't have to have just one middle, one place where the vertical axis crosses the horizontal like you have in high school. You can have two or three or four sets of axes, if you want to. There are formulas that will let you transfer from one set to another.

One day pretty soon I will see him again, probably this week. And I am going to hold out one of the bowls or a piece out of my pocket and say, "Hello there, Angelo. Would you like some more candy?"

(I will write it all down next time, everything he says and everything that I say, too. Everything that happens.)

He will look up then with those wonderful, scary eyes he has. What is he going to say to me, I wonder? Will he leave me the new wrapper?

Most of all, I wonder what it is he sees when he looks through me.

A Traveler in
Desert Lands

✦

He, coming up from the south as fate would have it, chanced to see a woman with a water jar upon her head. He was a courteous man, and sorely thirsty; tapping the knees of his camel, he made it crouch in the soft and shifting dust of the lost town of the dead before he asked for a drink.

"You would honor me by drinking," the woman with the jar said, "and by filling whatever skins and bottles you may have. If you empty my jar," her face convulsed as if to dislodge some brass-backed carrion fly that none but she could see, "it is a matter of no moment, for I can easily refill it at our well."

The traveler accepted the jar (which was gray-green and of ancient appearance) from her hands, put it to his lips, and slaked his thirst, drinking deep. When at last he returned it to her half emptied, he said, "I have five large canteens, and would like to water my camel, if that is permissible. If you will show me where your well is, I will take care of these things myself."

Replacing the jar upon her head, the woman nodded, turned without a word, and walked away. She was a very tall woman, both slender and emaciated, and there had been (the traveler thought) a touch of fever in her eyes.

The camel rose as though it knew what was expected of it, having caught the scent of water; it followed the woman, its head swaying to left and right as it contemplated bleak streets of tombs with arrogant eyes.

From its back, the traveler regarded them with less hauteur and more curiosity. Some remained sealed—or so it appeared. Others had clearly been broken into, looted, and abandoned. Still others gave evidence of habitation; and at the door of one he saw an old man seated, his dusty cheeks streaked with tears and his raddled face stamped with grief. The woman with the water jar halted to speak to this old man, though the traveler could not hear what she said; the old man nodded in response, his face perhaps a trifle less hopeless than it had been.

As for the traveler, he was tasting again the water he had drunk, now that it was down. It had no ill taste, and yet it seemed to him that its savor was of time immemorial. *By rains and a thousand wild winds I have been distilled from the blood of dragons,* the water seemed to say, *blood shed before the Lands of Man foundered. Ten thousand years I waited glacier-locked. I have washed the dead faces of a man whose spear was tipped with jasper and a woman whose god was a speaking tree.*

The traveler shook his head to clear it of such fancies. Where there were tombs and men who robbed them, there might be silver and gold besides, necklaces of emeralds and torques starry with opals. The thought revived him more, even, than the water had—for the traveler had been born of woman and suckled at the breast, and like all the breed was in need of money. "I might trade with them," he told himself, "or if needs must, they might make me a present to go away." And he patted the fantastically wrought-iron buttplate of the long-barreled jezail that reposed in a fringed rifle-boot to the right of his camel's saddle.

Meanwhile the woman with the jar had halted beside a stone trough some distance ahead; she pointed to the trough and emptied her jar into it, then indicated the mouth of a pit some score of strides beyond. "Your camel must drink here," she said, "for he could not descend our steps. You and I will go down together, if that suits you. I will refill my jar there, and there you may fill the containers you mentioned."

The traveler made his camel kneel, which was difficult with water so near, and dismounted. It rose again—tail first after the manner of all camels—as soon as he and his canteens were off its back, and hurried to the trough.

"Be careful on the steps," the woman with the jar cautioned the traveler, and she herself led the way down, descending more swiftly than he dared along a steep and narrow stair without a railing that circled the pit.

He wished to speak to her, to thank her profusely for her generosity and assistance, and to question her regarding the living inhabitants of the lost town of the dead, their wealth, numbers, and weapons; but the terror of the desert well (whose steps had been dished and broken by generations of thirsty feet, and whose twilight closed more securely about him with each such step he dared) held him silent; the capacious leathern flasks with which he was festooned obstructed him, chill vapors from the pool below intoxicated him, and the iron tip of his yataghan's sheath scraped soil as dry as gunpowder from the wall of earth to his left. He, looking to see whence it came before the light vanished altogether, beheld bones, ancient and blackened with niter.

The voice of the woman with the jar floated up from depths unguessed. "Here you may fill your containers, with a thousand more and you had them."

He clattered and scraped in pursuit of her words, and came to her nearly falling.

"You will find it a weary climb with your water." Her dusky wrappings rustled like dead leaves as she knelt; he heard the rush and gurgle of precious water as she refilled her jar.

He knelt beside her, his knees on cold clay. His questing fingers quickly found the water, and he asked, "Does it never drop lower than this?"

"No," she said.

"Nor rise higher?"

"No."

The traveler sought to recall her face. It had been long, certainly—a high, narrow forehead, close-set eyes yet large eyes, too, and lustrous. Long, flat cheeks, a slit of mouth that betrayed the teeth behind it, small nose, long upper lip, the chin prominent yet rounded. A face, he thought, past the first flush of youth but not altogether uncomely. By no means ugly or even homely, that face.

"You run a risk," he said, "going alone into such a place as this with a stranger." He divested himself of the first of his canteens and opened it.

"Understand that you are in no danger from me. I will not force you, nor do you any other harm."

"Alas."

The traveler thought her joking, although there had been no laughter in her voice; he thrust his canteen beneath the surface, and its burbling there was music beyond the skill of men. "I will have to empty all these into the trough to satisfy my camel," the traveler told her. "Then I must return to fill them again for myself. You need not accompany me." Too late it occurred to him that the old man he had seen—or some other— might be looking into his saddlebags at that very moment, that the jezail might be slung across another's back already, its horn of powder and the little bag of leaden balls bumping some other's thigh. He shrugged. At present, there was nothing to be done.

"I will accompany you if you will permit me first to deliver my jar of water to the house in which I dwell," the woman with the water jar promised. "I will carry three of your containers then, if you yourself will take the two that will remain."

"No, no," the traveler said. "I could not let you bear more weight than I."

"You have much else to carry."

By this time his eyes had fitted themselves to the darkness of the well; he saw her raise her jar, heavy again with water, and place it upon her head as before. The rectangle of daylight above them seemed very bright but very far as she began the slow ascent of the spiraling stair.

"Will you stay in our town tonight?"

"Yes, if you will allow it. I will buy food here, if I can." Frightful thoughts thronged his mind, but he said bravely, "Your people must have food."

"Goats," she told him. Her head did not turn as she spoke, though one long, graceful arm reached up to her water jar. "We have goats' flesh to trade, fresh or smoked. Sheep do not thrive here."

"I would not expect them to." He was filling the last of his canteens, and thought privately that nothing could be expected to thrive in such a place. Not sheep, not goats, not people, not even hyenas.

"We have goat cheese, too. Radishes, and a few other vegetables."

He stopped his last canteen, rose, and started after her.

The woman with the jar said, "I will show you a place where you can stable your camel, and the house where you can stay."

"I had hoped to stay in yours," he told her.

"It is our law."

"I have a tent," he said.

"But if you wish it I will be there as well."

His camel had emptied the trough. He poured the contents of all five canteens into it, and when the camel had began to drink again knelt to examine the carved and fretted stone-work of the sides and ends. Hooded figures walked with downcast faces there. There were garlands of rue and mandragora, and a god crowned with lightnings wept. "This is—was—a sarcophagus," he said. The woman with the water jar had already walked too far to hear him, or perhaps it was only that she made no reply, or that he failed to hear such reply as she made. He hurried after her.

Down one street of tombs and up another, and another, he pursued her, sweating through the dust stirred by his own boots, though the Sun was low and the swift chill of night had a foot in the stirrup.

At length she halted before a tomb somewhat larger than most. "This is where I live." She took the water jar from her head.

A second woman, somewhat smaller, possibly a year or two younger, appeared in the doorway.

"This is my sister Ahool."

"Welcome to our house," the sister said. Beyond the dim doorway, the traveler beheld a shelf upon which stood rows of gray-green jars yet sealed.

"We are not going into the house," the woman who had carried the jar told her sister. "We will return to the well. Then I shall show him where he can stay. You are not to follow us."

The sister eyed the traveler sidelong. "If you wish it," she said, "I will be there."

They went by other streets, again passing the weeping old man. "This is where you will stay," the woman who had carried the jar told the traveler. "Where you will eat."

The weeping old man did not look up at him; yet the traveler sensed that the old man's attention had flicked his face as one kills a fly with the lash.

"Has your camel drunk sufficiently?" the woman who had carried the jar asked as they approached the well again.

"Camels never get enough to drink," the traveler told her, "but I will water him again in the morning. That is one reason for my staying tonight."

"Am I another?" She had descended the first few steps, but she stopped to look back at him, her face twitching.

"What is one day more or less," he said, "when a lifetime would be insufficient to drink in your loveliness?"

Kneeling beside him in the darkness at the water's edge, she caught his hand. Her own was long and thin and hard, and telling of its bones, clawed, and hot as the hand of a woman who snatches fresh loaves out of the oven. "You fear you will have to take me with you," she said. "Two would greatly burden your camel."

He admitted it.

"I could run beside your camel like a wolf," she said, "but you will not have to take me with you." She steered his hand beneath the stained wrappings she wore until it cupped her breast. That firm breast was febrile and dry as the ashes from a forge, and it seemed almost that embers might linger in it, glowing and snapping.

As they carried his canteens back to the surface, the sister's hands caressed his back and slipped under the robe he wore, like two rats fashioned by a potter and hot from the kiln. "Linger," the sister murmured in his ear. "Linger a moment with me, Traveler. Taste my lips."

She remained behind in the darkness when they reached the surface. The Moon had risen, though the Sun had not yet set. The woman who had carried the jar prostrated herself and sang, saying when she rose, "This is our goddess, the white goddess of the bow. She comes to our town often, speaks to us, and gives us life—and the lives that come after life."

"In that case, the Sun must be your god," the traveler said. Privately, he wondered whether she knew her sister had followed them to the well, and how long the sister would remain there.

"Mahes, the Glaring Lion? Each month, when the bow of our goddess is strongest, we stone him. He is the Slayer of Men."

"Then you live in the houses he has provided."

After that the woman who had carried the jar said nothing until they came to the tomb before which the old man sat; there she led the way in, and the old man followed them. An old woman lay on the floor of the tomb with her face to the wall; the rasp of her breathing was like the slow cutting of a saw. "Here you will eat," the woman who had carried the water jar said.

With a nod, the old man added, "We hope to provide good fare for you."

"I must see to my camel," the traveler told them, for there was no food in evidence.

Outside again, he returned to the well. The sister had departed, or perhaps merely remained silent and unseen in the darkness there. Shrugging, he led his camel to a piece of level ground a hundred paces or so from the lost town of the dead and tethered it, unloaded it, and erected his tent. The powder in his jezail was fresh, he knew; but he opened the flash pan to make certain that the powder there was fine and dry, resealed the flash pan with wax, and pulled the hammer to full cock.

Then, slinging his jezail behind his back, he returned to the tomb before which the old man had sat. Both women were seated in the dust before it, and they (or perhaps the old man) had kindled a fire. Inside the old woman lay, the sibilation of her struggle for breath echoing and re-echoing in the stone chamber. "I would like to trade for food now," the traveler announced to the woman who had carried the water jar.

Her sister said, "You must ask our father," and both nodded.

The Sun, which had already crept far down the sky, hid his glaring eye behind the distant tombs on the hillside. Naked boys with sticks drove hurrying goats the length of the street, black, brown, and white. They vanished in the direction of the well.

The old man returned carrying a pot of blackened copper. From within the tomb he fetched a tripod of iron rods, which he erected over the fire, swinging the pot from a short chain at its apex. "I had hoped to have better fare for you," he said. "This is but goat's meat and turnips. Tomorrow we will have something better."

The two women nodded solemn confirmation, and the one who had carried the water jar glanced quickly toward the entrance of the tomb.

"If I can buy some food from you now," the traveler said, "there will be no need for me to remain here. I can leave in the morning. Your daughter told me that you might have dried meat for sale, or cheeses."

"Tomorrow I shall expound our beliefs to you." The old man might not have heard him. "Are you not a widely traveled man, blessed with an inquiring mind? You cannot but find them fascinating."

"I have a little jewelry to trade," the traveler told him, "but I feel confident you have much more than I, and better jewelry, too. Mine is only brass, but no doubt you have gold and gems, many truly precious things. I have spices as well—some very rare and valuable spices. If you could show me some of your jewelry, perhaps we might strike a bargain we would both consider advantageous."

"Spices?" Slowly the old man nodded. "Spices are good." He sighed. "Tomorrow. Tomorrow we will have better food to give you."

Both women turned their faces to the Moon and made it seated bows. Their right hands touched their lips, their left hands their stomachs.

That night in his tent, the traveler grew concerned about his camel, and after drawing his yataghan and testing the edge with his thumb, ventured out into the Moonlight to see to it. He found it on its feet, regarding him with rolling eyes; and although he poured out a little bag of spelt for it, it would not lower its head to eat.

When he had returned to the tent and sheathed his yataghan again, he stood perplexed for a moment, considering what else he might do. "I apprehend danger," he said to himself, "nor is the apprehension mere imagination. Horses, indeed, are creatures much given to fancies. Camels are not. I might saddle and load mine, and ride away—if I were not prevented. But I have ridden far already. My camel is near exhaustion, and so am I."

He pictured himself camping anew in the desert, all the weary business of unloading and erecting his tent a second time. By the time the poles were joined, the pegs driven, and the ropes tightened, night would be nearly spent.

And would it not be as dangerous to cross the desert by night as to remain where he was?

No, more dangerous. There might be lions or afrits. Wild lamias. Cruel witches and owl-eyed demons. Alfrs, fell spawn of dwarves and gods, and the long-legged hawks, too great to fly, that could outpace the swiftest stallion. Of necessity, he would camp in a waterless place, recalling the well of the lost town of the dead and the little copper pot of goat's flesh and turnips, and cursing himself for a fool.

Sitting upon his carpet, he pulled off his high-topped riding boots, rose, untied his sash, laid his yataghan beside his pallet and its piled blankets, removed his trousers, and blew out the lamp. Slipping into his bed, he found himself clasped by a woman so hot and lean and sere that she seemed almost a skeleton covered with parchment and animated by a fire behind her ribs.

One hand grasped his manhood; the other clasped him to her; she rubbed herself against him, cat-like and frantic, straddled his thigh, bit his shoulders, cheek, and neck. "Now!" Her spittle flew in his face. "I throb like a tymballa. Beat me! I steam, I smoke. Impale me upon your lance. Oh! Oh! Oh! *Oooooh!*"

With the last cry she was gone, howling and shrieking, his blankets hurled away and the flap of his tent thrown wide.

"It was the sister," the traveler told himself as he wiped a thick and reeking slime from his face, neck, and shoulders. "It can have been no other."

These thoughts he repeated to himself more than once that night as he lay listening to the howls and wails of many voices from the lost town of the dead. Trembling as he clasped his yataghan to him, he would repeat over and over that his visitor had been nothing more than the sister of the woman who had carried the water jar, a human woman whom he himself had beheld by daylight.

———

That woman and the woman who had carried the jar greeted the traveler the next evening before the tomb in which their father dwelt; and when he had returned their greetings and seated himself between them, the second remarked, "You slept late."

"He who cannot sleep by night must needs slumber by day," he replied.

The sister said, "Yet you are weary."

He nodded. "And you are not?"

"No."

The woman who had carried the jar smiled. "We, too, slept by day. Somewhat, at least."

"My camel had broken his tether and fled far from this place, whole leagues into the desert. Did you not know it?"

Both said that they had not, and the woman who had carried the jar added, "You must tether him more securely tonight."

The traveler felt a chill of dread. "I will endeavor to do so."

"You were fortunate to find him," the sister remarked.

"I was. But it is a weary business, recapturing a camel, when one is on foot."

"Doubtless it is," the woman who had borne the water jar conceded. "I have never done so, and for that favor thank the goddess." Some shading of her voice informed the traveler that her mention of her goddess had not been fortuitous.

"I might fetch my instrument and play and sing for you," the sister suggested.

"I have no doubt you play and sing charmingly," the traveler told her politely, "yet I would prefer to complete my business first. Then the three of us might make merry with whole hearts. I have brought samples of my spices in order that your father may examine them."

At these words, the old man thrust his head from the entrance of the tomb, saying, "You have brought your spices? That is well." He had vanished into the darkness within it before the traveler could reply.

"He is preparing our food." The face of the woman who had carried the jar writhed and twitched, but soon grew calm again. "Sumptuous Moon food, the sacred meal of our goddess, by which all share life."

"I could play my rebab for you," the sister suggested, "and sing of love while Heerhoor dances. She is a skillful dancer."

"Behold the length of these legs, Traveler." The woman who had carried the jar rose as a serpent uncoils and snatched to one side the rotting wrappings that served her for a skirt. "Behold also the length of my neck, the pride of our mother. I dance with cymbals of red gold on fingers and thumbs in the ancient manner, which in this degenerate time is called the Nautch of Necromancy, and is preserved in no other place."

The old man came out to join them, and the traveler, who by that time was anxious to change the topic of their conversation (and indeed to leave the place if he could with decency) asked, "Why have you no fire tonight? If lack of fuel prevents you, I will gladly collect as much as you require."

"What need of sticks and dry dung have we today?" the old man replied, and caught him by the sleeve. "You have brought your spices?"

"Small samples thereof," the traveler told him.

"Spices cannot be sampled unless they are consumed."

Reluctantly, the traveler agreed.

"Have you a spice for cold meats?"

"A most excellent one," the traveler declared, and produced a little vial of clear brown glass. "Herein are blended the peperi of ancient days, the black and the white, the pink, the red, and the green, confounded in strict accord with formulae renowned ere the foundations of my southern city of Mirouane were laid."

The old man displayed a clenched fist, breathed upon it, then opened it to reveal a massy gold ring set with a stone that blazed purple, then orange, in the level daylight. "This is the gem Hamalat," the old man confided. "The royal gem wrested from Mahes by the Moon. A thousand years it waited in the ruins of Endymion. Those who wear it can never suffer sunstroke or go blind. It has further powers in addition," his voice fell, "which I will confide to you only if you obtain it. The man who possessed it might soon shape a kingdom for himself."

"Then why have you not done so?" the traveler inquired, while greatly admiring the ring.

"I am glad you asked," the old man said, "and more glad still that you asked in my daughters' absence."

Looking about him then, the traveler realized for the first time that both women had left them.

"For it was only my devotion to our goddess that kept me here searching for it—and certain other things—and still more my wife's. If at midsummer you were to mount your camel and pursue the Moon across the sky, you would, if you were favored, attain to a certain hill, a broad hill but not high, and marked in no particular way. That hill, and this lost town of its dead, are all that remain of the great city of Endymion, that came down from the Moon. Know you the tale?"

Music sounded behind the traveler, and turning he beheld the sister with her rebab.

The woman who had carried the water jar knelt before him. "Lend me your sword, you who are the Moon and Sun to me, and you shall see such a dance as few men have ever seen."

"The King of the Moon leaned forth one day, and cast his lure across the seas," the old man began.

"You cannot dance with my sword or any other," the traveler told the woman who had carried the jar, "for I see that you have golden chimes upon the fingers of both your hands."

"But Leviathan took the lure and wound the line about him," her father continued.

"Gold is as nothing to us," the woman who had carried the jar murmured as she slipped the yataghan from its sheath, "we grind it beneath our feet, and so shall you."

"He fell for a year, a month, and day . . ."

Rising, the woman who had carried the jar began to dance to the music of the rebab, fevered music that was like to the flashing of the recurved blade she flourished aloft. Ever the chimings of the red-gold finger cymbals slipped through, around, and over the exigent strains, and in a minute or three (though it had grown dark) the fluting notes of a syrinx joined them, an eerie piping, more distant far in time than space, that railed against death and the desert, and like a child forlorn sobbed of wildflowers.

"Flitting down from the Moon they followed him," the old man said, "and built the city from which they might behold her always. Here they buried their dead."

"I see," the traveler said.

"It is a tale for children, and yet to those who know its secrets, it reveals much. And that is why we teach it to ours."

"By the Moon's gift we never die," the sister told the traveler, and she began to sing.

> *What death is there without decay?*
> *She walks with me the white Moon-way.*
> *Hand in hand and hand in mouth,*
> *Eat, thou traveler from the south.*

Nameless instruments joined the music, hissing and thudding, and the woman who had carried the jar danced now in a circle of torches, her rotting wrappings flying from her as dead leaves in a storm.

"By the grace of the goddess we never die," the old man explained. He had taken back his ring, and his tone was almost apologetic. "Our dead are consumed by the living, and come to share their lives. The more who eat, the more life for those who once eaten are undead. Our goddess, you must understand, is herself dead. Mahes gives her life, but though he hates us, she loves us. Give me the spice you brought."

The traveler sought to rise, but a dozen hands pressed him down.

"My wife died last night," the old man said. "Tonight we will share her flesh, all of us. She will make you one of us, a beholder and celebrant of the Moon, and for that she—and we—rejoice."

Presenting a covered dish, the sister knelt before the traveler, and the point of his own yataghan was at his throat. She removed the cover, which was of gold; its mellow ringing served notice that the music had ceased.

A human brain rested upon the dish.

The old man unstopped the vial and sprinkled the powders it contained, black and white, pink, red, and green, upon the brain, then thrust the ring beneath it. "Eat," he said. "Eat to the ring and the ring is yours."

A sigh escaped a hundred unseen throats.

"Refuse and die. Nor will anyone share life with you."

The traveler felt the points of spears and knives at his back, and the rebab sobbed.

"I will eat," he said. "I will eat because I must. But first I will speak the truth. I seldom do so—it is not wise for travelers, nor is it the way of traders. Yet it is time that the truth was spoken to you."

"Eat!" exclaimed a dozen voices.

"You have a disease. I do not know what it is called nor whence it came—out of these tombs, perhaps. I only know that you have it, and that you pass it one to another by this means. You are sick, though you think yourselves sacred. Delirious, you imagine that you see the Moon traversing these empty avenues. You also believe that this unfortunate woman will live on in us, when in truth it is only the thing that killed her that will live on in us."

A caravan would have passed by the lost town of the dead, but the man who led it saw the traveler's camel, which wandered free over the desert by day and returned to the lost town to drink with the goats at evening. Hoping to capture it for himself, he followed it; it led him to the town, and his four wives and his slaves entered it with him in search of water.

They were met by a man skeletally thin and dressed in the rotting cloths that had once clothed a corpse. He welcomed them and led them to the well; but when the leader of the caravan had begun to descend its steps, the man skeletally thin pushed him from them so that he fell to his death, and laughed as madmen do.

That night, with his long-barreled jezail, he shot a certain old man of the town in order that his new wives might eat; after which all five dashed howling and shrieking through the streets of the lost town of the dead, accompanied by the slaves, the Moon King and his gauze-winged subjects, the woman who had carried the water jar and her sister Ahool, and various others.

The Walking Sticks

✦

Jo saw something in the back yard day-before-yesterday, and that should have warned me right there. Got me started on this and everything. I should have gone to the big church over on Forest Drive and talked to somebody, yelled for the police and put this out on the net— done everything I am going to do now. Only I did not. It was a man with a funny kind of derby hat on and a big long black overcoat she said, and she went to the door and said, "What are you doing in our back yard?" And he sort of turned out to be smoke and the smoke blew away.

That is what her note said, only I did not believe her because it was practically dark, the sun only just up, and what does it mean when a woman says she saw a man in a black overcoat at night? So much has been happening, and I thought it was nerves.

All right, I am going to go back and tell all of it from the very beginning. Then I will put this on the net and maybe print it out, too, so I can give a copy to the cops and the priests or whatever they have over there.

Mavis and I got divorced six years ago. Guys always talk about what big friends they are with their ex. I never did believe any of that, and that sure was not how it was with us. As soon as it was final I went my way and she went hers. Mine was staying on the job and finding a new place to live, and hers was selling the house and taking off in our Buick for Nantucket or Belize or wherever it was she had read about in some magazine that month. Jo and I got married not too long after that and bought this place in Bear Hill Cove.

All right here I better say something I do not want to have to say. A letter came to Mavis from England, and the people that had bought our old house from her carried it over and stuck it in our box. I ought to have opened it and read it and written to the man in Edinburgh. His name was Gordon Houston-Scudder. I should have said we did not know where Mavis was and not to send anything, but I did not even open it. I thought sooner or later Mavis would turn up and I would give it to her. Now I wonder if she was not behind the whole thing.

Around the end of September a pretty big crate came from England, and there was a good-sized cabinet in it. Jo and I got it out and cleaned up the mess. The key was in the lock, I remember that. And then inside the cabinet there was another mess of wood shavings that got all over the carpet.

Under that was the canes, twenty-two of them. Some were long and some were shorter. There were all kinds of handle shapes, and a dozen different kinds of wood. The handle of one was silver and shaped like a dog's head. It was tarnished pretty bad, but Jo polished it up and showed me hallmarks on it. She said she thought it might be pretty valuable.

About then I remembered the letter for Mavis and got it out of my desk in here and opened it. Mr. Houston-Scudder was a solicitor, he said, and his letter was from what looked like lawyers, Campbell, Macilroy, and somebody else. He said the estate of some doctor from the 1800s had been settled and the canes were supposed to go to a woman named Martha Jenkins or something, but she was dead now and as far as they could see Mavis was her only relative so they were sending them to her.

I thought that was all right. We would just keep them for her and if she ever came back I would give them to her, and the cabinet, too. Those kids that got killed? I had nothing to do with that. *Nothing.* So help me God.

Anyway, that was that. We put the cabinet in a corner of the dining room, and I locked it and I think I put the key in my pocket. Only the cane with the German shepherd head was not in there because Jo wanted to keep it out to look at. It was in the kitchen then, I think, leaning against the side of the refrigerator.

Here I do not know which way to go. If I just tell about the walking and the knocking, you probably will not get it. Maybe I should say that the key is lost before I get into all that. I think I must have left it in my pocket, and Jo put my jeans in the wash. For just a cabinet it was a pretty big key, iron. I have tried to pick the lock with a wire, but I could not get it open. I could break the doors, but what good would that do?

The thing is that I do not deserve to go to prison, and I am afraid that is what is bound to happen. But I did not do anything really wrong. In fact nothing I did was wrong at all, except that maybe I should have told somebody sooner. Well, I am telling it now.

It started that night, even though we did not know it. Jo woke me up and said she heard somebody in the house. I listened for a while and it was *tap-tap-tap, rattle-rattle*. I told her it sounded like a squirrel in the attic, which it did. But to shut her up I had to get up and get my gun and a flashlight and have a look around. Everything was just like we had left it when we went to bed. The front door and back door were both locked, and all the windows were closed. There was not any more noise either.

Then when I had turned around to go back to bed, there was a bang and clatter, like something had fallen over. I looked all around with my light and could not see anything, but when I was going back to bed, passing the cabinet, I stepped on it. It was the one with the silver handle. That was the part I stepped on, and it hurt.

So I said some things (that part was probably a mistake) and leaned it back against the cabinet like Jo had probably had it, and went back to bed. Naturally she wanted to know, "What was that?"

And I said, "It was your goddamn cane. I must have knocked it over." Only I knew I had not. Then I asked why she had not told me there were little jewels like rubies or something for the eyes, and she said because there were not any, and we argued about that for a while because I had seen them, and went to sleep. Now I am going to have another beer and go to bed myself. I have locked the pieces in the trunk of my car, and it is not doing that stuff anymore anyway.

Here is what I should have written last week. The thing was that I had told it to go to hell, when I stepped on it, I mean. I think that was a mistake and I ought not ever to have done it, but a sharp place had cut my foot a little bit and I was mad. Only I know it walked that first night before I said anything. That was what Jo and I heard, I am pretty sure.

A couple of nights after that Jo heard it again, and next morning it was leaned up against the front door, which was not where we had left it at all.

So that night I put it in the bedroom with us and shut the door, which was a big mistake. About midnight it knocked to be let out, loud enough to wake up both of us. We got up and turned on the lights, and it was exactly where I had left it, and there were dents in the door. I said they had probably been there before and we had not noticed, but I knew it was not true. I took the cane out and leaned it up against the cabinet in the dining room again and went back to bed.

That was the first bad night I had, because it woke me up but it did not wake up Jo. I lay there for hours listening to it tapping on the bare floors and thumping on the carpets. It seemed like it was going through the whole house, room after room, and after a while it seemed like the house it was going through must have been a lot bigger than ours.

It was lying in front of the front door in the morning.

Jo said I had to throw it away, and we had a big fight about it because I wanted to take off the silver dog's head first and saw the wooden part in two, but Jo just wanted me to throw away the whole thing.

Finally I just put it in the garbage, because it was a Saturday and I did not have to go to work. Then when Jo went shopping I got it out and wiped it off and hid it down in the basement. When Jo got back the garbage had been picked up and she thought it was gone.

I know you must think I am a damned fool to do that, but I was wondering about it. In the first place, I was not really so sure anymore that I had heard what I thought I had. There were the dents in the bedroom door, but I got to where I was not really sure they had not been there already. Besides, what if I had left it in the garbage and the garbage collectors had taken it away, and I heard the same thing again? Squirrels or something. I would have felt like the biggest damned fool in the world.

Anyway, that is what I did. And that night I did not even try to go to sleep. I just lay in bed listening for it, and when it knocked loud on the basement door to be let out, I got up and put on some clothes and went to the basement door. It was really pounding by then. It seemed like it shook the whole house, and I was surprised Jo did not wake up.

When I put my hand on the knob of the basement door it felt hot. I never have been able to explain that, but it did. I stood there for half a minute or so with my hand on the knob while it pounded louder and louder, wondering what was going to come out when I opened the door, and whether I really should. I was trying to get my nerve up, I guess, and maybe I thought pretty soon Jo would come and there would be two of us. Finally I turned the knob and opened the door.

And what came out was the cane. Just that cane, all by itself, with a sort of cold draft from the basement. As soon as it came out it went up and broke the light over the basement door, but I had gotten a pretty good look at it first.

After that I followed it through the house to the front door, and when it tapped on that to be let out, I opened the door and let it go. After that I closed the door and locked it, and went back to bed.

When I went out in the morning to get the paper, I was expecting to find that cane out there, probably lying in front of the front door. I looked all around for it, in the bushes and everything, and it was gone, and the harder I looked for it and did not find it the better I felt. I was really happy.

But now I am going to bed. I should be able to wrap this up tomorrow night.

A cop came today asking questions. I told him I did not know anything about the dead girls except what I had seen on TV. He asked about Jo, and I had to tell him she had left me, which I think is the truth even if her car is still here, and all her stuff. After that he went next door. I saw him, and I think probably he was asking them about me.

Anyway, the next night I followed the cane again, only that time I followed it outside. I had heard it, I thought in the house. I had gotten up and gotten dressed very quietly so as not to wake up Jo and looked all around for it. Finally I heard it down in the basement again, walking and walking, tap-tap-tapping on the concrete floor down there, and I opened the door like before and let it out, and then I ran ahead of it and opened the front door.

And when it went outside, I followed it. I guess I kept about half a block back. Maybe a little bit less. There is no way that I can say how far it was. It did not seem to be very much walking, but pretty soon we were in a neighborhood I had not ever seen before, where all the houses were taller and a lot closer together, and the pavement was not even anymore. I got scared then and went back, and when I got inside I locked the door like I had before.

Only something had made Jo wake up, and I told her about how the cane had come back and gotten into the basement somehow, and how I had been following it. She said, "Next time let me throw it out."

So I said, "Well, I hope there never will be any next time. But if you can find it, you can throw it out." After that we went back in to bed, and I did not hear anything else that night. In the morning I got up pretty early the way I always do on workdays and got dressed, and Jo fixed my breakfast. Then I went to work the way I always do, figuring Jo would take off for her own job in about an hour. That was the last time I saw her.

When I got home that night and she did not come, I thought she was probably just working late. So I made supper for myself, a can of stew I think it was and rye bread, and drank a couple beers and watched TV. There was nothing on TV that night, or if there was I do not remember what. It got to be practically midnight and still no Jo, so I phoned the police. They said she had to be gone twenty-four hours and to call back if she did not come home, but I never did. That was the only time I called you.

While I was getting undressed somebody knocked on the door. I opened it and all the power went out. The light turned off, and the TV picture shrunk to nothing very fast, so I never did see the dog's head cane come in and by that time I had cut it up anyhow, only I could hear it. I stood as still as I could until I could not hear it anymore. Maybe it went down into the basement again, I do not know. I do not know whether the basement door was open or closed, either. It just sort of went away toward the back.

Well, I went in the bedroom and shut the door and moved the bureau to block it, and just about then the lights came back on and I saw there was a note on my pillow. I have still got it, and here it is.

Johnny,

There was someone in the back yard. I saw him as plainly as I have ever seen anything, a big man with a black mustache and a derby hat such as one sees in old photographs. He wore a thick wool overcoat, black or of some dark check, with a wide shawl collar, it seemed, and what may have been a scarf or muffler or another collar of black or dark brown fur.

I watched him for some time, wishing all the while that you were here with me, and asked him more than once what it was he wanted, threatening to call the police. He never replied; I know that you will laugh at me for this, Johnny, but his was the most threatening silence I have ever encountered. It *was*.

When the sun rose above the Jeffersons', he was gone. No. You would have *said* that he was gone, that with the first beams he was transformed into something like mist, which the morning breeze swiftly swept aside. But, he was still there. He *is* still there. I feel his presence.

I am not going to work today, having already called in sick. But, I am writing this for you to cleanse my spirit of it, and in case I should decide to leave you.

I *will* leave, if you will not destroy every last trace of Mavis's stick. I know you did not discard it as you promised me you would last night, and *will not* discard it. I left my poor Georgie for you for much less. I hope you realize this.

I will go, and once I have I will be out of your life forever.

Very, very seriously,

Jo Anne, with all my love

Now I think it is about over. I really do. Either over, or starting something different. Okay, here is the bad part, right up front. The bottom line.

Last night I thought I heard something moving around and I thought oh God, it's back. But then I thought it could not be back because of all the things I did. (I ought to tell about all that, and I will, too, before I turn in tonight.)

Anyway, I got up to see what it was, and it was all the other canes in the big oak cabinet in the dining room rattling around and knocking to be let out.

So it is not only the one with the silver top, it is all the rest, too. But if that one is still doing it, why would the others want to step up? So I think what it really means is I have won. Here is what I plan to do. I am going to call up Union Van Lines and tell them I have got a certain item of furniture I want taken out and stored. I will get them to move the whole cabinet for me. (Naturally it will still be locked, because I have lost the key like I said.) They will put it in a warehouse someplace for me. I think New Jersey, and I can tell them I am planning to move there eventually but I do not know when yet. Every month or whatever they will send me a storage bill for fifty bucks or so, and I will pay that bill, you bet, for the rest of my life. It will be worth every nickel to know that the cabinet is still locked up in that warehouse. I will call them tomorrow.

All right, here is the rest.

There was a night (if you read the paper or even watch the news on TV you know what night it was) when I followed the cane with the silver top outside again. After about four blocks it went to the same place it had before, where the big high houses were up against each other so close you could see they could not have windows on the sides. Where the streets were dirty, like I said, and sometimes you saw people passed out on the cold dirty old pavement. That pavement was just round rocks, really, but the streetlights were so dim (like those friendship lights the gas company used to push) that you could not hardly tell it except with your feet.

We went a long way there, a lot farther than the first time.

When we started out, I was trying to keep about half a block behind like before, because I thought somebody would grab that cane sure, and maybe ask if it belonged to me if I was too close. But when we got in among those old houses that leaned over the street like I have told about, I had to move in a lot closer because of the fog and bad light. It was cold and I was scared. I do not mind saying that, because it is the truth. But I had told myself that I was going to follow the cane that night until it came back to the house, no matter what. I did, too.

I kept thinking somebody would notice a cane walking all by itself pretty soon, but it was real late, very few people out at all, and nobody did.

Then there was this girl. She had blond hair and a long skirt, and a coat too big for her it looked like that she was holding tight around her, and hurrying along. I kept waiting for it to register with her that the cane was walking all by itself. Finally when it got real close to her it registered with me that was not how she saw it. Somebody was holding that cane and walking along with it, and even if I could not see him she could.

Just about then he grabbed her, and I saw that. I do not mean I saw him, I did not, but I saw that she had been grabbed and heard her yell. And then the cane was beating her, up and down and up and down, and her yelling and her blood flying like water when a car drives through it fast. It sounded horrible, the yelling, and the *thud-thud-thud* beating, too. I ran and the yelling stopped, but the beating kept right on until I grabbed it.

It felt good. I never hated to write anything this much in my life but it did. That girl was lying down on the dirty pavement stones bleeding terrible, and it was horrible, but it felt good. It felt like I was stronger than I have ever been in my life.

People started yelling and I ran, but before I got very far the houses looked right again, and the streetlights were bright. I was getting out of breath, so I started walking, just walking fast instead of running. I tried to hold the cane so nobody would see it, and when I looked down at it, it was looking up at me. Sure, the handle was bent because of beating on the girl. Or something. But it was looking up at me, a German shepherd or something with pointed ears. The red things were back in its eyes even if Jo had not ever seen them, and it seemed like I could see more teeth.

Then in the morning it was all over the news. I had the clock radio set to wake me up at five to go to work, and that was all they were talking about, this girl that had been a baby-sitter over in the Haddington Hill subdivsion (it is flatter even than here) and she was on her way back home when somebody beat her to death.

That night they showed the place on TV so you could see the blood-stains on the sidewalk, and it was not right at all, but when they showed her picture from the yearbook, it was her. She had been a sophomore at Consolidated High. I thought I would walk over there and have a look, and when I went out the door that cane with the silver dog on it was in my hand. It stopped me and made it hard for me not to go at the same time.

But I stopped, and that is when I did it. First thing I thought of was I would take off the silver head and put it in my safety deposit at the bank where it could not do anything. But when I twisted it trying to get it off, it unscrewed. I had not even known it was screwed on. There was a silver band under the part that came off that said some name with a J only too worn to read and M.D., all in fancy handwriting. It could have been Jones or Johnson or anything like that, but he had been a doctor.

Then inside that silver band the cane looked hollow. I turned it upside down and this little glass tube came sliding out. It was about half full of something that was kind of like mercury only more like a white powder, some kind of heavy stuff that slid around very easy in the tube and was heavy. I took it way back to the back corner of the back yard where I had noticed a snake hole the last time I cut the grass and poured it in. Jo wanted to know what I was doing there. (She had seen me out the kitchen window while she was washing dishes.) I said nothing, just poking around.

But the funny thing was, when I got back inside the cane was just a cane. There was nothing special about it anymore. I sawed the wood part in two down in my shop like I had planned to, but it was nothing. It was exactly like sawing a broom handle. The next day I took the silver dog head down to the bank on my way home from work, but it did not matter anymore and I knew it.

So I thought that everything was fixed until Jo saw that man and went away without taking her clothes or car or anything. Then just before I started writing this I saw him myself, and there was a woman with him, and I think it was Jo. That was what started me doing this. So this is all of it and maybe I will put it on the net like I said, and maybe I will not. I want to sleep on it.

———

Another cop came a couple of hours ago, and after he went out back I found these papers, which I had stuck in a drawer. (It is December now.) He was friendly, but he did not fool me. He said the New Jersey cops got a court order and broke into the cabinet for them. I said, "What were you looking for?"

And he said, "Jo's body."

So I said, "Well, what did they find inside?"

And he said, "Nothing."

"Nothing?" I could not believe it.

"That's what they say, sir."

Then I told him there had been a collection of valuable canes in there, and they did not belong to me, they belonged to Mavis. He hummed and hawed around, and finally he winked at me and said, "Well those Jersey cops have some real nice canes now, I guess."

I am not ever going to go near New Jersey, and I hope that those other canes do not decide to come back here, or anyway not many of them.

So then I told him about the trespassers and asked him to take a look around my back yard. He went to do it, and he has not come back yet. That makes me feel good and really strong, but probably I will have to call somebody tomorrow because his police car is still parked in front of the house.

Queen

✦

It was late afternoon when the travelers reached the village. The taller of the two led the way to the well, and they sat there to wait as travelers do who hope that someone will offer them a roof for the night. As it chanced the richest man in the village hurried by, then stopped, compelled by something he glimpsed in their faces. Something he could not have explained.

"I'll be back this way quite soon," he told them. "We have a room for guests, and can offer you a good supper."

The taller thanked him. "We were only hoping for directions. What is the name of your village?"

The richest man told him.

"We have come to the right place, then." He named the old woman.

"She's poor," the richest man said.

They said nothing; it was as though they had not heard.

"She hasn't a lot. Are you relatives? Maybe you could buy something and take it to her, then she could cook it for you. A lamb."

"Where does she live?" the taller asked.

"Over there." The richest man pointed. "At the edge of the village." He hesitated. "Come with me. I'll show you."

They followed him, walking side by side so silently that he looked behind him thinking they might have gone. Neither had a staff. That seemed strange; he tried to recall when he had last seen a traveler who had no staff to help him walk, no staff to defend his life, if defense of life were needed.

The old woman was still at her spinning, which surprised him. She let them in and invited them to sit. The travelers did, but he did not, saying, "There are things I have to do. I only brought them here because they didn't know the way, didn't know how to find your house. Are they relations of yours?"

She shook her head.

"Do you know them? It might not be safe."

She considered, her head to one side, remembering. "I think I know that one. Or perhaps not. It's been so long."

"You're not going to hurt her, I hope?" the richest man asked. "She has nothing."

Speaking for the first time, the smaller of the two said, "We have come to take her to the coronation."

"Well." The richest man cleared his throat. "She is an, er, um, descendant of the royal line. I had forgotten. However . . ."

"However?"

He coughed. "However a great many people are, and she has little with which to make you welcome."

"A little oil," the old woman said. "Some flour."

"So why don't I, ah, provide a bit of food? I could have my servants bring something, and dine with you myself." Suddenly unsure, he looked at the old woman. "Would that be all right?"

"I would like it," the old woman assured him.

When his servants had spread a cloth for them and loaded her small table with dishes, he dismissed them and sat down. "I don't know that all this is good," he said. "Likely some of it won't be. But some of it's bound to be good."

"Do you want to go now?" the smaller traveler asked the old woman. "Or would you rather eat first? It's up to you."

She smiled. "Is it a long way?"

The taller said, "Very long indeed. The place is very far from here."

"Then I would like to eat first." She prayed over the food the richest man had provided, and as he listened to her it came to him that he had never heard such prayers before, and then that he had never heard prayer at all. He was like a man who had seen only bad coin all his life, he thought, and after a great many years receives a purse of real silver, fresh from the mint.

"That is true," the taller said when the old woman had finished her prayer, "but food is good, too." It seemed to the richest man that this had been said in answer to his thought, though he could not be sure.

"I was about to say that I never expected to go to a coronation," the old woman told the smaller, smiling, "but now that I think about it, I realize it isn't really true. I used to dream that I'd see my son's coronation—that my son would be a king, and someday I would see him crowned. It was silly of me."

"Her son was a teacher," the richest man explained.

They ate olives, bread, and mutton, and drank wine.

"You won't be leaving in the morning, I hope?" The richest man had discovered that he did not want them to go; he would suggest they sleep in his house, as he had first proposed. They could rejoin the old woman in the morning.

"No," the taller said.

"That's good. You must be tired, since you've come a long way. You really ought to stay here for a fortnight or more recruiting your strength. This is an interesting part of the country, agriculturally and historically. I can show you around and introduce you to all the people you ought to meet. Believe me, it never hurts to be introduced, to have connections in various parts of the country. Too many people think that they can do everything through relatives, their families and their wives' relations. It never works out."

No one spoke.

"I'll see to it that you're welcomed everywhere."

The old woman said, "If we're really going to go to a coronation . . ."

"I can find a donkey for you," the richest man told her, "and I will. You couldn't keep up with these two fellows for an hour. I'm sure you realize it, and they're going to have to realize it, too."

She was looking at the taller. "Weren't you the one who came to tell me about my son?"

He nodded.

"I knew I'd seen you somewhere. Yes, that was it. You don't look a day older."

The richest man coughed apologetically. "You're not relatives of hers, I take it."

"No," the taller said. "We're messengers."

"Well, you're welcome just the same. I hope you'll stay until the new moon, at least."

"We will leave when she has eaten as much as she wants," the smaller told him.

"Tonight?" It was insane. He thought the smaller might be joking.

"Oh, I've had all I want," the old woman said. "It doesn't take much to fill me up these days."

The taller said, "Then we should go."

"I want to thank you," the old woman told the richest man. "What you've done for me tonight was very kind. I'll always remember it."

He wished that it had been a great deal more, and tried to say that he was sorry that he had never befriended her during all the years she had lived in the village, and that it would be otherwise in the future.

She looked at the taller when he said these things, and the taller nodded assent.

"You're a messenger," she said. "You said so. Just a messenger."

The taller nodded again. "A servant."

"Sent to get me." A shadow, as of fear, crossed her face. "You're not the messenger of death?"

"No," the taller told her. "I'm not."

"What about him?" She indicated the smaller.

"We should go now." The taller stood as he spoke.

The richest man felt that all three had forgotten him. More diffidently than he had intended, he asked whether he might go with them.

"To the coronation?" The taller shook his head. "You may not. It's by invitation only."

"Just to the edge of the village."

The taller smiled and nodded. "Since we are there now, yes, you may."

"You'll tell others," the smaller said when they were outside. "That's good. Because you're rich, they'll have to listen to you. But some won't believe you, because you're dishonest. That should be perfect."

"I am not dishonest," the richest man said.

They walked on.

"I've done some dishonest things, perhaps. Those things were dishonest, but not I."

The sun had set behind the hills, but its light still filled the sky. A breeze sprang up, swaying the lofty palm at the edge of his new pasture. The taller had been walking on the old woman's right; now the smaller took her left arm as if to assist her.

"Right here, I think," the smaller said. "There's a bit of a climb, but you won't find it tiring."

The taller spoke to the richest man. "This is where we part company. We wish you well."

The old woman stopped when he said that, and when she turned back to face the richest man, he saw that she was standing upon nothing, that she and they had climbed, as it appeared, a hummock of air. "Good-bye," she said. "Thank you again. Please tell everyone I'll miss them terribly, and that I'll come back just as soon as I can."

The richest man managed to nod, became aware that he was gaping, and closed his mouth.

"I suppose we ought to go on now," she said to the taller, and he nodded.

The richest man stood watching them follow a path he could not see up a hill he could not see, a hill that he could not see, he thought, because it had no summit. Only hills with summits were visible to his eyes. He had not known that before. When they had gone so high that the sun's light found them again, they halted; and he heard the taller say, "Do you want to take a last look? This would be a good place to do it."

"It's really quite little, isn't it?" The old woman's voice carried strangely. "It's precious, and yet it's not important."

"It used to be important," the smaller said; and it seemed to the richest man that it was the breeze that spoke.

The old woman laughed a girl's laugh. "Perhaps we'd better hurry. Do you know, I feel like running."

"We'll run if you like," the taller told her, "but we can't promise to run as fast as you can."

"We'll just walk briskly," the richest man heard the old woman say, "but it had better be very briskly. We wouldn't want to be late for the coronation."

"Oh, we won't be." (The richest man could not be sure which of her companions had replied.) "I can guarantee that. The coronation won't begin until you get there."

Night came as the richest man watched them climb higher; and at last one of his servants came, too, and asked what he was looking at.

"Right there." The richest man pointed. "Look there, and look carefully. What do you see?"

The servant looked, rubbed his eyes, and looked again; and at last he said, "Three stars, master."

"Exactly," the richest man said. "Exactly."

Together they returned to the old woman's house. There was a great deal of food still on the table, and the richest man told his servant to fetch the cook and the scullion, to gather everything up, and to return it to his kitchen.

"Is this your house now, master?" his servant asked.

"Certainly not." The richest man paused, thinking. "But I'm going to take care of it for her while she's away."

The servant left, and the richest man found the figs, selected a fig, and ate it. Some people would want to tear this house down, and time and weather would do it for them, if they were allowed to. He would see that they did not: that nothing was stolen or destroyed. That necessary repairs were made. He would keep it for her. It would be his trust, and suddenly he was filled with a satisfaction near to love at being thus trusted.

Pocketsful of Diamonds

✦

At supper, Aunt Mildred rapped her glass with a fork until all five children stopped to listen. "We will be welcoming new arrivals tomorrow." She beamed at the children, hoping for at least one smile in return, but got none. "Their names are David Apple and Candi Cotin, and that's all I can tell you about them until I've had a chance to talk to them."

Danny passed a bite of sweet potato to his sister Debbie, who had just passed him a sizable bit of her meatloaf. Debbie was a year older, and as he gave her his morsel of sweet potato, Danny's look loudly declared that it was up to her. Debbie was looking at him already. You're the man of the family, Debbie's look reminded him.

From the opposite side of the table, LaBelinda voiced the question that was on the mind of every child present. "Where they goin' to sleep?"

"We must welcome them both, and warmly," Aunt Mildred declared.

"Debbie 'n Danny got their big ol' room all to theyselfs 'cause they's sister 'n brother." LaBelinda shot them a look compounded of envy and dislike.

"I'm glad you mentioned that," said Aunt Mildred, who was not. "You see, Taffy—that is what David prefers to be called, according to the paper they gave me—and Candi are brother and sister, too. There was a divorce and some changes in name. You understand, I'm sure."

The children nodded. Divorces and changes in name were things they understood very well indeed.

"Well, *Ah* think . . ." LaBelinda began.

Luis, who hardly ever spoke, touched her arm and gestured graphically toward Danny and Debbie. "Dere," said Luis. "Weeth dem."

Later that night, while Danny lay in bed beside his sister, he found himself back in the kitchen of the little brick house on Second Street. Mom and Dad were kissing, standing up with their arms around each other in the middle of the room; and he knew that he should not make any noise or push between them to get hugged the way he had when he was small. But he knew also that when he went out of the kitchen something terrible would be waiting in the vast darkness beyond its glowing circle of light, a circle that spun around and tilted as he watched, yellow light from the overhead fixture, blue light from a burner on the gas stove, and red light from the telltale eye of the electric percolator, all turning and turning.

He blinked, and Debbie was shaking him. "Look! Look! You've got to see this."

Danny sat up rubbing his eyes, and Debbie was already back at the window, and the light coming through the window was not the colorless glare of the mercury-vapor lamp at the top of the steel pole but was red and green and yellow and blue, and even pink and orange. Then he was standing beside her, and there was something new and wonderful where the dirty, cracked walls of the old packing plant usually were.

From their window they got out onto the little porch roof, Debbie going first because she was oldest; and from the little porch roof they climbed down one of the ornamental iron pillars that held it up, Danny going first because he was bravest, and the man of the family.

"Now normally, folks," declared the tall man in the red-and-white striped sportcoat who stood on the platform at the gate, "admission is a mere one dollar and seventy-five cents for adults, fifty cents for children, and babes in arms free. Senior citizen discount of one dollar even." He was addressing Danny and Debbie as if they were a noisy crowd. "But I'll tell you what I'm gonna do."

"We haven't got any money." Danny thought it best to establish this at once.

Suddenly the tall man on the platform knelt, pushing back his yellow straw hat. "Your pockets are full of diamonds," he whispered to Danny. At once he rose again and continued as though there had been no such whisper. "For tonight—and *only* for tonight—admission will be free. Absolutely free! To one and all."

Danny wanted to show the tall man that there were no pockets as well as no diamonds in his worn flannel pajamas, but did not know how to do it.

"Now normally," the tall man twirled a slender bamboo cane, "normally we do not provide the promised free refreshment tickets to those lucky patrons who pay no admission. To babes in arms, for example. To those who have received the passes generously distributed by our management and those whose admissions have been magnanimously paid by their employers at a deep discount. But not tonight! Tonight is special. Tonight is golden, and tonight is pro-foundly *ab*normal. Let me tell you what we're gonna do. Tonight *only*, we're gonna provide the promised free refreshment tickets along with your free admissions!"

Bowing, he presented Debbie with a large piece of dark green cardboard, then handed another, brighter piece to Danny. A moment later, his bamboo cane was propelling them through the gate.

SKYROCKET
Rides—Free

announced a large sign. An arrow pointed in the direction they were going. "That sounds fun," Debbie said, "and it doesn't cost anything. We could go on that."

Danny was examining the piece of green cardboard the tall man at the gate had given him. "We could find the place where the free treats are, too."

"Step right up, kids," a new voice invited them. "They're all inside, and the last nine are free."

The speaker was a middle-aged woman in a purple dress, and she was speaking not to Danny and Debbie alone but to a little knot of very ordinary-looking people of all ages gathered in front of her platform.

But if the people in front of her platform were ordinary-looking, the people depicted on the canvas banners behind it were anything but.

"Just one diamond alone before our show's shown," chanted the woman in the purple dress. "Just one's all it takes, folks. That's why we call it the Ten-in-One. You pay once, and for that one measly little payment you get to see all ten shows. There're all alive except the dead one, and she's still dancing. Okay, who's first?"

A thin man in a well-worn denim shirt took something small and gleaming from a trousers pocket, handed it to the woman in the purple dress, and was admitted.

"All alive," the woman repeated; a moaning wind swayed and billowed the painted canvases, making them appear so. There was a monstrously fat woman and a sinister snake woman, a fire eater and a sword swallower, an alligator boy, a dead woman in a pink tutu, and a man with two noses, two mouths, and four eyes. Gaily colored lights glided across them all, rose, ruby, berylline, heliotrope, and canary.

A face that seemed not entirely human peeped around the curtain behind the woman in the purple dress, and the woman in the purple dress caught its owner by the arm and pulled her out. "This is Lobster Girl," she explained, and she held up the lobster girl's hand so that everyone could see it was indeed a pliers-like claw. "She eats children, but she never eats paid admissions, so you don't have to worry. You never do, do you Vamp?"

The lobster girl smiled, and her teeth were the teeth of a trap.

A fat lady in a black dress laid her hand upon Debbie's shoulder. It was a plump little hand in an immaculate white glove, and the fat lady smelled quite beautifully of lavender. "Wouldn't you children like to see the show?" She smiled at Debbie, and then at Danny.

Debbie shook her head.

"We haven't got any money," Danny explained.

"I have." The fat lady displayed a neat black purse. "And I'd like to see a woman fatter than I am." She laughed merrily. "Talk to her, too, if I could."

Dimly, Danny recalled a movie theater at which Dad had paid for four tickets. "Could we come with you?"

Debbie shook her head again, violently this time.

"You've been cautioned against child molesters, I'm sure," the fat lady said. "Stranger danger? But if I introduce myself, and you introduce yourselves to me, I won't be a stranger anymore, will I?" She held out her hand to Danny. "I'm Irma, and you are . . . ?"

"Danny."

Solemnly, she and Danny shook hands; then the fat lady held out her hand to Debbie. "I'm Bertha, darling. And you are . . . ?"

"You said your name was Irma," Debbie protested.

"Oh, I have a great many names," the fat lady explained, "but I ask only one of you. You are . . . ?"

"Debbie," Danny supplied.

The fat lady nodded and smiled. "Then come with me, Debbie and Danny, and we will see the show."

Danny took her hand, and she led him up to the woman in the purple dress while the lobster girl was dancing on all four claws, clattering around and around the platform and grinning over its edge at the people who gawked at her.

"My name is Lily," the fat woman told the woman in the purple dress, "and I would like to pay my own admission and the admissions of these two children in addition to my own." She took three glittering stones from her neat black purse and held them out.

"You're going to pay for them?" The woman in the purple dress sounded dubious.

"Yes, I am," the fat lady assured her.

Dubiously, the woman in the purple dress selected one of the glittering stones and held it up to the colored lights, which it transformed into purest crystal iridescence. "It's not regular," she said.

"Suppose I were to hand one to each child. That would be regular, wouldn't it?"

The woman in the purple dress frowned. "No, that wouldn't be regular at all."

"As you wish," the fat lady said. "Come along, children." Dropping the other two glittering stones back into her neat black purse and snapping it shut, she led Danny inside. For a second or two, Debbie watched them, trembling, before she ran to rejoin them.

"This is Sheffield, our sword swallower," announced a recorded voice. "Show them, Sheffield."

The sword swallower was a tall, emaciated, sad-looking man with a very pale face. He rose from the inverted bucket on which he had been sitting as the recorded voice spoke, and held out for their inspection a beautiful straight sword with a polished, double-edged blade. "People think the blade slides into the handle," he said, "but it does not"; his own voice was weak and tremulous, as colorless as his face. "You're welcome to examine it, sir, or to run me through the body, if you wish."

Danny accepted the sword and felt that it was weighty with magic. "Wouldn't you die?"

There was a lengthy silence during which the sword swallower appeared to consider the matter. At last he said, "It isn't terribly likely."

So timorously she could scarcely be heard, Debbie asked, "Are you really going to swallow it?"

The sword swallower shook his head. "I will only put the blade down my throat and pull it out again, madam. There is no actual swallowing, no peristaltic action involved in what I do. Watch."

He threw back his head and held the gleaming blade poised above his face for a moment that called for (but did not get) trumpets. His mouth opened, though not widely, and the blade slowly descended, down and down, until it seemed that he must surely be spitted like a calf for roasting.

At last the jeweled and gilded cross-guard touched his lips. He released the sword then and stood with arms outstretched, its gleaming hilt protruding from his mouth. Debbie clapped for him, the pattering of her small hands the only sound in the cavernous darkness of the show tent.

Slowly, both of the sword swallower's own thin and colorless hands reached for the hilt. More slowly still, he brought the sword up, an inch at a time. When it emerged at last, the point was red with blood.

"Thank you." He bowed to them, his right hand pressed to his stomach, his left still holding his sword. "Thank you all very much for your attention and applause." There was a bloody froth at one corner of his mouth.

"Doesn't it hurt?" Danny asked him.

The sword swallower shook his head. "There are no nerves in that part of the human body. Besides, it is my art. I have dedicated my life to my art." As they turned to leave, he righted his bucket and vomited blood into it.

"Five-alarm Forester is our fire eater," declared the recorded voice with obvious pride. "For your education and entertainment, Five-alarm will stuff a blazing torch into his mouth and extinguish it by that means."

"Oh, please don't!" Debbie exclaimed. "Not even if it doesn't really hurt."

The fire eater gave her a severe look, lit the torch he had been preparing, and ate it, munching and swallowing. He was a bent and wrinkled old man with rheumy eyes.

"How do you do that?" Danny asked.

"I will explain," the old fire eater said, "provided you will tell me your name, little boy."

Danny told him.

"Very well, Danny. Now give me a diamond—just one, Danny—and I will explain the whole thing and even let you try it, if you wish."

"I don't have any." Danny looked around the dark tent, seeking support from Debbie and the fat lady, and anyone else who might be inclined to give it.

"At your age, Danny, every pocket you have is full of diamonds." The old fire eater turned his own pockets inside out. They were quite empty.

"I don't even have any pockets," Danny said.

Wordlessly, the old fire eater pointed to the little five-sided pocket of Danny's pajama shirt.

"It doesn't work. The stitching came loose." Danny put his hand into it and wiggled his fingers when they emerged from the bottom.

"Then I will do it for a smile."

Danny smiled.

"Here is what I use," the old fire eater said, and he got out a mason jar and a big breadstick. "This clear liquid is one hundred and forty proof hooch. Would you care for a little drink?"

Danny shook his head.

"I would." The old fire eater sipped from the mason jar. "I can never take a healthy swig because it's too strong. The alcohol would barbecue the tissues of my mouth and throat. But I can do this." He dipped the end of the breadstick into the jar.

The fat lady said, "I see."

"Then you light it." The old fire eater did so, and it burned with a bright blue flame. "With enough experience, you know when it's about to go out, and when it is . . ." He thrust the blazing breadstick into his mouth and bit it off.

Debbie giggled nervously.

"It looks good," the fat lady whispered. "He's making me hungry."

Danny said, "Me, too."

The old fire eater chewed and swallowed. "If your timing's right, choking on a sesame seed is the chief danger. Now watch this, and I'll let you go. This is white gasoline." He picked up a bottle and filled his mouth, twisting a knob to dim the light above the four-inch dais on which he stood.

For a second or two, his worn face and bulging cheeks remained visible; then even that winked out, and they waited in total darkness.

A match flared, and a fountain of orange flame seemed to fill the whole tent, briefly illuminating more attractions than ten. The sword swallower waited with bowed head, seated upon his upended bucket; to his right, a dead ballet dancer had frozen in the act of tying one shoe, and a stock-still figure with half a beard flaunted a single female breast. Only the serpent woman on the opposite side of the tent moved, writhing and coiling between a magician and a woman embraced by a gorilla.

The flame vanished as abruptly as it had come. "Now you know where you are," the aged voice of the fire eater announced. Danny heard the fat lady's sharp inhalation, and Debbie took his hand, gripping it tightly.

The old fire eater said, "If you ever come back, Danny, I'll teach you to eat fire, exactly as I promised."

A tiny white light gleamed. "I keep this on my key ring," the fat lady explained. "It comes in very handy when I don't get home until after dark."

The recorded voice announced, "This is the Harpy, the bane of evildoers and the only animal in the world with breasts and feathered wings. You won't believe that she can fly, but she's going to fly for you."

"I don't want to see that," the fat lady said. "I'm going to go over there and see the snake charmer and the fat woman, and then I'm going to get something to eat."

Danny and Debbie followed her.

"This is so exquisitely sensitive of you, to say that I am charming, my most substantial sister," the serpent woman hissed. "Shall I give you a small and slight most gracious squeeze of thanks?" A bulb glowed to life above her dais, and Danny saw that although her head, arms, and upper torso appeared almost human, she was a prettily marked black-and-yellow snake from the waist down.

"I don't think so," the fat lady said.

The serpent woman simpered, yet reared herself higher and slithered into a rippling series of hairpin bends that to Danny appeared expressive of anger.

"Well, I like you," Debbie announced, and "I don't think you'd hurt us."

"So it is, small sister, and so it stays. Seek you wisdom? I, its sigil, make some women wise."

"My name's Debbie," Debbie told her.

"Simple and smooth, but possibly a smidgen saccharine, small sister. I sign myself Linda Lamia, though I was once called the Pythoness."

Debbie nodded and made the little curtsey she had been taught at dancing school. "Do you like being a snake?"

The serpent woman smiled. "I can scarcely say, since the chance of snakedom has thus far escaped me. It would be nice to possess a poisoned strike, possibly, but I've no personal experience of it." Her tongue flickered like a black flame.

"Will you make me wise? You said you would."

"Yes, since I promised. Listen sharp, small sister. First, this is no simple vision of sleep. Did you suppose so?"

"No," Debbie told her. "I know I'm not dreaming."

"Second, this is not consciousness as you have seen it until now. Nor as you shall see it once our supernormal show has struck its tents."

Debbie nodded. "Because the Sausage Works would be here instead."

"This Sausage Works you speak of is still here, you may be sure." For five seconds or more the serpent woman waited motionless, watching Debbie through slitted pupils. "Third, it is seldom wise, or even possible, to draw a hard and fast line 'twixt solidity and fantasy. But when you sketch yourself such a line, as you shall, you must trace a second such scribing 'twixt solidity and this."

The electric light above the serpent woman had dimmed as she spoke. Her eyes rolled upward and she writhed and swayed, coiling and uncoiling.

"You're going out of order," the recorded voice objected. "Everything's all confused."

"We want to see the fat woman next," the fat lady said, "and then we'll leave."

"I can't hear a word you say," the recorded voice told her pettishly.

A light glowed and brightened over the fat woman. "My name's Jolly Janie," she wheezed. "I weigh six hundred and seventy pounds. Around my gut measures eighty-four inches. You can't weigh me. 'Cause we don' have a scale big 'nough. But you can measure my gut. If you want to. I'll lend you a tape. Or you kin use yours." She was not looking at Danny, at Debbie, or at the fat lady, and appeared to be looking at nothing.

"I'm fat, too," the fat lady acknowledged, "and my name is Ermentrude."

"I don' eat but three meals a day. Jes' like you. I don' eat no big meals neither. But I jes' keep on gittin' fatter 'n fatter." Her tiny mouth was almost concealed by her bulging cheeks, and the sagging flesh of her forehead overshadowed her deep-set eyes.

"My name is Mina." Somewhat timidly, the fat lady reached out to touch the fat woman's hand, although the fat woman showed no sign of being touched. "I'm loyal and loving, orderly and very clean, a good cook, and fun to talk to. . . ." She waited for the fat woman to speak.

"I got to have help or else I cain't stand up. When I was with the circus they'd git a elephant to help lift me. Here it's that tow truck."

"I'm the woman ten thousand men ought to have married, and no man did." Again the fat lady touched the fat woman's hand, stroking it as she might have stroked a bird. "We could help each other, Janie. I know we could."

"You want to help me? You kin git me a triple-dip cone right outside there. Vanilla, strawberry, 'n chocolate." The bulb over the fat woman dimmed.

"I will. Trust me, Janie, I will. I'll bring it back to you, and then we'll talk." The fat lady took Danny and Debbie by the hand.

"Here you see Vamp the Lobster Girl," the recorded voice declared. "She eats children." Not far away a light brightened over the lobster girl's platform, and Danny and Debbie heard the *clack-clack-clack* of her claws.

"I don't want to go there," Debbie said.

"We're not," the fat lady told her. "We're going to get four ice-cream cones. Or something else, if you would rather have something else."

Danny explained about their pieces of green cardboard, and by the time he had finished they were out of the ten-in-one tent and standing in front of the refreshment stand.

"What'll it be, Doll?" inquired the middle-aged man behind the counter.

"Two triple-dip cones," the fat lady said, taking a diamond from her purse. "And how did you know my name?"

"Used to guess your weight," the man said. "Everything else, too. Where you live and what you do. You now, you're a schoolteacher from Indiana."

"Absolutely correct."

"I have to get the feel of you to get it exactly right. . . . But, oh, I'll say two hundred and sixty-two."

The fat woman smiled. "That's a bit flattering, but very close just the same."

"Tell you what I'm gonna do. If I get this next one right, your cones is free. Only if I miss, you gotta pay. You're here hopin' to meet a nice guy like me."

The fat lady nodded and smiled again. "You're amazing."

The man looked surprised and a little frightened.

"I must take one of the cones you're going to give me back to my friend Jolly Janie," the fat lady explained, "and while we eat our cones I'll have a little talk with her. After that, I'll come back here." She paused to smile once more. "I'm certain you and I have a great deal in common."

The man had taken two sugar cones from a jar; his hand trembled slightly as he scooped strawberry ice cream into each. "I still got a wife up in Maine," he said, "we ain't never been divorced."

The fat lady smiled and nodded. "How interesting! You must tell me all about her."

Debbie declared, "We're not going back in there," and drew Danny aside.

When the fat lady had gone, Danny showed the man his piece of green cardboard.

"This's for cotton candy," the man said, and fed shining crystal granules into his candy-floss machine.

"What is mine, Mister?" Debbie held up her piece of green cardboard.

"Cinnamon apple. You want it?"

Debby nodded, and the man selected one and gave it to her, then wound spun candy floss on a rolled-up stick of cardboard for Danny.

Danny held it up to admire it; it looked almost too pretty to eat. "What would you like to do next?"

"Go away from here," the candy floss whispered. Danny was so surprised he nearly dropped it.

Thinking that Danny had spoken, Debbie said, "Well, I won't go back in that tent."

Danny was stepping hurriedly away from the refreshment stand already, in deference to his candy floss. "We could ride the Skyrocket."

"Oh, yes." The candy floss opened clear blue eyes. "Ride the Skyrocket!"

"Or the Ferris wheel," remarked Debbie's cinnamon apple. "The Ferris wheel is great fun. Nobody ever gets off the Ferris wheel."

Debbie, who had never seen a talking apple before, gawked at it.

Danny caught her by the arm and pulled her through the hurly-burly of the carnival to a little booth in which people were throwing wooden rings at plastic prizes. "I think that man's probably going to want them back if he finds out they can talk," he confided.

"Mine didn't talk," Debbie told him, sounding none too sure of herself.

"The Ferris wheel is where the colored lights come from," her apple said in a fruity but very matter-of-fact voice. "That makes it the easiest thing to find on the whole lot. Besides, it's much closer than that other ride. That other ride is on beyond it, way out in the cornfields."

Debbie caught Danny's sleeve with her free hand. "Come on. We're going to the Ferris wheel."

"You can eat me while you ride," her apple suggested. "I'm red and delicious."

Danny's candy floss whispered, "I've a great secret to tell you once you get to the Ferris wheel, and you may eat me afterward."

Danny nodded; but Debbie said, "I don't want to eat you. I've never had a talking apple before."

"I can tell you much, much more from inside," the apple assured her. "Young and innocent though you are, I can make you very wise."

"As wise as the snake lady?" (Debbie was hurrying through the crowd, dragging Danny behind her. A young woman who had been dancing topless on the platform of the All Girl Review caught sight of them, and for a moment her face softened; but no one else appeared to notice them at all.) "She seemed like she knew everything."

"Yes!" the apple exclaimed. "That's it exactly, and she would tell you to eat me if she were here."

"No," whispered Danny's candy floss. But only Danny heard her.

The Ferris wheel was very large indeed, and except for a summer sky the most beautiful thing that Danny and Debbie had ever seen. Not only was it carved wonderfully, but all the carvings were alive; and it gleamed everywhere with colored lights that rivaled that infinity sign posed between earth and sun that is the king of rainbows. There were countless riders and countless more waiting to get on, and though most seemed very ordinary people, many more were strange beyond imagining.

"Look!" Danny pointed as he spoke. "That's a goblin with two heads."

"There's a clown with a slingshot." Debbie pointed, too. "And another clown holding the moon."

"Riding the Ferris wheel is great fun," her apple repeated proudly. "Nobody ever gets off."

"It is time for my secret," his candy floss confided to Danny. "Listen carefully, and never forget."

"I will," Danny promised.

"It is a great secret—one of the very greatest—and yet it is a simple thing, as all truly great secrets are. It is that you are already on the wheel."

"No," Danny told her.

"Yes, you are. You must stand here and watch until you see yourselves, no matter how long it takes. That is extremely important."

Debbie leaned closer so she could hear the candy floss above the noise of the crowd.

"You must watch until you see yourselves," the candy floss repeated. "Then you may eat me."

For moments that afterward seemed very long, Danny and Debbie watched the wheel, and the things that they saw would fill a thousand books much larger than this one—a bat that was almost a person, for example, and a fox just then removing his mask.

"There's the nice fat lady," Debbie said, and waved to her, "and there's the snake woman and the lobster girl. They're all riding on it. And there, and there . . ."

"It's us," Danny said, and his voice cracked under the strain of it.

"Eat me now!" demanded Debbie's apple.

"Eat me, please," whispered Danny's candy floss.

He nodded, and as Debbie was taking a big bite out of her apple, he took an even bigger bite of candy floss, and it tasted wonderful.

And then, as they always did, they traded bites.

The Ferris wheel spun faster and faster as they ate, and seemed to turn on its side like a gyroscope as it spun, becoming the carnival itself, so that there was only one Debbie and one Danny again.

And at last it was earth and darkness.

After that, they woke up and stood in line to wash their faces and brush their teeth (Debbie could still taste cinnamon) and went downstairs to bowls of cornflakes.

"Children," Aunt Mildred said, tapping her cereal bowl, "I'd like you to meet our brand-new arrivals. This is Candi Cotin."

Candi was a sweet-faced little girl with hair so blond as to be almost white.

"And this is her brother, Taffy Apple."

Taffy was bigger and older than Danny, with red hair and freckles, and looked as if butter would not melt in his mouth.

"Candi and Taffy, these children are Stephen and Luis and LaBelinda, and Debbie and Danny. Danny and Debbie are brother and sister, just as you are—"

"Half sister," Candi whispered. Perhaps no one but Danny heard her.

"And you will share their room with them. Debbie, Danny, listen to me. After breakfast I want you to show Candi and Taffy where your room is and where you hang your clothes, and make them feel right at home."

Debbie and Danny had looked at each other when she said that, and had no further need of communication.

Upstairs a few minutes later, Taffy glanced around their room and said, "This is just a *little* room."

"We know," Debbie told him.

"There's only room for one bed." Taffy waited for Danny or Debbie to contradict him, but neither did. "So I'm sleeping in it. You two can sleep on the floor with Candi. You got a problem with that?" He eyed Danny, hands on hips.

"In a way we do," Debbie told him.

"Because we won't be sleeping here at all," Danny said.

Debbie nodded. "Because we're going to run away. There has to be a better place than this is. A lot of better places, really. We're going to find one."

"But there's something I have to do here before we go," Danny told Taffy. The punch he threw was half uppercut and half roundhouse right, but it caught Taffy just below the jaw and was a much harder blow than could be expected from a boy Danny's age. In a moment more the two were rolling over the floor, and a moment after that Danny was seated astride Taffy, holding him by the ears and bumping his head against the floor as fast as he could lift it and slam it back down.

That went on for several minutes; and when it was over Danny said, "I had to show you I'm not afraid of you, see?"

Taffy only cried, so Danny bumped his head one more time to get his attention. "I'm talking to you," Danny told him, "and you better answer."

"All right," Taffy croaked.

"So listen. Someday we're going to run into you and your sister again. I'm going to talk to Candi, and she better tell me you slept on the floor. You hear?"

Taffy managed to say, "Yeah."

"And her in the bed. I'll be bigger then, so that's how it better be." Danny gave Taffy's head a final bang for not forgetting.

Later still, when the house in which Aunt Mildred boarded children for the Department of Corrections and Family Services had long been out of sight, and even the old meat-packing plant could no longer be identified behind them, Debbie asked Danny where he had learned to fight like that.

To which he replied, "The cotton candy showed me."

Debbie considered, and at last she said, "That doesn't seem right."

"Okay, but it seemed really, really right to me while I was doing it," Danny told her. "What I want to know is how about us now? Can we get by on our own till we find somebody who'll be nice to us?"

"Don't worry." Debbie put her arm around his shoulders, suddenly very conscious that she was a year older, and that Danny had a bruise on one cheek and a big scratch on the other. "We're not little anymore. Not little kids, like we used to be. We're just young, and that's good."

Solemnly Danny added, "We've got pocketsful of diamonds."

Copperhead

◆

The telephone in the study rang ten minutes before the news came on. The new President picked it up and said hello.

"Mr. President?"

"Speaking." Only eighteen people were supposed to have the number. For an instant, the new President wondered how many actually did.

"This is Marsha. Boone's killed himself."

The new President was silent, conscious that there were a thousand things to say and unable to say even the least of them. In his mind's eye he saw the leaves, a drift of red, yellow, and gold autumn leaves at the foot of the tree on the hill. Leaves still touched with green here and there, and the stirring under those leaves.

"He left a note. I haven't been able to find out what was in it."

"Don't."

"Don't?"

"It will be damaging to us in some way. They'll find out, Marsha, and they'll throw it in our faces. We'll know a lot more about it than we want to then, and you're needed for other things."

"He was my husband, Mr. President. The divorce—"

"I know."

"It wasn't—wasn't final. Not yet. I want to know why he killed himself."

He recalled it exactly. *"There was a crash in Idaho in August,"* the general had said. *"We found this in the wreckage."*

"Are you still there, Mr. President?"

The irony almost overcame him, but he managed to say, "Still here."

"He hung himself with—with a telephone cord from the chandelier in the dining room. That's what they told me. He stood on a chair, a—a chair on top of the table. He p-put the cord around his neck . . ."

The new President turned on the TV and pressed the Mute button. It was easy, he thought. All the buttons were so easy.

"I need to know, Mr. President. I need to find out."

"You know."

"I need to see the letter."

"Then do." He murmured comforting words, his friendship with Boone and Marsha, the great contribution Boone had made to his administration. After a time that seemed long, the silent TV showed him with Boone, with Boone and Marsha, with Boone at the convention. Eventually he hung up.

The phone rang again at once. He picked it up and said, "I ought to get call waiting on this thing."

"Yes, Mr. President, you should." There was no humor in Rance's voice, none at all.

"I was about to call you. Boone's hung himself."

"I was calling to tell you. This phone was busy."

"There's a suicide note. Do you have it?"

"No, sir."

"Get it. Don't let the press get it, and don't let Marsha see it. The cops will have it. Find out if they've made copies. If they have, destroy them."

"Do you want to see it, Mr. President?"

He did not. He knew what would be in it, and knew that it would sicken him. "No," he said. Elsewhere in the house another phone was ringing. He got up from his chair and kicked the door shut. Peggy would get it, and Peggy, seeing the closed door, would stall them. Or stall them anyway, door closed or not. "Maybe I'll want to see it later. Not now. I want you to find her and bring her here."

"Find who, Mr. President?"

"Who the hell do you think?"

"Jane Doe?"

"You're watching her, or you're damned well supposed to be."

"We are," Rance said.

"A hell of a lot of good it did. Bring her here. Now!"

"Won't you be going back to Washington, Mr. President?"

Rage would help nothing. He had told the general to leave the Changer with him. He had done that. He himself had pressed the button. It had pressed very easily. He made his voice calm, and was gratified to hear it. He did not sound like a man who was controlling his voice at all. "I'm going to stay here, George, until this blows over a little. First the murder, then this. Washington will be a zoo."

"I'm sure you're right, Mr. President."

"I know I am. Fortunately we've got three years until the next election."

"Longer than that, Mr. President."

"Nearly three years until the next campaign." Although no one was watching, the new President made himself smile. Smiles showed in your voice. "That's what matters. How fast can you get her here, George?"

"Can we play rough, Mr. President? If she doesn't want to come?" Rance was stalling, giving himself time to think. That showed in your voice, too.

"Yes. Absolutely."

"What about Karen?"

The new President had not thought of that, but he would need to talk to Karen. Karen wanted a big job, but had she earned one? Controlling the redhead was like neck-reining a tiger. Perhaps she had. Assistant Secretary of Labor might be enough. "Yes," he said. "Bring Karen, if she can come. If she can't, don't wait for her."

"Five hours, Mr. President."

He glanced at his wrist. "Eleven tonight, our time."

They arrived at ten fifty-five in a black Lincoln Navigator, three FBI agents, Karen, and Jane Doe. He had told the Secret Service to get out and stay out, and had telephoned the Secretary of the Treasury when they had refused. They were a hundred yards or more away from the house, every one of them.

Now he ordered the FBI agents to return to their vehicle and stand by, and waved Karen and Jane Doe in. The former looked smart, competent, and horribly tired; as always the latter was so lovely that it was only with difficulty that he kept himself from gawking at her.

"You're beat," he told Karen. "Jane and I are going into the den to talk. Alone."

Karen nodded, and the tall and superlatively graceful woman he had named Jane Doe smiled enigmatically and brushed hair the color of new copper wire away from her face.

"I know you've done a lot," he said. "I know you've done the best you could at an impossible job. I want you to understand that I know that, no matter what else I may say tonight and no matter what happens tonight. Do you?"

"Yes, Mr. President."

Her voice had been so low that he had scarcely heard her. As he spoke again, he wondered whether she knew about Boone. If she did not, this certainly was not the time to tell her. "It may be hours—I don't know. I may need more from you tonight, and I may not. I don't know that, either. I want you to go into my wife's bedroom and lie down. She's in Washington, so you won't be disturbed. If there's anything in there you need, take it. Cosmetics. Clean whatever. I'll square it with her."

"I'll be all right, Mr. President. Don't worry about me."

"Try to get to sleep. That's what I'm saying."

She nodded. "I will, Mr. President."

"I'm going back tomorrow, and when I get back I'll make a slot for you. Something in State, some nice, quiet country where they speak English, Madame Ambassador."

The other woman laughed, the summons of golden bells.

"You come in here with me," he told her, and shut the door behind them, and locked it.

" 'Ou douh nawt leek mee."

"My feelings about you no longer matter." He waited for her to sit down, then sat down himself. It was in his desk drawer, the left upper drawer.

He got it out, turned it over in his hands for a few seconds, and laid it on his desk. In appearance it was a lopsided oval of black plastic with three red buttons, remarkable only in that its black was the black of space, a deeper black than any human technology was capable of, and in that its buttons might easily have been drops of fresh blood.

" 'Ou 'ad dawt vhen Aw coom."

"Yes, I did." The sunlit hilltop, the accumulation of fallen leaves at the base of the tree were back, more vivid than ever. "I slipped it into my pocket." He cleared his throat. "I shouldn't have had it at all, and I had my hands full with you."

She laughed again; her eyes were of every conceivable color, depending as it seemed upon the lighting and her mood. Just now they, too, gleamed scarlet.

Like the eyes of a white rat, the new President thought. Could she have been a pet in the place from which she came? A laboratory animal? "I never told you about this," he said aloud. "I'm going to tonight, because I owe it to you. You don't like to listen—"

She smiled, and her perfect teeth looked both whiter and sharper than any other woman's teeth.

"Or sit still. You don't have to listen if you don't want to. If you want to get up and wander around, that's fine. But I'm going to say it."

"Aw siht awn 'ou lahp? Aw siht vher steal. Naw mahter 'ow meany vhertds, Aw lesson."

"No."

"Naw vahn vahtches." She was clearly amused.

He shook his head. "I had been working hard. Not only after my inauguration, but for more than a year before it. Working twelve or thirteen hours every day without a break. Spring came and my wife and I came back here; I meant to take three days off—a long weekend. Some people in Spokane started burning things again, and my three days turned out to be eighteen hours. I went back to Washington and back to work."

"Aw douh nawt vhork. Aw douh nawt naw ahbawt dhees." She rose more gracefully than any dancer, seeming to float from the chair.

"Fall came. Football season. I'd lost twenty pounds, and I was yelling at everybody. My wife had to stay in Washington, but I cleared my desk and flew back here. I wanted to drink beer and watch football. Most of all, I wanted to sleep."

She poked the fire as a child would, gratified by the cloud of sparks.

"I was here a day and a half when General Martens called. There had never really been a crash before. All that about Roswell was nonsense, but this time there'd been a real crash or something that looked like one, and they had an artifact that still worked. I should have kept my damned mouth shut, but I said bring it here. I wanted to see it."

"Dhees dhing 'ou shaw mee? Eet dhaws nawt eent'res mee."

"There are other universes." The new President's voice fell. "All the astrophysicists say so. The Changer accesses them. Point it at something, press a button, and you get its cognate. Sometimes. Maybe all the time, but maybe sometimes the cognate is so close you can't tell anything's happened. Did I tell you we went up on the hill?"

" 'Ou deed nawt." She sat down again and crossed her legs. "Aw rhe-member dhawt 'ill. Aw vhas colt."

He nodded. "You were naked. General Martens didn't want to talk in the house—he was afraid of listening devices, really paranoid about them. We walked clear across the big meadow and climbed the hill. I sat on a rock up there, and he on a fallen tree. I'd started to sit down beside him, but he didn't want that, and at first I didn't understand. Later I got it—he was afraid I'd grab it."

She laughed.

"Which I did, in a way. He showed it to me, but he didn't want me to touch it. I was President, goddamnit, and he was trying to give me orders. I made him give it to me and leave it with me. I told him I'd give it back to him when I was through with it.

"Then I sat there on that rock and watched him walk back to the house—back to his blue Air Force Chevy. I turned the Changer over and over in my hands, and I thought, By God, this President stuff can be fun once in a while. It's about time."

"Vhat ahbawt mee?"

"I'm getting to that. There's a big maple up there. It was fifteen or twenty feet from where I was sitting, and its leaves were thick all around it." He paused, remembering. "Half its leaves had fallen, or about that. After the general's car went into Three Mile Woods, I looked at them. I don't know why, but I did. Perhaps I had heard something."

He paused, cleared his throat. "Suddenly they moved, stirred. There was only a very light breeze so it wasn't that. There was something in there, something under the leaves, and I guess my hand tightened on the Changer. It must have, because there you were."

"Ahh!"

"Yes. You know the rest. You know a lot more, too. Things you won't tell about the place you came from." He knew he should pick up the Changer at this point, but he discovered that he was unable to do so. He pointed to it instead. "I'm going to change you again. You know why, unless you're a lot stupider than I think you are."

" 'Ou dheenk Aw dell 'ou vhife."

"No. No, I take it back. Yes, that and a couple of dozen other things. I'm going to offer you a last chance. Do you want to stay here?"

"Aw douh nawt car."

"I offer it anyway. You've always said you don't remember the place you came from, the other universe. I'll be frank, since this is likely to be our last conversation. You've lied to us. Tell me the truth, and it's possible—just possible—that something you say will change my mind. Do you want to try?"

She rose again and went to the window, staring out into the night. "Ees zo confuse."

He waited; and when she did not speak again, he said, "There are three buttons, and I don't know which one I pressed. I may send you back. But I may simply send you someplace else. I don't know. This is your last chance."

"Vhas a groose." She turned, and her eyes were the color of heaven, and she was the loveliest woman the new President had ever seen. "Nawt lak 'ou. Aw zay, 'ou vhill nawt neffer grawnt offer mee agan." She shruggcd. "Dhoss bhoyes, de vhun keels de odder. Aw douh nawthing."

He said, "The first time I heard you talk like this I fell for it hook, line, and sinker."

He had reached for the Changer as he spoke. Her hand had to travel twice as far, but it struck like a snake. For an instant—perhaps it was half a second, perhaps less—she held it and looked at him, savoring the moment; and her eyes were as black as the Changer itself, a blackness in which red sparks danced. Her thumb depressed one of the red buttons.

His clothing collapsed in a heap. She did not see it, seeing only the naked man who stood before the chair in which the new President had sat. So tall was he that his head nearly brushed the ceiling; and so glorious was he that one felt that the ceiling had risen so that his head would not brush it.

"Because you have done this, cursed be you." His voice was like an organ, his hand like a vise as he caught her by the throat. "Upon your belly you shall go, and the dust you shall eat, and I shall crush your head under my heel."

In his new realm, where Time sang like a brook, the new President picked himself up and stood stock-still to listen. The trees in a wood far away were barking; on the cliff that rose behind him, a mountain ram winded its horns.

The Lost Pilgrim

✦

Before leaving my own period, I resolved to keep a diary; and indeed I told several others I would, and promised to let them see it upon my return. Yesterday I arrived, captured no Pukz, and compiled no text. No more inauspicious beginning could be imagined.

I will not touch my emergency rations. I am hungry, and there is nothing to eat; but how absurd it would be to begin in such a fashion! No. Absolutely not. Let me finish this, and I will go off in search of breakfast.

To begin. I find myself upon a beach, very beautiful and very empty, but rather too hot and much too shadeless to be pleasant. "Very empty" I said, but how can I convey just how empty it really is? (Pukz 1–3)

As you see, there is sun and there is water, the former remarkably hot and bright, the latter remarkably blue and clean. There is no shade, and no one who—

A sail! Some kind of sailboat is headed straight for this beach. It seems too small, but this could be it. (Puk 4)

I cannot possibly describe everything that happened today. There was far, far too much. I can only give a rough outline. But first I should say that I am no longer sure why I am here, if I ever was. On the beach last night, just after I arrived, I felt no doubts. Either I knew why I had come, or I did not think about it. There was that time when they were going to send me out to join the whateveritwas expedition—the little man with the glasses. But I do not think this is that, this is something else.

Not the man getting nailed up, either.

It will come to me. I am sure it will. In such a process of regression there cannot help but be metal confusion. Do I mean metal? The women's armor was gold or brass. Something like that. They marched out onto the beach, a long line of them, all in the gold armor. I did not know they were women.

I hid behind rocks and took Pukz. (See Pukz 5–9) The reflected glare made it difficult, but I got some good shots just the same.

They banged their spears on their shields and made a terrible noise, but when the boat came close enough for us to see the men on it (Pukz 10 and 11) they marched back up onto the hill behind me and stood on the crest. It was then that I realized they were women; I made a search for "women in armor" and found more than a thousand references, but all those I examined were to Joan of Arc or similar figures. This was not one woman but several hundreds.

I do not believe there should be women in armor, anyway. Or men in armor, like those who got off the boat. Swords, perhaps. Swords might be all right. And the name of the boat should be two words, I think.

The men who got off this boat are young and tough-looking. There is a book of prayers in my pack, and I am quite certain it was to be a talisman. "O God, save me by thy name and defend my cause by thy might." But I cannot imagine these men being impressed by any prayers.

Some of these men were in armor and some were not. One who had no armor and no weapons left the rest and started up the slope. He has an intelligent face, and though his staff seemed sinister, I decided to risk everything. To tell the truth I thought he had seen me and was coming to ask what I wanted. I was wrong, but he would surely have seen me as soon as he took a few more steps. At any rate, I switched on my translator and stood up. He was surprised, I believe, at my black clothes and the buckles on my shoes; but he is a very smooth man, always exceedingly polite. His name is Ekkiawn. Or something like that. (Puk 12) Ekkiawn is as near as I can get to the pronunciation.

I asked where he and the others were going, and when he told me, suggested that I might go with them, mentioning that I could talk to the

Native Americans. He said it was impossible, that they had sworn to accept no further volunteers, that he could speak the language of Kolkkis himself, and that the upper classes of Kolkkis all spoke English.

I, of course, then asked him to say something in English, and switched off my translator. I could not understand a word of it.

At this point he began to walk again, marking each stride with his beautiful staff, a staff of polished hardwood on which a carved snake writhes. I followed him, switched my translator back on, and complimented him on his staff.

He smiled and stroked the snake. "My father permits me to use it," he said. "The serpent on his own is real, of course. Our tongues are like our emblems, I'm afraid. He can persuade anyone of anything. Compared to his, my own tongue is mere wood."

I said, "I assume you will seek to persuade those women that you come in peace. When you do, will they teach you to plant corn?"

He stopped and stared at me. "Are they women? Don't toy with me."

I said I had observed them closely, and I was quite sure they were.

"How interesting! Come with me."

As we approached the women, several of them began striking their shields with their spears, as before. (Puk 13) Ekkiawn raised his staff. "My dear young ladies, cease! Enchanting maidens, desist! You suppose us pirates. You could not be more mistaken. We are the aristocracy of the Minyans. Nowhere will you find young men so handsome, so muscular, so wealthy, so well bred, or so well connected. I myself am a son of Hodios. We sail upon a most holy errand, for we would return the sacred ramskin to Mount Laphystios."

The women had fallen silent, looking at one another and particularly at an unusually tall and comely woman who stood in the center of their line.

"Let there be peace between us," Ekkiawn continued. "We seek only fresh water and a few days' rest, for we have had hard rowing. We will pay for any supplies we receive from you, and generously. You will have no singing arrows nor blood-drinking spears from us. Do you fear sighs? Languishing looks? Gifts of flowers and jewelry? Say so if you do, and we will depart in peace."

A woman with gray hair straggling from under her helmet tugged at the sleeve of the tall woman. (Puk 14) Nodding, the tall woman stepped forward. "Stranger, I am Hupsipule, Queen of Lahmnos. If indeed you come in peace—"

"We do," Ekkiawn assured her.

"You will not object to my conferring with my advisors."

"Certainly not."

While the queen huddled with four other women, Ekkiawn whispered, "Go to the ship like a good fellow, and find Eeasawn, our captain. Tell him these are women and describe the queen. Name her."

Thinking that this might well be the boat I was supposed to board after all, and that this offered as good a chance to ingratiate myself with its commander as I was ever likely to get, I hurried away. I found Eeasawn without much trouble, assured him that the armed figures on the hilltop were in fact women in armor ("both Ekkiawn and I saw that quite clearly"), and told him that the tallest, good-looking, black-haired, and proud, was Queen Hupsipule.

He thanked me. "And you are . . . ?"

"A humble pilgrim seeking the sacred ramskin, where I hope to lay my heartfelt praise at the feet of God."

"Well spoken, but I cannot let you sail with us, Pilgrim. This ship is already as full of men as an egg is of meat. But should—"

Several members of the crew were pointing and shouting. The women on the hilltop were removing their armor and so revealing their gender, most being dressed in simple frocks without sleeves, collars, or buttons. (Puk 15) There was a general rush from the ship.

Let me pause here to comment upon the men's clothing, of which there is remarkably little, many being completely naked. Some wear armor, a helmet, and a breastplate, or a helmet alone. A few more wear loose short-sleeved shirts that cover them to mid-thigh. The most remarkable is certainly the captain, who goes naked except for a single sandal. (Pukz 16 and 17)

For a moment or two, I stood watching the men from the ship talking to the women. After conversations too brief to have consisted of much more than introductions, each man left with three or more women, though our captain departed with the queen alone (Puk 18), and Ekkiawn with five. I had started to turn away when the largest and strongest hand I have ever felt closed upon my shoulder.

"Look 'round here, Pilgrim. Do you really want to go to Kolkkis with us?"

The speaker was a man of immense size, bull-necked and pig-eyed (Puk 19); I felt certain that it would be dangerous to reply in the negative.

"Good! I promised to guard the ship, you see, the first time it needed guarding."

"I am not going to steal anything," I assured him.

"I didn't think so. But if you change your mind I'm going to hunt you down and break your neck. Now, then, I heard you and Eeasawn. You watch for me, hear? While I go into whatever town those split-tailed soldiers came out of and get us some company. Two enough for you?"

Not knowing what else to do, I nodded.

"Me?" He shrugged shoulders that would have been more than creditable on a bull gorilla. "I knocked up fifty girls in one night once. Not that I couldn't have done it just about any other night, too, only that was the only time I've had a crack at fifty. So a couple for you and as many as I can round up for me. And if your two have anything left when you're done up, send 'em over. Here." He handed me a spear. "You're our guard till I get back."

I am waiting his return; I have removed some clothing because of the heat and in the hope of ingratiating myself with any women who may return with him. Hahraklahs is his name.

Hours have passed since I recorded the account you just read. No one has come, neither to molest our boat nor for any other reason. I have been staring at the stars and examining my spear. It has a smooth hardwood shaft and a leaf-shaped blade of copper or brass. I would not have thought such a blade could be sharpened, but it is actually very sharp.

It is also *wrong*. I keep thinking of spears with flared mouths like trumpets. And yet I must admit that my spear is a sensible weapon, while the spears with trumpet mouths would be senseless as well as useless.

These are the most beautiful stars in the world. I am beginning to doubt that I have come at the right period, and to tell the truth I cannot remember what the right period was. It does not matter, since no one can possibly use the same system. But this period in which I find myself has the most beautiful stars, bar none. And the closest.

There are voices in the distance. I am prepared to fight, if I must.

We are at sea. I have been rowing; my hands are raw and blistered. We are too many to row all at once, so we take turns. Mine lasted most of the morning. I pray for a wind.

I should have brought prophylactics. It is possible I have contracted some disease, though I doubt it. The women (Apama and Klays, Pukz 20–25, infrared) were interesting, both very eager to believe that I was the son of some king or other and very determined to become pregnant. Apama has killed her husband for an insult, stabbing him in his sleep.

Long after we had finished and washed ourselves in this strange tideless sea, Hahraklahs was still engaged with his fifteen or twenty. (They came and went in a fashion that made it almost impossible to judge the exact number.) When the last had gone, we sat and talked. He has had a hard life in many ways, for he is a sort of slave to one Eurustheus who refuses to speak to him or even look at him. He has been a stableman and so forth. He says he strangled the lion whose skin he wears, and he is certainly very strong. I can hardly lift his brass-bound club, which he flourishes like a stick.

If it were not for him, I would not be on this boat. He has taken a liking to me because I did not want to stay at Lahmnos. He had to kidnap about half the crew to get us out to sea again, and two could not be found. Kaeneus (Puk 26) says the crew wanted to depose Captain Eeasawn and make Hahraklahs captain, but he remained loyal to Eeasawn and would not agree. Kaeneus also confided that he himself underwent a sex-change operation some years ago. Ekkiawn warned me that Kaeneus is the most dangerous fighter on the boat; I suppose he was afraid I would ridicule him. He is a chief, Ekkiawn says, of the Lapiths; this seems to be a Native American tribe.

I am certainly on the wrong vessel. There are two points I am positive of. The first is the name of the captain. It was Jones. Captain Jones. This cannot be Eeasawn, whose name does not even begin with *J*. The second is that there was to be someone named Brewster on board, and that I was to help this Brewster (or perhaps Bradford) talk with the Lapiths. There is no one named Bradford among my present companions—I have introduced myself to all of them and learned their names. No Brewsters. Thus this boat cannot be the one I was to board.

On the positive side, I am on a friendly footing now with the Lapith chief. That seems sure to be of value when I find the correct ship and reach Atlantis.

I have discussed this with Argos. Argos (Puk 27) is the digitized personality of the boat. (I wonder if the women who lay with him realized that?) He points out—wisely, I would say—that the way to locate a vessel is to visit a variety of ports, making inquiries at each. In order to do that, one should be on another vessel, one making a long voyage with many ports of call. That is my situation, which might be far worse. We have sighted two other boats, both smaller than our own.

Our helmsman, said to be an infallible weather prophet, has announced that we will have a stiff west wind by early afternoon. Our course is northeast for Samothrakah, which I take to be another island. We are forty-nine men and one woman.

She is Atalantah of Kaludon (Pukz 28–30), tall, slender, muscular, and quite beautiful. Ekkiawn introduced me to her, warning me that she would certainly kill me if I tried to force her. I assured her, and him, that I would never do such a thing. In all honesty I cannot say I have talked with her, but I listened to her for some while. Hunting is the only thing she cares about. She has hunted every large animal in her part of the world and joined Eeasawn's expedition in hope of hunting grups, fierce birds never seen west of our destination. They can be baited to a blind to feed upon the bodies of horses or cattle, she says. From that I take them to be some type of vulture. Her knowledge of lions, stags, wild swine, and the dogs employed to hunt all three is simply immense.

At sea again, course southeast and the wind dead astern. Now that I have leisure to bring this account up to date, I sit looking out at the choppy waves pursuing us and wonder whether you will believe even a fraction of what I have to relate.

In Samothrakah we were to be initiated into the Cult of Persefonay, a powerful goddess. I joined in the preparations eagerly, not only because it would furnish insight into the religious beliefs of these amoral but very superstitious men, but because I hoped—as I still do—that the favor of the goddess would bring me to the rock whose name I have forgotten, the rock that is my proper destination.

We fasted for three days, drinking water mixed with wine but eating no solid food. On the evening of the third day we stripped and daubed each other with a thin white mixture, which I suspect was little more than chalk dispersed in water. That done, we shared a ritual supper of boiled beans and raw onions. (Pukz 31 and 32)

Our procession reached the cave of Persefassa, as she is also called, about midnight. We extinguished our torches in an underground pool and received new ones, smaller torches that burned with a clear, almost white flame and gave off a sweet scent. Singing, we marched another mile underground.

My companions appeared undaunted. I was frightened, and kept my teeth from chattering only by an effort of will. After a time I was able to exchange places with Erginos and so walk behind Hahraklahs, that tower of strength. If that stratagem had not succeeded, I think I might have turned and run.

The throne room of the goddess (Pukz 33–35) is a vast underground chamber of spectacular natural columns where icy water drips secretly and, as it were, stealthily. The effect is of gentle, unending rain, of mourning protracted until the sun burns out. The priestesses passed among us, telling each of us in turn, "All things fail. All decays, and passes away."

Ghosts filled the cavern. Our torches rendered them invisible, but I could see them in the darkest places, always at the edge of my field of vision. Their whispers were like a hundred winds in a forest, and whenever one came near me I felt a cold that struck to the bone.

Deep-voiced horns, melodious and tragic, announced the goddess. She was preceded by the Kabeiri, stately women and men somewhat taller than

Hahraklahs who appeared to have no feet. Their forms were solid to the knees, where they became translucent and quickly faded to nothing. They made an aisle for Persefonay, a lovely young woman far taller than they.

She was robed in crimson, and black gems bound her fair hair. (Pukz 36 and 37) Her features are quite beautiful; her expression I can only call resigned. (She may revisit the upper world only as long as the pomegranate is in bloom—so we were taught during our fast. For the rest of the year she remains her husband's prisoner underground.) She took her seat upon a rock that accommodated itself to her as she sat, and indicated by a gesture that we were to approach her.

We did, and her Kabeiri closed about us as if we were children shepherded by older children, approaching a teacher. That and Puk 38 will give you the picture; but I was acutely conscious, as I think we all were, that she and her servants were beings of an order remote from biological evolution. You will be familiar with such beings in our own period, I feel sure. I do not recall them, true. I *do* recall that knowledge accumulates. The people of the period in which I find myself could not have sent someone, as I have been sent, to join in the famous voyage whose name I have forgotten.

Captain Eeasawn stepped forward to speak to Persefonay. (Pukz 39 and 40) He explained that we were bound for Aea, urged upon our mission by the Pythoness and accompanied by sons of Poseidon and other gods. Much of what he said contradicted what I had been told earlier, and there was much that I failed to understand.

When he had finished, Persefonay introduced the Kabeiri, the earliest gods of Samothrakah. One or more, she said, would accompany us on our voyage, would see that our boat was never wrecked, and would rescue us if it were. Eeasawn thanked her in an elaborate speech, and we bowed.

At once every torch burned out, leaving us in utter darkness. (Pukz 39a and 40a, infrared) Instructed by the priestesses, we joined hands, I with Hahraklahs and Atalantah, and so were led out of the cave. There our old torches were restored to us and rekindled. (Puk 41) Carrying them and singing we returned to our ship, serenaded by wolves.

———

We have passed Ilion! Everyone agrees that was the most dangerous part of our voyage. Its inhabitants control the strait and permit no ships other than their own to enter or leave. We remained well out of sight of the city until night. Night came, and a west wind with it. We put up the mast and hoisted our sail, and Periklumenos dove from the prow and took the form of a dolphin (Puk 42, infrared) to guide us through the strait. As we drew near Ilion, we rowed, too, rowing for all we were worth for what seemed half the night. A patrol boat spotted us and moved to intercept us, but Phaleros shot its helmsman. It sheered off—and we passed! That shot was five hundred meters if it was one, and was made by a man standing unsupported on a bench on a heeling, pitching boat urged forward by a bellying sail and forty rowers pulling for all they were worth. The arrow's flight was as straight as any string. I could not see where the helmsman was hit, but Atalantah says the throat. Knowing that she prides herself on her shooting, I asked whether she could have made that shot. She shrugged and said, "Once, perhaps, with a quiver-full of arrows."

We are docked now at a place called Bear Island. We fear no bears here, nor much of anything else. The king is the son of an old friend of Hahraklahs'. He has invited us to his wedding, and all is wine and garlands, music, dancing, and gaiety. (Pukz 43–48) Eeasawn asked for volunteers to guard the boat. I volunteered, and Atalantah offered to stay with me. Everyone agreed that Eeasawn and Hahraklahs would have to be present the whole time, so they were excused; the rest drew lots to relieve us. Polydeukahs the Clone and Kaeneus lost and were the subjected to much good-natured raillery. They promise to relieve us as soon as the moon comes up.

Meanwhile I have been leaning on my spear and talking with Atalantah. Leaning on my spear, I said, but that was only at first. Some kind people came down from the town (Puk 49) to talk with us, and left us a skin of wine. After that we sat side by side on one of the benches and passed the tart wine back and forth. I do not think that I will ever taste dry red wine again without being reminded of this evening.

Atalantah has had a wretched life. One sees a tall, athletic, good-looking young woman. One is told that she is royal, the daughter of a king. One assumes quite naturally that hers has been a life of ease and privilege. It has been nothing of the sort. She was exposed as an infant—

left in the forest to die. She was found by hunters, one of whom had a captive bear with a cub. He washed her in the bear's urine, after which the bear permitted her to nurse. No one can marry her who cannot best her in a foot race, and no one can. As if that were not enough, she is compelled to kill the suitors she outruns. And she has, murdering half a dozen fine young men and mourning them afterward.

I tried to explain to her that she could still have male friends, men other than suitors who like her and enjoy her company. I pointed out that I could never make a suitable mate for a beautiful young woman of royal blood, but that I would be proud to call myself her friend. I would make no demands, and assist her in any way I could. We kissed and became intimate.

Have I gone mad? Persefonay smiled at me as we left. I shall never forget that. I cannot. Now this!

No, I am not mad. I have been racking my brain, sifting my memory for a future that does not yet exist. There is a double helix of gold. It gives us the power to make monsters, and if it exists in that age it must exist in this. Look! (Pukz 50–58) I have paced off their height, and find it to be four and a half meters or a little more.

Six arms! All of them have six arms. (Pukz 54–57 show this very clearly.) They came at us like great white spiders, then rose to throw stones, and would have brained us with their clubs.

God above have mercy on us! I have been reading my little book by firelight. It says that a wise warrior is mightier than a strong warrior. Doubtless that is true, but I know that I am neither. We killed three. I killed one myself. Good Heavens!

Let me go at this logically, although every power in this mad universe must know that I feel anything but logical.

I have reread what I recorded here before the giants came. The moon rose, and not long after—say, three-quarters of an hour—our relief arrived. They were somewhat drunk, but so were we.

Kastawr came with his clone Polydeukahs, not wanting to enjoy himself without him. Kaeneus came as promised. Thus we had five fighters when the giants came down off the mountain. Atalantah's bow served us best, I think, but they rushed her. Kaeneus killed one as it ran. That was simply amazing. He crouched under his shield and sprang up as the giant dashed past, severing an artery in the giant's leg with his sword. The giant took a few more steps and fell. Polydeukahs and Kastawr attacked another as it grappled Atalantah. I actually heard a rib break under the blows of Polydeukahs' fists. They pounded the giant's side like hammers.

People who heard our war cries, the roars of the giants, and Atalantah's screams came pouring down from the town with torches, spears, and swords; but they were too late. We had killed four, and the rest were running from us. None of the townspeople I talked to had been aware of such creatures on their island. They regarded the bodies with superstitious awe. Furthermore, they now regard *us* with superstitious awe—our boat and our whole crew, and particularly Atalantah, Kastawr, Polydeukahs, Kaeneus, and me. (Puk 59)

About midnight Atalantah and I went up to the palace to see if there was any food left. As soon as we were alone, she embraced me. "Oh, Pilgrim! Can you . . . Could anyone ever love such a coward?"

"I don't ask for your love, Atalantah, only that you like me. I know very well that everyone on our boat is braver than I am, but—"

"Me! Me! You were—you were a wild bull. I was terrified. It was crushing me. I had dropped my bow, and I couldn't get to my knife. It was about to bite my head off, and you were coming! Augah! Oh, Pilgrim! I saw fear in the monster's eyes, before your spear! It was the finest thing that has ever happened to me, but when the giant dropped me I was trembling like a doe with an arrow in her heart."

I tried to explain that it had been nothing, that Kastawr and his clone had already engaged the giant, and that her own struggles were occupying its attention. I said, "I could never have done it if it hadn't had its hands full."

"It had its hands full?" She stared, and burst into laughter. In another minute I was laughing, too, the two of us laughing so hard we had to hold on to each other. It was a wonderful moment, but her laughter soon turned to tears, and for the better part of an hour I had to comfort a sobbing girl, a princess small, lonely, and motherless, who stayed alive as best she could in a forest hut with three rough men.

Before I go on to speak of the extraordinary events at the palace, I must say one thing more. My companions shouted their war cries as they battled the giants; and I, when I rushed at the one who held Atalantah, yelled, *"Mayflower! Mayflower!"* I know that was not what I should have said. I know I should have said mayday, but I do not know what "mayday" means, or why I should have said it. I cannot offer even a hint as to why I found myself shouting mayflower instead. Yet I feel that the great question has been answered. It was what I am doing here. The answer, surely, is that I was sent in order that Atalantah might be spared.

The whole palace was in an uproar. (Pukz 60–62) On the day before his wedding festivities began, King Kuzikos had killed a huge lion on the slopes of Mount Dindumon. It had been skinned and its skin displayed on the stoa, no one in his country having seen one of such size before.

After Kaeneus, Polydeukahs, and Kastawr left the banquet, this lion (we were told) was restored to life, someone filling the empty skin with new lion, so to speak. (Clearly that is impossible; another lion, black-maned like the first and of similar size, was presumably substituted for the skin.) What mattered was that the new or restored lion was loose in the palace. It had killed two persons before we arrived, and had mauled three others.

Amphiareaws was in a trance. King Kuzikos had freed his hounds, piebald dogs the size of Great Danes that were nearly as dangerous as any lion. (Pukz 63 and 64) Eeasawn and most of our crew were hunting the lion with the king. Hahraklahs had gone off alone in search of it, but had left word with Ekkiawn that I was to join him. Atalantah and I hurried away, knowing no more than that he had intended to search the east wing of the palace and the gardens. We found a body, apparently that of some worthy of the town, but had no way of knowing whether it was one of those whose deaths had already been reported or a fresh kill. It had been partly devoured, perhaps by the dogs.

We found Hahraklahs in the garden, looking very much like a lion on its hind legs himself with his lion skin and huge club. He greeted us cordially, and seemed not at all sorry that Atalantah had come with me.

"Now let me tell you," he said, "the best way to kill a lion—the best way for me, anyhow. If I can get behind that lion and get my hands on its neck, we can go back to our wine. If I tried to club it, you see, it would hear the club coming down and jerk away. They've got sharp ears, and they're very fast. I'd still hit it—they're not as fast as all that—but not where I wanted, and as soon as I hit it I'd have it in my lap. Let me get a grip on its neck though, and we've won."

Atalantah said, "I agree. How can we help?"

"It will be simple, but it won't be easy. When we find it, I'll front it. I'm big enough and mean enough that it won't go straight for me. It'll try to scare me into running, or dodge around and look for an opening. What I need is for somebody to distract it, just for a wink. When I killed this one I'm wearing Hylas did it for me, throwing stones. But he's not here."

I said I could do that if I could find the stones, and Atalantah remarked that an arrow or two would make any animal turn around to look. We had begun to tell Hahraklahs about the giants when Kalais swooped low and called, *"It's coming! Path to your left! Quick!"*

I turned my head in time to see its final bound, and it was like seeing a saddle horse clear a broad ditch. Three sparrows could not have scattered faster than we. The lion must have leaped again, coming down on Hahraklahs and knocking him flat. I turned just in time to see him throw it off. It spun through the air, landed on its feet, and charged him with a roar I will never forget.

I ran at it, I suppose with the thought of spearing it, if I had any plan at all. One of Atalantah's arrows whistled past and buried itself in the lion's mane. Hahraklahs was still down, and I tried to pull the lion off him. His club, breaking the lion's skull, sounded like a lab explosion.

And it was over. Blood ran from Hahraklahs' immense arms and trickled from his fingers, and more ran down his face and soaked his beard. The lion lay dead between us, bigger than any horse I have ever seen. Kalais landed on its side as he might have landed on a table, his great white wings fanning the hot night air.

Atalantah embraced me, and we kissed and kissed again. I think that we were both overjoyed that we were still alive. I know that I had already begun to shake. It had happened much too fast for me to be afraid while it was happening, but when it was over, I was terrified. My heart pounded and my knees shook. My mouth was dry. But oh how sweet it was to hold Atalantah and kiss her at that moment, and have her kiss me!

By the time we separated, Hahraklahs and Kalais were gone. I took a few Pukz of the dead lion. (Pukz 65–67) After that, we returned to the wedding banquet and found a lot of guests still there, with Eeasawn and most of our crew. As we came in, Hahraklahs called out, "Did you ever see a man that would take a lion by the tail? Here he is! Look at him!"

That was a moment!

We held a meeting today, just our crew. Eeasawn called it, of course. He talked briefly about Amphiareaws of Argolis, his high reputation as a seer, famous prophecies of his that had been fulfilled, and so on. I had already heard most of it from Kaeneus, and I believe most of our crew is thoroughly familiar with Amphiareaws' abilities.

Amphiareaws himself stepped forward. He is surprisingly young, and quite handsome, but I find it hard to meet his eyes; there is poetry in them, if you will, and sometimes there is madness. There may be something else as well, a quality rarer than either, to which I can put no name. I say there may be, although I cannot be sure.

He spoke very quietly. "We had portents last night. When we were told the lion had been resurrected, I tried to find out what god had done it, and why. At that time, I knew nothing about the six-armed giants. I'll come to them presently.

"Hrea is one of the oldest gods, and one of the most important. She's the mother of Father Zeus. She's also the daughter of Earth, something we forget when we shouldn't. Lions are her sacred animals. She doesn't like it when they are driven away. She likes it even less when they are killed. She's old, as I said, and has a great deal of patience, as old women generally do. Still, patience doesn't last forever. One of us killed one of her favorite lions some time ago."

Everyone looked at Hahraklahs when Amphiareaws said this; I confess I did as well.

"That lion was nursed by Hrea's daughter Hahra at her request, and it was set in the heavens by Hahra when it died—again at her mother's request. The man who killed it changed his name to 'Hahra's Glory' to avert her wrath, as most of us know. She spared him, and her mother Hrea let the matter go, at least for the present."

Amphiareaws fell silent, studying us. His eyes lingered on Hahraklahs, as was to be expected, but lingered on me even longer. (Puk 68) I am not ashamed to say they made me acutely uncomfortable.

"King Kuzikos offended Hrea anew, hunting down and killing another of her finest animals. We arrived, and she determined to avenge herself. She called upon the giants of Hopladamus, the ancient allies who had protected her and her children from her husband." By a gesture, Amphiareaws indicated the six-armed giants we had killed.

"Their plan was to destroy the *Argo*, and with most of us gone, they anticipated little difficulty. I have no wish to offend any of you. But had only Kaeneus and Polydeukahs been present, or only Atalantah and Pilgrim, I believe they would have succeeded without much difficulty. Other gods favored us, however. Polydeukahs and Kastawr are sons of Zeus. Kaeneus is of course favored by the Sea God, as are ships generally. Who can doubt that Augah favors Atalantah? Time is Pilgrim's foe—something I saw plainly as I began to speak. But if Time detests him, other gods, including Father Zeus, may well favor him.

"Whether that is so or otherwise, our vessel was saved by the skill in arms of those five, and by their courage, too. We must not think, however, that we have won. We must make what peace we can with Hrea, and so must King Kuzikos. If we fail, we must expect disaster after disaster. Persefonay favors our cause. This we know. Father Zeus favors it as well. But Persefonay could not oppose Hrea even if she dared, and though Father Zeus may oppose his mother in some things, there will surely be a limit to his friendship.

"Let us sacrifice and offer prayers and praise to Hrea. Let us urge the king to do likewise. If our sacrifices are fitting and our praise and prayers sincere, she may excuse our offenses."

———

We have sacrificed cattle and sheep in conjunction with the king. Pukz 69–74 show the entire ceremony.

I have been hoping to speak privately with Amphiareaws about Time's enmity. I know that I will not be born for many years. I know also that I have traveled the wrong way through those many years to join our crew. Was that in violation of Time's ordinances? If so, it would explain his displeasure; but if not, I must look elsewhere.

Is it lawful to forget? For I know that I have forgotten. My understanding of the matter is that knowledge carried from the future into the past is clearly out of place, and so exists only precariously and transitorily. (I cannot remember who taught me this.) My offense may lie in the things I remember, and not in the far greater number of things I have forgotten.

I remember that I was a student or a scholar.

I remember that I was to join the crew of a boat (was it this one?) upon a great voyage.

I remember that I was to talk with the Lapiths.

I remember that there is some device among my implants that takes Pukz, another implant that enables me to keep this record, and a third implant that will let me rush ahead to my own period once we have brought the ramskin back to Mount Laphystios.

Perhaps I should endeavor to forget those things. Perhaps Time would forgive me if I did.

I hope so.

We will put to sea again tomorrow morning. The past two days have been spent making ready. (Pukz 75–81) The voyage to Kolkkis should take a week or ten days. The capital, Aea, is some distance from the coast on a navigable river. Nauplios says the river will add another two days to our trip, and they will be days of hard rowing. We do not care. Call the whole time two weeks. Say we spend two more in Aea persuading the king to let us return the ramskin. The ghost of Phreexos is eager to be home, Amphiareaws says. It will board us freely. In a month we may be homeward bound, our mission a success. We are overjoyed, all of us.

Atalantah says she will ask the king's permission to hunt in his territory. If he grants it, she will go out at once. I have promised to help her.

This king is Aeeahtahs, a stern ruler and a great warrior in his youth. His queen is dead, but he has a daughter, the beautiful and learned Mahdaya. Atalantah and I agree that in a kingdom without queen or prince, this princess is certain to wield great influence, the more so in that she is reported to be a woman of ability. Atalantah will appeal to her. She will certainly be interested in the particulars of our voyage, as reported by the only woman on board. Atalantah will take every opportunity to point out that her hunt will bring credit to women everywhere, and particularly to the women of Kolkkis, of whom Mahdaya is the natural leader. Should her hunt fail, however, there will be little discredit if any—everyone acknowledges that the grups are a terribly difficult quarry. I will testify to Atalantah's prowess as a huntress. Hahraklahs offers his testimony as well; before our expedition set out they went boar-hunting together.

We are loaded—heavily loaded, in fact—with food, water, and wine. It will be hard rowing, but no one is complaining so early, and we may hope for a wind once we clear the harbor. There is talk of a rowing contest between Eeasawn and Hahraklahs.

Is it possible to be too tired to sleep? I doubt it, but I cannot sleep yet. My hands burn like fire. I splashed a little wine on them when no one was looking. They could hurt no worse, and it may prevent infection. Every muscle in my body aches.

I am splashing wine in me, as well—wine mixed with water. Half and half, which is very strong.

If I had to move to write this, it would not be written.

We put out in fair weather, but the storm came very fast. We took down the sail and unshipped the mast. It was as dark as the inside of a tomb, and the boat rolled and shipped water, and rolled again. We rowed and we bailed. Hour after hour after hour. I bailed until someone grabbed my shoulder and sat me down on the rowing bench. It was so good to sit!

I never want to touch the loom of an oar again. Never!

More wine. If I drink it so fast, will I get sick? It might be a relief, but I could not stand, much less wade out to spew. More wine.

No one knows where we are. We were cast ashore by the storm. On sand, for which we thank every god on the mountain. If it had been rocks, we would have died. The storm howled like a wolf deprived of its prey as we hauled the boat higher up. Hahraklahs broke two ropes. I know that I, and a hundred more like me, could not have broken one. (Pukz 82 and 83, infrared) Men on either side of me—I do not know who. It does not matter. Nothing does. I have to sleep.

The battle is over. We were exhausted before they came, and we are exhausted now; but we were not exhausted when we fought. (Pukz 84, infrared, and 85–88.) I should write here of how miraculously these heroes revived, but the fact is that I myself revived in just the same way. I was sound asleep and too fatigued to move when Lugkeos began shouting that we were being attacked. I sat up, blearily angry at being awakened, and in the gray dawnlight saw the ragged line of men with spears and shields charging us from the hills above the beach.

All in an instant, I was wide awake and fighting mad. I had no armor, no shield, nothing but my spear, but early in the battle I stepped on somebody's sword. I have no idea how I knew what it was, but I did, and I snatched it up and fought with my spear in my right hand and the sword in my left. My technique, if I can be said to have had one, was to attack furiously anyone who was fighting Atalantah. It was easy since she frequently took on two or three at a time. During the fighting I was much too busy to think about it, but now I wonder what those men thought when they were confronted with a breastplate having actual breasts, and glimpsed the face of a beautiful woman under her helmet.

Most have not lived to tell anyone.

What else?

Well, Eeasawn and Askalafos son of Arahs were our leaders, and good ones, too, holding everybody together and going to help wherever the fighting was hottest. Which meant that I saw very little of them; Kaeneus fought on Atalantah's left, and his swordsmanship was simply amazing. Confronted by a man with armor and a shield, he would feint so quickly that the gesture could scarcely be seen. The shield would come down, perhaps only by five centimeters. Instantly Kaeneus' point would be in his opponent's throat, and the fight would be over. He was not so much fighting men as butchering them, one after another after another.

Hahraklahs fought on my right. Spears thrust at us were caught in his left hand and snapped like so many twigs. His club smashed every shield in reach, and broke the arm that held it. We four advanced walking upon corpses.

Oh, Zeus! Father, how could you! I have been looking at my Pukz of the battle (84–88). King Kuzikos led our attackers. I recognized him at once, and he appears in 86 and 87. Why should he welcome us as friends, then attack us when we were returned to his kingdom by the storm? The world is mad!

I will not tell Eeasawn or Hahraklahs. We have agreed not to loot the bodies until the rain stops. If the king is among the dead, someone is sure to recognize him. If he is not, let us be on our way. A protracted quarrel with these people is the last thing we require.

I hope he is still alive. I hope that very much indeed.

The king's funeral games began today. Foot races, spear-throwing, all sorts of contests. I know I cannot win, but Atalantah says I must enter several to preserve my honor, so I have. Many will enter and all but one will lose, so losing will be no disgrace.

Eeasawn is buying a chariot and a team so that he can enter the chariot race. He will sacrifice both if he wins.

Hahraklahs will throw the stone. Atalantah has entered the foot races. She has had no chance to run for weeks, and worries over it. I tried to keep up with her, but it was hopeless. She runs like the wind. Today she ran in armor to build up her legs. (Puk 89)

Kastawr has acquired a fine black stallion. Its owner declared it could not be ridden by any man alive. Kastawr bet that he could ride it, laying his place on our boat against the horse. When its owner accepted the bet, Kastawr whistled, and the horse broke its tether to come to him. We were all amazed. He whispered in its ear, and it extended its forelegs so that he could mount more easily. He rode away bareback, jumped some walls, and rode back laughing. (Pukz 90–92)

"This horse was never wild," he told its previous owner. "You merely wanted to say that you nearly had a place on the *Argo*."

The owner shook his head. "I couldn't ride him, and neither could anyone else. You've won. I concede that. But can I try him just once more, now that you've ridden him?"

Polydeukahs got angry. "You'll gallop away, and my brother will never see you again. I won't permit it."

"Well, I will," Kastawr declared. "I trust him—and I think I know a way of fetching him back."

So the previous owner mounted; the black stallion threw him at once, breaking his neck. Kastawr will enter the stallion in the horse race. He is helping Eeasawn train his chariot horses as well.

The games began with choral singing. We entered as a group, our entire crew. I was our only tenor, but I did the best I could, and our director singled me out for special praise. Atalantah gave us a mezzo soprano, and Hahraklahs supplied a thundering bass. The judges chose another group, but we were the popular favorites. These people realize, or at any rate most of them seem to, that it was King Kuzikos' error (he mistook us for pirates) that caused his death, a death we regret as much as they do.

As music opened the games today, so music will close them. Orfius of Thrakah, who directed our chorus, will play and sing for us. All of us believe he will win.

The one stade race was run today. Atalantah won, the only woman who dared run against men. She is celebrated everywhere. I finished last. But wait—

My performance was by no means contemptible. There were three who were no more than a step or two ahead of me. That is the first thing. I paced myself poorly, I know, running too fast at first and waiting until too late to put on a final burst of speed. The others made a final effort, too, and I had not counted on that. I will know better tomorrow.

Second, I had not known the customs of these people. One is that every contestant wins a prize of some kind—armor, clothing, jewelry, or whatever. The other is that the runner who comes in last gets the best prize, provided he accepts his defeat with good humor. I got a very fine dagger of the hard, yellowish metal all armor and weapons are made of here. There is a scabbard of the same metal, and both display extraordinary workmanship. (Pukz 93–95)

Would I rather have won? Certainly. But I got the best prize as well as the jokes, and I can honestly say that I did not mind the jokes. I laughed and made jokes of my own about myself. Some of them were pretty feeble, but everybody laughed with me.

I wanted another lesson from Kaeneus, and while searching for him I came upon Idmon, looking very despondent. He tells me that when the funeral games are over, a member of our crew will be chosen by lot to be interred with King Kuzikos. Idmon knows, he says, that the fatal lot will fall upon him. He is a son of Apollawn and because he is, a seer like Amphiareaws; long before our voyage began, he learned that he would go and that he would not return alive. (Apollawn is another of their gods.) I promised Idmon that if he was in fact buried alive I would do my utmost to rescue him. He thanked me, but seemed as despondent as ever when I left him. (Puk 96)

The two-stade race was run this morning, and there was wrestling this afternoon. Both were enormously exciting. The spectators were beside themselves, and who can blame them?

In the two-stade race, Atalantah remained at the starting line until the rest of us had rounded the first turn. When she began to run, the rest of us might as well have been walking.

No, we were running. Our legs pumped, we gasped for breath, and we streamed with sweat. Atalantah was riding a turbocycle. She ran effortlessly, her legs and arms mere blurs of motion. She finished first, and was already accepting her prize when the second-place finisher crossed the line.

Kastawr wrestled. Wrestlers cannot strike, kick, gouge, or bite, but everything else seems to be permitted. To win, one must throw one's opponent to the ground while remaining on one's feet. When both fall together, as often happens, they separate, rise, and engage again. Kastawr threw each opponent he faced, never needing more than a minute or two. (Pukz 97–100) No one threw him, nor did he fall with his opponent in any match. He won, and won as easily, I thought, as Atalantah had won the two-stade race.

I asked Hahraklahs why he had not entered. He said he used to enter these things but he generally killed or crippled someone. He told me how he had wrestled a giant who grew stronger each time he was thrown. Eventually Hahraklahs was forced to kill him, holding him over his head and strangling him. If I had not seen the six-armed giants here, I would not have believed the story, but why not? Giants clearly exist. I have seen and fought them myself. Why is there this wish to deny them? Idmon believes he will die, and that nothing can save him. I would deny giants. And the very gods, if I were not surrounded by so many of their sons.

Atalantah says she is of purely human descent. Why did her father order her exposed to die? Surely it must have been because he knew he was not her father save in name. I asked about Augah, to whom Atalantah is so often compared. Her father was Zeus, her mother a Teetan. May not Father Zeus (as he is rightly called) have fathered another, similar daughter by a human being? A half sister?

When I congratulated Kastawr on his win, he challenged me to a friendly fencing match, saying he wanted to see how much swordcraft I had picked up from Kaeneus. I explained that Kaeneus and I have spent most of our time on the spear.

Kastawr and I fenced with sticks and pledged ourselves not to strike the face. He won, but praised my speed and resource. Afterward he gave me a lesson and taught me a new trick, though like Kaeneus he repeated again and again that tricks are of no value to a warrior who has not mastered his art, and of small value even to him.

He made me fence left-handed, urging that my right arm might someday be wounded and useless; it has given me an idea.

Stone-throwing this morning; we will have boxing this afternoon. The stadium (Pukz 101–103) is a hollow surrounded by hills, as my Pukz show. There are rings of stone seats all around the oval track on which we raced, nine tiers of them in most places. Stone-throwing, boxing, and the like take place in the grassy area surrounded by the track.

Hahraklahs was the only member of our crew to enter the stone-throwing, and it is the only event he has entered. I thought that they would measure the throws, but they do not. Two throw together, and the one who makes the shorter throw is eliminated. When all the pairs have thrown, new pairs are chosen by lot, as before. As luck would have it, Hahraklahs was in the final pair of the first pairings. He went to the farther end of the stadium and warned the spectators that his stone might fall among them, urging them to leave a clear space for it. They would not take him seriously, so he picked up one of the stones and warned them again, tossing it into the air and catching it with one hand as he spoke. They cleared a space as he had asked, though I could tell that he thought it too small. (Pukz 104)

He went back to the line at the other end of the field, picking up the second stone on his way. In his huge hands they seemed scarcely larger than cheeses. When he threw, his stone sailed high into the air and fell among the spectators like a thunderbolt, smashing two limestone slabs in the ninth row. It had landed in the cleared space, but several people were cut by flying shards even so.

After seeing the boxing, I wonder whether I should have entered the spear-dueling after all. The boxers' hands are bound with leather strips. They strike mostly at the face. A bout is decided when one contestant is knocked down; but I saw men fighting still when they were half blinded by their own blood. (Pukz 105–110) Polydeukahs won easily.

Since I am to take part in the spear-dueling, I had better describe the rules. I have not yet seen a contest, but Kaeneus has explained everything. A shield and a helmet are allowed, but no other armor. Neither the spears nor anything else (stones for example) may be thrown. First blood ends the contest, and in that way it is more humane than boxing. A contestant who kills his opponent is banished at once—he must leave the city, never to return. In general a contestant tries to fend off his opponent's spear with his shield, while trying to pink his opponent with his own spear. Wounds are almost always to the arms and legs, and are seldom deep or crippling. It is considered unsportsmanlike to strike at the feet, although it is not, strictly speaking, against the rules.

Reading over some of my earlier entries, I find I referred to a "turbocycle." Did I actually know what a turbocycle was when I wrote that? Whether I did or not, it is gone now. A cycle of turbulence? Kalais might ride turbulent winds, I suppose. No doubt he does. His father is the north wind. Or as I should say, his father is the god who governs it.

I am alone. Kleon was with me until a moment ago. He knelt before me and raised his head, and I cut his throat as he wished. He passed swiftly and with little pain. His spurting arteries drenched me in blood, but then I was already drenched with blood.

I cannot remember the name of the implant that will move me forward in time, but I hesitate to use it. (They are still shoveling dirt upon this tomb. The scrape of their shovels and the sounds of the dirt falling from them are faint, but I can hear them now that the others are dead.) Swiftly, then, before they finish and my rescuers arrive.

Eeasawn won the chariot race. (Pukz 111–114) I reached the semifinals in spear-dueling, fighting with the sword I picked up during the battle in my left hand. (Pukz 115–118) Twice I severed a spear shaft, as Kastawr taught me. (Pukz 119 and 120) I was as surprised as my opponents. One must fight without effort, Kaeneus said, and Kaeneus was right. Forget the fear of death and the love of life. (I wish I could now.) Forget the desire to win, and any hatred of the enemy. His eyes will tell you nothing if he has any skill at all. Watch his point, and not your own.

I was one of the final four contestants. (Pukz 121) Atalantah and I could not have been happier if I had won. (Pukz 122 and 123)

I have waited. I cannot say how long. Atalantah will surely come, I thought. Hahraklahs will surely come. I have eaten some of the funeral meats, and drunk some of the wine that was to cheer the king in Persefonay's shadowy realm. I hope he will forgive me.

We drew pebbles from a helmet. (Pukz 124 and 125) Mine was the black pebble (Pukz 126), the only one. No one would look at me after that.

The others (Pukz 127 and 128) were chosen by lot, too, I believe. From the king's family. From the queen's. From the city. From the palace servants. That was Kleon. He had been wine steward. Thank you, Kleon, for your good wine. They walled us in, alive.

"Hahraklahs will come for me," I told them. "Atalantah will come for me. If the tomb is guarded—"

They said it would be.

"It will not matter. They will come. Wait. You will see that I am right."

They would not wait. I had hidden the dagger I won and had brought it into the tomb with me. I showed it to them, and they asked me to kill them.

Which I did, in the end. I argued. I pleaded. But soon I consented, because they were going to take it from me. I cut their throats for them, one by one.

And now I have waited for Atalantah.

Now I have waited for Hahraklahs.

Neither has come. I slept, and sat brooding in the dark, slept, and sat brooding. And slept again, and sat brooding again. I have reread my diary, and reviewed my Pukz, seeing in them some things that I had missed before. They have not come. I wonder if they tried?

How long? Is it possible to overshoot my own period? Surely not, since I could not go back to it. But I will be careful just the same. A hundred years—a mere century. Here I go!

Nothing. I have felt about for the bodies in the dark. They are bones and nothing more. The tomb remains sealed, so Atalantah never came. Nobody did. Five hundred years this time. Is that too daring? I am determined to try it.

Greece. Not that this place is called Greece, I do not think it is, but Eea-sawn and the rest came from Greece. I know that. Even now the Greeks have laid siege to Ilion, the city we feared so much. Agamemnawn and Akkilleus are their leaders.

Rome rules the world, a rule of iron backed by weapons of iron. I wish I had some of their iron tools right now. The beehive of masonry that imprisons me must surely have decayed somewhat by this time, and I still have my emergency rations. I am going to try to pry loose some stones and dig my way out.

The *Mayflower* has set sail, but I am not aboard her. I was to make peace. I can remember it now—can remember it again. We imagined a cooperative society in which Englishmen and Indians might meet as friends, sharing knowledge and food. It will never happen now, unless they have sent someone else.

The tomb remains sealed. That is the chief thing and the terrible thing, for me. No antiquarian has unearthed it. King Kuzikos sleeps undisturbed. So does Kleon. Again . . .

This is the end. The Chronomiser has no more time to spend. This is my own period, and the tomb remains sealed; no archeologist has found it, no tomb robber. I cannot get out, and so must die.

Someday someone will discover this. I hope they will be able to read it.

Good-bye. I wish that I had sailed with the Pilgrims and spoken with the Native Americans—the mission we planned for more than a year. Yet the end might have been much the same. Time is my enemy. Cronus. He would slay the gods if he could, they said, and in time he did.

Revere my bones. This hand clasped the hand of Hercules. These bony lips kissed the daughter of a god. Do not pity me.

The bronze blade is still sharp. Still keen, after four thousand years. If I act quickly I can cut both my right wrist and my left. (Pukz 129 and 130, infrared)